MW00916101

Life,
Some Assembly
Required

Kaje Harper

Copyright © 2017 by Kaje Harper

First edition copyright 2015 by Kaje Harper

Edited by Linda Ingmanson

Cover by Angela Waters

Formatting by Beaten Track Publishing – beatentrackpublishing.com

All rights reserved. This copy is intended for the original purchaser of this e-book ONLY. No part of this e-book may be reproduced, scanned, or distributed in any printed or electronic form without prior written permission of the author. Please do not participate in or encourage piracy of copyrighted materials in violation of the author's rights. Purchase only authorized editions.

Image/art disclaimer: Licensed material is being used for illustrative purposes only. Any person depicted is a model.

This is a work of fiction. Names, characters, places, and incidents are products of the author's imagination or are used fictitiously and are not to be construed as real. Any resemblance to actual events, locales, organizations, or persons, living or dead, is entirely coincidental.

Content warning: For adult readers over the age of 18 only. This book contains explicit sexual situations between two men.

Dedication

For my husband, whose willingness to put up with my distractions and obsessions deserves some kind of medal. For my beta readers, especially Jonathan, who gave freely of their time to read and comment and make suggestions, and whose honest critiques helped me write a better story.

And for my readers, whose comments and questions about John and Ryan and their future together encouraged me to give the guys this sequel.

Contents

Chapter One

An annoying trickle of sweat slid down the side of Ryan's neck. He gritted his teeth, trying to ignore it. He had good reasons to be overheated, reasons for his palm to be wet where he clutched the phone. The kitchen was much too warm, and John was standing close, a solid, heat-radiating bulk at his back. Plus he'd just given John one hell of a blowjob, which was vigorous exercise of a sort. Then he'd gotten up off the floor too fast and tweaked his bad leg, and that always made him sweat.

It wasn't that he was scared to hear what his father was going to say. *Wasn't.* He pressed the silent phone to his ear.

His father had asked hopefully just a moment ago, *"You seeing someone special, Ryan?"*

"Someone really special," he'd answered, finally laying it on the line. *"Dad, I've met this man…"*

Now there was a long pause. Eventually his dad said tentatively, "And?"

Shit, he was going to have to put it plainly, in words. He cleared his throat, and the lingering irritation from breathing smoke yesterday made him break into a cough. *Dammit, not now.* He waited out his bout of hacking, then said as evenly as he could, "I'm dating him. Living with him, actually. It's John. John Barrett."

"Your landlord?"

"My…" What? *Boyfriend* sounded so juvenile; *partner* sounded like a business deal. "My lover." He made a face, because that was wrong too, but he couldn't find the right word.

The next pause was even longer. John hugged him close, and Ryan leaned into him for a moment. Then he shrugged free and took one step away, wincing as the stitches in his lacerated leg twinged. He didn't need to be supported. He should be able to do this on his own. "Dad?"

"Um. Okay. I didn't You're saying you're with him like gay?"

1

Ryan swallowed. His dad's tone was hard to read. "Bi. Bisexual. But I love John."

"Wow." Another silence. Ryan really wanted to pace, but that one step was all his damned leg was good for, so he just leaned on the counter and waited, hearing his father's breathing louder than usual, across the miles. Finally Dad said, "That's good. That you're seeing someone. Good luck with your classes. We'll have to talk again, real soon." The dead air over the phone told Ryan he'd hung up.

He unsmooshed the phone from his ear and stared at it.

After a moment, John reached out slowly, as if trying not to startle him, and took it out of his hand, setting it into the charger on the counter. "So? Good? Bad? What did he say?"

"Not much." Ryan took a breath that wasn't as steady as it should've been and fought back another tickle in his throat. His chest was painfully tight. "He said it was good."

"So that's going to be okay?"

"I guess." Ryan rubbed his forehead. "He hung up damned fast."

"Well, I'm sure it was a surprise. After all the girls you dated over the years."

No doubt. It'd come as a surprise to Ryan too, just a few months ago. One minute he'd thought of himself as a player, a guy who appreciated hot women but had no desire to settle down with one. The next minute, day, week, month Somehow, here he was, in love with a man, playing second father to John's teenage son and daughter, settled into a house and a yard. All they needed was a golden retriever to have suddenly become the gay version of his childhood. And Ryan had no clue how that'd happened.

His mind ran in circles, replaying every word of that odd little conversation with his dad. "I don't know why I said bi."

"Huh?"

"About me." He met John's gaze, his own eyes stinging and wet, still irritated from yesterday's smoky fun and games, of course. He blinked hard to clear them. *My John. Strong and steady and kind and just so completely mine.* "To my dad. I said I was bi. I told your kids I was gay, but for Dad I soft-pedaled it."

"Does it matter?"

"I'm not ashamed of being with you."

"It didn't sound like you were." John moved closer, still keeping every motion slow and easy, like he thought Ryan might spook.

"It's just that he knows about all the women I dated. They weren't a lie. I didn't want him to think I lied to him."

John put a gentle hand on his shoulder. "It's okay, really. The labels don't matter."

"Sometimes they do. Sometimes they hurt somebody." He wasn't even sure what his orientation was. He did still notice girls that way, his attention sometimes caught by smooth thighs and round boobs. But he didn't want to sound less than one hundred percent committed to John, and he was afraid he had.

John eased Ryan in close. He knew just how to tilt Ryan's body against his hip to take the weight off Ryan's bad leg. When had he learned that? Ryan sighed, coughed a couple of times hoarsely, and leaned harder. So good.

John kissed his temple. "You can say gay or bi or whatever. I got all I needed when you told your dad that I'm your lover, I'm someone special."

"God, yes." Ryan turned enough to find John's mouth with his. "Mm. You're everything. I should have said it better."

John kissed him back lightly. "He didn't give you a lot of time."

"I feel so strange." Ryan closed his eyes and hugged him. This was almost the best part of falling for a man, to have this much strength holding him when he needed it. "I told Mark about us a long time ago. Your ex-wife, her husband, the cops. A lot of people know. But this still feels like stepping off a cliff."

"It's your dad. The first person who matters more to you than to me."

Ryan thought about that and opened his eyes to kiss John again. "You're right."

"Of course I am."

"Smart man."

"A genius, almost."

3

"Don't push it." He took control, driving with lips and tongue, and felt John go with it, opening his mouth and relaxing.

After a while, John said, "We were about to take this upstairs."

They had been. But somewhere along the line, Ryan's raging hard-on from blowing John had faded. "I don't know. I'm kind of sore." His cut leg throbbed, although he'd lived with worse pain from the old burns. It was really pretty minor. An excuse.

John was immediately concerned, though. "Then you should get off the damned leg. Chair or bed?"

"Chair."

John lined one up under his ass before Ryan had time to even reach for it, and he eased down.

"Thanks."

"Can I get you something? Pain meds?"

"No. I'm good. Sit with me."

John folded his tall frame into the nearest seat.

Ryan reached for his hand. They didn't do sappy things like hand-holding often, but he played with John's long fingers, tracing the veins on the back of his hand and the knobs of his knuckles. John had calluses from years of outdoor work, and little scars from the knives he carved with. If you just looked at his hands, you might think he was a thirty-seven-year-old laborer instead of the bright college-educated landscape architect he really was. What would Dad see, looking at John? The lanky, redheaded outdoorsman, or the compassionate, steady guy inside? "I'm not sure what'll happen when Dad gets his head around what I told him."

"Well, he's a thousand miles away in Oregon, right? You have your own money to finish med school. You don't depend on him for anything. You talk once a month. We can give him time to figure it out."

That was all true. But in an odd way, that hurt too. There were other measures of how close two people were besides paying for shit, and just how often they talked. Maybe he and Dad butted heads over little stuff, but he'd always believed that when it came down to the important things, Dad would be there for him.

Ryan could remember two years ago, waking up in the hospital to find his dad at his bedside. It'd been Dad who'd put a surprisingly gentle hand on his forehead and told him, "You got caught in a fire, son. The roof came down on you. No one else on the crew got hurt, but you're going to be here a while."

Days later, Dad was still there at his bedside when the burn specialist told them how bad his leg injury really was. After the doctors were gone, when Ryan was pretending not to be holding back tears of pain and fear, it was Dad who'd told him, "I know you, Ry. First you'll work on healing the leg, then you get back to using it, and then you'll find a new career. Maybe even become a doctor, like you always planned. You'll get it done. I have faith." That faith helped carry Ryan though the agony of burn treatments, the tough year of rehab and all the challenges he'd faced. Ryan realized how much he hoped Dad's trust in him would stretch to cover his relationship with John too. "I really want him to be okay with this."

"Do you think he won't be?"

"I wish I knew." Dad was a pretty fair-minded guy, but he'd joked a couple of times that he was worried one of his sons might be turning out gay. He'd always meant it to be funny, but the underlying message wasn't a good one.

"Well, tell me what I can do to help, right?"

Ryan blew out a breath. "We'll see." He tried to lighten the mood. "A return blow job might ease my pain."

John clearly could tell that was more bravado than substance because he said lightly, without reaching for Ryan, "Sure. The guy who ran into a burning building to save my kid can have all the blow jobs he wants."

Ryan buffed his nails on his shirt. "Just doing my job as superhero." He pretended John's words didn't bring back the laboratory fire last night—standing on those smoke-filled stairs, telling John he'd go up after Mark, when every instinct screamed at him to get them both out right the fuck now, and let someone else be the hero. Somewhere he'd found the guts to go higher, deeper into the fire, into a replica of the hell he'd already lived through once. He swallowed back the memory of how close his injury two years ago had come to paralyzing him. He was no superhero. He'd stood in the doorway of that burning room, looking at Mark across the smoke, and almost turned away. He hoped John would never know he'd come within a breath of leaving Mark alone there, to live or die.

But in the end he'd got them both out alive. He'd defeated his demons. *Fuck you, fire and smoke. I won.* A cut leg, some irritation in his throat, and a few blisters were a small price to pay.

Hell, if he really looked ahead, the next few years of day-to-day parenting of teenagers were a lot scarier. He coughed, and gave John a sideways look. "What about the guy who picks up your kid's dirty socks off the couch? What does he get?"

John smiled, deepening the little wrinkles at the corners of his eyes. "Now *that* guy should stop being a wuss and make the kid pick up after himself."

Ryan laughed and aimed a kick towards John's shin, wincing and missing by inches. They both jumped as Ryan's phone rang. John said, "I'll get it." He stood, looked at the display and mouthed *your brother*, as he passed it over.

Ryan took it, glanced at it to see *which* brother and growled, "What do you want, Brent?"

"Nice to talk to you too, bro."

"Sorry." He made an effort to mellow his tone. "How are you? Why're you calling?"

"Maybe I heard someone started a major fire last night, at that podunk college you're at, and I wanted to make sure you weren't mixed up in it."

"You heard the word arson and immediately thought of me?" The banter came smoothly, from years of habit.

"Of course."

"I didn't set it."

"Moron. As long as you weren't caught in it this time."

A ceiling crackling with tongues of flame, tiles falling in a shower of sparks, smoke that rasps in my chest and throat. The taste of ashes in my mouth He shuddered, and fought back the urge to cough. Damned smoke irritation— that shit lingered. Brent didn't need to know. "I'm fine."

"Good. That's good to hear."

Ryan waited.

"Also, um, Dad called me and asked if I'd talked to you lately. He sounded weird."

"Weird?"

6

"Yeah, like, worried. Maybe? Anyway, that's why I figured I'd make sure you hadn't got yourself back in the hospital or something."

"Not this time." Brent was the last person he'd ever tell how close it'd been. "How are you and Anne doing? Thinking wedding yet?" Getting Brent's mind on his fiancée might head him off.

"We're fine. Planning on probably having the wedding this summer." There was a pause. "You're sure Dad had no particular reason to worry? I wouldn't want the old man to get an ulcer over your ungrateful hide."

"Nah. There's no big problems on this end. Little stuff. If you ever visit again, we can get drunk and I'll tell you all about my dissection lab and how to cut open the skull of a cadaver."

"Yuck, you would, wouldn't you? Okay, bro. Maybe call Dad and set his mind at ease, huh? Later."

Ryan set the phone down. He didn't look at John. "Well, there *isn't* a big problem." When that was greeted with silence, he added to his feet, "Okay, I'm chickenshit. Just say it." He met John's eyes eventually.

John looked surprisingly calm. "You just came out to your dad over the phone. I've met Brent, and I can totally understand not wanting to turn around and do the same with him."

"Right."

"It doesn't mean you're scared. Maybe you're smart."

It totally meant he was scared, but he just ducked his head, looking back down.

John deepened his voice. "So, as I remember it, before all this phone drama, we were headed upstairs for a couple of teenager-free hours."

"Yeah. We were." Ryan tried once more to recapture the moment. John had been so hot, so sexy, panting and groaning, coming in his mouth, and Ryan had thought he might come in his own pants just from doing it. He'd been so turned on— he should be desperate for it now. But somehow, his dick still wasn't interested.

"Come here." John held out an arm.

Ryan was hit with a wave of shaking. What he wanted now wasn't sex, but to just let John hold him. Jesus, he was becoming some kind of wimp. He pushed up out of the chair determinedly and went to John in one hard step that jostled John up against the counter, slamming their hips together. Oops, harder than he'd intended, but he covered for it by biting John's earlobe, along with some bump and grind. The familiar solid strength of John's body, the taste of his skin, and John's long arm that automatically wrapped around him, went a long way to getting him past those shakes.

John chuckled. "Upstairs?"

"Mm." But Ryan widened his stance, so their thighs pressed together. He angled his head for a real kiss, not taking his weight off John. Upstairs was a good plan, soon. Right now he wanted this, the hard press and slide of bodies and tongues that was him and John, together, and the rest of the world could go to hell.

John let Ryan kiss him wild and wet for a while, then eased back. "I really would like to get you off that leg and flat on a bed."

"The leg's fine." He was used to ignoring it.

"Yeah, but I'm planning to make you weak at the knees, so you might prefer to be horizontal."

"Big talk." Ryan couldn't help a smile. "You have a plan?"

"Several. But we only have two hours."

"Really big talk."

"It's been weeks since we had alone time."

"Tell me about it."

"I'm going to put a finger up your ass and let you feel how amazing that is."

"Jesus!" He hadn't meant *"tell me about it"* to be that literal. His cock jerked slightly, but his stomach lurched at the same time. Having his courteous, sweet John talking dirty in the kitchen was a turn-on. He wasn't sure if John's interest in his ass was, or not.

"If you want to," John added.

"We could, um, go up and discuss it."

John handed Ryan his crutches and insisted he use them, which eliminated any groping on the way upstairs. Anyway, his leg ached and the blisters pulled on the back of his left hand. He settled for getting into the bedroom, out of his clothes, and onto the bed in record time. He lay back, the sheet draped strategically over his scarred leg from long habit, and watched John pull off his briefs.

There was a sight worth seeing. John might be closing in on thirty-eight, but he was fitter than a lot of guys ten years younger. His outdoor job gave him long lean muscles, solid pecs, and a nice flat belly. Not six-pack ripped, but fit. A dusting of red curls across his chest narrowed down to a treasure trail leading to some of Ryan's favorite bits. After that kitchen blowjob, John wasn't hard, but he was still worth a look or three. John laid his clothes neatly on the chair, briefs on top, his gaze fixed on Ryan. His changeable hazel eyes had the amber brightness that Ryan associated with some of the best moments of his life.

"C'mere, John." Ryan scooted sideways to make room. The move twinged his leg, shooting a pain from his calf to his thigh, and he flinched involuntarily. John tugged the covers out from under him and lay down beside him, pulling the sheet up over them both.

"Hey. You're blocking my great view."

John rolled onto his side, propped up on his elbow, and slid his free hand under the sheet to stroke over Ryan's stomach and down. His touch was more friendly than sensual as he patted Ryan's unresponsive cock. "I get the feeling you're not really into the view anyway."

"I'm always into looking at you."

"Was it that thing I said? I actually practiced the *finger up your ass* line. But we don't need to do that."

Of course John had practiced. He did stuff like that. He tried so hard to get it right for them.

Ryan hesitated. He could cough a few times, tell John he wanted to suck him again instead, joke about come being good cough syrup. But if he started hacking, he wasn't sure he could stop, which was *so* not sexy in bed. Besides, he didn't want to start playing those half-truth games. He sighed. "It's not that. My stupid leg hurts and my hand hurts, and I guess I'm in a weird headspace." His conversations with Dad and Brent were echoing in his mind, and thinking about sex made him flinch. Not just because it was gay sex. Any sex and Dad was "I'm kind of stressed at the moment."

"How unreasonable." There was a touch of amusement in John's deep voice.

"Are you laughing at me? When I can't get it up?" He was half joking, but maybe half not.

"Never." John leaned over to give him a quick kiss. "Stressed sounds pretty reasonable. After all, it's been a crazy few months. You came here for medical school, a straight guy with a long string of women under your belt…"

Ryan's lips twitched at the phrasing. "So to speak, although you know it'd been a while since the last girl I'd slept with."

"Sure. But your dad and brothers know you as Ryan Ward, hot stud of the San Diego Fire Department."

"God, I hope not. I don't want my dad to think of me as the hot stud of anywhere."

John kissed him again. "You're sidetracking me. They think you're straight. Very straight. So did you, not that long ago."

He had. When he arrived on campus to start school in September, he'd thought he might end up dating the tall redhead in his class, the one with the nice boobs and the long, slim legs. Instead he'd fallen for the tall, redheaded landscaper with the wide shoulders and the five-o'clock shadow— the guy who'd picked him up when he fell, offered him a room when he needed one, and helped him discover what making love was really supposed to feel like. Between them, they'd figured out that "straight" was definitely not the right word for either of them. "Not anymore. I'm gay." It came out thinly, past his irritated throat. He clearly needed to practice saying that. "I'm gay."

"Or bisexual. Doesn't matter what you call it, as long as you're with me now."

"No place else I want to be."

"But still, it makes complete sense that it's hard to tell your family about us."

"I'm a coward. You told your family." John had been amazing. Just a few weeks ago, John's son Mark had run away from John's ex-wife and her SOB husband, Brandon Carlisle, and showed up on their doorstep. At the time, they'd been pretty much on the down low. But when the moment of truth came, Ryan had been impressed by the way John faced down his ex-wife and her lawyer husband. He'd said, *"I'm in love with Ryan. I live with him. Ryan's my boyfriend."* Now, after choking over the same words himself,

Ryan realized he hadn't been anywhere near impressed *enough.* "You were awesome."

"It was a different situation. Anyhow, you've told your dad."

"And I'll tell Brent. Somehow. And Drew, I guess." His oldest brother might not be too bad, but Brent would probably flip his lid. Ryan sighed. "This shouldn't even be a thing, you know? I should be able to say, 'Hey, guys, I've found someone to love.' What sex you are, which chromosomes you have, shouldn't matter."

"Maybe one day it won't. There are states with gay marriage now."

"Not this one."

"Not yet." John reached for him, tugging him over, their legs tangled together. Ryan went with it, suddenly exhausted. They slid around into a favorite position, John's shoulder under him, sharing a pillow. His bad leg was positioned just right, and John raised one knee to keep the sheet off Ryan's stitches. The room was quiet and cool.

John fumbled about and pulled more covers up over them. "You should sleep. I don't think you got much last night."

"No, not really." He'd felt the nightmares hovering. They'd dragged him back awake every time he dozed off.

Despite showering the moment he got home from the hospital— with John's help, a ton of shampoo, and a plastic bag over his stitches— he'd still kept thinking he smelled smoke. The thought of their home on fire made him nauseous. The odor came and went, sometimes strong enough to yank him upright, panicked and coughing, before abruptly vanishing in the quiet night air, leaving him breathing hard and unsure of his own senses. He'd tossed and turned, unable to hold still even for John's sake, so grateful for John's warm, live presence in his bed, and the sounds from Mark, sleeping with his door open down the hall.

He'd hoped that walking safely out of the inferno of Smythe Hall, knowing he could still do what had to be done, would put an end to his worst nightmares. In a way it'd helped. He'd had two years of nasty, whispering voices in the shadows of his mind calling him scared, a coward, telling him he'd never even see a candle flame again without a lurch in his gut. Those were now silent. Because he finally knew that even if his gut did clench and his heart hammered from just looking at a fire, he'd still do the right thing. He could walk *toward* the flames, and not away.

But clearly that wasn't going to be enough to lose all his bad dreams. Now, instead of the old well-worn scenes of falling beams, when he closed his eyes he saw Mark, crouching across the smoke-filled room that was sometimes the lab, and sometimes this house they were sleeping in. He saw Patrick, the boy they'd found shot and bleeding on the stairs, picturing him dead and staring, with ghosts in his eyes. He dreamed that the makeshift rope he'd used broke, that Mark fell out the window, that the stairs they'd gone down became filled with smoke so dark they never found their way out. He dreamed of Mark, and sometimes John, dying a dozen ways, dreamed of the walls of their home lit by flames, collapsing. Maybe all you ever did was replace one set of nightmares with another.

He pressed his face in tighter against John, closing his eyes and rubbing his cheek against the rough skin at John's hairline. Wavy short strands tickled his forehead. He sighed, his tension slowly seeping away. "We're good, at least, aren't we? You and me?"

"Of course we are." John laid a warm palm on Ryan's shoulder.

"Even if Dad's not okay with this, and Brent's an asshole, you and I are family. And Mark, and Torey, as often as we can have her here. We're settled in for the long haul."

"Yes." John was quiet long enough for Ryan to wonder if he was dozing, but finally he added, "When you and Mark were up there, trapped, in danger, I was as scared for you as for him. My heart was in that building, in that fire, living inside both of you. So yeah, we're a family."

Ryan's eyes prickled under his closed eyelids. Family. It sounded so good. He'd thought his life was over, back when he woke from firefighter hell to find his leg burned almost beyond saving, his job gone, girlfriend gone, his family so sorry for him they could hardly look at him. He'd tried to rebuild what he could, but he'd never in his wildest dreams imagined someone like John could be the one to bring him back to life. Now he couldn't imagine loving anyone else.

There were still a lot of details to work out. Parts of this life felt fragile and unsettled. Parts were still scary, still uncertain. But he hoped, wanted, *needed* the love he and John shared to be solid, a place from which they both could build. He brushed a kiss against John's temple, eased back on the pillow so John's hair quit tickling his face, and fell asleep at last.

Chapter Two

When the doorbell rang the next evening, John bolted up from the couch, almost dumping Ryan onto the floor. *Oops.* He slowed down, and steadied Ry, realizing they'd somehow fallen asleep with Ryan's head on his shoulder and an arm draped over him. He'd meant to work on his grounds-crew scheduling. Ryan had planned to study. They'd come in here after dinner, both said, "Soon," and then settled down together on the couch for a moment…

Ryan grunted, blinking, his green eyes bleary and dull. He coughed once, and John held his breath but it didn't trigger a scary bout this time. Ryan really was getting better; he was fine. No need to keep worrying. John pushed him farther back onto the cushions, though. "Stay put. I'll get it."

The couple on the front porch were strangers. He held the door half-closed in case they were reporters, but no one shoved a lens in his face. They just stood there in the yellow circle of the porch light, looking rumpled and tired.

"Can I help you?"

"Does Mark Barrett live here?"

John moved farther into the narrow opening of the door. "Why are you asking?"

"Could we talk to him?" When John frowned, the man added, "We're parents of a friend of his."

"Parents of ?"

"Patrick Remington? They were, they're, um, in a band together."

"Oh!" The last time John had seen Patrick, he'd been strapped onto an ambulance gurney, with blood from his gunshot wounds staining his shirt bright red, terrifyingly limp and unmoving. His blood had stained John's clothes too. "Sure. Is he okay? At least…" He wasn't certain he should let them talk to Mark, but they didn't deserve to stand out here in the cold. "Come on in."

"Thank you."

"Take off your coats and come into the living room." He closed the door behind them. "I'll make some coffee."

"That's not necessary. If we could just see Mark?"

"We'll talk about that." The woman stared at him, and John added, "Mark's fifteen. I'm his father. And I want to talk to you first."

"Fifteen? But it's a college band."

"Other than Mark, they're all college students, yes. But he's not. Why don't you go sit down?" John called into the living room, "Hey, Ry. We have company. It's Mr. and Mrs. Remington, Patrick's parents."

Ryan appeared in the doorway, one crutch under his arm. "Hey, come on in. How's Patrick's doing? We've been worried."

John held his breath at the question. The parents weren't glued to their injured son's bedside, which, yeah, either meant he was better or He let out a sigh when Mrs. Remington said, "They say he's out of danger. He's been awake, off and on, but not making sense. Which is why we're here. Because we don't understand…" Her voice trailed off.

"Come, sit." Ryan led the way. "I want to get off my leg, and you guys look beat. Take the couch. John'll make us coffee." He gave John a quick glance, possibly an apology for assuming command. Or maybe not.

John laughed and headed to the kitchen freezer for the beans. He was fine with letting Ryan start this conversation.

When he brought out four steaming mugs a few minutes later, Ryan was in the recliner, leaning forward to listen to Mr. Remington. He gave John a grateful smile. John set his cup down at his elbow first, then served the Remingtons.

Ryan turned to him. "They've told me Patrick should make a full recovery, but not for months, so he's going home to Pennsylvania with them."

"The band will miss him." John sat down across from Ryan. "Will he come back for summer semester then? Or in the fall?"

"We don't know." Mr. Remington frowned. "We talked to a detective yesterday, when Patrick was still in the ICU. Maybe we weren't hearing her right, but she mentioned drugs, and arson, and that Patrick broke in somewhere? It was all confusing and totally not like our son."

Mrs. Remington said, "I know kids change in college. Patrick's twenty now, and he's been on his own for two years. But still, he *never* did drugs. We used to worry, because the music scene is so full of that stuff, right? But he didn't. He was so focused. And now we don't know what to think."

John exchanged a glance with Ryan. Presumably nothing they knew was a secret anymore.

Ryan said cautiously, "Patrick wasn't involved in the arson. He was in the building, and the arsonist shot him."

"But *why?*" Mrs. Remington's anguished tone struck a chord with John. *Why my child?*

Mr. Remington added, "Patrick hasn't been awake much, and he mostly rambles, but he kept saying, 'Make sure Mark's okay. Mark knows. He was there.' This address was in his phone. So we'd really like to talk to Mark now."

John said, "Look, I'll tell you what we know. Then maybe you can talk to Mark, but you have to understand he's just a kid and this has been really hard for him." He laid it out as simply as he could. Explained that Patrick's boss, Dr. Crosby, had been doing potentially valuable antibiotics research that had gone very wrong when the medication turned out to have bad side effects. He told them about the accidental death of Patrick's fellow lab assistant, Alice, disoriented after using the drug, and about Crosby's murder of her roommate Kristin to silence her. In as few words as he could, he explained Crosby had burned down the lab to cover his tracks.

He faltered there, and Ryan took over, explained why Patrick had been there with Mark, looking for more medication, when Crosby showed up. "It's not like Patrick was doing drugs. It was supposed to be a safe medication, with a side effect he wasn't told about."

"But that's almost worse," his mother said. "He was taking some unknown thing? A drug no one understands? What if it damaged him permanently? And his employer was a murderer? And is still on the *loose?*" Her voice rose with each question.

"The police are pretty sure Crosby's out of the country and going to stay that way," Ryan said firmly. "As for the drug, hopefully Patrick will be fine once it's out of his system."

"But we don't know?"

"You should ask his doctors. I'm just a med student."

John said, "At least he's going to recover. That's huge. When I saw all the blood, I was afraid he was already dead."

"When you *saw* him?"

John bit his tongue. Ryan had brushed past the events of Friday night with, " then Patrick was found and taken to an ambulance, and the fire department put out the fire." He was giving John a dirty look now. They'd agreed to do everything possible not to let their part in the events become known. John backtracked ambiguously, "I was there, when Patrick was put into the ambulance."

"Oh. I don't…" Mrs. Remington rubbed her eyes, and her husband patted her shoulder. "Can we talk to Mark? Please?"

"I guess." John stood reluctantly. "I'll get him. But I don't want him upset. He was there when his friend got shot, and the building burned. He was trapped, scared, and that's hard enough for a teenager. Right?"

"We understand. We won't take long."

"Okay."

John climbed the stairs slowly, and hesitated in the hallway outside Mark's door.

His son had been in his room all day, emerging only to wolf down his dinner and go back inside to pick up his guitar. Mark's nightmares all night Friday had been bad enough to leave him shaking and needing John's hugs. Next morning, Mark had muttered something about "I'm done crying like a little kid" into his cereal. He'd made a visible effort to act normal all of Saturday, but he'd been up in the night again, and today he'd retreated to his room and his music. John had tried not to hover, but he wasn't sorry to have an excuse to check up on his kid.

He called through the door, "Hey, Mark?"

"Yeah."

"Patrick's parents are here. He's doing better, and they want to talk to you. You don't have to, if—" He was cut off by Mark's door opening. Mark blinked at him, guitar in his hand, visibly coming back to earth from some creative space. John added more softly, "I can tell them, if you're not up for it?"

"No. It's good. I want to know how he is." Mark set the instrument aside carefully, and rubbed his face. "Okay. They're here?"

"In the living room."

"Okay."

John was so proud of his son. Mark went down calmly, shook hands with the Remingtons, told them how sorry he was that Patrick got hurt and how glad that he was going to be okay. So mature. *God.* He got these glimpses now and then of the man that Mark was going to be, and it caught him in the heart.

Patrick's parents wanted answers Mark didn't have. Why did Patrick insist on going into the lab without permission? Why did Dr. Crosby torch the whole building? Did the drug make Crosby crazy?

Mark sat down on the arm of Ryan's chair, and Ry put a steadying arm against his back. Mark visibly leaned into his reassurance. John saw the Remingtons look back and forth between the three of them. He wondered if they were trying to figure out how he, his short, blond, California-tanned son, and a black-haired, fair-skinned, muscular guy like Ryan fit together.

He went and leaned on the back of Ry's chair to present a united front. "We can speculate all night. We may never know the whys."

Ryan added, "Crosby tried to destroy everything. Maybe so no one else could use his work. Or as an eff-you to the people who didn't appreciate his genius. Perhaps he thought a big fire would cover his escape, or, hell, maybe he just wanted to see it all burn. And Patrick unfortunately got in his way."

Mark asked, "Will Patrick be able to play the flute again soon?" He blushed but finished, "That sounds crappy. He's a friend, and the band's not all I'm worried about. But he's also, like, the real creative part of the band. I don't know if we can get by without him. We got together yesterday, and the other guys were talking about maybe breaking up if he can't play."

"It's going to take time," Mrs. Remington said. "We're bringing him home with us to recover, and I don't know if he'll ever come back here. I don't think we want him at this school again. There are lots of places he can finish his degree."

"Another school won't have his band and the songs he wrote for us."

"That's pretty minor."

"Not to Patrick!" Mark said loudly. "What about what he wants?"

"We pay his tuition, so it'll be our decision. Later. After he's healed up."

"But you'll ask him?"

"Sure." Mr. Remington's tone didn't hold out much hope, though.

The Remingtons stood, said general thank-yous and prepared to leave. Mark slumped against Ryan, while John saw them to the door. When he came back, Mark said bitterly, "They weren't very grateful to you for saving his life."

"I didn't tell them."

"Why not? They would owe you! They'd have to let Patrick come back here, if you asked."

And then there were times when he was reminded Mark was only fifteen. "Patrick has a lot of healing to do. Let's wait and see." *He might not want to come back to the place he was shot and almost burned alive.* John decided not to say that out loud. Mark had his own nightmares.

"I guess." Mark sighed. "Or if he wanted to keep writing songs for us, he could do that from home. Although they won't sound the same if he's not playing them. I really, really don't want this band to fail."

"I know. We don't either."

Ryan said firmly, "Even if it does, there will be other bands for you. You're one hell of a musician, and only getting better. This isn't the only chance you'll ever have."

"I guess," Mark repeated. "Hey, it's almost nine. Calvin said Chanel Six was doing a special news report on the fire. Can we watch it?"

"You want to?"

"Well, sure. He said they had some really awesome pictures on the previews."

John glanced at Ryan, who shrugged ruefully. "I will if you will."

John reached for the remote and clicked the set on. "Three more minutes. I'll get cookies." With enough sugar, he might be able to sit through pictures of the blaze that almost destroyed his family.

****

Ryan leaned against John on the couch and munched a chocolate-chip cookie. He was getting better at baking these. They were still too crunchy, instead of chewy the way he preferred them, but at least it was a good crunch, not one that might break your teeth. He focused on the cookie, not looking at the TV, but the narrator's voice rambled on regardless. " at Bonaventure College where the Biomedical Research building was severely damaged in an arson fire Friday night."

Mark drew a short breath and then said, "Wow! Look at that!"

Not looking. Not looking. Ah, fuck. Ryan turned his head. There was a jerky amateur video playing, showing the glow of gathering flames behind a fourth-floor window of Smythe Hall. Automatically he evaluated it. At that point, it was already spreading fast. That hint of light in the sixth-floor windows wasn't a reflection but the secondary source.

He watched as the glow became an inferno. A window burst with a shatter of glass. The resulting venting created a flash of light as the flames sprang higher behind it. Then the video cut to the other side of the building and someone's more professional camera. The two-floor sandwich of flames was obvious, with the fifth floor that had saved them still dark between the bands of fire. Jesus Christ, they'd been lucky.

A pan along the building showed the window he'd broken, already gaping open. The fire suddenly flared brilliantly behind it. He breathed out, willing his hammering heart to slow down. This part of the video was happening later, after he and Mark had made it to safety. They'd probably already been in the ambulance by then. *If we'd been caught inside when that flash-over happened, we'd never have made it out.* He shivered, and stuffed more cookie in his mouth.

19

The camera picked up the emergency units gathered around the building. Firefighters, cops, flashing lights, spotlights, hoses, axes, ladders going up. All the familiar controlled confusion of a major fire. Ryan ignored the announcer talking in an excited voice about millions of dollars in damage and the arsonist still on the loose.

Then a head-and-shoulders picture of a man in a white coat, blue shirt, and red power-tie came on the screen. "Doctor Lionel Crosby, a medical researcher and assistant professor at Bonaventure's medical school, has been identified as the prime suspect in the setting of the blaze."

"What do they mean, suspect?" Mark asked. "They know he did it."

"Not until he's convicted. You and Patrick and all the evidence could be mistaken."

"Hah," Mark muttered.

The announcer said, "Although it's believed that Dr. Crosby has left the area, anyone seeing this man, or with knowledge of his activities or whereabouts, is asked to contact the York Police Department. I have Detective Sharon Carstairs here in the studio to discuss the case further. Welcome, Detective."

Over her response, John said, "She looks really tired."

"No doubt." Ryan couldn't muster up a lot of sympathy for the woman who'd accused John of dealing drugs and possibly murder. Even if she had backed off later.

Carstairs said, "The number on the screen is our hotline. Or call 9-1-1, especially if you see the suspect. I want to emphasize that Dr. Crosby should be considered armed and dangerous. There were shots fired inside that building. Do not approach or try to apprehend this man if you see him. Contact us as soon as you can safely do so."

The announcer asked, "I thought Dr. Crosby fled the country that same night?"

"We believe he did. However, he's not in custody. Until he is, we must consider him a possible threat. We want the citizens of York to be aware of the situation. We would also appreciate any information that may help us successfully prosecute the case when he's apprehended."

"You said Dr. Crosby's also the main suspect in the murder of Kristin Saunders earlier this year..."

Mark muttered, "She says 'when he's apprehended' like she thinks they'll actually catch him."

Ryan shrugged. "She's a good actress, and she wants people to have faith in the cops. She told us privately he's long gone; I'd tend to believe that." He closed his eyes and tuned out the TV. Dimly, he knew that the announcer was rehashing, in his most sensational terms, the deaths on campus and the subsequent revelations. He opened one eye when John's name was mentioned as the man who found Kristin's body. But they didn't make a big point of it or show John's picture. *Good.*

The program wound down to its close. Ryan squinted at the TV. Carstairs was gone from the screen. The announcer sat in front of dramatic footage of the fire. He said, " many of the events of that night may remain a mystery until Dr. Crosby is apprehended, or young Patrick Remington has recovered enough to make a statement. We'll be bringing you the latest developments during our normal news broadcast at ten. This is Luke Laramie, for Channel Six News." The picture zoomed in on the fire, filling Ryan's vision with the glowing, ravenous destruction as flames devoured Smythe Hall. A section of roof caved in, driving a shower of brilliant sparks skyward against the darkness.

Ryan reached for the remote and turned off the TV.

John said, "Well. I'm not sure I needed to see that again, but at least you two are all right." He touched Ryan's wrist, above the healing blisters on his left hand.

Mark said, "I wanted to see it. But it still doesn't feel quite real."

Ryan fisted his hand, feeling the blistered skin pull tight, and then opened it again. "What doesn't?"

"Dunno." Mark shook his head impatiently. "It's like, I know I was in that lab with Crosby and a gun, and I was half crazy, excited and confused and freaking scared, and there was smoke and fire. But now, I'm eating chocolate chip cookies, watching it on TV. It's like something I dreamed."

"It's like that sometimes," Ryan said. "You can't hold on to that intensity, which is probably a good thing. But it can feel strange, to wonder how life can possibly go along so normally afterward." Even after David, after Mom, his leg life still kept on going.

21

"I have school tomorrow. I'm supposed to be studying for a history test tonight. When I sit down to study, it feels fake, like I should be doing something more real, um, more important. But when I try to think of what, there isn't anything."

John said, "Studying's good."

"I've had dreams But when I wake up, it fades. I've been trying to write a song. About the fire. And that feels even faker. Like, I'm milking the drama."

Ryan could've told him about those flashes when it did feel all too real, so real it swamped you and dumped you back in time, dragging you down into the smoke and dark, but he hoped Mark would never have that. He moved his leg, and the new stitches tugged, a sharp pain in the familiar, numbed scar tissue. The scars pulled too. He said, "Well, that history test is real, all right. And the consequences if you flunk it will be real too." Not that Mark had flunked anything since he'd arrived, but getting back to normal was best.

"Okay. I'll go study."

"And good luck with the song," John said. "Although, if it doesn't want to come out, then maybe let it wait awhile? You could let ideas simmer while you study." He gave Mark a warm smile.

"Okay. Thanks. G'night." Mark stood and went up to his room. They both sat silently, waiting until they heard the thump of his door closing.

John said, "Not that he wouldn't have a good excuse for messing up the test."

"He's probably better off with something straightforward like history to work on."

"True enough." John slid closer. "What about you?"

"I don't have a quiz until Tuesday."

John chuckled. "So does it feel real to you?"

"The fire? Oh, yeah."

"The burns hurt?"

"Nah. Well, a bit. But I'm well beyond disbelieving it when something burns. It feels real, but I don't need to dwell on it either. It's not a crisis, since no one died. There's always another day and another fire."

Ryan felt John's shudder. "Better not be."

"Well, not for me. I meant in general." Ryan stretched restlessly. The muscles in his good leg twitched. He was spacey from not sleeping, but he needed to work out. "Hey, how about we lift some weights and then have a shower."

"Should you keep taking showers with those stitches?"

"Sure. You can help me cover them. After we get sweaty together." He nudged John with his hip. He urgently needed to relieve the tightness that twanged every muscle and nerve in his body. Times like this, he really missed being able to run, but working with the weights was helpful, and showering with John might even be better than running. Maybe tonight he'd sleep.

****

John sat in the cab of his truck, looking past the safety barriers at the burned-out hulk of Smythe Hall. *Jesus.* He'd seen it two days earlier, but apparently there'd been some demolition. Or maybe some collapse. The room that Mark had hidden in was now a gaping hole in the side of the building.

Beside him, Ryan gave a long low whistle. "Well, they didn't get that controlled fast enough, did they?"

John cleared his throat. "You think they'll have to take it all down?"

Ryan eyed it, no doubt running his experienced firefighter gaze over the damage. "Probably. Fourth through sixth floors are shot. The lower levels held up better, but odds are it's structurally unsound. It's cheaper to rebuild than clean that up." He grinned. "On the plus side, my pharmacology prof had his office in there. If he didn't take the papers home, I might get to rewrite that midterm exam that I think I flunked."

"You've never flunked an exam in your life."

"This might've been the first time."

John shook his head. Ryan thought he flunked everything, right before he came home with another A. He was scary smart but a bit neurotic about his grades. Only Ryan would *want* to retake an exam.

John took a quick look at the landscaping damage that would be his responsibility. The trees along the building looked bad. As soon as the warning tape came down, he'd have to check them over. He had a sad feeling that most of them were done for. The grass was no doubt a wreck, although they wouldn't find out till spring, and there was no point re-sodding a construction zone. The bushes would need a lot of pruning, and some were crushed. He and his crew would have their work cut out for them.

Right now, though, he was delivering Ryan as close to class as he could, totally abusing the college-vehicle sticker on his truck. He pulled his gaze away from blackened walls and twisted pipes, and drove another hundred yards up the restricted drive toward Carlson Hall, stopping right by the steps. "You're going to be okay with the crutches in the snow? I could give you a hand."

"I'm fine." Ryan swung out, hooked his backpack over his shoulder, and fished in the back for his crutches. "I won't say no to a lift home, though."

As if he'd have let Ry take the bus today. "Just text me when and where."

He sat watching as Ryan navigated the slick walkway and stairs, until he was lost in the stream of students going in the doors. Then he drove slowly back across campus to his parking lot. Drove very slowly and very carefully. Students had no awareness of danger and a tendency to step off curbs without looking, earbuds firmly in their ears. He was amazed they didn't have a lot more accidents.

His office was warm. As he turned on the light, he was hit with a sudden memory— Mark's voice, hoarse and terrified. *"Dad, I need help."*

He pulled over his desk chair and sat down hard, his knees shaking.

What if I hadn't still been on campus? What if Ryan hadn't had the knowledge and the guts to go after Mark? *What if?* He put his elbows on his desk and his face in his hands. Only a week ago, he'd thought "disaster" meant his ex-wife showing up on his doorstep and flipping out when she found out he was dating a man. Now he had a whole different definition.

All weekend, he'd thought he was keeping it together so well. Ryan had been insomniac and strained; Mark had had nightmares. John had been solid and calm. He'd thought.

Now he hid his face in his hands and struggled to breathe. *Dear God.* A nightmare parade of could-have-beens sent tremors through his body. Mark burned, Ryan falling, while he was casually driving home, not realizing. *Jesus.*

The scrape of boots on the stairs outside his door gave him just enough time to pull himself together before Kwame and Juan, his winter crewmen, appeared. Kwame said, "Hey, boss. Big mess out at Smythe Hall. Lots of ice from all the water."

"Oh. Hell, yeah." He hadn't been thinking. Some of those walkways were probably skating rinks. "I should've been on top of that."

Juan shrugged. Kwame said, "That lady cop told us to get some sand and ice on it Saturday, so we did. No worries. But you might want to check on it now."

"Let's go look." He stood and gestured them out the door. "So Detective Carstairs talked to you?"

Kwame nodded. "She said the fire was arson. Some prof who went crazy. She was asking around. Not that we had anything to tell her. I don't think I ever met the guy."

The wind outside the door had a bitter edge. It might be the beginning of March, but the month was coming in like a lion this year. John pulled his hood up and hooked up a load of salt from the storage. "Show me what you've managed so far."

There was plenty to do, between salting the ice, inventorying damaged plantings, and showing a construction crew where to install a new chain-link fence to safely cordon off the damaged building. But all morning, John kept finding himself coming out of some distracted fugue, reaching for his phone that wasn't actually ringing, or turning fast toward a building that didn't have flames flickering in an upper window. It wasn't flashbacks, exactly, but maybe a feeling of disbelief that disaster had passed them by. As if some part of him couldn't believe it was over. He heard his phone ring, reached for it and found it silent. Again.

Screw it. He texted Ryan: *Meet me for lunch?* And Mark: *Stop by my office before band practice.*

He was late getting back to his office to meet Ryan. When he hurried down the stairs, Ryan was already sitting in the best chair with his feet up on the other one. Ryan's grin warmed John's chilled body better than the heater did.

"Hey, Ry. Hogging the chairs, huh?"

"Yeah," Ryan drawled without moving his feet. "Hoping my slave is bringing me food, because I really don't want to trek over to the student center for it. I forgot to pack a lunch."

"I remembered." John reached for his backpack and the vital thermos of coffee first. He handed Ryan a mug.

"Ah." Ryan inhaled the steam, took a long, slow sip and closed his eyes. "Bless you, my son. All your sins are forgiven."

"I haven't had time to commit many since you said that this morning." John found the sandwiches he'd made, put Ry's on a paper towel near his empty hand, and perched on the corner of the desk with his own.

Ryan took a bite, licked mayo off his thumb, and grinned at him. "Don't the Catholics think even imagining gay sex is a sin? If so, I've had plenty of time this morning to accumulate a few."

"I'm not Catholic. And I've actually been working."

"Wage slave."

"School brat."

They chewed in silence for a while. Eventually, Ryan said, "I had a text on my phone."

"Hm?"

"Dad. He wants to Skype tonight."

John swallowed, the piece of bread suddenly dry and sticky in his throat. "Is that good? Bad?"

"I'm not sure. He said to be sure you were there too." Ryan set his half-eaten sandwich down. "He's, well, a bit controlling. No, not that, really. He's more of a stage manager. He wants things to go right for his kids, and he's willing to push kind of hard to make that happen. Because he cares."

"How strange of him," John drawled.

Ryan peered narrowly at him, and John widened his eyes in innocence.

He managed to make Ry laugh. "Yeah, maybe it's the pot calling the kettle black. But that's part of the problem. We're a lot alike, and we tend to butt heads."

"It's just a Skype chat."

"True. Distance is good." Ryan downed the last of his coffee and rewrapped the sandwich remnant with jerky motions. "And I do want him to meet you. And you, him."

"So, this could be a good thing."

"I guess. At least we'll know what he thinks. Where we stand."

"Uh-huh."

After that aborted call Saturday, it hadn't escaped John's notice that Ryan had kept his cell phone closer to hand all Sunday. But neither his father nor brother had called back.

"You could conference Brent in," John suggested, not sure if that was a serious suggestion or an attempt at *it could be worse.*

Either way, Ryan actually shuddered. "God. No. Definitely not."

John determinedly finished off the last of his lunch and stood. "Well, we can't stew about it. You have classes, and I've got smashed forsythia bushes to deal with. Those firemen did a number on the plantings."

"Hey, if it's plants or people, the plants lose."

"I'm not complaining. You were one of the people."

Ryan eased his feet down off the spare chair and peered up at John's face. Whatever he saw made him scoot forward and lean his shoulder against John's thigh, hugging his hip despite the unlocked door. "So you'll replant a few bushes. No big."

"Yeah." John touched his hair lightly.

Ryan glanced toward the door, then struggled to his feet with John's hand under his elbow and kissed him, fast and dry. "Dead bodies await me. Is Mark going to band practice today?"

"Yeah. Four to six. He says they plan to keep the band going until Patrick gets better and comes back." *If he ever does.* Patrick had been shot twice in the abdomen, and John had seen those wounds firsthand. Whatever his parents said, John was still keeping his fingers crossed. It was going to be a long recovery, even for a young healthy guy.

"I'll meet you here at six, then?"

"It'll be the highlight of my afternoon."

"Always nice to know I beat out a squished bush." Ryan bumped against his shoulder and went out. John pretended he wasn't listening to Ry's uneven footsteps on the stairs to be sure he got up safely.

Chapter Three

They made it home from campus by six thirty. Mark, sitting between them on the truck's bench seat, was gloomy and silent. John wanted to say something wise and fatherly about the fire or the band or the friend who got shot, but he didn't know which one Mark was worrying about. Not to mention that acting wise was hard to pull off, especially in the eyes of a fifteen-year-old boy.

Ryan was just as quiet. Tired? Painful leg? Dreading the looming Skype with his dad?

John decided that telepathy would be good to have, if his guys were going to go all silent on him. When they got home, Mark mumbled something about not being hungry and took the stairs two at a time up to his room.

John called after him, "Dinner isn't optional."

Ryan said, "I need to check my email. Call me when it's ready?" He disappeared into the front parlor that had become his office, and shut the door.

John was left standing in the entryway. "Well, hell. What am I? Little Suzy Homemaker? *'Call me when dinner's ready?'* Really?"

He stomped upstairs and took a shower. The hot water and the noise soothed him, keeping him from knowing if Mark was studying or just playing three chords over and over on his guitar again, and from hearing if Ry was swearing at his computer screen. His cell phone could ring with news that the biggest tree on campus was down, and he didn't know and couldn't be expected to care as long as he was in the shower. It took the water getting not just cool but cold to finally drive him out.

He dressed, checked his phone to make sure that biggest-tree-falling thing was only in his head, and then went to the kitchen. It was his night to cook. Or to arrange dinner, since the fridge was papered with fliers from every takeout place in town. Most weeknights, they did that. But tonight he wanted to actually make something home-cooked for his guys.

He put frozen fries into the oven, frozen green beans into boiling water, pork chops in a pan. *See? Cooking isn't that hard.* He cleaned the counter while everything was cooking and wiped down the fridge. Swept the floor. Ryan would like that. Put out real plates instead of paper, thought about vacuuming, and then sat down hard at the table. *What the hell?* Maybe he really was some kind of frustrated housewife.

A sudden memory hit him, the first time he met Cynthia's father. Near the end of tenth grade, when he and Cynthia had already been dating for months. Her mother had been sick by then with the cancer that eventually took her, and her dad was doing everything. He'd looked at John, tired eyes locked on his. "You treat her right, you hear me?" And John had answered, "I will. Always. I promise."

They'd gone out with a bunch of friends on a boat on the lake. The boat was big enough to have a cabin, and three of the other couples had taken turns in there, enjoying the private space. But he and Cynthia had stayed on deck. He'd put an arm around her, watched the way her sunshine hair blew across her face, and felt a love and protectiveness so deep in his bones that it hurt. And then he'd taken her safely home with just a kiss...

Ryan came in limping with one crutch and looked at him. "Smells good. When will it be ready? We're supposed to Skype with Dad in twenty minutes."

Ah hell, John realized, it's meet-the-parents-night again. "Five minutes." He thought his tone was casual, but Ryan tilted his head curiously.

"Are you nervous?"

"Are you?" he snapped back.

"Fuck, yeah," Ryan admitted.

John had to laugh. That was Ryan. And despite the déjà vu involved in meeting Ryan's dad, surely it would be easier at thirty-seven than at sixteen. Although that bone-deep love was the same. "I am too. Let me feed you first." He shouted up the stairs for Mark.

They ate fast. The pork chops were kind of dry, and John let Mark escape back to his room without finishing. He exchanged concerned glances with Ryan, but their own ordeal was looming. He could only handle one emotional conversation at a time. Mark would have to wait.

Ryan brought out his laptop so they could set it up on the kitchen table and sit together facing it. John fidgeted, clearing the counter that would be behind them. There was no time to wash the dishes, so he hid them in the sink. He turned on the under-cabinet light, then turned it off when it cast a glare on the screen. Ryan sat at the table and typed, stopped, typed again and cursed under his breath.

"Come sit, John. He's showing up online."

"Maybe you should talk to him first. Alone. Then if he really wants to see me…"

"Get your ass over here in this chair, John Barrett. I am not doing this by myself. I need you."

John sat quickly. "You've got me."

"Thanks." Ryan puffed his cheeks, blew out a breath, and clicked the connection on.

John had a second to wish he'd combed his hair after cooking and put on a different shirt. Then he was looking at an older man in a navy blazer. John noticed a definite resemblance to Ryan, much clearer than in the few pictures he'd seen. Ry's father had the same dark hair, although shot through with silver and cropped short. His nose, his jaw, the way he looked at them with cool confidence Yeah, those two were family for sure. His eyes weren't Ryan's green, though, but something darker.

"Ryan." His voice was deeper too. "Good to see you."

"You too." Ryan shifted in his seat. "Sorry I haven't called more."

"You've been busy, I guess. Busier than I realized."

"Med school's not easy, even in first year."

"That wasn't what I meant." Phillip Ward gave John a small nod. "I'm Phil Ward, and you are ?"

"John Barrett." It came out hoarsely. John cleared his throat self-consciously. "It's good to meet you." He almost added "sir" but kept it back at the last moment. They were all equals here.

"Likewise. So. You and Ryan. You're actually together."

John breathed through his nose. Before he could find an answer to that almost-question, Ryan said, "Cut it out, Dad. I'm right here. If you have questions, you can ask me."

"All right. Have you thought this through?"

"Have I *what*?"

"This, um, relationship. I'm not trying to run your life, but..."

"It sure sounds like you are."

John said, "Give him a second, Ry."

Phil nodded. "Thank you. Now, Ryan, you've told me John has a home and a permanent job there, two teenagers, an ex-wife. He has a lot going on and two kids who look to him for stability."

"And?"

"And you have medical school, which is only going to get harder, demanding all your time, and then you'll do a residency, and probably move out of town in three years. Is it smart to dive into something, um, new and difficult on the relationship front right now?"

"Being with John isn't difficult."

"It won't be easy either. I've been thinking about it the last two days. Heaven knows, I don't want to sound prejudiced but..."

"You're doing a pretty good job of it, for someone who doesn't want to."

"No, really, Ry. I asked myself, what if it was a woman you were with, a woman who was settled with a job and teen kids? And truthfully? I'd advise the same thing. Not to get too serious, to slow it down."

"Slow down."

"Yes. You won't have any time to give to a family for years. You remember when your cousin Linda was in med school, and she fell asleep right in the middle of Thanksgiving dinner? Plus, you'll be moving out of York again soon. If you want a good, worthwhile residency, you won't get it at some little country clinic. So you'll be leaving, and John is settled there."

"Dad, stop." Ryan slapped the table. "Just stop."

"Ryan, I simply want what's best for you."

"What's best for me is John."

John added, "And for me, it's Ryan."

Phil's smile was less than wholehearted. "That's good. That you both say that. But it doesn't change the fact that this— a serious relationship between you two— will be complicated."

"A gay relationship. Don't bullshit me, Dad. You were all pleased I'd met someone, until you found out it was a man."

"I admit, it wasn't what I, um, expected."

"It wasn't what you wanted."

"Don't put words in my mouth, son."

"I don't have to. You pretty much said it, when you told me to slow it down."

John's stomach churned. He felt like the guy caught in a field between two angry bulls, about to tear into each other. He wanted to step between them, but he had the feeling neither one would welcome that and he might end up worse off.

Phil said, "If you can tell me this isn't a distraction to your work, that being in a gay arrangement won't impact your grades or your future opportunities, I'll shut up."

"It's not an *arrangement*, it's a relationship. It won't affect my grades. Anyway, I'm *in* med school already. I just have to pass. *Jesus!*"

"You see? That's not like you right there. Grades still matter for your residency possibilities. You said so yourself last fall. And what if the best opportunity is in Texas, or Alabama? Are you going to tell them you're bi or gay or whatever? Parade John in front of them. Or lie about it?"

"No one's parading. And that's two years away."

"So this is temporary?"

John pressed his fist against his gut and kept his mouth shut.

Ryan snapped, "No! But given that I almost died three days ago, you'll have to excuse me choosing what's important *now*, not what *might* be, two or three years down the road."

"You *what?*" The picture on the screen was crappy, but John could see the shock on Phil's face.

For a moment they were silent. Then Ryan said, more quietly, "No big deal. Just a near-miss. But it helped remind me what's important. Yeah, I still want a successful, interesting career. But if I don't have John, I think none of the rest will matter."

"You're not hurt, are you?"

"Nah. Nothing like that."

Phil nodded slowly. "This is that important to you?"

"It is. He is."

"Even after all the women you dated?"

"Especially after all the women."

"Enough to come home at spring break and introduce John to your brothers and the neighbors, and tell everyone about him?"

John heard Ryan take a sharp breath, but before he could say anything, Ryan grinned fiercely. "Yes, Dad. Even that much. Get Brent and Andrew there for break, and I'll tell anyone you like. I'll wave the fucking rainbow flag in their faces."

Phil and Ryan stared at each other across the miles, both breathing faster. Phil said, "I'll pick you up at the airport. Let me know when."

Ryan said, "We'll rent a car."

"Send me your flight times." Phil clicked off his camera and was gone.

Ryan blew out his breath and turned to John. "What the fuck did I just do?"

"Told your dad we'd visit him and come out to your brothers for spring break?" John suppressed an urge to giggle. He wasn't sure it would sound like humor. "That's the first time the welcome mat has sounded worse than being rejected."

"Yeah. No. I don't know." Ryan coughed. "Damn. He's not a bad guy, but we can't talk about important stuff. It ends up like that."

"So are we actually going?" It sure didn't seem appealing.

"I said we would."

"And you wouldn't want him to think you're backing down?"

34

"Maybe." Ryan slumped in his chair. "It's probably a busy time for you."

"Yeah. Last week of March. The ground will be thawed, most of the snow gone. I have a lot of projects planned."

"So we have a good reason not to go."

Perversely, John said, "I could maybe take a couple of days. A weekend would be best."

"What are you saying?"

John leaned back and looked into Ryan's eyes. "I'm saying this is your call. They're your family. Whatever happens won't make or break me. I'm not some scared sixteen-year-old, and I'm out already to the people who matter in my life."

"Dad can be really hard to take when he's on a roll. Brent is kind of homophobic."

"So yeah, they can probably find ways to make me feel bad, but not enough to really count. I can handle two days of almost anything. But it will matter a hell of a lot to you. So this is your call."

Ryan nodded slowly. "All right. Okay. Let me look…" He leaned over the keyboard, checking some sites online. "Okay. Torey's spring break is the week after ours, so she won't be coming to visit till April second. If we want flights we can't go Friday Maybe Saturday morning, returning Sunday night. We could get tickets for about three hundred apiece."

"Six hundred, to visit for one day? You could always stay longer, even if I have to come back to work."

"No!" Ryan gave him a hard look. "We go together and we come back together. If we do it at all. And what about Mark?"

"He can't stay here alone," John said quickly. Mark might be mature for fifteen, but staying a night alone while both his parents were a thousand miles away was not acceptable.

"We could send him to visit his mom. Or get a sitter. Or bring him along, although it might get messy. Of course, Brent might have to be more civil if Mark was around."

"I'm not using my kid as a shield."

"We'll figure something out," Ryan said. "Maybe you should talk to Mark? See what he thinks?"

"I guess." John stood slowly. "Are we going to be sleeping in your childhood room or anything?"

"Hell, no. For one thing, my dad sold the old house when my mom died. For another, we're getting a hotel. I don't care what it costs. I want a place to go to that doesn't belong to my dad."

"Should we even do this at all? We could invite him here."

Ryan was silent for a long time. John watched expressions come and go across his face, uninterpretable, fleeting. Eventually he said, "I want to go. I can afford it for both of us, or even all three. And I want to get this over with, all at once. Like ripping off a Band-Aid."

"What a compliment," John said dryly.

"Damn." Ryan closed his eyes. "I'm doing this all wrong, aren't I? I hate arguing with Dad. I bet all the crap I've said makes you want to run away fast."

There had been things that had hit John where he lived, but most of them hadn't come from Ryan. Phil had gotten in a few zingers. John didn't want to think about Ry's residency and maybe having to move, although someday they'd have to face that. He also wasn't eager to give Phil a weekend to take more shots at them up close and personal, especially with Brent added.

But he could see that Ryan was holding himself stiffly, eyes squeezed shut and waiting, as if expecting a blow. So he bent and kissed him lightly. "I only remember one thing. You said that without me, nothing else mattered. That's how I feel about you. So let me go ask Mark where he wants to spend that weekend."

****

The flames cast a harsh light behind the sixth-floor windows of the tall building. John squinted upward, his heart pounding so hard he couldn't breathe. Mark stood at a window, silhouetted. Below him, on a lumpy white rope, Ryan swung against the brickwork, his cane in his free hand. He was going to do it; he'd save John's boy. The window he aimed his stick at cracked And then a blast rocked the building. Flames shot out with a vicious roar. Mark and Ryan were blown outward, helpless, tossed into the air fifty feet up like rag dolls. They fell through the sky, clothes sparking, catching flame, flung over John's head, crashing toward the concrete, where he would never be in time to catch them, where he'd never catch them both, but he ran, he reached, cried out—

John woke gasping, arms shaking, bolting upright in bed in his own dark bedroom. For a second, it still felt so real he hesitated to turn, to look or reach across the bed for Ryan. Then when he did turn, the other side of the bed was empty. His heart did one more nauseating flip.

But the sheets were in disarray and there was a dent in the pillow. He laid his palm on it and felt the faint warmth from Ryan's head. As he glanced around, a line of light under the bedroom door was added reassurance. He'd put the hallway light on a motion sensor so if any of them woke in the night and left their rooms, that warm glow would show them the quiet house around them. None of them were sleeping well yet.

He pushed the covers off and stood. His robe hung on the door, but Ryan's was missing. John wrapped the thick flannel around himself over the sweatpants he'd worn to bed and slipped out of the bedroom. Soft voices from Mark's room, through the half-open door, told him there was no need for silence.

Mark and Ryan both looked up when he pushed Mark's door wider. They were sitting side by side on the bed, with Mark snugged against Ryan's side. In the mellow lamplight, they both looked pale and tired, and Mark's cheeks glistened wetly. John went to them. "Room for me on the other side, son?"

They slid over, and he eased down on the bed beside Mark, not caring that the pillow made an awkward lump under him. He wrapped his arm around Mark's shoulders above Ryan's, far enough to brush his fingers against the bare skin of Ryan's neck. For a few minutes, they just sat like that, silent. All there. All still breathing.

John said, "I had a hell of a nightmare. It's good to be here with you two."

Mark twisted to look up at him. "You too?"

"Yeah."

"About the fire?"

"Mm. You?"

Mark shrugged and leaned in against John. "Not really. About Patrick. Weird shit. Like he was climbing stairs and telling me there was a secret at the top. Endless stairs, up and up, with something really bad behind us. And then we got there and he pulled open the door at the top and it opened onto nothing, just a cliff. Empty space. And he stepped out anyway, and fell..." He shuddered, then sighed, becoming less rigid under John's arm.

Ryan stroked Mark's back in small circles. "As a firefighter I used to be fine with heights, but I tell you, I'm getting less fond of them." Ryan stopped rubbing, shifted to ruffle Mark's hair. "No sky-diving holidays for us, huh?"

"Nope." Mark's voice was steadier.

"So this nightmare. Was there a musical soundtrack?"

"I uh..." Mark frowned, tilted his head.

"The scary stuff usually has a soundtrack, right? *Ba-dum, baaaa-dum.* I figured for you, bad dreams probably have one too."

"I don't know..." Mark's voice trailed off. "I don't remember but, well, maybe."

Ryan slid his arm free of their warm tangle to lean off the foot of the bed and snag Mark's acoustic guitar from its stand. He slid down the bed to make more space and held it out to Mark. "Want to try? Put music to it?"

"Um." Mark took the instrument.

Ryan said, "You don't have to, but I figured it might help take away the power if you dissect it a bit. Separate out the music and control that. Right?"

John stood up and leaned against the wall beside the headboard to make room. Mark cradled the guitar, plucked a tentative note, then two. "Maybe..." He tried again, a run of sounds in a minor key. Then another, lower. "Hm. Not quite." He noodled around, tuned a string a fraction, tried a few chords. When he rubbed his cheek with the back of his hand, it was a fast, absent gesture. He bent his head over the guitar, played something haunting and sad.

Ryan stood too, holding the footboard of the bed. "I like that."

"Too sweet, too smooth," Mark muttered. "I need more dissonance. I think..." He played something slower, harsher. "Hm."

John settled his shoulders against the wall. For another ten minutes, he and Ryan stood there as Mark played a few notes, then a line or two, then a ten-note phrase over and over, then a variation. Eventually he looked up. "There's something there. Maybe I'll try and write it out tomorrow." He held the guitar out to Ryan and rubbed his face. "I'm tired."

Ryan stood the guitar back up in the rack. "Want one of us to stay a bit longer?"

"Dad?" Mark's eyes were still shadowed. "Is that okay?"

Ryan gave John a mock shove. "Hey, you. Hang out with your kid while I get back to sleep without you rolling around and snoring." He went out of the room, limping heavily.

Mark said softly, "You think he really doesn't mind?"

That Mark had chosen John to stay? Or that John had let Ryan go off to bed alone? Either way, "Nope. He's fine. Ryan says what he thinks. You know that." He tugged Mark's covers straighter. "Here, slide back in."

Mark lay down under the blankets, and John perched on the edge of the bed. "I liked that little bit that you played. Not the last thing, but the next-to-last one."

"Mm. I think it could be good." Mark turned on his side, not touching John, but close enough that John felt his body heat against the hand he was braced on. He slid the hand over to press against Mark's chest, and Mark didn't pull away. "It did help, to try to play it. I wonder how he knew it would."

"Ryan's pretty smart."

"Yeah. And he says he has nightmares too, and some from even before, from stuff he did as a firefighter. So it's not about being scared, really."

"Nope." John searched for the right words. "Everyone has them. Sometimes stupid stuff, like going to the wrong room for an exam, can make you wake up breathing fast. I still have those, twenty years out of school. And bad stuff like the fire? Or Patrick getting hurt? You have to expect it to show up in dreams."

"Will they still happen in twenty years too, you think?"

"Maybe. But not bad like this. Living through the fire, saving yourselves like you did, that will always be part of who you are. A strong part. You maybe have to pay for it with nightmares, but you gained something too."

"Mm. It's kind of embarrassing, though. I've woken you guys up four times this week."

"We don't care. And I'll tell you a secret." He leaned close to put his mouth near Mark's ear. "Ryan wakes up even more often than you do. And I might have both of you beat. I just don't yell as loud. We'll get through it. All right?"

"All right," Mark murmured.

John leaned and brushed a kiss on his son's temple, the rough teenager skin as precious as the baby softness of those first days of wonder. He ached to make things perfect for his boy, even knowing it never could be done. "Get some sleep."

"Okay. Dad?"

"Yeah?"

"Can I come with you and Ryan? When you go to Oregon?"

"I thought you were going to stay here with a sitter."

"I changed my mind. Can I?"

"Yes, of course. If you want to."

"I think I'd rather." Mark closed his eyes, and took a slow breath. "It's better with you and Ryan around."

"Sure. We'll do that." John had to admit he'd rather have Mark with him too, not a thousand miles away.

"Good." Mark's voice was low and slurred. "Tired."

"I'll stay till you drop off."

"Thanks."

It took less time than he expected for Mark's breathing to slow. John stood carefully and went out, leaving the door slightly ajar. The door of their own room was shut, but when he eased it open, he wasn't surprised to see Ryan propped up on pillows, reading a textbook.

He hung up his robe and slid in beside him. "Not sleepy?"

"Not yet. I was awake when Mark went off this time."

"I didn't hear either of you," John admitted.

Ryan glanced at him, then leaned over to kiss his hair. "Good if one of us could get some rest."

"Well, it didn't end well."

Their eyes met, and Ryan's rueful look acknowledged the truth. "We're all fucked, aren't we?"

"A bit." John squirmed his head into the pillows, trying to get more comfortable. "I think it's getting better. Mark fell asleep a lot faster this time."

"I hope so. If he seems like he's having trouble much longer, we should go looking for a therapist."

"Maybe we can get a group discount."

Ryan rubbed John's leg through the covers. "I think we'll be okay. After I got hurt, it took a while for me to quit reliving it at night, but it did fade."

"He said the guitar helped."

"Good. In my case, I threw myself into getting better. Into exercise, working out, every moment I wasn't studying. Doing something productive and absorbing, and that helped me."

John ran a finger over the rounded, wide curve of Ryan's impressive biceps. "With side benefits."

Ryan actually smiled. "That too. I think music will be that for Mark. We need to do what we can to keep his band going, or at least make sure he's absorbed in playing."

John nodded, then, because he could, he pressed his lips to the firm muscle where his finger had been. "And you and I need to exercise."

That bought him a chuckle. "Couldn't hurt."

He mouthed across Ryan's skin, not really trying to start anything, just drawing in the taste and scent of his man. "Mark wants to come to Oregon with us," he mumbled.

"Oh. Okay."

He lifted his head to glance at Ryan's face. "You're sure?"

"Yeah. I'm glad, actually. If I wake up at two a.m. with the desperate need to be sure he's safe in his bed, I won't have to catch a plane or make him Skype in the middle of the night."

John pressed a kiss against Ryan's neck. "That's pretty much what he said. I love you, you know."

Ryan set the textbook aside, turned out the light and rolled to take John in his arms. "Back at you. In many, many ways."

Kissing was always good. They could do that for as long as it took to drift off, and never consider the time wasted.

Chapter Four

Three weeks later, they landed in Portland in the driving rain. That was normal for the season, other than the force with which it was coming down, and Ryan tried not to take it as an omen. He looked at John, instead of out the window where Mount Hood and the rest of the local peaks were invisible behind gray clouds, the beauty of the West Coast drenched and subdued. The plane bounced as it touched down, buffeted by a gust of wind. Mark leaned a palm on his rain-streaked window and sighed. "I was hoping it'd be warmer than back home."

"I'm sure it is," Ryan said. "But wetter. Sorry. Give it an hour and it may clear up. Weather changes fast here."

The three men in the seats opposite them had watched videos on their devices the whole flight, and were now making packing-up motions. They hadn't even noticed he and John existed, as far as he could tell. And yet the whole flight, he'd still been aware of their presence every time his arm brushed against John's, and every time their knees bumped and he didn't immediately pull away. This was so fucked up. He was so fucked.

John said quietly, "We could just hang out in the hotel until tomorrow and come back home."

"Huh?"

"If you frown much harder, your face will stick that way."

"Idiot." Ryan elbowed him in the ribs, but not hard. "I'm second-guessing myself. For the hundredth time."

"Wouldn't that be 'hundredth-guessing'?" Mark said.

"Maybe two-hundredth." He chewed on his lip and then admitted, "After Dad thought about it some more, which took a few days, he called and asked me if he should tell Drew and Brent not to come. Make it just him and us this first time. And I said no."

43

John said slowly, "You didn't ask my opinion."

"No. I'm sorry." Ryan felt a lurch in his gut. He hadn't thought it would matter to John. He couldn't do this if John was mad at him. "Is it all right?"

"I suppose. They're your family."

"Yeah." He sighed. "I just want to get it over with. Whatever shock or surprise or yelling or stupid cracks they're going to make, I want to have it all done with and move on."

"Will they be mad about you-know-what after all?" Mark asked, glancing at the people across the aisle and lowering his voice. "I thought you said it would be okay."

Damn. He hadn't meant to worry Mark. He really wasn't in control like he should be. "They won't be nearly as bad as your stepdad, I promise. But, well, it'll probably be weird. You can hang out at the hotel if you want. I picked one with an indoor pool and a game room. We can get reactions over with, and then if everyone's calmed down, you can come meet them later. I do promise that in our family, kids always come first. They'll be good to you."

"I'm not a kid," Mark muttered, but he relaxed back into his seat.

John bumped Ryan's shoulder. "It might not be that rough. Your dad did call me to say I was more welcome than it might perhaps have sounded."

Ryan snorted, because he could imagine Dad saying exactly that. "Sounds like him."

"And I've met Brent, and I can take him."

He had to laugh. "True. Although that's not saying much. Even with this leg, *I* can probably take him."

They stood in their turn, and he let John get down the bags. Those long arms had to be good for something. Besides wrapping around him, of course. He shivered. They worked their way off the plane and headed for the exit. John fumbled for his phone as it rang in his pocket. "Forgot to turn that off."

Ry hadn't forgotten his, and hadn't turned it back on either.

John said, "Unknown area code," and answered it. "Hello? Yes, it is. Um, sure, he's right here." He held out the phone toward Ryan and said, "Your brother Drew?"

Ryan took it reluctantly. "Yeah, Drew, what's up?"

"I'm sorry about calling John's phone. Dad gave me his number, and yours is off."

"So?"

"So I see your plane landed, and I'm here to give you a lift."

Ryan stopped short enough that Mark bumped him. "You're what? I told Dad we'd rent a car."

"You know Dad. He said it's stupid to pay fifty bucks for a rental when he has two extra vehicles sitting around that need to be driven."

"So he sent you?"

"Yep. I'm parked in the pickup lane. I've got the Frogmobile."

"Frogmobile." Ryan closed his eyes for a second.

John said softly, "Problem?"

Drew coaxed, "You can cancel your rental. Come on— it'll save you fifty bucks. And I promise I won't say a wrong word the whole trip back."

"All right." Ryan started walking again. "We'll look for you at the curb. At least you didn't bring the Trans Am."

"That one's up on blocks now," Drew said. "See you in a bit."

Ryan passed John's phone back. For several minutes, as they made their way through the steady stream of people, both John and Mark managed not to ask anything. Ryan got a sour satisfaction out of betting which one would break first.

Sure enough, it was Mark. "Trans Am? Frogmobile?"

"The Trans Am belonged to one of my brothers. Dad keeps saying he's gonna sell it, but he never does." It had been David's. It was never going to be sold. "The Frogmobile is a VW bus that was once bright green. It broke out in these rust spots all over it, like warts, probably ten years back, and that name stuck. But it usually runs, and has lots of room for four."

John said, "Drew's here to give us a ride?"

"Yeah. I'll call and cancel the rental. It does make sense."

"Sure."

Ryan glanced at John, but he looked unruffled. Sometimes his easy calm drove Ryan a little nuts. On this trip, he had a feeling it was going to be a saving grace. "At least it's not Brent."

"True."

Sure enough, the Frogmobile was easy to spot along the curb. The bright green rounded shape stood out, even in the dull drizzle that was still falling. They slung their bags in the back, and Ryan hesitated. Front seat for John, with his leg length, or for Ryan? John might be safer in back, farther away from Drew. Drew got out and came round to the curb before he'd decided.

"Hey, Ry, good to see you." He gave Ryan a hug. It felt the same as always, and Ryan wondered if his dad hadn't explained why they were suddenly having a family meeting, or if Drew seriously didn't care. He stepped back and looked at Drew, who seemed to be the same quiet, brown haired, brown eyed, casual, sweatshirted, boring, comfortable self as always. Ryan tried to decide if Drew was looking at John like he knew what they were to each other. Drew was looking at Mark, though.

"Hey, you must be Mark. I'm Ryan's big brother, Andrew, and most people call me Drew. Why don't you come sit up front? Dad says you haven't been to Oregon before, and you'll get the best view."

"Of the rain," Ryan muttered.

"Until ten minutes from now, when it'll be sunny. Come on, let's go before I get a ticket for parking too long."

Ryan couldn't think of a good reason not to, so he and John climbed into the second-row seat and buckled the lap belts. The narrowness of the seat meant his hip was pressed against John's, but he seriously didn't mind that. He set his cane on the floor at their feet. Up front, Mark commented tentatively about how tall the trees were. Drew pointed out a mountain playing hide-and-seek through the thinning overcast. John stared out at the green Oregon landscape, and Ryan watched the back of his brother's head, the set of his shoulders, the angle of his jaw, for some kind of clue.

He waited silently, if not patiently, for Drew to give him a hint, until they were cruising northwest along the highway, clearing the suburbs, and he couldn't stand it anymore. "Did Dad tell you why we're all gathered here today?" He couldn't help the phrase or the tone.

Drew replied easily, "He didn't mention a wedding. But yeah, he said we were meeting your friend John and his son."

"Because…" Ryan didn't want to open the topic in the car, if it was news. But he needed to know.

"Because you had a chance to visit."

Ryan blew out a dissatisfied breath, and Drew chuckled, damn him.

"I'm yanking your chain. At first, I wasn't going to come just to hang out with a friend of yours, even if I wouldn't mind seeing you. I don't get a lot of time off, with the kids and all, and we had plans. So Dad told me you were in a kind of relationship with John, and it was important we should get to know him. I admit, I was surprised." Drew steered easily, one hand on the wheel. Ryan glanced up in the rear-view, but Drew's eyes were on the road, not looking back at him that way.

"And?"

"I might even go so far as saying I was shocked, but not because it's a bad thing. I live in a pretty liberal part of town. I have a couple of friends who are gay. It doesn't bother me."

"How open-minded of you," Ryan muttered, and then wheezed as John elbowed him hard.

"Be nice," John said firmly. "Your brother's saying what he thought, and it doesn't sound half bad to me."

Drew added, "I lost count of the girls you dated, and we never heard about even one guy. So it took me a little while to put you and gay together. Then I really got curious to meet John. I wanted to see the guy who could make you hold still for a relationship, of any kind."

"It snuck up on us," John said.

"Well, you must be doing something right. Because there were a hell of a lot of hot babes trying to get a ring out of this guy, and none of them got anywhere past the second date."

The thought that Drew could be okay with this warmed Ryan. His tension headache receded for the first time all day, but he had to say, "It's not like we're actually getting married."

"You're bringing someone home to meet Dad. When was the last time you did that?"

Ryan tried to remember. *Junior prom, maybe. And only because we'd agreed to meet at my house.*

Drew nodded at his silence. "Yeah, that's what I recall too. Never. We saw you out on the town with girls, but there wasn't one of them you wanted us to get attached to."

Mark said, "So this, with my dad, is a good thing? Right?"

Ryan cursed himself silently. He should've insisted that Mark should stay home for the weekend, no matter how much the kid didn't want to. Plain speech and keeping Mark feeling safe weren't going to mix well. "I love your dad, Mark. My family needs to know that."

Drew made a soft "ha" sound. "John, you and I are going to have a long talk about what kind of magic you practice. Mark, it's a very good thing. Even I can see that. Our brother Brent and our dad may have their issues, but it's obvious to me. Don't worry."

John said, "That mountain over there. Is that a volcano?" He pointed out the back window to the right.

Everyone but Drew turned eagerly to look at it. Drew said, "Yeah. Mount Hood. They say it's dormant, but I've seen predictions as high as a ten percent chance of an eruption in the next twenty years."

Mark said, "Cool! I didn't know there were, like, active volcanoes here."

Drew began to talk about the Mount St. Helens eruption, thirty years ago. Ryan leaned against John's shoulder and just listened. Drew encouraged Mark to ask questions, and then to talk about himself. Drew was definitely Ryan's favorite family member right now. Maybe favorite of all time. He didn't realize he was shaking until John's hand closed over his knee, squeezing him reassuringly.

Ryan wanted to put his own hand over it and hold on to John, but the open interior of the bus meant they might be within Drew's sight. There was being okay with something in theory, and there was being comfortable with seeing it, and he didn't want to find out where Drew stood. He forced himself to stillness and murmured, "Thanks." After a moment, John smiled tentatively and let go.

Ryan liked coming to Oregon at this time of year. In Wisconsin, the trees were mostly bare, first leaves at most a wispy veil along a few branches. Oaks still wore the ragged brown of fall, and the long, dead winter grass was barely touched with new green. Here, spring was well underway. The roadsides were covered with wildflowers, an expanse of white and yellow clusters in the grass below the towering West Coast pine trees. There were bushes everywhere, blooming white, pink, and gold. As the rain cleared and the sun came out, the colors struck him with their brilliance. The warmth outside the van was an odd contrast to the chill in his gut as they got closer and closer to home.

They turned north, and then west again, on smaller roads, until a hard right turn put them on the tree-lined gravel drive heading for the house.

"You didn't grow up here," John said. "Right?"

"Nope. This is Dad's retirement place. He was a cop, did twenty-five years, and then came here. Now he does security consulting and grows cabbages."

"Ick," Mark said.

Drew laughed. "Not just cabbages. He has an organic vegetable plot and sells lots of different produce to a couple of local restaurants."

They turned the last corner, and the house came into view. It was an ugly place, two stories of a wood-sided rectangular box on a concrete foundation, but the property was gorgeous. The trees that circled the house topped it by a good fifty feet, shading it from the brightening sunshine, and the woods and fields rolled out green and lush on either side.

"Needs new paint," Ryan muttered, to hide the way arriving made his heart both leap and flinch.

Drew said, "Dad bought some paint. If the sunshine holds out, we can help him do it this weekend. Makes a nice group project." He pulled around and parked beside an unfamiliar red compact car.

"Is that Brent's?"

"Rental. He got in yesterday."

Ryan stared at it. "I forgot. We'd planned to go to the hotel in Saint Helens first and check in." *And drop off Mark out of the way of the first reactions.*

Before Drew could answer, the dogs came into sight around the house. They both frolicked up to the bus, panting and waggling their shaggy butts, displaying doggy grins. Mark grinned back. "Cool dogs! Can I pet them?"

John said, "They look friendly."

Ryan sighed. "They are. Knock yourself out, Mark. Just don't let them knock you over. Sarge, the big one, probably outweighs you."

Mark wriggled out of his seat belt and half fell out of the bus into the enthusiastic greetings of the dogs. John smiled to see it. Ryan muttered, "He's going to ask us for a dog. You just wait."

"I might think about it," John whispered back. "Look at that grin he's got."

Ryan was watching, and it took him a long time to raise his gaze past the boy and the dogs to where two men stood on the porch. They weren't looking at Mark, and they weren't grinning. His dad looked pensive. Brent looked like he'd bitten a lemon.

Ryan unlatched his seat belt and nodded their way for John's benefit. "Showtime." He leaned forward to put a hand on Drew's shoulder. "Do me a favor? Get Mark out of here for a bit? Let him take the dogs for a walk, show him the garden or the neighbor's horses. I'll text you when we're good with Dad." *If they managed that little feat.*

"Sure." They all got out and went around to Mark. Drew said, "Come on, Mark, you probably need to stretch your legs after all that travel. Why don't we take the dogs along and go see Mr. Harris's heavy horses?"

"Heavy horses?" Mark paused with a hand on Sarge's upturned head.

"Percherons. Big ones. Like what knights in armor used to ride."

"Dad, is that okay?" Mark glanced toward the house and then back at John. "Maybe I should stay here."

"Go with Drew," John said. "Have a good walk."

"Don't listen to any of his lies about when I was a kid," Ryan teased. "He'll tell you all kinds of crap. Remember he's my brother."

Mark managed a small smile that had a hint of "you're not fooling me" in it. But he ruffled Sarge's ears, looked at Drew and said, "Okay."

Ryan stood beside John, watching, as Drew gathered up boy and dogs, and led the way toward the woods. They waited, eyes on Mark, until the little group rounded a clump of trees. Then as one they turned back to the house.

John moved ahead of Ryan when he slowed for the front steps, and reached the porch first. He said, "Phil, good to meet you," and held out his hand.

"John." Dad shook his hand briefly and let go, his expression cool.

"Brent, nice to see you again."

"You too."

Ryan had the impression Brent said it through clenched teeth, but at least he said it. John kept a pleasant smile in place, as Ryan reached his side.

Dad said, "Why don't we go on in, and give Ryan a chance to sit down?"

It was Ryan's turn to clench his teeth, but he followed Dad into the living room. John stuck close to his side. Ryan deliberately chose to sit on the couch, far enough to one end to make it clear he wanted John to sit right beside him, leaning his cane against the cushions to block off the other side. The couch dipped nicely under John's weight. At least he was bringing home a partner whom Dad couldn't just out-bulk.

Dad said, "So. Did you boys have a good flight? Did it rain as hard down in Portland as it did here?"

"It was pretty wet," John agreed.

"It's a pity you have to head home so quickly. It's supposed to be unusually dry the next few days. You could see Oregon at its best."

"The drive up was pretty."

"The blossom will really open up with a bit more sun. I hear you like plants."

"They're kind of my job."

"Stop," Ryan said. "Enough already. Can we just talk?"

Dad gave John a smile without much humor in it. "How do you put up with him?"

"He usually makes sense," John said, without sounding in the least sarcastic.

Dad turned to Ryan. "What did you want to say?"

Fuck. He'd expected to be reacting, not starting the conversation. He'd anticipated some kind of argument, a question, an insult, something to get the ball rolling. Instead his damned father was looking at him with his cool, enough-rope-to-hang-themselves, interrogation expression.

Ryan sat up straighter. "So. John and I are boyfriends." This part he'd practiced. "Our relationship is important to me. Long-term. I want us to be treated the same as you treated Grace and Drew when they were dating. Or Anne, if Brent brings her here. Will that be a problem?"

Brent said, "Well, it's not exactly the same, is it? For one thing, you're not planning to get married."

"You never know," John said. "We've only been together a few months so far."

"I mean, you can't. It's not legal."

"It is in Massachusetts," Ryan said. "And Canada and plenty of other states, some even without residency, so we could drive somewhere and do it. This is 2011, not the dark ages. I'd bet it's only a matter of time for Wisconsin."

"You've checked into it?" John turned a pleased smile on him, as if the other two weren't there.

"I might've," Ryan admitted.

"That's beside the point," Brent muttered.

"I thought you said it was the point?"

"Yeah. No." Brent frowned and subsided.

Dad said, "I don't pretend to know how a guy who's been straight all his life suddenly becomes gay, but that's not my real concern."

"It isn't?" Ryan crossed his arms and waited for Dad to talk himself out of this one.

"No. I'm worried about you, son. About all the changes in your life, in so short a span. I'm concerned about what you might lose if you get too deep into a relationship, while trying to get through medical school." He glanced at John. "Any relationship. That's not meant to be an insult to you."

Ryan allowed a hint of sarcasm to leak through. "So when I called you up and said I'd met someone special, that pleasure in your voice was an illusion? The pleasure that went away when I told you my lover was a man?"

"I was pleased you'd come out of your shell," Dad said slowly. "But then I thought about it some more..."

"And hung up on me."

"I didn't hang up."

"You sure as hell did."

"I needed to think."

"And what did you come up with?"

Ryan had thought he had Dad on the ropes, but at that question his old man said, "That you're finally on track to becoming the doctor you always wanted to be. Not the firefighter that losing David made you. You gave up your dream once, out of the wrong kind of love. And I didn't want to see that happen again."

Ryan's heart stuttered, and his chest felt tight. "The way I reacted to David's death wasn't wrong! Neither is what I feel for John!"

"What you did for David almost got you killed. If you do a residency in some inadequate, podunk hospital and become a GP instead of the neurology specialist you wanted to be, you'll be selling yourself short again."

"No! That will be adjusting my goals for an important reason."

"And I also have some say in that," John interjected in his deep voice. "I don't know what kind of relationship you think this is, but I'm not going to let Ryan sacrifice his career for me. If he needs to go somewhere else to become the doctor he wants to be, even if it takes years, I'll be the first one to tell him to go."

"Hah, you '*won't let Ryan*,'" Brent said. "You'll even '*tell him.*' Right. He's more stubborn than a rhinoceros. I bet I know who wears the pants in your house, and it wouldn't be you."

Ryan took a breath to blast that "pants" comment and coughed it out as John pinched him hard, his hand hidden between their knees.

John said, "You're mistaken. There are two men in this relationship. We both wear pants. And sometimes take them off each other."

Brent opened and closed his mouth like a fish.

That pinch had somehow brought Ryan back from the furious edge. He added, "And seriously? *Rhinoceros?* Anyway, John is like a tree. A redwood. He doesn't get moved unless he chooses to. Not even by me."

Dad added, "Brent. Be civil or go outside."

Brent sat back, grumbling under his breath.

Dad turned back to Ryan. "Look, all I want is for you to take this slowly, all right? Don't dive into things and burn your bridges like you did last time. Maybe you really are, um, gay, and this will be the relationship of your life. Or maybe it will turn out to be a college fling. I just…"

"It's not a goddamned *fling!*"

"I used the wrong word. I didn't mean not serious, but maybe not long-term. Like when Drew and Ellen were so hot and heavy, and we all thought they'd get married. Ellen went away to graduate school, and they drifted apart. Then Drew met Grace, and she fit him and his life the way Ellen hadn't."

"Ellen was boring." It was a crappy comeback.

Dad smiled slightly. "Yeah, she was. But Drew really loved her, for a while. If it'd lasted, we'd have welcomed her and made adjustments for her OCD about arranging the kitchen and her obsession with giant pieces of abstract sculpture. And if you stay with John, we'll adjust to that too. Just go slow. That's all I ask."

"First time I've been compared to a sculpture," John said.

Ryan could tell he wasn't as amused as he was trying to sound, but like so often in arguments with his dad, the ground seemed to be shifting under Ryan's feet. "So you'll *adjust* to me being gay."

"Are you gay? Or are you just interested in John? If you weren't with John, would you date a woman or another man?"

Ryan managed to stay cool under the intent stares of both Dad and Brent. "I'm bi." He'd decided after a lot of thought that was the truth. "I'm with John right now, though. I can't imagine dating anyone else, guy or girl."

John gave him an odd look, which only clicked when John said, "I'm bi too. I loved my wife, until she left me. And I love Ryan. Right now, and for as long as he'll let me."

Ryan winced. He hadn't meant *right now* as any sign he wasn't committed. It was just a phrase, an acknowledgment that things could change, and Hell, his dad had his brain all twisted around. "I love John," he said. Because John shouldn't be left to wonder. "There's no one else I've ever said that about. No one else I've ever brought home. So what I need is to know that he's as welcome as any woman I might have introduced the same way."

"I can't promise that," Dad said. "I promise I'll try. I'm an old man, and the world is changing, and this is one more thing I have to adapt to."

John said, "I feel so sorry for the gay men who went through this fifty years ago. Or a hundred."

Dad blinked. "I suppose. Yes, at least I don't have to worry about a mob dragging you two out and lynching you."

John shook his head. "I was really thinking about the number of fathers who wouldn't have even tried to understand back then. The way those gay men had to simply expect to be rejected. So thank you."

"Ah." Dad actually dropped his gaze. "You're welcome."

Ryan didn't feel like they'd come up with a reason for gratitude, but he'd follow John's lead. People liked John. He murmured something similar, but narrowed his eyes at Brent, to show he wasn't included in the thank-yous.

John glanced at the window. "It looks pretty sunny out there. Drew said something about wanting to get house painting done, with the dry spell on the way? Can we help?"

"Sure." Dad popped out of his chair as if propelled by springs. "If you're up for it."

"I'm not good at sitting idle," John said, standing too.

"I can lend you two a couple of old sweatshirts."

"Sounds good."

"There's a bathroom through there." Dad pointed. "Unless, Ryan, have you changed your mind about spending the night here? I have room."

"Nope." Fifteen minutes of conversation, and he had the beginnings of an ulcer. "But I'd be happy to help paint."

"Tough to do with a cane," Brent said.

"I'll manage."

Brent headed out via the kitchen. Ryan got up and stood next to John, just listening as Dad went up the stairs and came back down with the old shirts.

John took them and put his hand lightly on Ryan's arm. "Ry? Painting clothes? This way?"

"Huh? Yeah. Sure."

The downstairs bathroom was small, but John steered him in and closed the door behind both of them.

"Fuck." Ryan leaned forward and rested his forehead against John's shoulder.

John wrapped those wonderfully long arms around him and folded him in. "What? I thought it went okay. A hell of a lot better than with Cynthia and Brandon, anyway."

Ryan huffed a laugh against his neck. "High praise. Yeah, I guess it did."

"But?"

Ryan shook his head, enjoying the way John's chin rasped against his forehead. "Arguing with Dad is always like that. He twists me in a pretzel."

"He was kind of twisty."

Ryan lifted his head and leaned his good hip against the sink. "His last eight years on the force, he was their main hostage negotiator."

"I bet he was great."

"No doubt."

"Well, he didn't kick us out, or condemn us to hell."

"True." Ryan met John's eyes. What had Dad implied? "You have to know I don't think this— you and me— is some kind of college fling. And you're not the gay equivalent of the six-legged metal cow that Ellen convinced Drew to invest in."

John's lips quirked. "Good to know."

56

"I might say stuff to Dad that doesn't sound so good. He gets me going sometimes. But if it bugs you if there's something I say that hurts you, tell me? In private, maybe, but don't assume it's gospel just because Dad drags it out of my mouth."

"Because what? Sometimes you're just trying to score a point on him?"

"Yeah." Ryan felt sheepish. "Nice, huh?"

"Human, I guess. I appreciate the reassurance about the cow."

"Idiot."

"What about Brent? Do you think he'll be trouble? He wasn't enthused."

"No." Ryan reached for the smaller of the sweatshirts and began pulling it on. Through the fabric across his face, he said. "He's a moron. But he won't do more than talk. And Dad and Drew will keep him in line around Mark, I'm sure."

"Fair enough." John shoved his arms into the other shirt. "Let's paint the house."

****

John didn't get a chance to catch Brent alone until it was almost time to leave on Sunday. By then he was actually feeling pretty good. He was nearly certain both Ryan and Mark had managed to sleep through without nightmares. Mark loved the dogs, and the woods, and Drew was great with him. The weather had held, and they'd managed to complete one coat of light beige paint on the whole house over the two days. So he was calling the visit a success, except for the way Brent was avoiding both him and Ry, refusing to meet their eyes and ducking out of conversations the moment John chimed in.

Ryan had gone inside to wash up after they finished painting, taking Mark with him. Phil was putting the leftover paint in the basement, and Drew was on the phone with his wife. So John took down the ladder and shouted to Brent, "Hey! Help! Can you get the other end of this?"

Brent had turned away, but he looked back reluctantly, then came and lifted the dragging end off the ground. They carried it into the garage and hung it on the hooks along the wall. When Brent would have whirled around and left, John grabbed his arm. "Hang on a minute."

"What?"

"Look." John let go and tried to sound casual. "You met me in York, and I thought we got along okay. Now all of a sudden you can hardly stand to be in the same room with me. So what changed?" Not that he didn't know, but he wanted Brent to say the words. This coming-out was a strange place to be, for a man who was almost thirty-eight. But he wanted it up front, where he could react directly.

Brent said, "Well, it wasn't me that changed."

"Nor me. Ryan and I were already together then."

"But I didn't fucking know it, right? I didn't know you'd turned my brother gay!"

"I did *what*?"

"You heard me." Brent made a disgusted face. "I've known Ryan for thirty years, and he has never been interested in men. Not *ever*. Then he moves in with you, and suddenly he's gay? I had a cool brother who was going places, and you made him queer!"

The accusation was just ludicrous enough that John was left without a comeback as Brent whirled and stalked out the front. John stared after him. Eventually he said to the open space, "I was the one with the wife and kids. Maybe he made *me* gay. Did you ever think of that?"

He turned away and found himself looking straight at Ryan, standing in the open door to the house with a startled look on his face.

"Oh hell!" John smacked his own head. "Hey, Ry, remember how you said your dad makes you say stupid stuff? Apparently your brother has the same effect on me."

Ryan's smile seemed a little forced. "Brent has that effect on a lot of people. He's surrounded by his own personal stupidity field, and other people get sucked into it. I was going to ask if you knew why he just peeled out of here without waiting to give us a ride to the airport, but maybe I have a clue?"

"Yeah. I said something. He said something. Frankly, I'd rather spend a hundred bucks on a cab than ride with him right now."

"I expect either Drew or Dad will drive us."

"I should give your dad back this sweatshirt and pants and clean up, I guess."

Ryan stood back, holding the door open for John to come inside. In the doorway, John paused, close enough to feel the heat of Ryan's body, inches from his own. "Are you worried I might have meant what I said?"

"Not really." But John saw Ryan's gaze drop.

"What you made me," he said softly, "was happy. When I wasn't sure I would ever be again. Gay or straight doesn't mean anything, compared to that."

Ryan's voice was equally low. "I'd kiss you but you have paint all over you. Go get changed."

"Ten minutes."

When he passed through the kitchen, heading for the bathroom, Phil intercepted him. "Hey, you look like a man who could use a shower. Mine's free. Through the master bedroom. Left at the top of the stairs."

"My clothes are in the half bath." He held up paint-smudged hands to show why he didn't want to carry them elsewhere.

"I'll bring them up and put them outside the door."

"Okay. Thank you." John climbed the stairs and turned left. He tried not to look around too much as he passed through Phil's room to the bathroom. He got an impression of neat, stark masculinity, and a wall-length bookcase. The bathroom door was open, and he went in.

There was a clean towel draped over the sink in obvious invitation. The shower stall was fogged from someone else's turn. John wiped his hands on the paint-smudged sweatshirt, stripped and got in under the water. He soaped fast, working the beige smears out from under his fingernails as quickly as he could. They still had about an hour until they had to head out, but using Phil's shower and Phil's shampoo made him twitchy. Despite the hours they'd spent together, painting, then eating dinner yesterday, and sitting around with a beer afterward, and painting again today, John didn't feel like he knew Ryan's father at all.

Phil was calm and controlled, watchful and reserved. He'd even kept Mark at arm's length, despite Ryan's statement about how much his dad liked kids. You couldn't prove it by this weekend. Thank goodness Drew had stepped up to hang out with Mark. Between Drew and the dogs, John thought Mark had enjoyed the visit.

John stepped out of the shower, dried off, and pulled his briefs on. When he cracked the door open to look, his clean clothes were on the floor. And Phil was standing by the window, not looking his way. John grabbed his jeans and tugged them up quickly. That went a long way to feeling less exposed. He slid his arms into his shirt and began buttoning it.

Phil said to the window, "Thanks for the painting job. I hadn't planned to make you work on your holiday."

"No, it was good to have something to do. Better than sitting around ignoring the elephant in the room. Or arguing about it."

"Hm. That's one way to look at it."

"Maybe we'll be back sometime?" John let his tone make it a question.

"You're always welcome. You and your boy, for as long as you're with Ryan."

"Really? I wasn't sure."

Phil gave him a startled look. "Why not?"

"You kept your distance. Not just from me but from Mark." That was what hurt, John realized. Not for himself. He could fully understand that. But treating Mark like there was something wrong with him, because of who John was, didn't sit well.

Phil said slowly, "I hadn't realized. He's a great kid. Maybe I didn't want to get attached."

"You *what*?"

"I miss having the boys around the house. But if things don't work out with you and Ryan, then I won't see Mark again." Phil's steady stare was a challenge.

"So I should stay with Ry so you get another grandson? Or you're so sure we'll break up that you'll protect yourself at Mark's expense."

Phil chuckled unconvincingly. "I think between Solo licking his feet and Sarge licking his face, the kid didn't have time to notice me."

60

"I think you're underestimating what Mark notices. But yeah, you probably don't hold a candle to the dogs, for him." John was disappointed to see no sign that little insult went home. "So, you think this is something temporary for Ryan?"

"I don't know. But I think perhaps for his sake it should be."

John frowned. "You want to explain that, in small words?"

"I don't need to rehash it. You heard me the first time. He gave up his dream of being a neurologist for eight years to live David's dream. I don't want to see him give it up a second time to live yours."

"What if my dream turns out to be his too?"

"You might be able to convince him of that," Phil said. "But is that really the right way to show you care about him? Will you act in his best interests, or yours?"

John swallowed uneasily. One thing he did know, though. "Ryan won't thank me for making any kind of decision for him."

"But he'll try to do what's right for you. That's how he is. If, in three years, he gets a great training opportunity in Boston or Rochester, will you be able to let him go take it? Be away from him for years? What if the spot he wants is in Mississippi and he's competing with straight candidates? Will you make him put you and the kid first?"

"In three years, Mark will be eighteen and heading to college anyway."

"And your daughter? And your job?"

John shook his head. "I'm not going to look that far ahead and borrow trouble. If we're still together in three years, odds are I'll have asked him to marry me, and I might even follow him wherever."

"*If* you're still together." Phil headed for the door. "Drew will give you a ride back to Portland. I need to get some of my planting done in the garden while the weather holds. Have a good flight."

John cursed silently as he pulled on his socks and tied his shoes. He left the paint-spattered shirt and sweatpants on the bathroom floor. Let Phil clean them up. Damn the man. He couldn't fault Phil for wanting what was best for Ryan, but he sure as hell could fault him for having some narrow definition of "best". And for making both himself and Ryan say *"if"* about their future in one weekend. Dammit. No wonder Ryan got so uptight around his dad.

He went down the stairs two at a time. Ryan was in the kitchen, talking to Drew. John suddenly needed to kiss him. But he didn't. He went and stood next to him, elbows brushing, and waited until they were done. Then he dredged up his best smile and said, "Let's go home."

Chapter Five

Ryan decided being back home with John but on break, with their routine messed up, felt weird. The weekend at Dad's had just made it feel weirder. By Friday afternoon, Ryan was very ready for spring break to be over.

There was a rhythm he'd gotten into all term, waking with John, getting up early and riding in together, then a full day of classes and labs and an evening of studying. Being so busy had kept him from thinking too much. He'd realized he missed that this week. Especially since John had been out working extra hard while the campus was quiet, so there was no one to share the pleasure of sleeping in with.

He wandered into the empty kitchen, set a second pot of coffee to brew, which he didn't really need but was going to indulge himself with, and sat down at the table with his computer. His email showed a dozen messages waiting in the inbox. Mostly junk, a couple via his university address, and then two potential time bombs— messages from Dad and from Brent.

He flushed the spam and then hovered over the rest. Should he do the school stuff, as calmly as he could with the others hanging over him, or bite the bullet? He slid the cursor up and down the list, then closed his eyes. *Hand of Fate.* He slid the mouse up and down and clicked without looking.

He opened his eyes. Dad. Okay.

Hey Ryan,

I had a call out of the blue from our old neighbor, Steve Bosco. You remember, the guy with the twins who are your age? I thought you might like to know that Dirk is apparently a lawyer (why am I not surprised) and Lauren is out your way, in Minnesota, doing research at the Mayo Clinic. Still single. He said you should give her a call when you're thinking about summer jobs or internships, and she might be able to help steer you to something there. The Mayo is the best. I've linked her contacts.

I've also attached a couple of pictures from this weekend, off my cellphone. I was glad you could visit. Keep in touch, and think about what I said.

— Dad

Ryan clicked on the attachments. There was a great picture of Mark, rolling in the damp grass with Sarge, the boy half-hidden by the big dog but clearly happy. One of Ryan himself, up a ladder despite everyone and their uncle having tried to keep him safely on the ground. He had his good leg braced against the rungs and an expression of concentration that was almost a scowl. Or maybe that had been about the time it had started to really fucking hurt. Not flattering. He closed it.

Then a close-up of him and John. They weren't hugging or even really touching each other beyond a brush of sleeves. But somehow the tilt of their heads and the direction of their eyes was intimate. It didn't scream *gay lovers* but it was nice. He emailed it and the one of Mark to his own phone and sat looking at the one of himself with John on the screen.

Talk about mixed messages. He had no clue what Dad had been thinking when he sent all that. Lauren had hung out with him in high school, and they'd dated for about two seconds before deciding they were better friends. So the message sounded like "go find a nice het relationship away from John", but the picture suggested something more accepting. He rubbed his forehead. Understanding Dad had always been an uphill battle, far more so than just defying him.

He heard John's truck pull into the garage. A minute later, John came inside, bringing a gust of air that was warm and smelled of grass and rain.

Just seeing him made Ryan feel better. "You're home early. There's fresh coffee."

John gave him that smile that made him gooey inside, like a melting marshmallow. "I think I love you." He poured himself a cup and cradled it in his long fingers. "It's too wet to do much, so I gave the guys a break. We'll work tomorrow."

"You do remember Torey's coming?"

"Of course. I'll be done before it's time to go get her." John shifted so he could see the picture of them on Ryan's screen. "That's nice."

"Yeah. Dad took it."

"Can I get a copy?"

Ryan suddenly remembered John saying *"I want to have your picture on my phone and hug you when I see you..."* They didn't do couple stuff on campus. Not yet. He ignored stupid butterflies in his stomach and said, "Sure. I'll send it over. There's a nice one of Mark too." He clicked Send.

It annoyed him that he'd hesitated. Coming out affected little things and big things, and he really fucking resented that sometimes. If John had been Lauren, he wouldn't have thought for a second about whether a picture of them together was going to be her phone's wallpaper.

"Did your dad have any news?" John asked casually, turning to dig in the pantry cupboard.

"Just gossip about old friends." Ryan closed the email and moved it to his "Dad" folder.

Which left the other lurking one. *Get it over with.* "There's one from Brent too."

John came over and sat beside him, putting a cookie on the table by Ryan's elbow, not saying anything. He just sat there, big and solid and comfortable. Ryan picked up the cookie, took a huge bite to fill his mouth and opened Brent's mail.

Ryan,

It was good to see you looking healthy and all, even if I didn't say so. But finding out you think you're gay Did we even know each other at all as teenagers? I wish you'd said something back then. I had no clue.

Ryan frowned. He'd had no clue either as a teen. Maybe a few times, a flash of thinking some guy looked hot, a brief interest in some naked ass in the locker room that was more visceral than aware. If he thought about it at all, he'd assumed that guys' asses looked a lot like girls', and he had a well-proven interest in girls' asses. He wasn't sure where Brent got the idea he'd been in the closet all his life.

I remember stuff I said that probably wasn't cool. I don't mean to come off anti-gay because I'm not. But...

Okay, this is going to sound cold. After I just said I was okay with you being gay. But I have to say it.

Anne and I have set the wedding date— June 11. It's going to be pretty small, back in her hometown outside Houston. Her family is great, but they're pretty conservative, and so I have to just tell you. You're invited. I really want you to be there. But I don't want you to bring John.

I like him okay. I guess, if you have to be with a man, at least he's not all swishy or loud. But if people get an idea what you two do, it'll just ruin the wedding. So you should just come alone. I'm not asking you to bring a woman, like a fake date or anything. Just come by yourself and keep it quiet. Okay? I bet summer is busy for John with his gardening anyway, right? And it's not like he's really part of our family, just because you've been with him for a couple of months.

Anne says she's looking forward to meeting you. I'd like you to meet her too.

— Brent

Ryan tried to take a deep breath and ended up inhaling cookie crumbs. By the time he was done coughing, spraying spit onto his laptop and cleaning up, he was past the first urge to put his fist through the screen. Not past the boiling anger that churned deep in his gut. "Motherfucking homophobic idiot! I'll not-family him!"

"Ry. Don't choke to death, okay?"

"That sanctimonious prick!"

John patted his back and moved the computer farther away on the table. "Compared to Brandon Carlisle accusing me of a gang bang of my own son, that's not too bad."

"But you knew Carlisle was a bastard. I thought…" His throat tightened.

"Compared to Cynthia, then." John shook his head. "Okay, still not the same. But he's not telling you not to come."

"He's telling me not to get my gayness on his nice Texas wedding. Fuck that. If I go, you go. I wonder if I can find pink tuxedos the right size for both of us."

"Ryan." John pinned his mouse-clicking hand to the table. "Stop. Relax. Just let it go for a bit. Don't do anything dumb."

"Aarrrrgh." Ryan made a sound that had no words, but John's hand was warm over his, and he gradually came down off the fury high.

"Give him time," John suggested. "After all, you and I have known each other less than a year. We *have* only been together a few months. It's maybe no big surprise he doesn't believe we're that important to each other."

"If you were a girl, he would invite you to come as my date, no matter how casual we were."

"Yeah. Still, sometimes it's good not to burn your bridges. When I told my dad I was going to marry Cynthia before starting college, he was ready to lock me in my room and bribe someone to send her off to Alaska."

"Really?"

"Yeah. He thought she got pregnant on purpose. By the time we got to the wedding, he was willing to come and glower at everyone from the head table. And when Daniel was born and died…" Ryan heard John drag in a breath. "By then, he was there with us all the way. Six months from 'the girl's a tramp out to trap you' to 'you need to take care of her because you're both hurting.' Maybe Brent will come around too."

Ryan didn't figure Brent's learning curve would be anywhere near that fast. But maybe he wasn't the most objective about this. "What should I tell him? I really want to blast his ears off."

"Would you let me? Answer your personal email?"

"Hell, yeah." Ryan pushed the computer over.

"So two options." John tugged it into position. "I can act like I'm you and just tell him I need to think about it for now. Or I can let him know I'm me and that you're letting me take point here."

"I like that." Ryan took a sour satisfaction in the thought of Brent realizing John had seen his comments. "Write away, Mr. Barrett."

"Okay." John hesitated, then typed.

Brent,

Ryan is letting me answer this, because he's mad enough to damage the keyboard. I get it, though. You don't think we'll be together long-term, and you're not willing to risk a problem at your wedding for what you see as a temporary insanity of Ryan's.

Well, he doesn't want to come to the wedding without me. But I don't think it pays to draw lines in the sand right now. Ask him again in a month. I'll still be here. He'll still want me included. But you'll have had a month to get used to that, and I know he wants to meet Anne. So give it time and a bit of thought.

— John Barrett

Ryan frowned. "That's way too friendly. Can't you at least address it to 'Brent, you freaking hypocrite'?"

John gave him an odd look. "How many of your classmates have you told that you're dating a man?"

Ryan could feel heat rise in his face. "I don't socialize with them much."

"Mm. Well, I've told exactly one of my ten grounds crew guys."

"Okay. You're one ahead of me."

Their eyes met. Ryan reached over, shifted the mouse, and clicked Send.

John leaned back in his chair. "The other question, of course, is do you actually *want* to come out to everyone at a Texas wedding?"

Ryan had to admit he had a pretty sharp point there. "Maybe not. But I want to have the right to have you there with me, even if we decide to wear cowboy boots and belt buckles the size of dinner plates and stand three feet apart."

John laughed.

Ryan suddenly felt warm, in a far better way. He glanced at the clock. "Hey, John, we have more than an hour before Mark comes home."

"So we do. I knew there was an advantage to knocking off work early."

Ryan closed up his email and powered down the computer. Anything else could wait. "Want to go prove how gay we are?"

"No." John stood suddenly, looming over him, but he was smiling and his hands on Ryan's face were gentle. "But I do want to go upstairs and take you to bed. Without having to prove anything."

Ryan turned to kiss John's wrist and laid his cheek in one rough palm. Sometimes it drove him crazy how calm and right John could be. But sometimes it was really, really nice. "I could be persuaded."

John bent over and kissed him. They were getting really good at this. The touch of John's mouth, the slow, insistent press of his tongue, the pinch of his teeth on Ryan's lower lip, could get them both hard in seconds. Having John hold his head still and take over the kiss was pretty freaking hot. Ryan pulled his mouth free to breathe. "Upstairs?"

"Pretty damned easy to persuade, aren't you?"

"That was a serious kiss."

"Up you get." John's hand under his elbow lifted him forcefully, but Ryan wasn't about to complain.

They had learned better than to neck on the stairs, ever since the time when John had failed to keep him from losing his balance. But it was no hardship to follow John's work-toned ass, just barely hinted at in his loose jeans, up those familiar stairs.

In the hall outside the bedroom, John said, "You get into bed naked. I'll clean up a bit."

"No shower," Ryan said, trying for a growl. "If you don't get into my bed pretty soon, I might not wait for you." He palmed himself blatantly.

"Keep your hands warm for me. Five minutes." John hurried down the hall to the main bathroom.

Ryan went through the bedroom to the master bath. He pulled off his sweater and glanced into the mirror. He hadn't shaved that morning, so his jaw held a shadow of dark stubble. His hair stood up unevenly, like he'd been running his hands through it. He probably had been. He unbuttoned his shirt, leaned his hip against the sink to take the weight off, and thought about choices.

There'd been a time when he cruised along in life without making big decisions every day or even every week. Hadn't there? He felt a vague nostalgia for that, but overriding that was the growing warmth of knowing John was down the hall, getting naked for him.

He got clean and ready too, and made his way to the bed. The room was cool, but he stripped down the covers and stretched out on the clean sheet. His leg pulled uncomfortably, scars stretching and twinging, but he could ignore it in the rising excitement that had his cock stiffening against his belly. John appeared in the doorway, all long muscles and furry skin and visibly ready for fun. For a moment, they grinned at each other. Then John pounced.

Ryan rolled them together, grabbing at John's wrists, trying to pin him. The edge of the bed sank under his hip, and he squirmed back, getting a leg over John's. They wrestled, both going for underarms and ribs, because by now they knew each other's ticklish spots. Ryan managed to get a finger out from where he gripped John's wrist to jab it lightly against his side, *there*. John giggled and writhed away.

Yep, that spot. Ryan managed another poke and then a tickle and felt John's muscles weaken. "Gotcha." He went for the win, taking ruthless advantage as John kicked unsuccessfully at his good ankle and bucked under his weight. He bit John's collarbone in the spot that always made him moan and got his fingers deep into John's side, wiggling them mercilessly.

"Uncle," John said through his snorts and groans. "Uncle already."

"Hah." Ryan let go of his other wrist and slid down his body, pressing his cheek against John's skin to feel the ruffle of curly hair. He reached the tip of

John's erection, standing damp against his belly, and licked it. John's groans deepened. Ryan licked him again and then sucked that fat, rounded head into his mouth, rolling resilient flesh against his tongue.

John cupped his head in firm hands, stilling him but not pulling him off. "I thought it was my turn."

"Objecting?"

"Never."

"Good." Ryan sucked harder, pulling John's stiff length between his lips and letting it slide out. This was fun. This was easy. So odd that the gay sex, which was the thing he'd always shied away from even imagining, had turned out to be the sweet, simple part of being with John. He loved this, the feel and the taste and the control. Making a big, strong man shake and moan and even beg. Making John, of all people, tremble and need, incoherent and driven, until he would actually thrust roughly into Ryan's mouth, all careful consideration lost in that frantic urgency.

He sucked and plunged, taking John deep in his throat, drawing a hoarse gasp from him. Then he backed off, licking slower, more gently, until the muscles of John's thighs were taut and shaking under his hands. Ryan pushed John's legs wider apart, and slid a hand down to rub his furry balls.

"I won't last if you do that," John murmured.

"I like knowing that." Ryan kissed the tip of his cock, spreading shiny precome around with his lips. "A year ago, if someone called me a cock-sucker, I'd have punched them. Now I want to say, 'Hell, yeah. I'm an excellent cock-sucker.' At least I want to say it to Brent."

John laughed. "So I'm getting an exceptional blowjob because you want to piss off your brother?"

"No. You're getting the bj because I love making you come apart. Knowing it would piss off Brent is just added spice. I'm bi, and I like dick, and that's just how it is. In fact..." Ryan pulled back and sat up, looking at John. He took a slow breath and licked his lips. "I want you to fuck me."

John frowned. "No."

"What?"

"I'm not going to get inside you for the first time to prove some stupid point about how gay you are or how equal we are."

"That's not what this is!"

John reached down and wrapped his hand around Ryan's cock, stroking gently. "Then why did you get softer instead of harder when you said it?"

He had? Ryan hadn't realized. But that hint of sadness in John's eyes needed to go away. Ryan shifted to stretch out beside John and kiss him, stroking him in return. "I might be a little anxious. But this isn't just some whim or a reaction to that email. I bought stuff for prep weeks ago. I've…" He'd touched his own ass, more than once, pushed a finger inside, finding out why the first hint of pressure against prostate was enough to make John shudder. It was good. He *was* ready. "I've thought about it. I want to."

"Maybe another day?"

"No. I Please. Today. I need it."

John was silent. For a minute, they lay there, facing each other, then John began kissing him quietly, slowly, their tongues barely stroking, his hands just keeping the need at a simmer. Ryan went with the change in mood, although he was achy with unsatisfied want, and it was hard to lie still. John slid a hand across the bare skin of his hip, warm fingers trailing. A fingertip circled a raised scar where one of his skin grafts had been taken, rubbing, stroking, moving from numb to sensitive and back again. Ryan's arousal got hotter and harder to ignore. He *did* want this.

He almost said, *Unless you don't want my ass for those scars.* But that would be pure manipulation. John had kissed every one of those scars, time and again. He'd brushed lips and tongue over them, murmured honest words of appreciation for Ryan's ass, until even Ryan couldn't manage that hypocrisy. He might find his own skin ugly, but he had full and abundant proof that John didn't. Which meant all he could say was, "Please?"

"For real?" John dipped his finger lower, toward his cleft.

Ryan squirmed in anticipation, achy, unsettled desire building. He was definitely not getting soft now. "Oh yeah."

"And it's just the two of us in this bed? This isn't about anyone else?"

72

"This is about switching because I know how amazing it feels from on top, and I want you to feel that. And I want to know…" He gasped and opened his thighs as John's rough fingertip pressed between his ass cheeks. "Yeah. Want to know what it feels like to have you in me."

John leaned closer, stroking him in front and in back, then let go and murmured, "Roll over, on your other side."

Ryan was caught between sensations to the point where he had to think about that before managing to follow directions. He rolled, putting his back to John. John spooned him, kissing his neck, hugging in far too close to do anything interesting. His hard length was pressed flat against Ryan's back. It was sweet, familiar comfort, but not what Ryan needed now. He bumped John with his ass. "Lube."

"Sure."

Ryan closed his eyes and listened as the drawer opened and shut, the cap clicked open. He tensed as John's fingers came back with cool lube, gliding, slicked and feather-light along his crack. He pushed back again, wanting a firmer touch.

"Okay." John pressed against his opening, easing a finger in against the clench of his ass.

It didn't hurt. Ryan had done this himself several times now, and although John's fingers were bigger, he'd figured this part would be easy. What he hadn't expected were the little ripples of sensation, odd switches from *yes/good* to *really weird/backward,* the moments when all he could think was that he needed *more*, and then seconds of recoil. Then John brushed against his prostate and it was all *more.*

He bit his lip against a whine and pushed back. John held his hip with one hand, while rubbing with his finger in maddening little touches deep inside. Ryan shoved his ass onto that finger harder, deeper. "Go."

"You're sure? You haven't taken much yet."

"Yeah." He wasn't, but the electric ache inside him needed something, more, different. "Fuck me. Right the fuck now."

John's finger pulled out of him, a sensation that made him shudder. There was the sound of the lube again, and then a much bigger pressure against his ass. He grabbed a fistful of sheets and held his breath. The pressure built, and he grunted, trying to relax for it. John said, "Jerk yourself. Maybe that'll help."

"You're big." Ryan slid a hand to his half-hard shaft, stroking himself roughly. It felt good, but his whole body was focused on the spreading of his asshole, tight, burning, not sexy. "You might have to just force it." It got better, right? When the guy was inside?

John kissed his shoulder, then his neck. "You need more prep."

"I'm okay."

"No way." John eased back, and Ryan couldn't help a tiny sigh of relief as the pressure eased. "Let's try more fingers."

Suddenly, Ryan was done with it, for tonight anyway. He rolled over and took John in his hand, sliding to line their cocks up in his fist. John was hard and slicked, he was softer and dry, but that was going to change fast. He pumped them together. The not-hard problem went away immediately, in the delicious slip and rub against John's big dick. He moaned and tightened his hand, speeding the motion.

John kissed his open mouth, adding his hand to Ryan's. "Gonna come like this pretty fast."

"That's okay. Me too." Ryan kissed him back, then focused on doing his best to touch as much of both of them as he could. He jolted, slipped out of his hand, adjusted.

"Easy." John grabbed more lube, pushed his hand away. "Let me."

"Mm. 'Kay." That was so good. Slippery, wet, sliding heat and the sight of John's big cock alongside his own. John's fingers cupping his balls with his other hand, managing a tug and rub that sent warmth shooting through Ryan's groin. He grabbed John's shoulders and concentrated on that feeling. "Serious skills there. Great hands. Yeah. More."

Heat built; the outside world dimmed. Ryan's attention narrowed to just this space and time, fast breaths and strong hands, warm skin under his palms and perfect, rubbing, squeezing, pulling, pressing, oh yeah, more, tight, almost, almost, perfect. He came hard, spilling over in John's grip, dizzy with the release of it. John kept the rhythm going until Ryan whimpered with overload, then opened his hand. Ryan pulled away, kissing John's shoulder, mouthing his neck, while John used both hands to jerk himself faster, harder, his head thrown back, rolling his own loose sac in one hand as he pulled his cock. A few seconds later he came too, pulsing over his slick-shined fingers, his breath harsh and loud.

Ryan sucked hard on the thin skin under John's collarbone and then kissed him there. "Wow. Nice."

"Nice?" John managed to pant.

"Fucking, damned sexy." Ryan flicked his tongue over the corner of John's mouth.

"Better." John relaxed slowly, wiped his hands on some random part of the sheet and then pulled Ryan in against him. He kissed Ryan more gently, tenderly. "That wasn't what you planned."

"Next time. It was excellent."

"Yeah." John nuzzled against him, rubbing a hand over his hip. "Love you."

"Mm. You too." He moved closer, ignoring the stickiness, rolling enough to take his weight off his bad leg.

John pushed him over more, easing him back into a comfortable spoon. "You do know you never have to bottom in order for me to be happy."

"Next time," Ryan repeated, and meant it. He had some kind of hang-up, but he'd be damned if he'd let it fester. A few more private sessions with more fingers might be in order, but he was determined to get there. Right now he was floating on a sea of endorphins and mushy sentiment. He hugged John's arm against his chest. "How did I ever find you? I wasn't looking. I'd never have dreamed I could have this. And yet here you are."

John rubbed his chin against Ryan's neck. "Here we are. I'm just going to assume I did something right in a previous life."

"Works for me." Ryan closed his eyes. Just for a minute. "You'll wake us before Mark gets home?"

"Yeah. Sleep if you want."

Ryan hadn't done much all day, hadn't even done much in bed, but suddenly he was melting into the mattress, cradled against John. "Mm. Just might."

"Is it creepy for me to say I like to watch you sleep?"

Ryan wriggled closer and sighed. "Ask me when I wake up." John chuckled and nipped his ear, but even that wasn't enough to keep Ryan awake for long.

Chapter Six

John had managed to fit a fair bit of work into a rainy week by Saturday, when he took his "Unaccompanied Minor" paperwork to the airport to claim his daughter. He went through security and located the gate for Torey's flight. She'd complained about being handed off and signed for like a package. She was almost thirteen and pushing her independence for all it was worth. But he'd be damned if he was going to have her wandering around the airport alone, even if the airline had been willing.

He found the gate and waited as passengers streamed out of the jetway looking tired and rumpled. The flight had run three hours late, well into the evening, and while he'd been able to delay his trip to the airport to match, these poor folk had clearly not had a fun time. One after another, strangers one and all, they hurried past him and off toward the exits.

He was almost ready to start panicking when finally a flight attendant appeared with Torey in tow. Torey was frowning, and her hair was spiky and probably not the style she'd left home with, but she looked damned good to him. "Hey, sweetheart!" He opened his arms.

For a second, he was afraid she'd decided she was too grown up for hugs, but then she came and leaned into him and let him wrap his arms around her. "Hi, Dad."

The flight attendant said, "That was a tough flight. I just need your ID and signature, and then you can get this young lady out of here."

Torey wrinkled her nose at the term "young lady" but said nothing as John went through the formalities. When he was done, John reached for her carry-on backpack. "Did you check a suitcase?"

"Well, *duh*." Torey stepped back. "I can carry this. But I'd never get a week's worth of clothes into it."

"Oh. Right." Whatever had he been thinking, huh? "Baggage claim is this way."

"I know." She headed out fast enough to make him take two long steps to catch up.

As they walked side by side through the airport, he debated opening a conversation, but her prickly attitude made him hesitate. There'd be an hour in the truck driving home, without an audience. Time enough then to figure out why she was hardly looking at him.

They got her bag and made it out to the parking lot. As soon as they were in the truck, Torey said, "I'm tired. Gonna nap." She closed her eyes and leaned her head against the window. It didn't look very comfortable.

John shrugged out of his light jacket. "Here, fold that under your head."

Torey glanced at him for a moment, almost shame-faced, but then she took the jacket, mumbled "Thanks," and did as he suggested.

He drove quietly, navigating the freeways out of the airport. Beside him, Torey pretended to sleep, but the tension of her body and her restless fingers belied that. After fifteen minutes they were out of the city and on the open roads. He said, "Are you mad at me about something?"

He thought she might not answer, but then she opened her eyes. "Huh?"

"The silent treatment. Usually when I see you I get to hear all about how you've been." Usually he had a hard time getting a word in edgewise.

"Maybe I'm tired."

"Are you?"

"Yeah. But Things are okay. I'm not mad."

"Really?"

"I said so, didn't I?" She glared at him. "What? You don't believe me?"

"I'd believe you better if you didn't look like you wanted to kick my shins right now."

"Jesus, Daddy, I'm not three! I'm almost thirteen."

He managed not to say *then act like it.* "I know that, hon. So there must be something making you crabby."

"Crabby." She closed her eyes.

"Sorry. Upset. Angry."

That got a big sigh, but when he was about to give up, she said more quietly, "Why did you make me stay with Mom and *Him*, when Mark didn't have to?"

Uh-oh. John said carefully, "I thought it was a mutual decision."

"Yeah, mutual being you and Mom and Ryan and Brandon. Not me."

That wasn't how he remembered it, but he said, "Oh?"

"I know you like Mark better."

"Torey!" He let himself sound stern. "You know that's not true. I love you both equally."

"Then it wasn't fair!"

"It was the best solution we could come up with. Are you having problems?" He really hoped not. It was a fragile peace, this arrangement he had with his ex-wife, where Torey lived with Cynthia and her new husband, and Mark lived with him and Ryan. Technically, legally, Cynthia should have had both kids. He'd go to bat for Torey if she really needed him to, but he didn't have any actual right to change custody arrangements. If he tried, he had no doubt that Cynthia would make life hard for all of them. Maybe even insist a judge send Mark back. He'd browsed the Internet and seen enough cases of kids' custody being ripped away from good but gay parents to make his blood run cold. He really, *really* didn't want to risk everything on some judge's acceptance. "What's wrong?"

Torey made a face. "It's just not fun. Nothing is okay. Mom and *Him* are fighting, and Mom is all stressed and tired. Now that Mark's not there, Brandon keeps giving me these talks about how to be successful in life. Which always means doing stuff I don't want to do."

"Like what?"

"Like running for student government next year instead of doing theater. Because it will look better on a college application."

"Unless you want to get into a theater program." John didn't think Torey was really destined for the stage, but right now she was very into that.

"Exactly." She nodded. "Which I do. But he says that's not a serious major."

"Well, it's a long way off, right? College? You're still in middle school."

She shrugged.

He decided a change of topics might be smart. "How's your mom? Getting fatter?" The baby was due in June. Even though it wasn't his baby this time, he remembered Cynthia at seven months pregnant with each of the kids, starting to get bigger, clumsier. He had a moment of concern. "Is she taking care of herself?"

"I guess."

"Are you helping plan the nursery?"

"Not really. Mom's being all weird about it."

"Weird how?"

Another shrug. "She keeps saying she doesn't want to rush."

"Well, I guess she has a couple more months." He remembered Cynthia being obsessed with baby planning. Maybe the fourth time wasn't as exciting, even with a lot more money to spend. Or maybe she wasn't feeling up to it.

"So. Can I stay with you and Ryan for the summer?"

"Don't you want to be there to see your little brother or sister?"

"Babies just sleep and poop and cry all night."

"Says who?"

"Janet at school. Her little sister is two, and she says it's been the longest two years of her life." Torey heaved a theatrical sigh.

John held in a smile. "I liked having babies. Even with dirty diapers and getting up in the night."

"I bet Brandon won't, though."

He looked away from the road for a second to meet her eyes. That was hard to refute, but, "It's different when it's your own baby. Wait till he has that little one in his arms. He might surprise you."

"By *not* dropping it on its head and going off to play golf?"

"Torey! That's uncalled for."

"I don't care."

John sighed. He was worried about Torey. Maybe even about Cynthia, although it wasn't really his business what Brandon did with his own wife and child. Torey was, though. "How about we try to have fun for the next few days, and then you and I can have a chat with your mom. Okay?"

"I guess. I really, *really* want to spend the summer here."

"Even if you have to share a bathroom with your brother?"

"*Da-ad.* I mean it."

"We'll talk to Mom." And Ryan, although John was pretty sure Ryan would be onboard with whatever Torey needed from them.

Torey lost some of her stiffness. "Thanks. So anyway, other than the stuff that sucks, the school play is going to be pretty awesome. As long as Brandon lets me stay in it." Torey rattled on, much more her usual self, about her first theatrical role. John was able to listen and ask the occasional question when there was a lull. By the time they reached the house, he pretty much had his Torey back.

As soon as he parked, she jumped out, grabbed her backpack and flew up the front steps. Ryan opened the door for her. "Hey, squirt."

Torey jumped into his arms, and he staggered as he hugged her, then swung her around. "You've grown."

"A bit."

John got her bag out of the back, watching them, realizing he was jealous of Ryan for that uncomplicated greeting. He fought it off, lugging her suitcase up the steps. "Hey, you two, get out of the doorway, huh?"

"Sure." Ryan gave Torey a loud, smacking kiss on the hair. "Come into the kitchen, have a snack. Tell me what you're going to cook for dinner tomorrow."

Torey laughed at him. "Cook?"

"Yeah. That's why you're here, isn't it? To be our domestic servant for a week?"

John left them heading for the kitchen, bickering happily, and lugged the suitcase upstairs. When he'd set it in Torey's room, he stopped at Mark's door and knocked.

The guitar sounds stopped. "Yeah?"

"Your sister's here. Come on down and have a snack with us."

"Oh. Okay." There was a pause, then Mark opened his door.

As they walked toward the stairs, John couldn't help asking, "When you talk to Mom, do things sound okay with her?"

"I guess. We don't talk that much."

"Ah." He caught Mark's sideways glance but didn't answer it.

In the kitchen, Torey sat at the table, while Ryan was busy at the stove. He looked up as they came in. "Hey guys, Torey said she didn't get any dinner on the plane, so I'm making mac and cheese. Want some?"

"At nine at night?" John asked. "We already ate."

"Sure," Mark said, sitting down.

Ryan laughed. "Good for you. I need this eaten. Leftover Kraft mac is gross."

Torey glanced at Mark. "Hey."

Mark flicked his eyes toward her. "Hi. Late flight, huh?"

"Yeah. Worst ever."

"Sucks."

"I might stay here forever and not fly back. For real."

John was suddenly the target of startled looks from Mark and Ryan. He raised his hands. "I bet that sounds tempting after three hours sitting on the runway, huh? What do you guys want to drink with your mac and cheese? And don't say beer."

Mark laughed, and the moment passed.

But later that night, after the kids had gone to bed and the house was quiet, Ryan rolled over in bed to face him and said, "You look worried. Problems?"

"I'm not sure. Torey said she wasn't having fun at home."

"That doesn't sound *too* bad."

"No. But she also said she wants to spend the whole summer here."

"Well, I'd be okay with that, but I can't imagine Cynthia would be. You get Torey for a month and then in theory she gets Mark for a month, right?"

"Yeah." John sighed and pressed his face against Ryan's neck. The weight of Ry's arm across his shoulders was deep comfort. "It's so damned complicated. What if Mark flat-out refuses to go?"

"Depends on how much pressure you're willing to put on him, I guess."

"Yeah. And then Torey. What if *not having fun* is the tip of the iceberg? What if there's something else going on?"

Ryan hugged him tighter. "We have a week. I think we can probably find out. Unless she's changed drastically since Christmas, Torey can't keep a secret to save her life."

"True." It was a comforting thought.

"You've got some time off to have one on one chats with her. And I'll take her out to a movie or something. Between us, we'll get the low down on what has her so touchy."

"You noticed that?"

"Yeah. Could just be hormones. When we were in our teens, Mom used to sometimes say, 'Thank goodness you're not girls,' after talking to her friend who had three teen girls in the house. Apparently, female hormone surges are a fearsome thing."

"Maybe. I hope so. I mean, I hope that's what it is."

Ryan kissed his temple and slid a leg across his thighs. "And if not, we'll figure something out."

John let himself relax into Ryan's hold. "God, I'm so glad I have you."

Ryan's chuckle was affectionate and low in the dark room. "It must be love if I'm taking on a hormonal preteen for you."

"Must be." He was damned lucky it was. He hoped with all his might that it would never change. They were both tired, and he'd worked a full day before heading to the airport, but John pressed in against Ryan, enough to feel a warm ache of wanting. He didn't do anything about it but savored the low edge of desire that came and went as they moved gently against each other, drifting down toward sleep.

****

Ryan pushed away from his microscope in Histopath lab and tried to work the crick out of his neck. He was short of sleep, and for once it wasn't his own fault. They'd spent yesterday helping Torey redecorate her room into something fit for a teenager, but she'd been uncharacteristically quiet, even sullen, despite the new posters and curtains. John hadn't said anything about it, but he'd slept so restlessly Ryan thought he had John's elbow-prints on his ribs. He rubbed his eyes.

Beside him, Donna sat back, rolled her shoulders, then gave him a quick smile. "I think I'm going cross-eyed."

"Me too." He rubbed his hip. "Getting too old to bend over for two hours in a row."

"Hah. Bet I'm older than you."

He glanced at her. It was possible. She was blonde, attractive in a wholesome way, and there were a few tiny lines around her eyes. "I'm thirty," he said.

"Thirty-two."

"Beat me."

She smiled. "I was a nurse for eight years before deciding that I was as smart as any of the doctors who kept telling me what to do, and I was damned well going to prove it."

"Firefighter." He pointed at himself.

"Yeah, I know. You're famous."

Ryan could feel himself stiffen. "Oh, right." He wasn't looking down at his leg. Not at all.

Donna touched his sleeve. "In a good way. You're a hero, and you're hot. Half the girls want to do you, and half the guys are jealous."

"Really?" Not that he was interested, but that kind of shit was never hard to hear. Automatically, he said, "What about you?"

"I'm famous too," she said with a teasing smile. "Twenty-two bedpans in one hour. World record."

"I'm impressed."

"Well, I'm lying about the number. But I'm sure I've done impressive stuff, if I only thought to keep track."

He said, "Nursing is hard. A good nurse makes a helluva difference." He rubbed his thigh.

She gave him an approving look. "You're going to be a better doctor for knowing that." She clicked off the light under her scope. "So, I'm done. Some of us were thinking about going out for a beer and greasy bar food around four, before diving back into the books. Care to join us?"

He almost said yes, then remembered, "I can't. Promised to take my boyfriend's kid to an early movie."

For a second, he didn't understand why her face went blank, then his own words echoed. *Boyfriend.*

"Oh." Her face fell, and he realized maybe she'd thought he'd been flirting. Maybe he had. Old habits were hard to break. She managed a nice smile, though. "So the boyfriend's why you don't hang out much?"

"Um. Yeah." He pressed his lips together and kept his panicked impulse to try to take the word back under control.

"Maybe he'd like to join us sometime."

"Oh. Yeah. Maybe." He wasn't sure he was ready to think about that. "Not this week. His kid's visiting." Torey deserved all the time they could give her.

"Well, he'd be welcome." She took a closer look at him. "Seriously. Stella brings her girlfriend sometimes. Most everyone's cool with it."

Meaning some people wouldn't be. But he already knew that. "Thanks."

She stood up, stacked her papers together. "He's a lucky man. Your boyfriend."

Ryan managed to dredge up a grin. "I tell him that all the time."

As Donna left, he bent over his own scope again. Not looking around the room. Not wondering if the people at the next lab bench had heard their quiet conversation. The stained tissue section under the scope blurred before his eyes. What was this one for again? Spindle cells? He no longer remembered.

Abruptly, he stood, putting the prepared slides away in their box and gathering his notes. He knew this stuff well enough. No point in going blind staring at it. He slung his backpack over his shoulder, picked up his cane and headed out. He didn't think anyone looked at him longer than usual. For sure, no one said anything.

Outside the building, the spring day was a welcome relief, the air finally warm and sweet. He eased carefully down the steps, silently cursing his scars. In the past, in another life, when he was obsessing over something he used to go running. Half an hour of pounding pavement and sucking air didn't leave room for confusion. Not possible now, though.

He had an hour for lunch. Without thinking, he turned toward John's office. The building was open, and he headed down to the basement. John's office door stood ajar, and when he went in, Torey was at John's desk doing something on the computer. Ryan stopped just inside the doorway. "Oh. Hi. Is your dad around?"

She waved toward the ceiling. "Out there somewhere, digging stuff. I got a splinter, and he sent me back here to take it easy."

Ryan sat carefully in the other chair. "Want me to look at the splinter?"

"He got it out. It's nothing." But she held out her hand.

He took it, checked the little redness at the base of her thumb. It looked clean, no remnants he could see. "That shouldn't be too bad." He gave her fingers a light squeeze, let go. "So, princess…"

"Don't call me that. I'm not a baby."

"I know, hon. Getting to be a teenager." He laughed. "You're scaring your dad a bit with all the growing-up stuff."

"Good," she muttered.

He leaned over enough to push the door shut. "Want to tell me what's up?"

She shook her head, but then said, "It's all so complicated now."

"Something in particular?"

"Not really. You and Dad. Mark being gone. Mom and *Him* aren't getting along so good anymore. They had a big fight, I don't know about what, and now it's like living with, with, I don't know, strangers. Mom's all weepy and then angry and then worried about shit."

Ryan saw the little look she slid him with the swearword, and didn't comment. There were worse things than bad language for an almost teen.

"And Brandon? What does he do?" *If he's hurting you, John will punch his teeth down his throat, and I'll hold the bastard still for it.*

Torey shrugged. "He's not around much. Like, even less than usual. When he is, he talks like a robot. He used to be on Mark's case about everything, and now he *acts* like he cares about my grades and my future. But he doesn't really. Sometimes I wonder if he'd even recognize me if I cut my hair or put on glasses."

"Oh, hon. He's lived with you for years. Hopefully that's a bit harsh."

"Well, maybe. But he asked if I was getting good grades in French. Mark was taking French. I have Spanish."

"Maybe there's something going on and he's distracted."

She pulled a strand of hair into her mouth and bit it absently. "I don't care. I mean, I don't really want him to pay that kind of attention to me, like he used to with Mark. It's just sometimes I feel like I could disappear, and no one would notice."

"Your dad and I would."

"Yeah." She bit her hair harder.

He reached out and snagged the strand away. "Don't do that. Maybe you do need a haircut."

She eyed him oddly. "Could I get one here? Anything I like?"

"Um."

The door opened, and John came in. Ryan felt a flash of relief. "Hey, your daughter was asking if she could get her hair cut while she's here."

"Don't see why not." John smiled at her. "Tired of having it long, sweetheart?"

"Kind of." She flicked it back over her shoulders. "I want something cooler."

Ryan said, "Cooler like for summer, or cooler like cutting edge?"

"Both?" She glanced between them.

"Sure," John said. "No shaving and no permanent color without asking your mom. Does that work?"

Torey's grin was his reward. "Yeah. I can live with that."

John looked at Ryan. "Not that I'm complaining, but I thought you were going to study through lunch for your exam."

"My eyes couldn't take another hour." He hesitated, then said without emphasis, "Some of my classmates were going out for drinks after, but I told them I was taking my boyfriend's daughter to a movie." Well, *told her*, technically. But he figured it would be *them* soon enough.

John gave him a long look, then came over, bent and kissed him. "First time?"

Torey looked puzzled but didn't say anything.

Ryan blew out a breath and let go with the hand he'd somehow tangled into John's hair, to let him straighten up. "Yeah."

"Problems?"

He shook his head. "You're invited along sometime."

John gave him a softer version of the smile. "That's good, right?"

Torey said, "If you guys want to get mushy, I can go somewhere else."

"Nope," Ryan told her. He suddenly felt lighter, as if his body could float. "How about if I take you both to the student center for lunch. On me."

"Ooh. Big spender." John reached down for him.

He let John's work-rough hand and welcome strength haul him to his feet. Really, this, compared to thinking about taking Donna out and maybe getting some girl-sex in a one-time hookup? No comparison whatsoever. He smiled at Torey. "C'mon, squirt. Let's see how bad they can mess up pizza this time."

"Don't call me squirt," she muttered, but she shut down the computer without complaint and led the way up the stairs.

It was a bit weird going back to class after lunch, but there was the exam to claim his attention and everyone else's. Then physiology class afterward. No one looked at him differently or said anything. He got a few random greetings, shared some general bitching about the projection quality of the exam slides. Either Donna could keep a secret or no one really cared. Maybe he should just get over himself.

He met John and Torey at the truck at four. "What's the plan?"

John said, "I'll come back for Mark after band practice, and we'll go to his teacher conferences directly. So we can head out now."

"Groovy," he said, mostly to make Torey roll her eyes.

"Old people," she muttered, getting into the middle seat.

"Keep it up and I'll make you go to a film with subtitles, squirt."

"You said I could choose."

"Old people have bad memories."

She punched him, unintentionally hitting his bad leg. He sucked in a sharp breath. John said, "Easy, hon. Don't break my boyfriend."

"Oh God. I'm sorry." Torey's eyes filled with tears. "I'm so stupid. I can't do anything right."

Ryan met John's gaze across her head. He said, "No problem. I'm not that fragile. And you're not stupid. Hey, tell you what. There's a hair place just down from the theater. How about if we make you an appointment while we're there."

She leaned forward so her hair shadowed her face. He could see where the blonder highlights were growing out. "You'll hate what I want to do with it anyway."

John said, "It's your hair, hon. And it'll grow back. I admit, I like my little girl with the long hair, but I can handle a change. Go for it."

"I hate changes," she muttered. "And then I want everything to change. That sounds stupid, doesn't it?"

"Sounds like a teenager to me," Ryan said.

"It was easier to be a kid."

"Yeah." John's voice was gentle. "Not better, though. Just easier."

Torey nodded, but she looked more doubtful than reassured.

They spent an hour at home getting changed and then Ryan kissed John good-bye in the kitchen. "See you in a few hours. I'll feed her something totally unhealthy."

"As long as it gets her to talk to you," John murmured.

"Yeah. I'll try."

They took Ryan's car, with Torey uncharacteristically quiet in the passenger seat. He parked in the theater lot and eased out of the seat. His thigh still ached, but he was damned if he'd let it show. "So. Movie first, or hair and food? There's a show at five thirty, and at eight."

"Can we check out the hair place?"

"Sure." They walked together down the half block, past a bar and an antique store. The salon was open, and they went in. Ryan glanced around. It seemed clean enough. The prices on the board made him choke a bit, and he was very glad John had said no color, but if it made Torey feel better, it was worth it. The woman at the front counter said, "Hi. Do you have an appointment?"

"No." Ryan looked around. Only one chair was occupied. "Any chance of a walk-in?"

"Sure." She smiled brightly. "For you?"

"For Torey here." He put a hand behind her shoulders.

"Absolutely. We'll make you look wonderful, sweetheart." She glanced back at him. "You're sure we can't give you a trim too? Otherwise you'll be hanging around for half an hour waiting."

"Um. You think I need one?" He glanced in one of the dozen mirrors, ran a hand through his hair and tried to remember his last cut. It had been a while, for sure. Although he loved having John's fingers tangled in it. "I don't want it short."

"You could use a shaping, though. Show off those gorgeous cheekbones a bit."

He laughed at her blatant flattery. "All right."

She picked up her phone. "Hey, Tina, Drake, we have customers."

The first person to come out of the back was a young woman with hair striped in half a dozen colors, none of them found in nature. Torey's eyes lit up brilliantly. Ryan said quickly to the hairdresser, "No shaving. No permanent colors. She goes back to her mom in a week."

Torey glared at him, although it didn't look serious. "Spoilsport."

"I promised your dad."

90

"Don't worry," the hairdresser said. "Hi, hon. I'm Tina. And we can make you look awesome without any of that. C'mon."

Torey went with her toward a chair in the back, already chatting happily. Ryan had to smile to see her so animated. He'd missed the old Torey on this visit. A hand tapped his shoulder and he whirled, then wobbled. The slim man beside him caught him with a surprisingly strong hand under his elbow. "Sorry. I thought you'd heard me. I'm Drake, and I hear you're all mine."

Ryan planted his cane firmly and nodded. "Lead the way."

Drake gestured him toward one of the chairs. "Want a shampoo?"

"Nah. Just cut it." His attention was caught by a giggle from Torey's direction. The stylist was holding her hair looped up on one side. Looped very short. Torey was grinning. Oh well, as long as she wasn't going for the clippers.

Drake said, "If she's yours, then you have aged very, very well."

Ryan did stop and think about it this time, through several heartbeats, before saying, "She's actually my boyfriend's kid." Calmly and slowly, without emphasis.

"Really?"

Now Ryan had to look, because Drake sounded happy. Drake grinned at him. "So, is he blond and cute like her?"

"Nope. She looks like her mom. He's tall, redheaded."

"Ooh, a ginger." Drake's voice had become lighter and sunnier. "Very nice. I bet you two look great together. So, what do you want done with your hair?"

"Just, you know, shorter. Not too much shorter."

"Leave it to me." Drake moved behind him and met his eyes in the mirror. He ran his fingers through Ryan's hair and then took a grip on each side of his head. "Keep some length here?" His eyes sparkled.

Ryan cleared his throat. "I guess."

"You've got it." Drake picked up a bottle and spritzed his hair to dampen it. "So, I don't remember seeing you around?"

"I'm a med student." He had a moment of stupid panic, imagining Drake mentioning him to some other med student. *Oh yeah, the guy with the cane and the boyfriend.* That was pathetically paranoid, even for Ryan's crazy brain. And what would it matter? He was coming out. Slowly, maybe, but he'd sworn he would.

"Nice. All this and a doctor too." He reached for scissors and combed up a section of Ryan's hair to trim.

"Are you g…" Ryan half swallowed the word *gay*. It was really none of his business.

Enough must have come through to be understood, though. Drake cut his hair with expert, smooth gestures. "I'm bi. I love the ladies to death, but you know, if you and that tall redhead of yours wanted a third guy to squish in between you, I might say yes."

For a moment, Ryan had a vision of himself, pumping into John while John bent over some lithe, smooth twink. He shook his head quickly, before realizing it wasn't a good idea while getting a haircut. "Oops. Sorry."

Drake laughed and picked the scissors up off the floor, setting them aside for a new pair. "My fault. And I was mostly joking. But you thought about it, huh? For a moment?"

His open enjoyment was hard to resent. Ryan said, "Life is complicated enough right now without that."

"Well, let's get you looking good to meet the complications, then." Drake combed, cut, combed again.

"I'm new in the area," Ryan said, because it was easier than *I'm new at this.* "What's it like being, um, out, in this town?"

"Better than some places, not as good as others, I guess." Drake's fingers were cool against his scalp, parting sections along the side. "It's small, but it's a college town. There's an LGBT student society at Bonaventure, of course, and there are a few adult places here in town. I'm not the one to ask, really. You could check with Tina. She flies her flag pretty loud and proud."

"Oh." Ryan rolled his eyes toward where Torey was sitting. He hadn't realized the stylist's wild rainbow hair was more than a fashion statement. He wondered if Torey had made the connection. If so, it hadn't fazed her. She was clearly chattering away happily as Tina worked on her hair, more animated than she'd been since she arrived. "Okay."

Ryan's cut was done first, and he had to admit it looked good. It'd been a while since he'd cared about anything other than getting it out of his eyes. Drake had left enough length to be grabbed, while somehow making the effect sharper and more classy. "Great, thank you."

"It was my pleasure. Definitely."

"How much longer do you think the kid will take?"

Drake looked over there, head tilted slightly as he evaluated with a professional eye. "I'm betting on at least twenty minutes. There are some magazines up front."

Ryan pulled out his phone. "That's okay. I have reading to do."

He was squinting at the little screen, trying to decide if he was getting old or the font really was blurry, when Torey said, "What do you think, Ryan?"

He looked up. She stood in front of him with the stylist hovering behind her. Torey's pose was confident, hip cocked like a runway model, but her expression was anxious. The cut was different. The stylist had stuck to the no-shaving rule, but one side and the back were cropped to about an inch and layered like a boy's hair. The right side was longer and angled down to a point at chin level. When Torey dipped her head, the longer side swung forward against her cheek, and she tossed it back with a quick jerk. "Well, *I love* it," she said brightly, still watching him.

"That's what counts." He saw her slump as some of the tension went out of her posture. "Your dad will be surprised."

"D'you think he'll be mad?"

"John? Nah. It looks good, and even if it didn't, he saves getting mad for bigger stuff than a haircut. It's one of the best things about him. If you're happy and tell him about it, he'll be pleased." He did wonder how fast a girl's hair grew. Not enough in a week, he'd bet. "I can't speak for your mom."

"I don't care. Anyway, I didn't put the colors in at all, so she can't complain."

"Colors?"

"Tina said she could do temporaries and make it like hers but just on the side, like a rainbow strand. But she said it costs extra and takes another half hour, so I decided not to."

"Ah. That's good."

Torey glanced over her shoulder. "Sometime I want to, though. It's so cool."

Tina smiled. "You come back one day, and we'll see what we can do. But this is the look you were going for, and I'm not sure the colors would make it better."

"Yeah." Torey peeked over at a mirror and smiled wider. "I love it."

Ryan paid for the cuts, adding good-sized tips. Torey bounced at his side as they walked along to a café and got a table. While they waited for the food to arrive, she talked nonstop about Tina and fashion and singers on YouTube that Ryan had never heard of, and Tina and drama class and Tina. "And she has a girlfriend who rides a motorcycle, so they're going to ride it in the Pride parade in June, she says. Even if they're the only Dykes on Bikes in the whole town."

"Pride parade?" Ryan blinked. "I wouldn't have expected York to have a parade."

Torey gave him a scornful look. "Of course they do. Well, she says it's not really a full parade, more like a park day where there's booths and people get together and walk around. But they'll ride the bike around the park anyway."

"Oh."

"Do you think you and Dad will go?"

"Go where?"

"To Pride in the Park?"

Ryan opened his mouth and found he had nothing to say. Not one syllable.

Torey chattered on, "You should. Show everyone how it's okay that you love each other. You could get a T-shirt or something. I saw one online that said 'I'm With Him' with an arrow, and you could both wear them."

Ryan managed to finally corral his scattered wits. "I don't think we're ready to make big public statements yet."

"Oh." Torey looked downcast for a minute. "But you're not, like, in the closet? You told Mom. You told Brandon, and I guarantee he won't keep it secret."

"No, we're not closeted." *Not really. Not anymore.* "But there can still be a difference between not being closeted and letting everyone know about it in public like that."

"I don't get it." Torey frowned at him. "I figured you'd want to show everybody that homophobic people like Brandon are stupid."

"I'm not sure marching for Pride would do that."

"It's solidarity, right?"

Ryan grabbed for a change of topic. "Homophobic? Solidarity? Are you studying for your SATs already?"

"I'm thirteen, pretty much. I can use big words. And I think everyone who's gay should stand together, out in the open, and show them how many gay people there really are."

"It's not that simple for everyone, princess."

"Well, duh. I know that. There's people who would get thrown out of the house for being gay. Or lose their jobs and stuff. But if enough people come out, then they can't treat us all bad, right?"

"That's the general plan, yeah." His brain caught up with his ears. "Us?"

Torey flushed and looked down at her hands. "Well, I'm the kid of a gay dad, right? So if they, y'know, discriminate against him, then it matters to me."

"True." He eyed her face. The longer wing of hair was half over her eye on the right, but he could still tell she was nervous. "So if you were in town in June, you would go to Pride?"

"Totally!" She looked up eagerly. "It'd be cool. And I will be here, right? Because I'm supposed to be here for June, to get me out of Mom's hair while she has the baby."

"I don't think that was exactly it, but yes. We're hoping to have you for the month."

"So I'll get to go. I hope Tina does ride with her girlfriend on the Harley. That would be excellent."

"You liked Tina?"

"Yeah. She's great. She said she lived in LA for a while, but it was all plasticky fake. So she came back home to Wisconsin. She said…"

Ryan listened through the meal, and ice-cream for one, and the walk to the theater. And wondered. When they were in the movie and the hero and heroine got into a passionate clinch, he murmured to Torey, "Who do you think is better looking? Jake or Kate?"

She didn't answer, though, leaving him to wonder distractedly which one he preferred himself. Kate was ten years younger and a lot smoother. A year ago, he'd have had no doubts. Something had clearly shifted in his thinking, because he could now imagine kissing her pretty well, but not half as easily as he could imagine Jake's rough stubbled face against his own.

****

John slid over in the bed that evening, to give Ryan more room to stretch out. Sometimes Ry wanted to lie wrapped up together, other nights he was restless and it was dangerous to John's softer parts to be too close. This was clearly a watch-your-balls night. John winced as Ryan's knee hit his thigh.

"Sorry," Ryan muttered. "I was just thinking."

"With your knees."

"Sometimes I think my knees have more brains than my head."

"Hah. You have a big head." John risked a hand on Ryan's dick, to rub the curved cap suggestively.

"Even bigger when you do that." But Ryan's tension slacked off a bit. He turned to face John across the pillows. "So, how did Mark's teacher conferences go?"

"Fine. He still has catching up to do, but they say he's working hard. It was good."

"Did you happen to mention, um, us or anything gay to anyone?"

"No. You know Mark prefers us on the down-low around school. Why would you think I did?" *Had someone said something to Ryan?*

"Well, I kind of told the stylist that Torey was my boyfriend's kid."

"You did?" John decided he liked that. Liked the idea of Ryan talking about him to a stranger in ways that showed they were together. "And what? You think that weird haircut of hers was the stylist's revenge?"

Ryan huffed a breath. "No, quit that! It's the way Torey wanted it. Anyway, I told my stylist, not hers."

"Well, yours did a good job." He ruffled his hand through Ryan's dark hair, disarranging it, but it fell neatly back into place. "You look good."

"He thought so too. He offered to join us in bed, if we wanted to play with a third guy."

"He *what*?" John's fingers tightened inadvertently, and Ryan caught his wrist.

"Watch the pulling."

"Sorry. But what did you say?"

"It's kind of flattering, when I think about it." There was enough tease in Ryan's tone to make John relax. If there'd been anything serious about this, Ry wouldn't sound like that. "He was willing to take you on, sight unseen, because he thought I was seriously hot."

"Well," John said ponderously, trying to tease back, "how good-looking was he? Should we put it on the bucket list?"

Ryan rolled quickly to pin him to the bed. He kissed John, fast and hard. "Not on your life, tree man. You only get one guy in your bed, and that's me."

John chased his mouth, arching up to kiss him back. "Good."

"Although I did think for a second that it would be hot, watching you fuck him."

"Seriously?"

"Until I realized I'd probably try to kill him." Ryan kissed him again, differently this time, slower and sweeter. "I have nothing against people who like a little spice in their love life. I'm not even saying I'd never go there. But not for a long, long time. Right now, it's you and me, exclusively, and that's what feels right."

John ran his palms down over the planes of Ryan's back and took a handful of nicely muscled ass in each hand, and yeah, one side was more developed and who the hell cared? Ryan was so hot strangers were hitting on him. And secure enough to tell John about it. "Exclusive suits me." He was a one-person guy and couldn't see that changing.

Ryan let his weight slide over John as he nibbled and licked along John's jaw, but he seemed less than fully involved. John moved his hands to Ry's hips to hold him still. "Something else going on?"

"Not really. I was impressed by how pro-gay Torey was. I wondered..." Ryan paused, then shrugged, his chest rasping against John's. "Well, just wondered."

"Might be part of her campaign to spend more time here."

"It's her mom she should be trying to convince, though. She knows we want her here, as much as we can get."

"I hope so." Since sex seemed to be fading off the agenda, John rolled them into a spoon, with Ryan turned on his good side and pulled in tight, his back to John's chest. He wrapped an arm around Ry, pressing his palm where he could feel Ryan's heartbeat. Sometimes they talked best this way, close together but not looking in each other's eyes. "What about you? If she convinces Cynthia to let her spend more than a month here? Are you up for that?"

"You really think that's likely?"

"No, but there's a chance Cynthia will be glad to get a moody teenager out of the house for a while. Or alternatively, she might want the in-house babysitting. Hard to say."

"Moody teenager is right. Although she seems better now than when she arrived."

"I think so too. And you're avoiding the question."

"Not on purpose." Ryan pushed back harder against John. "Yeah, I'd be fine with it. She's a good kid, mostly. Although I'm not sure I want to wear an 'I'm With Him' T-shirt to Pride."

"A what where?"

Ryan laughed. "Ask Torey. She wants us to be loud and proud." His voice sobered. "It's all so damned new, this coming out."

"Yeah."

"It's like, it never stops. We told the kids, we told your ex, my dad, my brothers, a coworker. And yet I'm still making those choices. Do I say 'boyfriend' to the probably gay guy who's cutting my hair? Do I say it to a professor who asks if I'm interested in an externship halfway across the country? Do I ?"

"Wait. The externship. Is that a real thing?"

"Maybe. I need a summer job. I applied to a whole bunch of things that would look good on my record, or be interesting. Not many of them are local, though."

"Oh." John had kind of expected that would be a joint decision. "Anything I should know about?"

"Not yet." Ryan rolled over and backed up enough to meet his eyes. "I'm not hiding anything. Some of them I applied for before we were even together. And once I was on some of the out-of-town lists, I figured I'd keep applying for anything that sounded good. There's a lot of competition. I might not even get an interview. I figured if I did, that'd be the time to talk to you about it."

That sounded so reasonable John couldn't understand why he felt let down. "Sure. Makes sense."

"I don't want to spend three months away from you, though. No matter how great the position is." Ryan reached over to run a finger along John's lip.

John nipped lightly at it. "I guess we'll wait and see."

"I put in applications at some of the local clinics and the hospital too. And in some other bigger towns nearby. But the competition's fierce, with the med school here. Unless I want to empty bedpans."

"That'd be a waste of your talents." John ran a hand over Ryan's naked hip. *Speaking of talents.* "You know, you don't have to work this summer if you don't want to."

"Well, I guess. I have the disability income. But I can't imagine doing nothing for three months, and there's tuition to pay."

"You might find other distractions." John rolled over enough to get his other hand in on the stroking act. He was about to suggest he could hire Ryan for summer work crew, but stopped himself short as the scars under his fingers reminded him not to be stupid. Sometimes he forgot Ryan had physical limits, because he seemed so competent. Occasionally, he forced Ryan to remind him, which wasn't good. "Anyway, I'm sure you'll find something. You're brilliant." He leaned up to kiss Ryan's shoulder. "Hard-working." *Kiss his neck.* "Talented." *Throat.* "Gorgeous." *The hollow of his collarbone.*

Ryan pulled him up into a real kiss. "Is all this flattery in aid of something?"

John tried a hopeful smile. "You give stellar blowjobs."

He felt good when Ryan laughed, openly and without restraint. "Not something I'll put on my résumé. But in a pinch, I'll have you give me a testimonial." He eased his way down John's body to add to the evidence, and John tangled his hands in the flattering new haircut and stopped thinking about anything much at all.

Chapter Seven

John watched from the cab of the truck as Torey said her good-byes on the front porch. She and Mark traded playful shoves that didn't quite become hugs. Mark said, "See ya round the Net, squirt," and headed back into the house.

Torey yelled after him, "Don't call me that, metal-head!" She turned to Ryan, who gathered her in for a real hug.

John swallowed against a sudden lump in his throat. The fierce way they clung for a second and then pushed apart warmed him. His falling in love with someone new could've made things so much harder with the kids, and instead, Ryan made things easier. It was such a gift. Ryan reached out as if to ruffle Torey's hair, and she smacked his arm. "Don't mess my hair."

"But it's so tempting." He grinned at her. "Take care, Skype often, and break a leg with your performance."

"I will."

She hesitated, looking at him as if she wanted to say something else, until John called out the truck window, "Come on, hon. Don't want to miss your flight."

"Yeah, I do," she muttered, loud enough to hear. But she gave Ryan another quick hug and then swung up into the passenger seat.

All the way down the driveway and into the road and for half a block until they turned the corner, she sat twisted around, looking back. John said, "You really like Ryan."

"Duh." She turned around finally. "He's fun."

"June is only two months away."

"I know." She sat in silence for a while, then asked, "Dad?"

"Hm?"

"Why didn't you fight for us?"

His stomach rolled queasily. "What do you mean?"

"In the divorce. Why didn't you try to at least get joint custody?"

"A lot of reasons," he said, wondering if he could explain it. "You were both much younger then, and I was working full time and more. Your mother was home full time. She was the one who was there if you were sick, or needed something. She took you out places, kept track of your schedules. If I'd had joint custody, it would have meant disrupting your lives over and over and hours spent with sitters or daycare when I was at work. How could I want you to be in daycare when you could be with your mother?"

"A lot of kids go to daycare."

"Your mom and I always agreed that she'd stay home, as long as you kids were young enough to need that. We both felt kids were always better off with a parent than shoved into care."

Torey played with the longest strands of her hair. "You said there were other reasons?"

"Well, your mom wasn't budging on joint custody, and I'd have had to fight her in court to get it. I didn't want to drag things out, or have you get involved in a nasty court case, that'd make things worse between us all. Plus..." He hesitated, then added, "That was such a huge part of your mom's life, you know. You kids. Being there for you, taking care of you, making all that day to day stuff go well. It was kind of what defined her, and I didn't want to fight her and rip it away. She was a good mom, and she loved you so much."

"But you do too."

"Yes, of course."

"So how was that fair?" There was a hitch in Torey's voice. "She was the one who cheated on you. How was it fair that she got to keep us?"

"I don't know. It wasn't a matter of fairness, I guess. It just felt like the best choice. I thought it would be easier for you too. I didn't know she was planning to move. I thought I'd be around a lot, even without formal joint custody."

"Well, it really sucks." Torey turned away to stare out the window.

"Um, plus at the time, I didn't know she was already cheating on me," he said. "In fact, even now I don't know for sure…"

"Come on, Dad." Torey's voice held a wealth of teen scorn. "She said it herself. I can do the math."

"It doesn't change the fact that she's a good, loving mother and took excellent care of you," he said stoutly. He had to believe that.

"I guess." Torey sighed. "It was okay when I was little. But the longer she's with Brandon, the more she acts like him. I really miss the old days, when you were together. I miss the way Mom was back then. She was softer. Not so stressed. She was better when she was with you."

"There's no way to go back to that," he said evenly. "I'm sorry."

She turned away, staring out the window. "It's tense back home, like we're waiting for some kind of explosion."

"You're waiting for the baby. Shouldn't that be a good thing?"

"I guess. Maybe it will be when it's actually born. Maybe Mom will relax and Brandon will be happy. Especially if it's a boy."

"You don't know yet?" Cynthia had always wanted to know ahead, to plan the nursery and buy the right clothes. Surely by seven months along, she should know?

"No one's told me." Torey sucked the long side of her hair into her mouth.

John said, "Don't chew your hair, sweetie. You don't want to make me a liar."

That got him a brief smile. "Yeah. Thanks for that, Dad."

He'd offered to Skype with her, to introduce her new haircut to Cynthia at a distance. There'd been a few fireworks, but they'd claimed the shortness was an effort to help Torey break her habit of chewing on it, and Cynthia had subsided amazingly quickly. She'd looked tense and distracted, and kept the chat short. It hadn't been anywhere near as bad as he'd expected.

They drove along in silence for a while. The landscape in America's Dairyland was bursting into spring at last. Trees were leafing out, some in full regalia, others still tender and light green. The grass in the fields was already tall enough to ripple in the breeze. Warm Sunday sunshine bathed everything in that special winter-is-gone glow. They passed pastures with cows, some small herds of dark Angus beef cattle, some rangy black-and-white Holsteins. Occasionally a paddock with horses came into view. Torey followed those with her eyes as they passed.

"I miss this too," she said eventually.

"What, hon?"

"Just the way it looks. The way it's all green and growing. Around LA, it's only green if someone's constantly watering it; otherwise, it's brown and olive and dry. It still doesn't feel like home."

He nodded and didn't offer any platitudes about how it would someday.

"You're right, though."

"Hm?"

"When I'm here, I miss Mom too. Almost like I miss you when I'm there. I guess I'm a stupid kid who wants to go back to being little with Mommy and Daddy."

For just a moment, he wished it too— to have the kids small again, big-eyed with wonder, simple and fierce in their affection, to have easy neck-strangling hugs, tossing a ball with them in the evenings, the problems no worse than a missed catch or a lost page of homework. He ached, remembering. "That's not stupid. We all sometimes wish we could turn back time."

"But you wouldn't want to be without Ryan, would you?" She turned her gaze on him, watchful and intent. "You wouldn't want to go back to being straight and with a wife and give up Ryan?" She sucked in a breath and held it.

He wasn't sure why this question seemed so vital or what she wanted the answer to be. Did she still hold some forlorn hope he and Cynthia would reconcile? He could only answer honestly. "No. The early years when I was with your mom were wonderful, when you kids were small. But I'm not the same man I was then. Now I love Ryan. I wouldn't give him up, even to have those days back again."

Her breath went out with a whoosh. "Not even if people treat you and Ryan bad? I've been reading a lot. Some douche bags are really nasty about, like, gay people." She wrinkled her nose, her eyes fixed on him.

He winced at the word but let it go. "Not even. And no one's really given me a hard time yet for being gay."

"Other than Mom and *Him*."

He managed a little smile. "Other than that. And I think your mom was mostly surprised, maybe insulted that I picked a guy over her. Maybe worried that I was lying all those years about being attracted to her."

"But that's dumb, right? I mean, bisexual is a real thing. I read up on it."

"Yeah, it is. I was head-over-heels for her back then. I didn't lie to her. Then or now."

Torey nodded. "Okay. That's okay, then."

He wasn't sure exactly what he'd said right, but for the rest of the drive, she relaxed and talked quietly and easily about drama class and her friend's mountain cabin and about choosing courses for next year. It was the closest she'd been to her old self all visit. When he hugged her at the gate and turned her over to the flight attendant's care, she clung to him and whispered in his ear, "I'm *fine* with you being bi, Dad."

He watched her go down the jetway, returning her last glance with a little wave, staring after her as she vanished into the crowd of strangers. He wished they'd had more time and the chance to talk more. It seemed like she was finally opening up, and then it was time for her to go. Well, he'd look forward to her next visit. Which wouldn't be too far off, after all— his little girl would be with him again in a couple of months. Still, he had to rub his eyes to clear his vision as he headed back through the airport toward the truck.

****

Promptly at five the next Tuesday, Ryan knocked on his physiology professor's door, trying to sound firm and confident. He'd thought his midterm the day before had gone well. Maybe even better than well. But this afternoon, as Dr. Vernon went past Ryan's seat in class, he'd tossed off a quick, "See me during office hours, please." Wondering why had tied Ryan up in knots for the last two hours.

He heard, "Come in."

As he opened the door, he took a quick look around. Dr. Vernon was clearly a type-B professor. The type-A's could generally eat off the top of their shiny desks. Here, sliding stacks of journals lay on top of full shelves, the desk had uneven paper piles, and a spare chair was occupied by textbooks, draped with at least two white lab jackets. It was a good sign, since Ryan usually liked type-B's better.

"Close the door and sit down." Dr. Vernon gestured to the one empty chair.

Ryan did as he was told, waiting, trying not to show any worry.

"I have something to discuss with you, that might affect your career," Dr. Vernon began, "But wait, let me find it." He dug through the papers on his desk. Ryan clenched his teeth against a rush of crazy what-ifs. Had he flunked? Was it his leg the prof thought might hold him back? His unconventional background? His gay relationship? He'd made a point of casually mentioning John to his classmates several times now. He'd gotten a few blank looks, and he had the impression a few of his fellow students were more distant. But so far no big problems. He'd wondered what would happen when word got back to his professors He knew that was paranoia talking— Bonaventure was a private college, but not religious— but he couldn't help a quick breath.

"Here it is." Dr. Vernon pulled out a paper and passed it to him. It was his exam after all, with a big 100% circled at the top.

"I don't get it." He pushed it back across the table. Did the prof think he'd somehow cheated?

"That's one of the best, most complete exam papers I've had in a while. You have a very good grasp of the concepts of physiology and of experimental method in the bonus question as well."

"Um, thank you?"

"Have you already taken a summer position anywhere?"

"Not yet," Ryan said cautiously, beginning to relax.

"Well, I have a friend, a colleague of mine who does research in Cerebral Palsy. Very cutting edge. He was complaining to me that the student he'd lined up as his freshman summer intern can't take the position after all, and his second two choices have committed elsewhere. It's a very competitive program. He likes to start one new student each year, have them come back every summer. If things work out, it's a great foothold into a research position."

"It sounds like it. But…"

Dr. Vernon raised his hand. "Hear me out. I looked at your application essay. You have a pediatric neurology interest, right? You also say you want to do clinical medicine, but frankly you have two things going against you. One is your injury, which will make the long, physical hours of a clinical residency difficult. The other is your being gay."

"My *what*?" He knew he'd heard right, but that still was unexpectedly blunt, and the fact that yes, his professors clearly had found out about John was like a body blow, jolting the air out of him.

"Mr. Ward, I have nothing against LGBT students or doctors whatsoever. But in the real world, you have to know that pediatrics is not just about the patient but very much about the parents, and the other doctors who refer to you. You can try to keep your private life out of the office, but unless you go back into the closet completely, there will be times it becomes an issue. I'm not saying it's fair. And I'm not saying you shouldn't try to follow your dream, if that's what it is. I'm just saying, realistically, it's another strike against you."

"Oh." He tried to breathe normally, sit quietly, take this as calmly as Dr. Vernon was.

"Now, on the plus side, you're extremely bright, focused, old enough to have a well-reasoned world view. You have practical life experience, and you work hard. Those *might* be enough to get you a top-notch career in pediatric neurology. But they absolutely *would* be enough to get you an excellent position in neurology research."

I don't want to do research. Not forever. He nodded.

"And if you do cling to the idea of a clinical practice, you'll still want every advantage you can get. Three years in Dr. Modahl's lab would be well worth having on your résumé."

"Yes. I'm sure you're right."

"So." Dr. Vernon folded his hands on top of his papers and looked at Ryan. "Are you interested? I can either tell my friend that I know just the summer student for him, so he wouldn't have to open the search process up again. Or I can commiserate with him and leave it at that."

"Where's his lab located?" Ryan asked.

"He's at Johns Hopkins University."

"Baltimore?"

"Yes." Dr. Vernon paused. "There's often cheap student housing available for the summer, if that's a concern."

"No. Well, yes, but it's not just the cost." Ryan's head was spinning. He almost started to tell Dr. Vernon about John and Mark, about Torey coming in June and how he and John were so new at this. But it wasn't his professor's problem. "Can I have a little time to think it over? I need to check on a few things."

"Yes, of course," Dr. Vernon said. "But only a day or two, I'm afraid. He'll be interviewing other candidates right away."

"Sure. A couple of days will be fine."

"You could still apply to interview with the rest, of course. But there'll be a lot of competition."

"Yes. I can imagine." He gripped his cane and stood restlessly. "Thank you, sir. Either way, I appreciate it. That's a big vote of confidence."

Dr. Vernon stood too and held out his hand. "You earned it. I hand out very few hundred percents. I'd like to see you have a stellar career."

"Thank you," he said again, accepting the handshake.

Ryan had texted John that he'd take the bus home. But as he got to the bus stop, John's pickup pulled over to the curb and the window went down. "Give you a ride, stranger?"

He slid in gratefully. "Thanks. No Mark?"

"His practice was canceled." John gave him a glance before pulling back out into traffic. "So how'd it go? You don't look like he flunked you."

"No. Not flunked." Ryan rubbed his chin, trying to get a grip on what had happened. "I do want to talk about it. Maybe later, when you're not driving."

"That sounds a bit ominous."

"I don't know. He was very complimentary. I aced the exam. But Well, we'll talk later."

When they got home, Mark was in the kitchen. Ryan stuck his cell phone in his charger, a new one John had made, carved like the open mouth of a fish. Mark didn't look over as Ryan leaned on the counter. "Hey, whatcha making?"

"Dinner," Mark grunted.

"Ooh, I like that. Given that it was actually my turn to cook."

"Well, I wasn't doing anything else, and I'm sick of takeout and spaghetti and hamburgers."

"What are you making?"

Mark frowned at the bowl in front of him. "Meatloaf. I looked up a recipe online."

"Sounds good."

"It still has to cook for like an hour, though. I forgot that."

"An hour is fine." Ryan dropped into a seat at the kitchen table. "It'll take your dad that long to have his shower."

Mark smothered a chuckle and reached for the loaf pan.

"So, you're home more lately. Problems with the band?"

Mark shrugged, although his posture tensed at the question. "Patrick's not coming back ever. We Skyped. He says his parents won't go for it. So we're taking a week off, to think about what to do next."

"That doesn't mean the rest of you can't make it work."

"Maybe." Mark shot him a look. "They want me to write more stuff. Like Patrick did. What if I let them down? I don't want them counting on me."

Ryan bit back automatic reassurance. "You'll have to talk it over some more."

"Well, they have a bunch of midterms. Then Cal says he might know a guy who plays sax. So we'll meet up next week."

That didn't sound too dire. Ryan relaxed a bit. "And in the meantime you're cooking. I approve, young padawan."

"Torey says she cooks sometimes at home. I guess Mom has morning sickness."

"Still?" Cynthia was into her third trimester. But that wasn't really his problem. Let Brandon worry about his wife. "Does Torey like cooking?"

"Dunno. She said she liked being here and not doing it for a week." Mark dolloped ketchup onto the top of the loaf and slid it into the oven. "There. I think that's okay."

"We can throw some oven fries in with it later," Ryan said. "Thanks."

"If Torey can cook, I can."

"Do you miss her? Torey, I mean."

Mark gave him a look and shrugged.

"She'll be here for a month this summer. Almost like old times."

"I guess."

Of course, right about that time Ryan would have to head for Baltimore. If he went. "What do you think? Would it be better if it was just the three of you for a while, you kids and your dad, without me?"

Mark's look became a flat stare. "Why would you ask that?"

Ryan cursed his clumsiness. "It was just a question."

"I thought you and Dad were, like, forever, not going anywhere."

"We are," John said from the doorway.

"Absolutely," Ryan said, turning quickly to face John. "But you know, I could, like, take a short vacation if you needed family time."

John frowned. "You're family too, Ry."

"Yeah." He struggled to his feet. "I thought you'd be in the shower."

"I forgot I had my phone in my pocket." John set it in his own charger, in the cradling wooden hands he'd carved.

Ryan looked at the smooth lines of the wood. "How about if I come up with you?"

"Sure."

Mark said, "Dinner's in an hour, Dad."

"Sounds great. Thanks," John said.

Ryan followed him up the stairs, for once hardly seeing the way John's ass looked two steps above him. They went down to the bedroom, and John waved. "Sit down. You're gimping worse than usual. And talk to me."

110

Ryan eased onto the bed. John almost never mentioned the limp. Idly, he scratched at the itch along his bad thigh, then forced his hand away. Scratching was bad, and thinking about how the scar was bugging him more lately was just a distraction. He looked up to where John was leaning on the wall with his usual patience. Or not quite his usual, because the groove between his eyebrows was deeper than normal, and his fingers were curled in loose fists at his sides. His attention was intently focused on Ryan.

"I didn't mean anything drastic down there," he started.

"Why would you think the kids and I need time without you?"

"Well, it was more like a speculation. A possibility?" He tilted his head, looking up at John. "Not because I don't love being with you and the kids, 'specially with you. But, well, I got offered a summer job out of town. And if you'd *wanted* me gone for a bit, that'd make the decision easier. It'd be a reason to take it, right?"

"Oh." John eased his hip onto the corner of the dresser, looking slightly more relaxed. "Tell me about the job. Where? How long?"

"Baltimore. Three months."

"Ouch."

"Yeah." Ryan scratched over his scar again, stopped himself. "I don't want to be away that long. I really don't. But it's a big deal. A research internship."

"Well, if you want to, if it's important to your career, you should," John said. His tone was unconvincing, though.

"It's over eight hundred miles. More than twelve hours to drive. Too far to come back on weekends, even if I didn't have lab duties, which I might." He'd checked the distance on his phone, as soon as he'd left Dr. Vernon's office.

John winced again. "Maybe we could, I don't know, meet in the middle?"

"Not while you have Torey here, at least. You won't want to leave the two of them alone overnight."

"Crap. True. Or I could get a sitter, maybe."

"I don't know." Ryan shifted on the bed, trying to ease the ache in his knee. "I should just say no. I really don't want to spend three months living alone, or have both of us on the road for hours to spend a day together. It's dumb to even think about it."

"If you were alone, would you do it?"

"Sure."

"Well, then it's not dumb to at least think about it." John caught his gaze and held it. "The one thing your dad said that made sense was that being with me will make your career tougher. I hate that. I don't ever want to be the reason you don't become the doctor you want to be."

Ryan shoved up off the bed and took two steps to John. He noted the way John's arms, thighs, whole body, opened for him to come in against that solid bulk. He hugged John, rubbing his face against the rough skin of his jaw, sighing as John's arms wrapped around him. "No."

"No, what?"

"No, I'm not doing it. Dad's right, but also wrong. Yeah, bending my life to accommodate the people I love will make it more complicated. But compared to not having you? Bending is so worth it."

John slid a hand to Ryan's hair and tipped his face back to meet his eyes. "You're worth waiting for too, if that's what makes the most sense. I'd miss the hell out of you for three months, or a year later on, or whatever it takes. But we're solid enough to get past that."

"I know. I don't want to."

"You'd be good at the job, I bet."

Ryan shrugged. He didn't want to be in some lab halfway across the country for months, wondering if John slept okay or if Torey was having a fight with Cynthia or if Mark's band was coming apart. Was it wimpy to admit he didn't want to be eight hundred miles away when he really needed a hug? Or when John did?

"You shouldn't decide too fast. I bet it would be a good reference, good experience."

"Yeah, but..."

John touched his lips, then kissed him quiet. "Think hard, then, before you decide. I don't ever want to hold you back." He bent to kiss Ryan with more serious intent. "I have other *pressing* thoughts right now."

Ryan leaned up against John harder, rotating his hips against John's thigh. "You were going to shower. Want company?"

"I might be persuaded. It makes sense to conserve hot water."

Ryan nipped at John's neck and then under his jaw, loving the little shiver John gave as his head tipped back for more. "Of course it does. I always make sense."

John chuckled. "Suuuuure you do. But this time, I'm not arguing." He pushed Ryan off, keeping a secure hold on his arm. "Come on. We only have an hour."

Ryan went with it, forcing summer jobs and future years to the back of his mind. Sex was good. Sex with John was wonderful. He'd make sure John knew that whatever he decided, they were always damned fine together.

****

In front of his computer that evening, Ryan reflected that it had been a truly excellent hour. Or forty minutes anyway, because neither of them had held out that long. Slowly making out in the tight space of the bathroom, followed by slippery, soapy hand jobs in the shower, always made him feel better. John was getting quite creative with his hands, and Ryan had stopped jumping in surprise when a fingertip breached him. He shifted in his seat, warm at the memory. He really wanted to try to bottom again. Sometime, when they had privacy, time, and a bed. And lots of lube.

He pulled up his file of job applications and looked through it. He'd promised John he'd think hard, and he knew what he'd have done if he was alone, what his dad and his professor and everyone would recommend for his career. It was a great opportunity. He'd applied for plenty of other summer positions just as far away and much less prestigious.

He pulled up the lab's webpage, reading the famous names who'd worked there, the groundbreaking information that'd come out of the work they'd done. Wasn't that what he'd gone into medicine for? To make a difference? These people made a real difference.

Overhead, he heard Mark's footsteps crossing the hallway and then back again. Faintly, Ryan picked up the deeper bass notes of some music. Not Mark's own playing. Ryan tilted his head, trying to pick out the tune and recognized a black metal band Mark listened to when he was feeling down. He made a note to check on the kid later, see if he needed a friendly ear.

The music wasn't too distracting. Mark was pretty good about keeping it quiet, but the lower register traveled farther than he realized.

Not for hundreds of miles, though. Not to Baltimore.

If he did the internship, he'd be too far away to pick up on how Mark was feeling, or what John looked like coming home from his day.

They were all sleeping better, even though he hadn't found a therapist with a wait time of less than two months, unless he thought Mark was suicidal. Which, thank God, he didn't. But Mark still sometimes woke with a shout about falling, or played his guitar in the middle of the night. John still had times when he got up at two a.m. and went down to the workshop to carve another cane. In addition to the four Ryan now had, plus the scarred-up one that'd saved his life. If he was off in Baltimore, he'd never know about that. And when he himself woke, with the crackle of hungry flames in his ears, the other side of the bed would be cold and empty.

When he came home from a great day at the lab, he'd have to reach for a phone to share it.

When he'd, no doubt, get an email from his dad at that lovely summer job, full of carefully crafted little barbs about how he'd chosen well by putting his career first, he wouldn't be able to shrug it off by plowing John into the mattress from several states away.

He pulled up the photos from Oregon— John looking at him with love in his eyes; Mark, a carefree kid for a moment. He put the lab website on a split screen. If he'd wanted to do exactly that kind of research as his career, then maybe he'd have to go. It would be too crazy not to. But he didn't want to work in a lab after graduation. He wanted to work with people. Dr. Modahl was looking for someone who'd want to do this again every summer. Three months apart again, every year.

Upstairs, the music changed to Mark's guitar. He was working on something dissonant and minor-key. After several false runs his playing stopped. Ryan waited, listening, but there was only silence. Mark had been playing a lot less lately…

He sat there for a long time, reading the job postings he'd bookmarked, checking the descriptions of residencies he might want to pursue, weighing his options. He realized that even as he was reading and thinking, he was waiting for that guitar overhead, waiting for John's laugh, waiting for something to push him forward or pull him back. There was nothing but the sound of his own thoughts.

He opened his email and sent letters to all the positions he'd applied for that were more than an hour away, to let them know he'd decided not to follow through at this time. He used all his verbal skills to sound polite, grateful for the chance to apply, to let them know he was notifying them immediately so as not to waste their time. Good manners never hurt. There was an email from Dr. Vernon, with details of the externship. He replied to that too. "I truly appreciate your vote of confidence, but my partner and I have teenage kids, and I don't feel comfortable spending that much time away from them."

There. Done.

He gave himself permission to waste some time on the Net as a reward for making up his damned mind. He was deep into a story about the development of the typewriter, for no reason he could recall, when his Skype chimed.

Torey. Huh. He clicked it on.

"Hey, Ryan." Torey looked unhappy, despite the smile she pasted on for him. "Is Dad around? I texted him, but he didn't answer."

"He's in the workshop." Ryan had been subliminally aware of the sound of sanding from back there for the last half hour. "Hang on. I'll get him."

He got up stiffly and walked back to find John. His scars twinged as he moved, and he rubbed at them absently. Maybe he needed to skip the kneeling in the shower *Naaaah. Worth it.* He was smiling at the memory as he opened the workshop door. John looked up from the curved piece of wood he was working on.

"Hey, Torey's on Skype. She wondered if you'd chat with her."

"Sure." John set the piece aside. "Let me wash my hands first."

Ryan tilted his head. "What is that thing?" It had a lovely shape, but most of John's stuff was functional as well. He couldn't figure this one out.

John blushed and didn't say anything. That was unusual. Ryan said, "What? Giant dildo?"

That got a laugh, and John's flush receded. "Nope. If you must know, I had this driftwood piece, and I thought maybe a rail on the bathroom wall, next to the cabinet. It'd look decorative, but useful…"

Ryan remembered bracing on the wall awkwardly as John coaxed a hand between his thighs. "Oh yeah. I like that thought."

"Figured you might. I just need to make sure it's really smooth and solid."

"I'll help test it out."

John brushed against him on purpose, as he headed for the half bath, and Ryan got a whiff of the sawdust-and-sweat smell of his man. Mm.

He went back to his study, pulled the second chair in front of his computer and sat. "Hey, kiddo. John'll be here in a minute. He's washing up. How was your flight home?"

"Okay."

"Did your friends at school like the haircut?"

That brightened her eyes for a minute. "Yeah. They thought it was great."

John came in and sat next to him. "Hi, sweetheart."

Torey's face crumpled. "Dad. I want to come home!"

Ryan exchanged a dismayed glance with John, who said, "You mean back here? What's wrong?"

"I think while I was gone, Brandon and Mom had a big fight."

John said urgently, "Is your mom all right? Brandon wasn't too hard on her? He didn't hurt her?"

Ryan bit back a snarky comment about Cynthia having claws of her own. John was right to be concerned, even if the deep worry in his voice made Ryan irrationally jealous.

Torey said, "I don't know what happened. They're not talking to each other. When one of them comes in, the other one goes out. I think Brandon's eating in restaurants, and Mom slams things around the kitchen and cries, and she doesn't eat much. And if they do talk, they sound mean It's just awful."

"You're safe, though?" John said. "Not scared?"

"Not really scared. Just sad, and mad, and I wish I was back with you. I hate it, Dad." Torey's eyes filled with tears. "Even when you and Mom were getting divorced, you didn't fight like that."

"Do you think Brandon…" John stopped. "No. That's none of my business. But if you and Mom agree that you'd be better here, you're always welcome. Always. You can come any time. Can I talk to Mom?"

"She's lying down with a headache." Torey bit the longest tip of her hair angrily, then flicked it back. "I asked her if I could go back to Wisconsin, but she said no. She says everything's fine and I need to concentrate on school."

"Maybe it'll blow over," John suggested carefully. "Maybe she and Brandon can work it out."

"I don't care. I just want things to go back to normal. Ever since Mark left, it's been getting worse. Except it got better for him, 'cause he *left*."

"Honey, he didn't have it all easy."

"Yeah, but it is now, right? He didn't even think about what Mom would be like to me if he ran away."

John sighed. "Torey, that's not fair."

"Well, she's sad all the time. And that makes her mad too, and nothing I do makes her feel better. I hate it here. And Mark gets to live with you. Can't you let me come back?"

"I'll talk to Mom, I promise. But Torey, I can't send you a plane ticket without her agreeing to it. If she decides to go to court over custody, I might lose time with you completely."

"You mean because a judge might get all prejudicy about you and Ryan?"

John glanced at Ryan. Ryan tried to hide a wince, because it was another coming-out problem that they hadn't really discussed out loud. John said, "For a variety of reasons. Your mom tends to dig in her heels if she thinks she's being pushed around, and she has the law behind her."

"Stupid laws."

"Maybe, but they're on Mom's side. Right now she's still trying to do what's best for you and Mark, even though she's not happy with me."

"If she wanted best, she wouldn't have married Brandon."

"Torey." John shook his head.

"Well, it's true." Torey slouched visibly. "Okay. So what do I do now?"

"Baby, you do your best." John moved closer to the screen. "Do your schoolwork, your theater group, hang out with your good friends as much as she'll let you. Try to remember that nothing your mom and Brandon argue about is your fault. I'll talk to your mom, I promise. For now, you can call me, as often as you like…"

"Daddy, but…" Torey wiped away a tear.

Ryan stood silently, touched John's shoulder. "Talk to her," he murmured. "I'll go study." As the door closed behind him, he heard John's voice, sweet and deep, murmuring to his daughter.

Ryan was upstairs under the covers, reading, when John finally joined him. He set his e-reader aside and pulled back the sheets. "Come on. Come to bed."

John stripped down to boxers and climbed in beside him. His long legs were cold as he tangled them over Ryan's. Ryan wrapped an arm across his shoulders. "How's Torey?"

John shrugged under his arm. "I persuaded her to go to bed. She's so unhappy, but there's nothing I can do."

Ryan hugged him harder. "You listened to her. That's not nothing."

"It's not enough." John pushed his face into the crook of Ryan's neck, his breath warm and damp. "I want to snatch her away and bring her here. But that's not possible."

"It might not be best either. She loves her mom, and her friends, however unhappy she is right now. A big battle with Cynthia would hurt Torey." Ryan wanted to yank her away too, but Torey would feel worse if John and her mom burned their bridges.

"I made sure there's no physical fighting." John sighed. "From what she says, Cynthia's clearly depressed. Torey's protective of her mom, and it sounds like things are bad between her and Brandon."

"People fight and make up," Ryan said. His own parents had never gone to bed mad, but they had occasionally stayed up all night. "Hopefully it'll work out."

"I told Torey she could call either one of us, any time. Is that okay?"

"Of course. I might not answer during class or an exam."

John kissed the tender spot under his ear. "I'm not asking you to be Superman. But it's so good to know she has someone for backup if I'm not available." His tone was raw with distress.

"I can do that."

"I feel like a horrible parent."

"*You* are a great parent."

"It was easier when they were little. I could swoop in and save them, you know?"

It was probably the lateness of the hour that made Ryan reach for a platitude. "You can't save everyone all the time."

John pushed away a few inches. "She's my child. My youngest. If I can save *anyone*, it should be her."

"Sh." Ryan touched his face. "I'm sorry. I didn't mean it like that. It's not that bad, is it?"

John shrugged one shoulder. "I didn't think so, but she was crying and saying how her life was awful and she might as well be dead."

"Seriously?" Ryan propped himself on one elbow.

"She calmed down after a while. We talked about her school play, and this new girl she's trying to be friends with who's one of the leads. She seemed better, calmer, by the end."

"That's good."

"I left a message on Cynthia's voice mail, to tell her Torey seemed really unhappy and to keep an eye on her."

"So you're doing everything you can." Ryan eased down, pulling John back against him.

"It doesn't feel like enough. And now Mark's band is breaking up. If I can't keep my kids safe and happy, what good am I?"

Ryan discarded lots of answers to that. He loved the kids by now, but it didn't go bone deep yet, the way the desperation in John's voice did. Although if Torey was really talking about wanting to be dead An ice-cold, helpless feeling in the pit of his stomach said he cared more than he'd realized.

Nothing they could do tonight. He had to trust that John had calmed her down. Any kid with John as a dad had to know she'd always have someone to count on In the end, he hugged John close and brushed kisses over random bits of skin, until they both got too sleepy to do more than lie quietly together.

Chapter Eight

It'd been a tough week. John jumped every time his phone rang. Torey had called twice, although never as tearful and desperate as that Tuesday night. She said things seemed calmer at home. John let himself breathe easier. So it rocked him back on his heels when the doorbell rang Friday evening, and he opened it to find Torey on the porch, a backpack slung over one shoulder.

Behind her was Cynthia, her belly big and distracting. Next to her, one step down, stood an unfamiliar man with dark, weathered skin. A taxi was parked in the driveway.

For a moment, none of them moved.

Then Torey said, "Hi, Dad."

He opened his arms and gathered her in, looking at Cynthia over her head. Cynthia bit her lip and said, more uncertainly than he'd heard in a long time, "My credit card is canceled. Can you pay the driver?"

"Um. Okay." He reached automatically for his wallet and passed a card to the waiting man.

The driver said, "A hundred and twenty-six dollars. Is it okay?"

John winced but said, "Yes. From the airport?"

"Yes, sir."

"Put a fifteen dollar tip on it too."

"Thank you. I'll get your receipt." The man took his card and headed for the front of the cab.

Cynthia said, "Thanks, John. I didn't know what else to do."

John kept his arm around Torey's shoulders but pushed the door wider. "You'd better come in. Let me get my receipt." Cynthia stepped past him into the hall, her eyes downcast. The driver brought two suitcases up and set them beside the door. John signed the slip and hefted the bags into the entry. He ushered Torey inside and closed the door.

Torey leaned against him. That at least was good, was wonderful, to have her here, safe, where he could see her. He said, "Let's all go to the kitchen."

He expected Cynthia to sit at the table, but she leaned up against the counter. "I'm sorry, John."

"You might've called," he said as evenly as he could. "What's going on?"

"It's a long story, and not a good one." She flicked a glance at Torey.

John said, "Tor, why don't you grab a couple of cokes and take one up to your brother. Let Mom and me talk for a bit."

She tossed her head. "I'm not a baby. I can hear adult shit."

Cynthia said, "Watch the language!" at the same moment that he said, "Maybe it's easier for your mom not to have you hear it."

Torey heaved a deliberate sigh, looking only at him. "All right. But I'm not going back to California. Ever."

Cynthia managed a tired smile. "No. We're not. Don't worry."

"Okay, then." Torey bent to the fridge, pulled out two cans and headed up the stairs.

John waited until her footsteps passed the landing, then said, "Cynthia, what's going on?"

Cynthia put a hand on the bulge of her stomach. "I've left Brandon."

"Does he know that?"

"Oh yes. Actually, he asked for a divorce first."

"Bastard," John muttered. "How long till the baby's due?"

"Less than two months. June tenth. That's part of the problem."

"I thought he wanted a child."

Cynthia's smile twisted bitterly. "Oh, he did. A perfect son to carry on his name. The problem is, I had an amnio and this baby's a girl. And she has Down syndrome."

"Oh, hon. I'm so sorry." He put a hand on her arm.

"Brandon wanted me to have an abortion, of course. Even though I was almost twenty weeks along when we got the results. I said no."

John rubbed her arm gently.

She looked up at him, her eyes full of tears, which she scrubbed away roughly. "John, I'm not going to lose another baby. Not ever!"

His throat ached as he met her eyes. He knew both of them were taken back to that long-ago day when Daniel died. He gathered her against him, her big belly awkward. She clung to him, whispering, "Damn Brandon anyway. I'm raising this child."

He laughed damply and kissed her hair. "That's the spirit." And looked up into Ryan's eyes as he came into the kitchen.

Ryan's face shuttered, like blinds dropping over all emotion. He said blandly, "Hey, John. Cynthia. I saw Torey run upstairs."

John set Cynthia away from him carefully. Not fast. Not guiltily. He had no reason to feel guilty. "Hey, Ry. Cynthia was telling me that Brandon has decided he doesn't want a baby after all. Which just shows what an idiot he is. There's nothing more wonderful than a child."

"Of course." Ryan limped a couple of steps closer and pulled out a chair. "You should sit down, Cynthia. You look tired."

John held her elbow until she was safely seated, and then stepped back. "Ryan's right. Can I get you some water? Tea?"

"Water would be good."

They were all silent as he went to the fridge, found a bottle, opened it for her. She took a small sip. Ryan leaned against the counter, eyeing her.

She set the bottle on the table, playing with the ring around the neck with a fingertip. Eventually she looked up at them. "I'm sorry about coming here without notice, but I had to move fast."

"Why?" John scowled. "Did Brandon threaten you?"

"Not like that. But…" She glanced at Ryan. "My baby has Down syndrome, and Brandon wasn't happy. First he wanted me to have an abortion. Once I passed the legal limit for that, he started talking about finding a good institution for her. I said no. I'm going to raise her and take care of her. When he finally believed I meant it, he flipped his lid. Told me he'd divorce me if I kept her."

"Aw, wouldn't that be just too bad," Ryan drawled. "You're better off."

"Maybe." She dropped her gaze. "He's a flattering, generous guy when things are going well. He always treated me like I was important, beautiful.

Took me on trips, bought me things, showed me off to people, let me help plan our lives and entertain powerful people and make connections for him."

John stayed quiet with an effort.

After a pause, she sighed. "I knew he was a perfectionist, but so am I." She flicked a glance at John. "That was part of why John and I didn't stay together. I wanted things done right, and he just wanted them smooth and easy."

"I don't think that's quite fair," Ryan started to say.

John shook his head at him. "Go on."

"Well, Brandon's even more like that than I am. When things were good, we had lovely homes and traveled, and it was fun. Even the first year in California was fine. And we both really wanted a baby. But he doesn't want *this* baby." She touched her belly again.

"And you do." Ryan's voice was less harsh.

"Yes. I'm not happy that she'll be handicapped. Of course I'm not. But you don't throw a child away because they have a flaw. She's still a baby. Of course I want her."

"And so you came here," John said. "I guess I'm flattered."

"I wasn't sure where else to go." She clenched her fingers on the edge of the table. "You have to understand, Brandon's a lawyer. So he's used to getting his way. If it's not happening on its own, he'll make it happen."

"You said he wanted a divorce."

"Once he realized I wasn't going to be bribed or threatened into the abortion. But that's not enough. He said he doesn't want this baby 'hanging over his head.'"

"Meaning what?"

"He asked me not to put his name on the birth certificate."

"He *what*?"

She gritted her teeth. "He offered me a million-dollar settlement, on top of the standard California fifty-fifty deal. As a trust fund for the baby. As long as I'd sign away her rights to any other child support and not give her his name or tell her about him."

Ryan's eyes met John's. Ry said, "I can go kill him now, right? Or at least damage him?"

124

John had to smile. "Maybe later. So, Cynthia, I do get that you couldn't live with him. But why come here?"

"Well, I got mad and said no to the settlement. I said he was her father and he'd have to step up to that."

"Ah."

"Yeah. We fought about it. He said he knew a lot of the local lawyers and judges, and he'd see to it that I came out of the marriage penniless if I didn't agree to his terms. I told him what he could do with his terms and his money. Then last night, he said I'd find out what it was like to live without his money. And when I went to buy groceries this morning I found out he'd canceled my credit cards."

"Son of a bitch," John muttered.

Cynthia's smile was bitter. "Canceled the cards, moved all the money out of our joint accounts into his personal one. Even went through my purse and took all my cash. I had to let them put the groceries back on the shelf."

"What did you do?"

"I called him, of course. I was so damned mad! God, I wanted to kill him! He said from now on I'd have to ask him for every penny I spent, and by the time the divorce went through, I'd be begging to accept the deal. I told him to think again."

John rubbed his face. "He really doesn't know you, does he?" Cynthia had never done well if you backed her into a corner.

"I guess not. You'd already bought an open ticket for Torey to come here. I booked it for this afternoon. I had some cash stowed away for mad money, and I bought a ticket for myself. Then I took everything valuable I could put my hands on and left."

Ryan said, "Why not go to a friend closer by?"

"I thought about it. But all our friends in California were really his friends first. Other than some parents of Torey's classmates, there wasn't anyone I knew who didn't know Brandon better. And I wanted to be farther away from him."

John said quickly, "You don't think he'd be violent, do you?"

"No. Well, I doubt it. But he might try some other dirty trick. Maybe something to get at me through Torey. And she'll be better here with you. I

125

haven't been feeling well lately, and she needs more attention than I've been able to give her."

John wanted to rip apart the guy who'd tried to hurt his girls. But all he could do was make them safe here. "Well, you're welcome. You and Torey and the new baby when she's born."

Ryan said coolly, "Yeah. Torey can stay as long as she likes. And you too, if you don't mind sharing house room with a couple of fags."

John frowned at him. Now was so not the time to bring that old hurt up. But Ryan was staring at Cynthia. She shrugged uncomfortably. "I'm still not happy with that. I admit it. But Torey needs her father right now."

"And you have no place else to go, and even this house of perversion is better than nothing?"

"Ryan!" John snapped. "Not now. We'll worry about that tomorrow." Cynthia was looking drawn and pale, and she kept unconsciously rubbing over the baby bulge like it hurt. He remembered the last two months of her previous pregnancies. She'd had sciatic nerve pinching and false labor cramps off and on for weeks. "Cyn, you should lie down. Unless you could eat something?"

"No, I'm kind of nauseous. Lying down would be great."

"Couch?" Ryan asked. "Torey's room?"

Cynthia kept her gaze on John. "I'd rather avoid the stairs for now."

"Sure." He reached down to help her get up.

She leaned into his hand as she got to her feet, then smiled at him and took her arm away. "Thanks, John. I'm sorry about this. I knew, out of the people I might go to, you were the one I could really count on."

"Of course." He picked up her bottle of water. "Come on and lie down. I'll find a blanket and get your bags up to Torey's room."

"I'll get the bags," Ryan said.

"You should leave the black one for John," Cynthia told him. "It's pretty heavy."

"I'll manage." Ryan limped out toward the door.

John thought about following him and taking the heavier bag, but he didn't think Ryan would let him right then. Cynthia was pressing a hand to the small of her back as she headed for the couch. He might as well get her settled.

He was spreading a throw blanket over her legs when Ryan dumped the two suitcases inside the living room door. "Do you need both of these upstairs? That black one does weigh a ton. What's in there? The good silverware?"

Cynthia had her eyes closed, but she cracked one open to peer up at John. "My jewelry, and every valuable piece I gave Brandon in the last two years too. Some silver out of the wedding presents, actually, yes. And Brandon's baseball card collection."

"His what?"

Her smile was sharp. "It was in the safe. He took all our bank accounts. I took the cards. He always claimed they were worth thousands of dollars. I guess I'll find out."

"Oh."

She patted his arm. "You know what else I brought? Mark's baseball player and Torey's horse that you carved. I didn't want Brandon to get those."

John's throat tightened. "That was nice, that you thought of it." He always tried to let his artwork go, when he gave it away, but he couldn't deny he'd hate knowing that Brandon was taking an axe to the things he'd made for his kids.

"He's a bastard," she said, her voice slurring. "He doesn't get to keep anything important."

"You should sleep for a bit," he told her.

When he reached the doorway, Ryan took his arm in a firm grip. "We need to talk."

"Huh? I was going to check on Torey."

Ryan looked frustrated. "Oh. Yeah, sure. After that."

They climbed the stairs. Torey's room was dark, but they could hear voices from Mark's. Ryan followed, as John went to Mark's open door, and knocked on the frame. Mark was sitting on the bed, his guitar in his lap. Torey perched on the desk chair, her legs drawn up to her chest. They both looked at him.

Torey sobbed and jumped up, slamming against him to bury her face in his chest.

He hugged her close. "Hey, honey. It's okay. You're home. It'll be all right."

Mark said tentatively, "She said Mom and *Him* are getting a divorce."

John smiled at him over Torey's head. "Yeah. It looks like it."

"I still get to live with you, though, right?"

"If you want to."

"Yeah. You and Ryan."

"Me too," Torey mumbled against his shirt. "And Mom."

John hugged her. "Now, hon, I can't promise that, all right? We'll see."

Ryan said, "We can help your mom find a place to live somewhere not too far away."

Torey sobbed again, burrowing deeper against John, and he frowned at Ryan, "Not now, all right?"

Without a word, Ryan headed off down the hall toward their room. John turned back to his kids. "So guys, I don't know how this will work out. But we're all here now, which can only be a good thing. For tonight, maybe Mom can have your bed, Torey? You can use Ryan's old room for a day or two." He knew better than to suggest Cynthia have Ry's room, even if it was mostly used as an extra closet these days. "Is that okay?"

Torey said dramatically, "I'd sleep on the hard floor forever if we can stay here."

"I think we can manage better than that." He'd never been more glad of having bought a big house. They had lots of options.

Mark said, "Should I go talk to Mom, you think?"

"I'm sure she'd love to see you, but she's asleep on the couch right now. I'll tell her to stop by your room when she wakes up."

"Okay." Mark picked out an intricate run of notes on his guitar, looked up again. "I'm glad she's leaving Brandon, but I'm still mad at her."

"That's okay. I understand. And she will too, I'm sure." He hoped. "We'll take everything slow."

"You're not breaking up with Ryan?"

"God, no. Of course not."

"Okay, then." Mark went back to his playing, ignoring John and Torey. It was kind of rude, but John wasn't up to pointing that out right now.

He drew Torey out of the room with him and eased the door most of the way shut. "C'mon, honey. Why don't we get what you need for a day or two out of your room and into Ryan's. Then you probably need to rest too."

"It's not that late, 'specially in California." She took his hand, like a much younger child, and hefted the backpack on her shoulder. "Dad, I don't get it. Mom was better, and then all of a sudden, she told me to pack a bag and we were leaving. She wouldn't wait for anything. All my stuff is still at home, pretty much, other than this. What happened?"

"What did Mom tell you?" he temporized.

"She said Brandon went too far and they were getting a divorce. And that we should stay with you for a bit, because you'd help take care of me. But I'm not a baby."

"Huh?"

"I don't need taking care of. And I *hate* when she doesn't tell me stuff."

"Well." He swung open her own door for her. "Has Mom said anything about Brandon and the new baby?"

"Nope." Torey went to the dresser and opened the top drawer, digging out a few bits of clothing. Her lip twisted in a sneer. "What happened? Did they find out it was a girl?"

John managed not to react to that. "I wasn't there, so I think it's up to Mom to tell you about it." He reached over and turned on the bedside light. The sheets should be fresh for Cynthia. He'd washed them after Torey's visit. "In the morning, maybe. I think we all need a good night's sleep."

"Can I Skype with Char? I didn't even get a chance to tell her we were leaving."

John rubbed his face. Torey would miss her friends, and her school would need to be notified, and probably a hundred things he wasn't thinking of. "I guess. You can use my laptop. It's in the office. You remember your password?"

"It's been, like, a week, Dad. I think I remember."

"Okay. Have fun. But tell her we don't know how this will work out, okay? Until we all have a good talk."

Torey stuck out her lip stubbornly. "Well, I'm not going back there, no matter what Mom says. But I'll miss Char."

He sighed and held out his hands. "Here. Give me your stuff, and I'll put it in Ryan's room. Go talk to her. Do you want me to bring you something to eat?"

"No, thanks. I'm not hungry. Anyway, I know where the kitchen is."

When she'd hurried off, he wandered down to Ryan's old room and pushed the door open. The space was tidy, the bed neatly made. He couldn't remember the last time Ryan had slept there. Ry had offered to, the time he'd had a bad cold and a cough in March, but John had pulled him into their big bed instead.

He set Torey's things on top of the covers. With sudden anxiety, he pulled open the bedside drawers, but there was no lurking lube, no condoms, no sexy underwear. Nothing that needed to be hidden. An assortment of Ry's clothes, a couple of paperbacks at the bedside, both mysteries. He pushed the drawers closed.

From the light under the door at the end of the hall, he assumed Ryan was in their room. But he had the impression that somehow Ryan blamed him for Cynthia showing up out of the blue. He didn't want to deal with that right now. He turned and went back downstairs.

Torey was in his office, her voice muffled but not sounding distressed. He glanced in, and she gave him a wave. Well, she knew the routine. He stepped back, shut the door, and went through the house to check that everything was set for the night. He turned out the porch light.

When he reached the living room, the couch was empty, the blanket thrown back. The sound of retching from the downstairs bathroom was a good clue, though. He picked up Cynthia's water bottle from the coffee table and waited outside the door. When she came out ten minutes later, he handed it to her. "Have a sip."

"Thanks." She drank slowly. He saw that her hand was shaking.

"How sick are you, really?"

"Not that bad." She sighed. "This pregnancy has been harder than the other times. I'm bigger and more unbalanced, and I guess I'm older, and the nausea is happening at the end, not just at the beginning."

"But you're medically okay?"

"Sure. My doctor wants me to rest, take lots of fluids. She threatened to put me in the hospital if the nausea got worse, but it's been okay if I mostly lie around and don't move too fast."

"I'm surprised she cleared you to fly."

"I didn't ask. But I don't have high blood pressure or anything. I didn't figure it would be dangerous, just uncomfortable."

He nodded. "Brandon Carlisle is a total bastard."

She smiled without humor. "He pointed out a bunch of times that the morning sickness would go away if I had an abortion."

"Right. Bastard." He put a hand under her elbow. "Instead of going back to the couch, why don't you go up to Torey's room? I can bring you up some soup or something."

"No food." She pressed a fist under her breastbone. "But yeah, going to bed now makes sense."

He guided her up the stairs. There were already rails on both sides, for Ryan's benefit. In fact, all the added supports he'd put in around the house over the last few months would be perfect for a very pregnant woman too. At Torey's door, Cynthia turned. "John. Thank you. I know I wasn't very kind about you and Ryan, before. But it means a lot that I knew I could still count on you." She stretched up suddenly to brush a kiss on his chin.

"That's okay," he said, stepping back. "Let me know if you need anything. I'll be down the hall. You know where the bathroom is. I'll put out some fresh towels. We'll sort it out in the morning. Oh, and you might look in on Mark before you go to bed."

"You think he'll talk to me?" Her eyes were shadowed.

"Sure. You're still his mother. As long as you don't act like you might take him away from here, you should be fine."

"Oh, good. I've missed him so much." She sighed. "I'm not lying when I say I missed you too."

"I'll get those towels," John said.

He puttered around in the main bathroom for a while, getting extra towels hung up, filling the soap dispenser, and grabbing a fresh box of tissues. But eventually he headed to his room. *Our room.*

Ryan was stretched out on the bed, still dressed, reading a textbook. He didn't look up as John came in and shut the door. John hesitated, then began undressing. He was down to boxers when Ryan turned a page and said, "Torey okay?"

"She's chatting with Char on Skype."

"Mark?"

"I think so." The sound of the guitar had stopped, but it was pretty late by now.

Ryan turned another page slowly and drawled, "The ex-wife?"

"Once she got through vomiting in the bathroom, yeah, I think so." He knew his tone was a bit acid, but really, what was he supposed to do? Turn a sick, pregnant friend away at the door, because she was his ex?

"Did she clean it up?" Ryan's acid matched his.

"Dammit." John reached out and took the book out of Ryan's hands. "If you want to talk, look at me, not the pages."

"Okay, John." Ryan glared back at him. "So where's your ex-wife sleeping tonight? My room?"

"Of course not. She's in Torey's room. Um, Torey's in yours."

"Hah." Ryan grabbed a pillow and propped himself higher. "How convenient that you have enough rooms."

"Well, it is. She was sick. I'm not going to make her go off to a hotel."

"Not tonight. Of course. But you shut me down when I said we'd help find them a place."

"I just said we should wait." John rubbed his aching eyes. "Let's not do this tonight, all right? Let's all get some sleep and see how things are in the morning."

"Sure." Ryan swung his legs over the side and sat up. "I'll accept that. But I'm not sharing you with her."

"I wouldn't ask you to. Can't I be kind to her, as a friend, without it touching you?"

"You'd think. But will she go along with that?"

"What do you mean?"

"When things got tough, she ran to you. And she's being awfully nice to you."

"She trusts me with Torey."

"Sure. But John, she's losing her home and her income and her man. Is it too much to imagine that she might want to get you back instead?"

He remembered the little kiss outside her door. But surely that was just habit and gratitude? "I promise, when we got divorced, she was very done with me. There's no going back."

"I hope so."

He got into bed, watching as Ryan undressed all the way down to skin. He seemed stiff, less easy in his movements, and he kept his bad side turned away from John, the way he had at first. John pulled the cover back. "Come on, get in."

Ryan slid back in beside him. John turned out the light, but Ryan didn't ease into a spoon. Instead he plastered himself over John, kissing him, nipping, his hands busy over John's chest. John kissed him back but said, "I'm tired. And the kids are still awake."

"I don't care." Ryan bit his collarbone harder, sucked on his shoulder, hard enough to raise a mark.

John shifted under him, half aroused, half uncomfortable. "Easy."

"No way." Ryan sucked on his earlobe, then gave it a bite. He moved to the other side of John's chest, drawing his skin tight with lips and teeth. Automatically, John opened his thighs to cradle Ryan's hips.

"Oh yeah." Ryan kissed him on the mouth, his lips sloppy and wet, his tongue forceful. John whimpered involuntarily. Ryan breathed in his ear, "I'm going to suck you and mark you up, and then turn you over and fuck you deep, until you feel me in your throat."

"I don't want marks where the kids will see them."

"Dammit." Ryan bit him over his nipple, hard. "I'll keep them down here. You can wear a shirt. But you are *mine*."

"Ouch. All right." He cradled Ryan's head in his hands, bemused and actually turned on by his sudden possessive tone. Ryan was all over him like a tidal wave, licking and sucking and biting. At first, John tried to do the same, but Ry kept moving, pinning him with weight and hands, and eventually John gave up and let himself be taken.

Ryan licked down John's stomach, pushing the covers back with his shoulders. When he got to John's boxers, he yanked them off roughly enough to tweak his hard cock.

"Careful." John reached down. Ryan grabbed his wrist and pinned it. He looked up, meeting John's eyes, then slid over and sucked the tip of John's cock between his lips. For a moment, he paused, mouthing around the crown, flicking the slit and frenulum with little tongue movements. Then he bent over and sucked John down all the way to the back of his throat, his lips brushing John's copper curls.

John's hips came up off the bed and he barely managed not to shout. Teeth clenched to keep his voice to kid-sleeping-down-the-hall levels, he groaned, "Ngh. Jesus! Ryan!"

Ryan pulled back, John's length sliding wetly out of his mouth, then plunged again. John gripped Ryan's hair, trying to slow him down. "I'm gonna come in ten seconds if you keep that up."

Ryan pulled off. "Not yet. No way. Roll over."

John rolled onto his side. Behind him he heard Ry digging the lube out of the drawer. He raised one knee, and almost immediately, Ryan's hands were on him, spreading his ass cheeks apart. John reached down to rub his own spit-damp cock, ramping up his arousal. Ryan had many moods, but this one didn't feel patient or slow. Sure enough, Ryan breached him with at least two fingers, gradually but without stopping. John bit his lip and breathed, pushed into it, stroking himself faster to stay hard. Ryan's hand was heat and possession, stretch and claim. He closed his eyes, focusing on relaxing to that touch, allowing it.

Ryan's knuckles brushed his ass as a fingertip stroked his prostate, hard enough to color his darkness with sparks of light. Then Ry pulled his hand out, lined up his dick, and pushed in.

They'd gotten good at this, but he'd never done it with this little prep. For a second, his body fought to resist it. But then he found his focus, found the place where burn became warmth, pain became need, and *out!* turned to *in, in, in!* He grunted and pressed back, helping, asking to be filled. Ryan's fingers dug into his hip as he worked John open in small, demanding, rolling movements, always deeper, always more. John dragged in a rough breath and bucked against Ryan's hips.

"Yes." At first Ryan's voice was a bare thread, almost inaudible. "Yes. Like that. Let me. Take it." He shoved deeper, spreading John wide. "Gonna fuck you, have you, all of you. I need you."

"Yes," John grunted. "Please."

"God." Ryan stopped, more than half-sheathed, to bite John's shoulder, then the back of his neck, and then lick over the marks.

John pumped himself, his hand speeding over his shaft restlessly. "More."

"Hell, yeah." Ryan began thrusting in earnest, one hand gripping John's thigh, pulling up and back, his hips flexing. He dragged almost out, lunged in. John gasped. Ryan did it again, faster.

"Love you." Ryan's fingers dug into John's leg as he plundered his ass. "Fuck, fuck, yeah. I love you, love this. You're mine." He slammed in deep, until John imagined his own dick touched from inside. Ryan stopped there, plastered against John's back. "Say it. Say you're mine?"

"Yours," John ground out. "Don't stop."

"Never." Ryan took up the rhythm again, his voice low and intense. "I'm yours, you're mine. This, what we have, all of you and me. No one gets to touch that."

"No," John gasped, stroking frantically, teetering on the brink.

"You want me."

"You. Please."

Ryan hiked John's leg higher and reached under to add his hand to John's on his cock. "Gonna make you come. You'll taste it in your throat when I come too. No one else gets this."

John was past speech. He braced one hand on the bed, rubbed himself with the other and took what Ryan was giving him, every inch, every bit of stretch and pull and hard, tight, sweaty, cock and hands and breath. It was long and rough and perfect in the dark of their bed. Until Ryan grated out, "John. Come."

And he did, flying apart under Ryan's driving weight. He might have cried out, might have shuddered. All he knew was that at last, at last, at final last he was flying off that cliff, tension arcing free. His cock, balls, groin flashed with exquisite heat, and he sprayed in sticky, warm, sudden relief. Ryan thrust into him again, jerky, grunting, short fast strokes. It was almost more than John's sensitized ass could bear, but then Ryan groaned and froze, shaking against him. John reached back with his wet hand to pull Ryan in closer against his body.

They both breathed through the trembles of aftershocks. Then Ryan eased out of him slowly. John couldn't help a wince. Ryan reached down and rubbed gentle circles around his opening. "You okay?"

"Perfect." John felt like blissed-out Jell-O. He let his hand flop limply to the sheet.

Ryan rustled around behind him, getting the wet wipes, cleaning John's fingers and then gently wiping the lube off his ass. Ryan moved about, leaned, then came back and plastered himself over John's shoulders. His soft dick nestled into the small of John's back. He kissed John below his right ear. "I love you." His voice was calmer, the earlier edge gone. "Not just for the sex, not just the fun. I love you. I'm sorry if it felt like I was doubting you."

John got up the energy to turn over and indulge in some slow kissing. "I'm sorry if I gave you a reason."

"You didn't. Really. I have to remember that's who you are. You'd never turn away someone in need, not even Cynthia. You being kind to her is you being the John I love." Ryan rose up and bent to kiss him properly, tenderly, bare brushes of lips and mingling of breath. "Although I don't trust Cynthia. I'm sorry, but I do think she's realized what she lost, and wants you back."

He doubted it but wasn't in a mood to argue, in this comfortable, warm place in their bed. "Well, she's out of luck. I'm yours."

They spent a while longer trading gentle touches, until Ryan quieted and relaxed. He seemed to have dropped off, but John lay there for a long time, unable to keep himself from turning over all his worries in his mind— the kids, custody, Cynthia's pregnancy, Ryan's summer job. He was willing to bend over backwards to make life smoother for all of them, if he could only figure out what everyone needed. Eventually, he heard Torey come upstairs, and then her door shut and the house was still. Some undefined time later, still trying to decide how to take care of everyone he loved, he finally fell asleep.

Chapter Nine

Ryan woke to the nudge of John's morning wood against his hip. For a minute he thought about taking that somewhere. But his bladder was asking for attention, and his leg itched fiercely. As he rolled over, John moved and then sucked in a painful breath.

"What?" Ryan asked. Some of the night before drifted vaguely through his mind. "Ass sore?"

"You wish." John kicked his shin with bare toes. "You bit my nipple. It smarts."

"Sorry." Although he wasn't, very.

"I'll have to wear a loose shirt."

"All your shirts are loose, unfortunately. It's such a waste." He snickered, then sniffed as the faint aroma of bacon reached him. The full events of the night before came crashing back. "Cynthia."

At the same moment, John said, "Torey."

Ryan sat up. At least John's first thought wasn't of his ex-wife. That was promising. Not that he'd expected different, but last night had unsettled him, with John being all soft and caring to Cynthia. And he was *damned* certain she had her eyes on more than just a night without having to find a hotel.

They both rolled out of bed to get dressed. John beat him downstairs. When he got to the kitchen, John was at the table and Torey was dishing bacon and muffins onto plates. "Wow," Ryan said. "Hey, John, can we keep her?"

He realized his mistake when Torey turned hopeful eyes on them. "Can I? I promise I'll help cook. I'm learning to bake too. These are actual muffins from scratch, except you didn't have chocolate chips, so I used raisins."

"Isn't it some ungodly early o'clock on California time right now?" he asked, sitting beside John.

"I set an alarm." She placed glasses of juice in front of them too. "I wanted to show you I can be useful."

"I'm sure you can, hon," John said. "But we still have to talk about a lot of other things."

She shrugged, trying to look unconcerned. "I know. But I really have been learning to cook. I thought you should know."

Ryan picked up a muffin and took a bite. "Hey. Not bad, squirt."

She frowned at him. "Don't call me that."

He gave her a smirk, still trying to lighten things up, and took a bite of his bacon.

John said, "Sit down and eat with us, hon. This is great."

Torey perched on the edge of a chair and nibbled at a muffin. "Mom doesn't eat much in the mornings. It's nice to have company."

"Are you buttering us up?" John asked.

She ducked her head. "Maybe a bit. I really want to stay here."

John sighed. "At least it's Saturday, so no one has to rush out. Why don't we enjoy the nice breakfast you made, and then when your mother and Mark are up, we'll all sit down together and figure things out. We want you, hon, you know that. But there's still the legal custody order and figuring out what's best for everyone and what your mom needs."

Torey sighed. "It wouldn't be so bad living with just Mom, I guess, if Brandon isn't around. But is it wrong that I want *both* of you, Dad?"

John said, "Honey, you know it's not wrong. Just complicated."

Ryan stuffed his second strip of bacon in his mouth. She'd said, *"Both of you"*, not *"All three of you."* Of course she'd only known him a few months, so it was pretty egotistical to wish she'd put him in with John. He pushed his plate aside and stood. "I need to study. I'm going to go put in a couple of hours. Call me when we're ready to hash this out?" He knew both John and Torey followed him with their gazes as he left the room, but he didn't look back.

Unfortunately, studying was not happening. He sat at his desk in the ex-parlor that was now his office, with his class notes open. He had four different highlighters, colored pens, and a set of multicolored index cards. If he was six years old, he'd have the makings of a great first-grade art project. He tried to make an origami swan out of a pink index card, then crumpled it in his fist. His toss bounced off the rim of the trashcan and skittered across the floor. Of course it did. He let it lie there.

He bent over his notes and made a determined effort to at least write up some flash cards. Eventually the discipline that'd let him study through pain and anxiety and noise in the hospital kicked in, and he made better progress. He was startled by Mark's knock on his half-open door.

"Dad says we should meet in the living room."

"Oh." His stomach lurched, even though there was no real disaster looming. He trusted John. It would be fine.

He put his cards inside his notebook, set it aside, and followed Mark down the hall. Cynthia was enthroned in the armchair with a tall glass of ice water at her elbow. Ryan had to admit she looked short of sleep, pale and hollow-eyed. Torey was curled up in the recliner, her feet tucked under her. John sat on the couch, and he gestured Ryan to join him, while Mark dropped onto the old leather hassock. Ryan sat next to John, close enough to bump his knee in the process. He took heart from the fact that they were side by side and hopefully allied.

After a silent moment, John cleared his throat. "So. The question is, where is Torey going to stay, and where Cynthia will live, in the short- and medium-term, at least, before the baby comes."

Cynthia glanced at Torey and said, "Isn't that really an adult discussion, John?"

He shook his head. "The kids are both teenagers now, or nearly. They deserve to hear the truth and have their say, so they can understand the decisions." He looked at Torey. "This isn't going to simply be a vote, though. We want to know your thoughts, but there are other factors we have to deal with. The adults will have the final say, all right?"

She nodded but turned big, hopeful eyes on Ryan. He shifted uncomfortably in his seat. Cynthia's big baby belly kept drawing his eye. It was damned unfair that he couldn't separate the woman from the baby right now. He had nothing against the baby.

John said, "Cynthia, what was your plan when you came here?"

She flushed, the color blotchy on her pale skin. "I mostly wanted to get some distance from Brandon. And I hoped you would help with Torey. I've been sick a lot, and I'm not supposed to lift things or overexert myself. That makes it hard to move or set up a new household by myself."

John said, "Ryan and I are always happy to have Torey stay here. If you like, we can keep her with us, while you take care of yourself until the baby's born."

"That's fine with me too, Mom," Torey piped up.

Cynthia's eyes filled with tears. "Just like that, you're going to take both my kids away and send me off where? Some seedy motel?"

"There are plenty of decent hotels," Ryan said. "Or extended-stay places that are furnished. If John pays you next month's child support, you can afford something like that, for a while at least."

Cynthia straightened her shoulders. "I was planning to pawn the stuff in the suitcase. Or maybe sell it on eBay. Then I can find somewhere nicer, for Torey *and* me."

Torey looked at her, then at John. "I don't want to be far away again."

John said, "I don't either, hon. Maybe we can find your mom something really close by."

"But this changes things, doesn't it, Dad? I mean, we're not in California, and Mom doesn't have a house. You're the one with all the space now." Torey turned the beseeching look on Cynthia. "Why can't we all stay here? It would be so perfect."

Cynthia's lip curled fractionally. "I doubt Ryan thinks so."

He didn't, but he also didn't want to be the bad guy. He said, "What's your medical situation? You look like this pregnancy's been tough on you." *Yeah, you look like crap.* It was really petty to be pleased about that. He went on, "Do you need to be close to a hospital? We're about twenty minutes from York General, longer in rush hour."

She shook her head. "I'm fine. Just queasy off and on. All I need is some quiet and less stress. I don't expect to have to hurry in unless the baby's actually coming."

"So we need to find you somewhere peaceful for a couple of months. We can house the teenagers here, so you can rest."

"But maybe Mom shouldn't be alone," Torey said. She lifted her chin, her eyes on Ryan. "If we really can't both live here, then I guess maybe I should stay with her to help out."

"Thanks, honey," Cynthia said.

John said, "Mark? Any thoughts?"

Mark shrugged. "As long as I keep my room, and my school, and I don't have to turn down my amp all the time or eat extra-healthy crap, I guess I don't care."

John winced. Cynthia said, "You know I'd love to see more of you, honey. That's part of why I decided to come here to Wisconsin."

Mark eyed her without enthusiasm. "Well, I'm kind of busy with music and stuff. Things are pretty good with John and Ryan and me. But if you're around, I guess that's okay."

It wasn't a wholehearted endorsement, but it wasn't a rejection either. Which put Ryan in the hot seat again. He threw a glance at John, looking for clues, but John was the same calm, warm, infuriating guy he always was. Before Ryan could come up with words, Cynthia hauled herself up out of her chair. "Excuse me." She hurried off toward the bathroom.

The rest of them looked at each other. Ryan blew out a frustrated breath. "What about a week?" he said.

"A week what?" Torey asked.

"If we take a week to figure things out. You and your mother stay here, at least temporarily, while we get you registered for school and figure out the money and look around for housing. If we register you with the local school, I'd bet your mom won't want to move far enough to change that. That keeps everyone close at hand."

"Sure!" Her face brightened.

John held up a hand. "Let's wait for Cynthia." They sat silent as the toilet flushed and then Cynthia made her way back to her chair. John said, "Ryan suggested that maybe we shouldn't make decisions too fast. You could stay with us for a week and rest up, figure out your options. Look around for housing. Would that work?"

Cynthia gave Ryan a cool look. "I don't want to impose."

141

"No imposition," he said, equally coolly. "It makes no sense to rush into things and spend extra money on a hotel for the short-term. You might as well stay for a few more days, till you can get settled somewhere more permanent."

She turned a warmer look on John. "I admit, not rushing anywhere sounds really appealing right now."

"It's settled, then," John said. "We'll take a week to make the best of this. To make good decisions."

Ryan said, "I can take some time this morning to check rental listings and see if there's anything close by."

Cynthia flicked him a glance. "Thank you. Although I have no idea what I'll be able to afford yet."

"I can look at the options. See what price range we're dealing with."

"That sounds like a good idea," John agreed. "Meanwhile, we can figure out what needs to be done to get Torey registered at the middle school, and you'll want to find an obstetrician."

Cynthia sighed. "Yes. There'll be plenty to do. You have no idea how much I appreciate you taking us in on short notice. You too, Ryan."

He shrugged. "We'd do almost anything for Torey. But." He hesitated, then decided it needed to be said. "We won't act different around the house for you. If I want to kiss John, I'll do it whether you're in the room or not. We're out as a gay couple to the community, and I'm not going to hide anything."

She stared at him. "You mean you've told *everyone* already? About, um, you two? Told strangers?"

John said, "We've been together for months. Of course we've told people."

"Oh. Well. *I* think it would have been smarter to keep private stuff private, but clearly I can't tell you how to live your lives. Are you going to be all gay and proud at the kids' schools too?"

Ryan hid a wince, because no, they weren't really out at the high school. Mark had enough issues without two gay dads in evidence. He was saved by Torey saying, "Of course they are. Right? I'm sure I won't be the only kid with a gay dad. It's the twenty-first century. People will have to get used to it. Right, Ryan?" She gave him a sunny smile.

"Right. At your middle school, you call the shots about how out you want me and your dad to be. Like Mark does for his high school."

Torey nodded. "I don't want you to hide it. Is that okay?"

Cynthia said, "Torey, honey, you might want to wait and see."

John said to Torey, "Thanks, sweetheart. I like that."

Torey bounced up out of her seat. "So. That's settled. Ryan, do I get to keep your room this week?"

"Sure, hon."

"Then I'm going to move more of my stuff out of Mom's and see what clothes I have that I can still wear. I think I grew since Christmas. Last time I was here, I didn't bother to check." She whirled over to John, gave him a hug, then did the same with Ryan and Cynthia. "This is going to be fun, fun, fun!" she warbled and hurried out and up the stairs. Ryan glanced at John and saw the same uneasy expression he was no doubt wearing.

Mark sniffed. "It's always about clothes."

"Don't worry," John teased, "I won't make you share yours."

Mark got up, hesitated as if about to speak, then shrugged and followed his sister at a slower pace. Which left the adults sitting there. Cynthia rubbed her stomach. Ryan scratched at his thigh, then forced his hand away. John glanced between him and Cynthia. "So, what do we need to talk about between us right now?"

Cynthia said, "This is your house. I'm just a guest. I'll do my best to stay out of the way while I'm here and not impose on your daily routine."

"Don't be silly," John said. "You *are* a guest, which means we'll do our best to make you comfortable. Especially with the baby. You should let me know if you need anything."

"Oh no, I'm fine."

Ryan said, "What's most urgent task for you? Should we get a list of local obstetricians? Do you need John to give you a ride to a pawnshop, maybe?"

"I'm not sure I'm up for that this morning. Maybe later, John?"

"Sure. Take your time," John assured her.

She sighed. "I wish I knew more about selling jewelry. I bet a pawnshop won't give me a fraction of what they're worth. Maybe I should try eBay for that too."

Ryan pushed up off the couch. "John can lend you his computer to do some research. I should get back to studying. I have a midterm on Monday."

He left John and Cynthia sitting there and limped back to his books. He'd just had time to push his crabby mood aside and dig into sample questions when there was a knock on his door. "Come?"

John stuck his head in, then slipped into the room and shut the door. "Hey, Ry, how goes the studying?"

He closed his book on his page of notes. "Fine."

"Are you mad at me?"

"Why would I be mad?"

"I don't know." John sat slumped in the chair across the desk. "It feels like you are."

"Well, I'm not." Ryan had to pause, because that wasn't quite true. "I'm not mad at you, just at the situation. It seems like every time I get the hang of life and I think, 'Okay, now I can move forward,' then something new comes along."

John muttered, "Me too."

"I love your kids, more every day, but even with just Mark here it's already tough to find time for the two of us. If we have Torey and Cynthia in the house, I wonder if we'll ever get the chance to be alone."

"There's always nights."

"It's not just for sex. Although even then Last night, we at least knew Torey was still downstairs and out of earshot. What about when she's right down the hallway?"

John ran a hand over his hair. "I know. I thought about that too. If she'd come up at the wrong moment..."

Ryan pushed his chair back and went around the desk to kneel beside John. He didn't do it often because his leg didn't like it, but right now he needed to look up into John's eyes. "I love you, John Barrett, with everything

I am. But I'm still learning what it means to be half of a couple. Especially a gay couple. And med school is no picnic, and I feel stretched thin."

John took his head in rough palms and kissed him. "I'm sorry. I guess I'm not an easy guy to love."

"Oh no, you're easy. It's everything else that's complicated." Ryan slid down to sit on the floor and leaned his head against John's knee. "I know Cynthia's pregnant and you're worried about her and the baby. I want to help the baby too. But she still doesn't like me, and I don't want to spend what time we *do* have worrying about what she thinks."

"Then don't. What she thinks doesn't matter anymore."

"Hah. Say that to my face. Tell me you'll put your hand on my ass with her in the room." Ryan leaned back to look up at John.

"Well, it shouldn't matter." John's gaze slid away from Ryan's.

"Right." Ryan rubbed his face on John's thigh, feeling his stubble snag against the worn denim. "If she's right here, taking little potshots, looking sideways at us, that's going to be hard to ignore."

"She might come around. She's not half as bad now as she was with Brandon here."

"I hope so, for all our sakes, if she's going to stick around York. But I don't want to have to live with her day and night while she's figuring it out." Ryan felt a wash of shame. Was it wrong, to not want her in their happy home, poisoning the atmosphere in the heart of his personal life?

John shivered hard enough to shake his body under Ryan's cheek. "Truthfully? I don't either."

"Oh, thank God." Ryan pressed a kiss to his leg.

"I still have mixed feelings, though. Cynthia being pregnant reminds me of when we had Daniel and Marcus and Torey. I loved it when she was carrying my children, and seeing her big like that brings it back. I feel protective. Like I should take care of her."

"Mm."

"And then there's the baby. Brandon wants to throw her away, stick her in some institution, and it makes me really want to be there for her."

145

Ryan said neutrally, "You're a sucker for kids. I kind of am too." It was a *good* thing the baby came with Cynthia attached, actually, or he'd probably be setting up a nursery. And John would be carving a crib.

John nodded a couple of times. "Well, we have to remind each other we can help this baby thrive without adopting her, right?"

"Yeah."

"And without letting Cynthia move in with us."

"You're sure?" Ryan asked.

"Positive." John stroked his hair. "A week is good. It's smart, really, because this way I don't feel like I'm dumping Cynthia and the baby into the street. We'll find something that works."

Ryan leaned in harder, rubbing his head against John's stroking hand. "We have time. I shouldn't have pushed so hard. No matter where they live, Torey can hang out with us over the summer. Depending what job I get, I might have more free time once school finishes."

"What job? I thought you were pretty serious about Baltimore?"

"What?" Ryan realized with one thing and another, he hadn't told John. "No, hell, I'm done deciding. I told my professor I was flattered to have the offer but I didn't want to spend that much time away. I have applications still out for positions nearby, but who knows what I'll get? I'm staying here, though."

John stood abruptly, turning to face him. "Because of Cynthia arriving? You don't trust me alone for three months if she's around?"

"What? Where the hell did that come from?"

"Well." John flushed but didn't look away. "You said she was trying to get us back together. And next thing, you're turning down the job you wanted."

Ryan frowned. He pushed up stiffly to his feet too, aware that for once John didn't automatically reach out to give him a hand. "And you assume it was because I don't trust you?"

"Well, I thought you were going, and now…"

"I was never going."

"Sure you were. And you should. I'll be fine. *We'll* be fine."

"I should?" Ryan felt a little seasick. "You *want* me to go?"

"No, I didn't mean that."

"Maybe it's you who's changing your mind with Cynthia here." Ryan tasted acid in his throat. He knew he was being unfair but couldn't stop. "Maybe you'd like having me away for a while so you can have your kids and your wife and a baby in the house without any arguing. Sex isn't on the table, but you could play at being a happy family again."

"What?" John stared at him. They were both breathing fast.

Ryan clung to his mounting anger. It felt good after the gnawing guilt and anxiety to be in the right for once. Maybe John really did want him out of the way. Maybe he did feel like it would make things easier. He opened his mouth to say something cutting, and noticed the light from the window, reflected in the sheen in John's eyes. And stopped.

They stood silently. John swallowed twice, the sound loud in the small room. He reached out toward Ryan and then hesitated, misery on his face.

Ryan dug his fingernails into his palms, then opened his hands, letting it all go. So he was pissed at Cynthia and the whole situation? That was no fucking, damned excuse for taking it out on John. He inhaled, exhaled slowly and said the words he'd usually tried to wriggle out of. "I'm sorry."

John shook his head. "For what? I don't get it."

Of course not, because John was a much more straightforward person who didn't escalate a fight just to come out on top. "John, I declined the summer job before Cynthia ever showed up."

"You did?"

"I did."

"Oh."

"And I trust you. Completely." He moved closer. "I'm sorry I made it sound like I didn't. Her, I trust as far as I can kick her, which, with my leg and the baby, is not far at all."

John's lips twitched, but his eyes didn't warm up yet.

"She's not used to being on her own. No surprise if she tries to grab on to you."

"I don't think she's likely to want any man right now, after what Brandon did."

Ryan thought that Cynthia would very much like John's warm, reliable support. But he said, "Either way, you'll try to help her. And I'm not worried you'll let her get between us on purpose. Just Sometimes you see people in the best light. So before you say yes to any reasonable-sounding ideas of hers, check with me. All right?"

"Of course."

"Yeah. And you actually mean that." Ryan stepped in against John and was enfolded in a hug without hesitation. He closed his eyes, leaned hard, and vowed to try to take John at his word and to keep his loathing of Cynthia under control. "You're a wonderful guy."

"Thanks."

"I'm sorry I forgot to tell you about turning down the Baltimore job."

"No. That's okay."

"It wasn't on purpose. Life got crazy."

John's laugh still held a hint of shakiness. "It sure did."

"But there's no one I'd rather share the craziness with than you. Do you think we could send everyone out for lunch later, so I can appreciate you properly?"

"Probably not today, if Cynthia's still feeling sick. But soon."

"Right. Very soon." Ryan could wait a week for some loud, naked alone-time with John, although not happily. He vowed to do his best to be patient. And to find a new home for Cynthia, ASAP.

Chapter Ten

John was in Ryan's office Tuesday evening, looking over Ryan's shoulder at the apartment listings he'd found, when the doorbell rang. He glanced out the parlor window that overlooked the front porch, and swore.

Ryan glanced up fast. "What?"

"It's Brandon. He's got some nerve coming here." John hurried out, hot anger rising in his chest. *That son-of-a-bitch!*

Mark was almost to the door, but John grabbed his arm and pulled him back. "Let me."

Mark stared at him in confusion. "What? Calvin's coming over to talk."

"That's not Calvin. It's Brandon."

Ryan caught up with them as he reached for the doorknob. "Hang on. Either of you have your phone on you?"

John shook his head. Mark said, "Yeah."

"Can you set it to video?"

"I guess."

Ryan said, "He's a lawyer, John, and he's threatened a nasty court case. We want everything on record."

"Oh, good thought." John turned to Mark. "Can you start it and give it to me?"

Mark stepped back. "I want to know what's happening. I'll film from here."

John preferred to send the kid away from the unpleasantness, but Brandon rang the bell again and then knocked loudly. So he nodded to Mark and pulled open the door. "Yeah?"

Brandon Carlisle was shorter and younger than John, but he drew himself up stiffly and puffed out his chest. "Barrett. You have my wife here."

"I don't *have* anyone." He blocked the doorway and felt Ryan step in close behind him, looking past his shoulder. "And you're not welcome here."

"I want to talk to my wife."

"Then you can call her first and ask her."

"She's not answering her cell phone."

"What, did you forget to cut it off with the credit cards when you took all the money out of the joint bank accounts?"

Brandon glared at him. "I don't have to answer to you. Tell Cynthia I want to see her."

"About what?"

Brandon took a half step closer, getting up in his grill. "None of your business."

"If you're threatening to push your way into my house, then I think it is."

"She's *my* wife."

"She's stressed and tired and pregnant. With *your* child, I might add."

"That has nothing to do with me."

At his shoulder, Ryan laughed. "Really? You need a gay guy to explain the facts of life to you?"

Brandon turned a hard glare on him. "I don't need you for anything." He returned his stare to John. "You've wrecked my life enough already."

"Me?" John blinked. That was out of left field.

"Yeah, you. Stealing away the kids. Making Cynthia all soft in the head. She'd have stayed home where she belonged if you hadn't let her come running here. She'd have done what she was told."

"*Cynthia* would? What've you been smoking?"

"She was an excellent lawyer's wife. She knows I'm up for a partnership. She wouldn't have done anything to jeopardize that if you hadn't interfered with our family. Everything was working fine."

"Until you told her to get an abortion." Anger rose to choke him. "How could you do that? Don't you *know* how she would feel about killing her baby?"

"It's a fetus, not a baby. It's defective. She never used to be sentimental."

John kept his temper by a thread. He didn't punch Brandon's defective mouth. Instead he managed a slow breath and shook his head, anger turning to disgust. "I don't think you ever knew her at all. Yeah, she's ambitious, and practical. But she loves her kids. All of them, including yours."

"That thing's not mine."

"Then you can get off my porch." John took a step forward, and Brandon reflexively stepped back.

Ryan said quietly, "I'll see if Cynthia's awake and wants to see him. Don't let him hurt anybody until I get back, all right?"

John was about to snap that he was more likely to hurt Brandon when he caught Ryan's nod at Mark, still videotaping from the dimness of the hallway. "Oh. Right."

As Ryan walked away into the house, Brandon said, "Look, I didn't come to fight with you. She stole something from me, and I want it back. That's all."

"What about all the money you stole from her? Moving every penny to your personal accounts was pretty low."

"What? I should've let her blow all my money on some fuck-you shopping spree? I don't think so."

"She had to put back *groceries*, you creep."

Brandon smirked. "I told her I'd give her whatever money she needed. She just had to *ask* me for it."

Behind John, Cynthia said, "I wouldn't ask you for water if I was on fire."

Brandon's attention snapped to her. "Fine. I don't care. We're getting a divorce and you hate me. Fine. But you stole my personal possessions, and I want them back."

"Oh? What on earth could that be?" Cynthia's tone was the one John had come to hate most, toward the end of their marriage— amused, superior, uncaring. It should've made him feel better, to have her turn it on Brandon now, but somehow it didn't.

"My baseball cards, you cunt!" Brandon's hands curled into fists. "That was my father's collection before it became mine. You have no idea what you have there. They're very valuable, and I want them *back*."

"California's a community property state. What's yours is mine."

"I'm the lawyer, not you. Community property doesn't apply to anything I owned before we got married. Give them to me, or I'll have you arrested for theft."

"Just try it," Cynthia said. "What do you think would happen to your chance of making partner when I tell the papers that you threw your pregnant wife in jail and left your stepchildren penniless and homeless over a few stupid baseball cards?"

"*Stupid?* There are 1915 Cracker Jack cards in there. There's a Hank Aaron rookie card, Pete Rose, a Topps Mickey Mantle. They're worth more than your damned engagement ring."

"Ooh. I wonder what I can get on eBay for them."

"Arrested for selling stolen merchandise is what you'll get."

Ryan said, "Hey, how about we cool this down? Cynthia, you don't really want the cards, just a decent amount of money to live on, right?"

John glanced over his shoulder and saw her fold her arms over her belly and smile nastily. "I don't know. I'm enjoying watching him beg."

Brandon snarled, "This isn't begging. This is you behind bars if you don't hand them over."

John saw Cynthia open her mouth for some no doubt nasty comeback and spoke loudly over her. "Ryan's right. Cynthia and the baby need enough cash to live on. If you want the cards that much, why don't you put a reasonable sum into a bank account she can access, and I'm sure" —he gave her a hard look— "she'll get the cards back to you right away."

"That's extortion."

"No," Ryan said in a hard voice. "Extortion would be threatening to upload a video to YouTube of you calling your ex-wife a cunt and your unborn child a thing and admitting you took away their grocery money."

Brandon stared at him, then his gaze darted to the hallway where Mark stood with his phone. "Damn it. Marcus, bring that here. Now!"

John held out a hand behind him. "Why don't you give it to me and go upstairs, Mark." He kept his tone steady. His stomach twisted at the realization that his son had been watching all the grown-ups in his life fight like this. That couldn't be good. "Go on, son."

"I'm fine," Mark said tightly. "It's pretty cool to see the real Brandon Carlisle come out."

Brandon's eyes flicked back and forth between them.

Time to stop all this before something unforgivable happened. Something more unforgivable. "Look. We all want to come out of this with the kids taken care of, and everyone free to go their own way."

"Speak for yourself," Brandon said. "I want what's mine."

"Then stop acting like an evil dictator."

Brandon looked at Cynthia. "You're going to have to come back to California, you know. You can't take a minor child out of state during a divorce. As soon as you get your papers served, you'll be bound by the rules."

She hugged her stomach. "I'm sure my obstetrician won't want me to travel anytime soon, and anyway, I thought this wasn't your child?"

He visibly ground his teeth.

John rubbed his forehead, feeling a headache beginning to throb. "That's all later, right? For now, can we get a damned cost-of-living payment and then give this bastard back his dumb cards?"

"I don't know," Cynthia drawled. "I might prefer to burn them."

"Then you'd be on the hook for the value of them," Ryan pointed out. "Not worth the satisfaction. Come on, Brandon, help us out here. You know what they say about *hell hath no fury*; if you want those cards back intact you'd better bend a little. Especially if you don't want to look like a cheap bastard to fifty thousand YouTube viewers."

Brandon huffed a few breaths through his nose, then turned to John, visibly dismissing Ryan. "So. You give me the cards, I cut her a check for ten thousand?"

John said, "I don't trust you not to stop the check once you have them. You come with us to the bank tomorrow and transfer the money. Then we give you the cards."

Cynthia said, "Better make it fifteen thousand. California divorce takes at least six months."

Brandon's icy glare had probably put the fear of God into hostile witnesses, but on John's own doorstep, with family at his back, he wasn't impressed. Finally, Brandon said, "All right. First thing in the morning, though. Time is money, and *I* have clients depending on me. I'll have to get a flight out by noon. Which bank?"

They made arrangements in short terse sentences. John stayed in the doorway until Brandon's car cleared the end of the street. Then he turned back inside and shut the door.

Mark, Ryan and Cynthia were all still standing there, staring at each other. Cynthia gave her head a toss. "I don't know what I ever saw in that idiot."

John had wondered that too, but he said, "Where's Torey?"

"In her room, well, Ryan's room, with her headphones on," Mark said.

"Well, thank goodness for small favors."

Ryan said, "Mark, maybe you could copy that video to your dad's computer. Then take it off your phone. You don't need to keep that crap around."

Mark's fingers turned white on the cellphone. "I want to do what we said, upload it to YouTube. I want everyone to see what he looks like when he's not all cool and fancy suits and superior."

"I'm sure you do." John kept his tone calm, as he reached for Mark's phone. "But we want things to go as well as possible for your mom and the new baby, right? A threat only works until you follow through. We want him worried and cooperating, not just mad as hell."

"I like making him mad." Mark looked at Cynthia. "I told you, Mom. You see? I told you what he was like."

Cynthia licked her lips and shrugged. "But your dad's right. We need to keep that in reserve."

"He doesn't care about us kids, unless we're making him look good. He doesn't care about anyone."

"He's mad at me right now. He doesn't like not getting his way."

Mark scoffed. "I bet he has another whore already."

"Mark!" John took one quick step and eased the phone out of his son's grasp. "Apologize to your mother."

"For *what*?"

For implying she was his last whore? Maybe it was better to let it go. "Never mind. I'll get that video copied and give you back your phone."

"You'd better mean Ryan'll do it." Mark turned to Ryan. "Promise you won't let him mess with it. I just got all the settings the way I want them."

Ryan moved up beside John, leaning into him in a wonderful way that settled John's churning stomach. He took the phone out of John's hand and smiled at Mark. "I've got this. You go on back to your homework."

"I'm done. Calvin's coming over."

"We'll let you know when he gets here," Ryan promised.

"Well, all right." Mark hesitated, glancing at his mother.

Ryan tilted his head at Cynthia, and then smirked up at John and kissed him under the ear. "I'm so glad *you're* not a rabid weasel with dollar signs for a heart."

Cynthia huffed loudly and stalked off, or as close to a stalk as her pregnant waddle could manage.

Ryan turned to Mark. "Everyone makes mistakes. Your mom is figuring out that Brandon was a big one. I really shouldn't rub it in."

"No," John said, trying to sound severe. "You really shouldn't." He kissed Ryan lightly. "I'm glad you're not a weasel either."

Mark laughed. "You two are nuts." His voice had a younger, lighter sound, and John was glad of it.

"But we're your nuts," Ryan said. "No, wait. Rewind. That didn't come out right." Mark snorted, and Ryan smiled at him. "Go on to your room. I'll send Calvin up. Does that mean you're still playing together?"

"Maybe." Mark looked happier. "The saxophone guy didn't work out, and I thought we were screwed. But Cal says he met this guy who's a wizard on the violin. I think it could work. So Cross Cut might live again. He's going to help me go through a few songs and write out violin parts, and then we'll audition the guy."

"I hope he's good." John slid his arm around Ryan, pulling him closer. "It's about time things got better. You know I love to hear you play."

"Me too," Ryan said. "And violins are lightweight. Easy for me to roadie."

Mark said, "Thanks. Really."

John held Ryan, watching as Mark disappeared up the stairs. Eventually he said quietly, "So was what we did really extortion?"

Ryan shrugged, his shoulder digging into John's and tried for a Star Trek voice. "I'm a doctor, Jim, not a lawyer."

John kissed him again, slow and deep. "And thank goodness for that."

Ryan turned to face him, rubbing up against him, and lowered his tone. "Hey, wanna step into my office and have your prostate examined?"

"Not sexy," John muttered.

"But this is." Ryan took a firm grip on his hair and kissed him senseless, right there in the dim hallway.

Yeah, he had to admit, that was.

****

Ryan glanced around the bar at his classmates drinking, laughing and unwinding. He wasn't quite sure how he'd ended up here. He'd been hanging out in the hallway at eight o'clock, after a goddamned evening exam, agreeing with everyone else that neuroanatomy was the work of the devil, and that dissection preps never looked like either the book or your own specimen. Then someone shouted, "Beer. Must have beer!" And he'd been carried along with the tide.

He picked up his bottle and took a long pull. A four-piece band was playing upbeat but mediocre dance music. Some of his classmates who had energy to burn, or more caffeine than red cells in their veins, were dancing. Over near the little stage, a bunch of the guys were doing some kind of drinking game that involved balancing shot glasses. He wasn't sure how it worked and in fact wasn't sure they knew either. Mostly it seemed like a reason to alternate between drinking whiskey and spilling it. So far, they were tipping generously enough for the servers to bear with them, but being students, the money would probably run out soon.

At one of the bigger tables, a bunch of the grinders in the class were sharing a pitcher and trying to scare each other with how wrong all their exam answers were. After being at it for an hour, he wasn't sure how many of them could still pronounce *musculocutaneous nerve*, but they were trying. Someone's voice rose. "But if you ducked down and looked underneath, it actually wrapped around from the palmar surface, so in fact I'd bet it was an atypical..." The rest was lost in cheering and cat-calls from the shot glass crowd.

Ryan took another drink. He'd thought he would have to hurry home after this exam, to get Cynthia and Torey packed up and moved into a new place. But although the planned week was up, the best rental they'd found didn't come available till the first of the month. Which meant another week of sharing.

A pair of pretty women, enthusiastically dancing together, bumped up against his chair. They apologized cheerfully and danced off. He eyed their retreating backs, wondering if they were really together or just hetero friends without dance partners. Then he wondered why it mattered. He pulled out his phone to see if John had texted him back, but there was nothing new.

Donna dropped into the other chair at his little table. "Drinking alone?"

He tipped the bottle at her. "Not anymore."

She smiled. "So where's your boyfriend? You should get him down here to say hi."

"I did text him. Although now I'm not sure I want him to meet you all this way." He squinted. "*What* does Joe have on his head?"

Donna glanced over. "Looks like women's underwear."

"Do I want to know why?"

"Probably not."

"We've only been here an hour."

"Yeah, but everyone's drinking on two hours of sleep and no dinner." She raised her own glass at him. "Congratulations on being the most sober med student in the place."

"Don't say that." He upended his bottle.

"Why not?"

"I feel old."

"That again?"

He shrugged. It was the truth. Especially now with two teens and a pregnant houseguest. It seemed like he spent every minute being responsible and helpful and boring. Well, maybe not every minute. A vivid flash of John's hands on both of them, stroking hard and fast until he saw stars, reminded Ryan that his life had its compensations. But still, he was thirty and sometimes he felt fifty. He'd thought tonight might be a chance to cut loose, but so far it wasn't working.

Donna looked up over his shoulder and smiled warmly. "Well, *hello* there, nice not-too-young guy."

"Where?" Ryan tried to twist around.

"Oh no, I call dibs on this one. He's *hot*."

"Hm?" Ryan managed to turn, and then he had to smile. There was John, working his way across the crowded dance floor toward him. For once, his man was dressed in clothes that showed off his work-honed, lean form. The black jeans actually fit, the pushed-up sleeves of the Henley bared his veined forearms and hugged his wide chest and shoulders. "Sorry. You're out of luck."

"What? You think he plays for your team?"

"Nope. I *know* he does." He stood as John neared them. "Hey, you made it."

"Yeah, I was going to text but then I figured I'd drive over." John smiled at him and stopped half an arm's length away.

In a sudden fit of affection and beer, Ryan reached out, pulled him close and kissed him hello. Just fast and dry, but sweet, because it was John's mouth against his. When he was done, Ryan resisted the temptation to look around. Nothing changed, though. The band played loudly, the shot-glass folks whooped and laughed at each other, the type-A students shot down a theory about cranial nerves with drunken disdain. No one had noticed, or no one had cared.

Except Donna, who raised her glass to them. "Damn. The good ones are always taken or gay, or both."

John smiled. "Hi. I'm John Barrett."

"My boyfriend," Ryan added, in case that hadn't been obvious. Maybe he was drunker than he thought.

"I'm Donna, Ryan's classmate. Sit down, have a beer."

"Sure."

Ryan sat, listening as John and Donna got through the first meet-and-greet formalities. John ordered them each a beer, with another screwdriver for Donna, and eased back in his chair. "So how was the exam?"

"Almost the death of us. Thus the embalming you see all around you." Ryan waved his hand.

"Meaning you might have gotten an A minus?"

Donna laughed. "Bite your tongue. I'm sure wonder-boy aced it."

"I'm not." Ryan toyed with the label on his beer morosely. "I think I got the last specimen all wrong."

"You always think that," John pointed out.

The band changed gears, striking up a slow, soft song. On the small dance floor, dancers broke apart and reformed in a galaxy of swaying couples. The two girls were still dancing together, the shorter one with her head on the taller girl's shoulder. He didn't recognize them and wondered if they were students or townies.

Donna said, "You two should dance. Don't mind me."

"I don't dance," Ryan said.

"No?"

He slapped his scarred thigh lightly. "No."

Donna shrugged. "Slow dancing is just swaying in place. I bet your big strong guy would hold you up. Lucky you."

"I still don't. Not anymore."

"Oh well." Donna glanced at John. "Want to dance, then? Just platonically. I know you're spoken for."

John gave Ryan an odd look, then said, "Sure. You don't mind, Ry?"

He waved his hand. "Nah. Go ahead."

They got up and moved onto the crowded floor. Donna was tall enough that her chin was against John's shoulder, and he held her loosely but close in.

John had his head turned away, but Ryan could see Donna's face. Her eyes were half-closed, and she looked relaxed and happy. She and John made a nice couple, really. Not beautiful, but strong and attractive and intelligent-looking. They moved easily in a tight circle, and as they turned, Ryan saw that John's eyes were wide open and looking straight at him. As they rotated, John watched him over Donna's head until he couldn't anymore. And when they came around again, he could tell John was searching until he found Ryan's table again.

Ryan stood up, leaving his cane hooked over the chair. He moved slowly onto the floor, letting dancers dodge him rather than trying to get around them, until he was right behind John and could tap him on the shoulder. "Can I cut in?" he asked.

John and Donna paused and stepped apart. For a moment, Ryan froze. He could still do the conventional thing and hold out a hand to Donna. John would be fine with it. But tonight he'd kissed John, in front of whoever the hell had been looking. Ryan thought he might not be the bravest or fastest to embrace his inner gay, but he wasn't going to take any damned steps backward. He reached for John.

John's smile was his reward, as they came together. Donna grinned and headed off across the floor, and John folded Ryan into his arms. "Want to lead?" he murmured in Ryan's ear.

"Nah," Ryan said back, against John's neck. "Let's hold each other up and turn in circles."

"That works." John's hands on him were definitely tighter and more possessive than the way he'd held Donna.

Ryan closed his eyes and leaned in, letting John take a bit of his weight. He moved his feet, following John's lead after all. Someone had to steer, and it wasn't going to be the half asleep drunk guy. Although having John's hand warm on the small of his back, and the smell of John's skin in his nose, was waking him up, in embarrassing ways. He wasn't too sorry when the music stopped and switched to something more active. He eased back enough to see John's face. "I don't think I'm up for this one."

"How about another beer?"

"Sure."

As they walked past the bar to get to their table, John's big hand still rested lightly against his back for everyone to see. Ryan was aware of a new kind of feeling. Connected. A little possessive. Not like he owned John, but like they fit together and they weren't hiding it anymore, from anyone. Like John was his as much as he was John's and anyone else who might've looked over when John came in the bar and thought, *oh yeah, hello there big boy,* was out of luck. Forever.

That was the moment someone said, "Why don't you go off to some faggot bar and leave normal people alone? You're disgusting."

160

It came like a punch in the gut, leaving Ryan stunned and scrambling for words. John stepped in front of him, glaring at the business-suited middle-aged guy who'd spoken. Before Ryan could muster a good comeback, Donna shoved her chair back and stood up fast. "Why don't *you* go off to some stupid ugly-person bar and leave normal people alone?"

The guy swung around to look at her, his balance wobbly enough to show he was pretty drunk. "What's it to you, bitch?"

She tossed her head. "You're polluting my space with your ignorant bullshit."

He gaped at her, then muttered, "Fag hag."

"Yeah?" Tom suddenly stepped up behind her. "These are my friends too. I bet you don't have any friends."

The drunk looked around the bar as if expecting support, but most people were oblivious. The few close enough to have heard him didn't seem inclined to back him up. A couple of classmates gave Donna a thumbs-up. The locals looked away, obviously not wanting to get involved.

"You're all fag lovers," the guy said.

Tom moved closer. "You know what? You can walk out the damned door and head south. Take a right in Alabama. I bet there's a red-neck dive down there where you'd fit right in."

The man turned to the bartender. "You gonna keep this bar decent or not?"

The bartender set a glass down in front of one of his customers and shrugged. "As long as people don't make trouble, they're welcome in here. As far as I'm concerned, you're the one making trouble."

"Jesus *Christ*! What's this world coming to?" The drunk slammed his hand on a table, glared at John and Ryan with clear loathing and then pushed his way toward the door.

A ripple of silence followed him, but as the door shut behind him, conversations sprang up again. Ryan felt hot and cold, his face flushed but a chill like ice sliding down his spine. He couldn't feel John's touch, couldn't tell if John had moved his hand or if his skin was numb. His feet were glued to the floor.

John murmured, "Let's sit down, huh?"

He swallowed against the dryness of his throat. "We should just go."

Tom said, "The hell you should. Come on, sit down. I stole your guy's chair, Ry. He'll need to grab another one." He and Donna sat back down at the table, waving at him and John to join them. Which was nice and ordinary, and Ryan still couldn't move. His eyes stung and he thought his knees might be shaking. It wasn't fear, but hate so pure he wanted to chase the guy down and beat him to death with the cane John spent days making for him. Punch out the eyes that dared to look at John like that.

He realized he could feel John's hand again, rubbing circles on his lower back. He took a breath.

"Come on, Ry," Donna coaxed, pushing his chair back farther in invitation. "Sit with us. I promised Tom he'd get to meet your boyfriend."

"She said he's smarter than you," Tom joked. "This I gotta see."

"No one's smarter than Ryan," John said, still not moving from his side.

This was ridiculous. They should go home. Or sit down, or anything but stand here like specimen A and B of the gay American male for everyone to stare at. He dared another look around. A couple of people were watching them, but most weren't. His heart slowed as no one else seemed inclined to start up where that guy left off.

Sitting would be easier than walking right now. He took the five steps to his chair and eased down into it. John pulled another one over and sat close beside him.

Tom said, "Another round? I'm buying."

"Coffee for me," Donna said. "I have to drive eventually."

"Me too," John agreed.

Ryan managed a little wave of the hand that Tom took for agreement and watched him head over to the bar. When he came back holding four mugs, he said, "The bartender gave these to us on the house."

"Nice of him." Donna looked over there and raised her mug to the guy with a smile.

"Agreed." John took a slow sip of his own.

Ryan curled his fingers around the hot mug and let the conversation wash around him. The other three shot the breeze for a while. John was a good sport about all the gross medical stuff that Tom and Donna chatted about, and eventually Ryan managed a comment or two. Then Tom found out John was another obsessive baseball fan, and it was Donna and Ryan's turn to get bored.

The ice inside Ryan slowly thawed. The band played on, no better but no worse than before. A couple of other classmates stopped on the way past the table and introduced themselves to John. No one talked about the homophobic elephant in the room, but Ryan thought they went out of their way to be nice. Eventually Tom stood to join some other group who were urgently flagging him over. "Keep bringing this guy around, Ryan," he said. "He's smarter than you where it counts."

"I'm smart." Ryan was maybe not sober yet, though. At least something was still muddling his thoughts. He made an effort and added, "Bet I still kicked your ass on the exam."

"Well, yeah." Tom grinned. "But you cheer for the Padres. Seriously!"

Donna stood too. "I should go home. I'm helping my mom watch my nieces tomorrow. I need to rest up for it."

John stood politely when she did and instead of sitting back down, he bent and retrieved Ryan's cane off the floor. "How old are they?"

"Two and four."

"Oh yeah, sleep and a good stock of aspirin." John's smile was fond, though. "That's a great age." He passed Ryan the stick. That meant Ryan should try to get to his feet. He was willing to give it a shot, and it turned out he was less wobbly than he'd feared. John hovered but stepped back casually as soon as he realized Ryan had this without help.

Donna led the way out, with John close behind her. Ryan followed them toward the door. He thought he caught a couple of less-than-friendly looks among the mostly oblivious crowd, but no one said anything or threw fruit, so he decided to try not to care.

As John pulled the door open for Donna, Ryan froze. *What if he's waiting for us out there?* A lurch of anxiety caught him by surprise, followed by a surge of pure anger. He'd never been afraid to simply walk through a door before. Not unless there was a wall of fire on the other side. Who the hell was that bastard, to make him feel this way?

John glanced back at him, still holding the door. Ryan made himself put one foot in front of the other. Hopefully John would just think he was still drunk. The cooler air outside the bar was good on his face, and he headed for the truck without looking around. John was half a foot taller than Homophobic

Moron Guy, and Ryan had his cane in hand. They were fine. It was all in his head anyway.

Donna got into a battered old car, gave them a wave and drove off. John opened the truck door for him, then went around and swung up into the driver's seat. It was later than Ryan had realized. He stared at the dashboard clock as John pulled out into the street. He didn't look back. Didn't listen for another car behind them. They drove on through the quiet nighttime streets.

John handled the truck with easy competence, one hand on the wheel, his other elbow on the windowsill. Not one thing about him said that the ugliness in the bar had affected him. Ryan's anger was washed smooth by a sudden surge of love that wanted to overflow and spill everywhere. John was so strong and so dear, with his integrity and his quietness and his big solid frame and the character of his face. Ryan loved him, and he didn't want to simply stop hiding that now, he wanted to fucking flaunt it. *This guy chose me! And* fuck *anyone who tries to make me ashamed of that.*

He was trying to find words when his phone rang. He fumbled for it in his pocket, dropped it by his feet. John pulled over to the curb and stopped, so he could take his seat belt off and reach down for it. The display said, "Brent". He frowned at it, then answered. "Hey, bro. Is there a good reason you're calling me at halfway to midnight?"

"Oh. Oops." Brent sounded odd. "I'm at Dad's, and I forgot the time change."

"Is something wrong with Dad?"

John glanced over, and instead of pulling away from the curb, he shifted the truck into park.

"No, he's fine," Brent said.

Ryan took an easier breath. "Then *what?*" That came out harshly, but after all, the last time they were together Brent had peeled out in his rental car in an "eat my dust, faggots" reaction. And then pointedly un-invited John to his wedding. Ryan resented being reminded of that tonight.

"Well, I thought we We were just talking, um."

A woman's voice in the background said, "Give me that," and then louder, "Hi. Ryan? This is Anne, Brent's fiancée."

"Oh, hi, Anne." Ryan rolled his eyes at John, then put his phone on speaker, because if he was going to be rude to a woman in front of John, he wanted the reason to be obvious.

She said, "I asked Brent why we hadn't heard back that you were coming to the wedding. He showed me the email he sent you, and your answer."

"And?"

"Ryan, I really want you there. I know it's pretty obvious that Brent hasn't been okay with finding out you're gay, but he cares about you. When we were first dating, I heard more about you than about anyone, even Drew's boys."

"When I was the injured firefighter," he said, "Not the suddenly gay brother."

"Yeah." Anne actually laughed. "No doubt. The thing is, Brent's both right and wrong about this. My parents *are* conservative, and if you stood up in the church and kissed your boyfriend, you could cause a big problem. But I think there's a middle road. I want you to come, and bring John if you like. Be together, but quietly, so if the stuffy members of my family want to, they can ignore what you are to each other."

"Pretend to be straight, you mean?"

John gave him an admonishing nudge with his elbow, but Ryan frowned back. He was done with beating around the bush.

"Not necessarily straight. But maybe not too obvious? Brent planned for you to be one of his groomsmen, and we'd still like that. I'd like you and John to both be here. But you will make my family relations easier if you keep it to something Uncle Bo can at least pretend not to see."

"That's a change of tune, isn't it? What does Brent say?"

"I'll let him tell you."

There were some fumbling sounds, then Brent said, "She's right. I always figured if I ever found the right girl, Drew would be my best man, and you'd be right there next to him."

"And now?"

"Yeah." Brent took an audible breath. "Look, I can't say I understand the gay thing or approve of it. But you're my brother, and I want you at the wedding. If Anne isn't worried about her parents blowing a gasket, then that's all that matters."

165

"So you're telling me I can bring my boyfriend to your wedding?"

"Um. Yeah."

"And wear a rainbow tie and dance with him at the reception?"

"Eeeerr." Brent's noise was almost a squeak.

John said, "Hi, Brent. He's messing with you. He'll wear whatever the groomsmen are supposed to wear, and he has two left feet anyway."

Ryan said, "Hey, I thought we danced pretty well tonight."

"Sure, but only because you were drunk and let me lead." John leaned closer to the phone. "So thanks for the invitation, Anne. When's the wedding again?"

Brent said, "June eleventh, Saturday, at four p.m."

John hesitated. "Well, we'll try to be there, but we have a friend with a baby due on the tenth, so depending on that I might be tied up. Ryan can come either way, though."

"No, he can't," Ryan said. He didn't want to go see Brent tie the knot in a conservative Texas wedding without John there. He'd probably end up punching someone. He needed John's good influence.

"Well, I hope you both make it." Brent almost sounded sincere.

"And if your new in-laws figure out you have a gay brother?" Ryan asked.

Anne's voice came from a little distance, "They have to live in the twenty-first century sometime. You know, having you two test the waters might actually be a good thing for one of my younger cousins. And Brent and I will be living in Seattle, so we'll be far enough away for things to cool off."

"Seattle? I thought you were based out of Boston, Brent?" Although he traveled so much, Ryan could never keep track.

"I'm moving," Brent said. "Kind of a lateral move with a small pay cut, but then I'll be able to stay home a whole lot more."

"Oh. That's nice." Ryan bet Dad hadn't tried to get Brent to give Anne up, because she was bad for his career.

"Well, I should let you get to bed," Brent said. "I mean, to sleep. We just wanted you to know."

"Don't put me in the wedding party," Ryan said. "Find some other groomsman. But we'll try to be there to see it."

"Oh. Okay. Well. Um, maybe it's just as good if you won't have to do all that standing around up front. That might be bad for your leg, you know. You can sit down quietly in the pews."

"Yeah. Just as good," Ryan managed and hung up.

John rubbed his shoulder. "Breathe. He's coming around, anyway. Slowly."

"Hah. There are faster tortoises." At least they'd invited John this time. He only realized now that it had hurt to think of missing Brent's wedding, almost as much as it'd hurt to imagine going when John wasn't welcome. "Well." He blew out a breath. What a night.

John would have pulled away from the curb but Ryan put a hand on his leg. "Wait."

"What?"

He'd kissed John in public, danced with him, and the world hadn't ended. They'd been called fags in public by a stranger, and their friends had stood up for them. He'd had his moments of freaking out and of being scared of the consequences, and gotten past that. And then Brent. Maybe this was the night to do it all. He hit another contact on his phone, keeping it on speaker. "One more call." He didn't remember Andrea's schedule at the firehouse. She might be sleeping, or out on a run.

But she answered, not sounding like he'd woken her. "Yeah? Ryan?"

"Hey, how are you?"

"Pissed. Again."

"Um, why?"

"Remember when you said you would keep in touch? What was that? Christmas. And this is Let me see. April. I get what, a quarterly phone call?"

"I emailed you," he protested. "A fair bit." He'd made a point of it, in fact.

"Yeah. I now know all the courses you're taking, how tough the exams are, and which lab partner you never want to have again. And nothing about your real life."

"Hey, I'm in med school. That stuff is my real life."

"I call bullshit. What about the girl you were crushing on?"

"I was *what*?"

"When you called me, lo these many months ago, to say nothing much about anything and ask random questions. Tell me you didn't have a crush on someone."

"Jesus, how do you *do* that?" He didn't remember saying anything that would even remotely lead to that conclusion.

She sounded smug. "So it was true. C'mon, what's she like?"

"Um." Ryan took a breath. He could do this. Andrea was as tough as a woman had to be to do her job in a firehouse full of guys, but she wasn't judgmental. It would be fine.

He'd hesitated long enough for her tone to soften. "Are you okay? Did you break up?"

"No. In fact, I'm better than okay." He caught John's eyes, smiled as he said, "I'm in love."

Andrea whooped. "Finally! Ryan Playboy Ward found someone worth more than a fast fuck. Who is she?"

"His name is John."

There was a long enough silence from the other end for Ryan to start feeling queasy, before Andrea said, "This is for real, right?"

"Yeah. For real. He's three inches taller than me, red hair, great voice, does wonders with a piece of wood and a carving knife."

"Okay." She hesitated. "I'm rearranging some stupid assumptions."

"Not stupid. I never said anything. I didn't know myself until…"

"Christmas, right?"

"Yeah. Well, even before that, but I wasn't admitting it."

"So were you bi all along?"

"I presume." He shrugged, although she couldn't see it. "Not really a safe thing to be in my high school or a firehouse and I did like girls, a lot, so I dated girls and everything was fine. I didn't even realize I liked guys until John scraped me up off the pavement one day, and I started having trouble getting him out of my head."

"That's great!" Andrea's voice was warm. "He sounds excellent. Anyone who could jolt you out of your speed-dating mode must be something special. I need pictures."

"Well…" He thought about taking a picture of John right there, the way he sat with a tiny smile and hint of a blush, listening. But the overhead light was dim and his camera wasn't great. "Hang on." He texted her the picture of the two of them that his dad had taken. "Sent you one."

"I'm pulling it up now." There was a pause. "That's John with you? He's great. God, Ry, you look so happy. I don't think I've seen you look like that before."

"I am," he realized. Under all the tensions and frustrations of the crowded household, past the anxieties of coming out to family and friends, despite exams and itchy scars and giving up on the externship and bastards in bars and all his fears, he really was. "John makes me happy." He grinned at the way John's smile got bigger. "And now, if you'll excuse me, I want to go make him even more *happy*. Wanna know how?"

"TMI," Andrea said. "Call me some other time, though. You're not getting off this easy. I want the whole story."

"I'll do that."

"Ryan? Is this, like, a secret? Or can I mention it to people?"

For one more moment, he thought about asking her to keep it to herself. He could say he wanted to tell people his own way. But really, he was never going back to the firehouse. If the guys didn't like him turning gay, fuck 'em. It would have no impact on his real life. "Sure, whatever you want. Just let them know if anyone says anything nasty about John, I'll pay you to fill their turn-out boots with bullshit. The real kind."

"Hard to come by in suburban San Diego, but I'll get some if I have to. Good night, Ry. Call me. And…"

"What?"

"I'm glad you've found someone special. I'm happy you finally told me. And by the next time you call, I might be over being fucking pissed about the fact that *it took you four months to trust me.*"

The green symbol on his phone went red, showing that she'd hung up. He slid it into his pocket and glanced back at John. "She always did like to have the last word."

"Seems like it."

"So now everyone knows." He could feel the wide smile tugging his lips. "Everyone who matters."

"You don't look upset about that."

"Hah. Definitely not." He leaned over and kissed John. He'd meant it to be symbolic, but somewhere along the line it became hot and needy and impatient. He leaned into John's chest, tangled his hands into John's hair and held him still to be plundered. John closed his eyes and opened his mouth. A while later, Ryan broke off enough to say, "How far are we from home?"

"Ten minutes."

"Too far."

"Mm." John's arms felt wonderful, wrapped across his back, and his end-of-the-day stubble rasped perfectly against Ryan's upper lip. Ryan nipped that strong chin and traced his jawline before resuming the kiss.

After another minute, John pushed him away. "We can't do this here."

"Right." Ryan leaned back in.

"Really can't do what I want to do to you."

"Oh?" That caught his attention.

"Ten minutes. A big bed. Lube."

"I'm thinking about it."

"Put your seat belt on. I'll drive fast."

Ryan buckled back in, adjusting carefully as the lap belt came across sensitive territory. "Don't get us pulled over, though."

"Yeah. Definitely not."

They made the drive uneventfully through the dark streets, got inside and stumbled up the stairs with John's hand on Ryan's back. Ryan was glad of the support. He didn't think he was still drunk. But he felt punchy and floaty, light as air one moment and almost bursting out of his skin the next.

They tried to be as quiet as possible going down the hallway. Ryan stumbled once and was very glad Cynthia's room was the opposite end from theirs. They made it into their own room safely, without anyone looking out of doors or any lights coming on. John pushed him back against the closed door and kissed him. "Now what?"

"You had plans," Ryan pointed out.

"Yes." John pressed into him, hard enough that Ryan could feel the movements of his chest and the ridge of his cock inside those nice jeans. John kissed him under the ear and then murmured, "I want to strip you down, suck you off, and then, when you're all relaxed, I want to get my fingers inside you."

"Jesus." Ryan reached up to hold John's head still and bite his lower lip, pulling it gently and then letting go. "Did you practice that too?"

John's brilliance dimmed slightly. "Was it obvious?"

"Only because I know you." Ryan kissed him, softer, slower. "I loved it. I love that you spend time figuring out how to talk dirty to me."

"I guess I need to work on it."

"Practice. You need *lots* and *lots* of practice." Ryan wriggled out from under him. John eased back enough to make it possible but not easy. And still, when Ryan's knee buckled as he slid free, John touched his elbow just enough for balance and then let go casually.

"I love you," Ryan said quietly. "Come to bed."

They undressed and lay down together, the urgency suddenly transmuted to honey-slow sweetness. Ryan worked his way around, reversing position until he was facing John's thighs. A little pushing got him a nice firm hairy pillow for his cheek as he sucked John into his mouth. A minute later, John did the same for him. They didn't sixty-nine often. Ryan found having John's tongue and lips on him were a distraction from the serious fun of trying to get John's cock farther into his throat, so they usually took turns. But tonight, this was good.

Tonight he could suck and lick, nuzzle in around John's furry balls and inhale the musky, slightly acrid scent that now made every nerve in his body stand up and take notice. He could pause and feel the lush slide of John's tongue over his cockhead in counterpoint and then give the gesture back in long, slow loving. He savored each taste, each touch. There was no rush tonight.

Eventually his body began to make demands. He sucked harder, pulling John as deep as he could without choking. John did the same, his head bobbing, rubbing against Ryan's thigh. They wound each other up, breaths getting shorter, mouths faster and more urgent. When Ryan came it was like a wave, building, building, a swell of sensation and heat, until it broke over him. The rush was fast and hot, tugging him under. He fought to keep his mouth on John and not jolt free, but the best he could do was hold still, panting around that rigid fullness against his tongue. Until the wave receded enough to close his lips, suck hard and deep, and swallow fast as John let go with a soft moan.

When they were done with the shakes and could move again, John helped tug him around and up to the pillow. They kissed, sticky, salt-sweet, slow and silent. John eventually murmured, "That's one way to solve the being-too-loud problem."

"Works for me."

John hugged him in closer, then ran his fingertip into the crack of Ryan's ass. "So. What about the next part of the program?"

Ryan shivered. "Maybe."

"With lube, of course." John reached into the drawer for it and moved up and over Ryan.

Ryan tried to relax back into that mellow boneless just-came state and simply let things happen. John's hands on his ass, digging, massaging, followed by kisses and little bites That was good. He let his legs fall open wider. John's slick finger brushed his opening and he tensed, but didn't let himself move. John was beautifully patient, touching and rubbing until he relaxed and softened. The drizzle of more lube was cool but not unwelcome. The breach of a broad fingertip went smooth and easy.

He kept his eyes closed and his head in the crook of one arm, as John worked deeper. It was strange but good, even starting to turn him on again. He shifted his hips, rubbing against the sheet, as he felt the itchy warmth of returning want.

John murmured, "That's sexy."

"Mm."

John slid out and came back with two slick fingers. That was different. It wasn't too much. There was stretch but no burn. But the pressure made him pant against his elbow, and his shifting became writhing, until John's fingers tugged and torqued against his motions. He grunted and arched. John's fingertip hit his prostate, and suddenly it was too much. He wanted to shout and push back and pull away and cry and for fuck's sake, when did sex make him cry? The next touch buzzed up his nerves like a static shock, as much pain as pleasure.

"Stop!"

John's fingers froze. "Does it hurt?"

Ryan pulled free, and John let him. Ryan reached for a wipe and cleaned himself, even the damp brush of the paper on his hole a confusing mix of unpleasant and *more, please.*

John wiped his own fingers slowly. "You don't have to keep pushing yourself. I'm happy in our bed the way things are. Ecstatic, even."

"I want to." Ryan rolled over, tugged John in against his shoulder and lowered his voice to a thread. "It's just intense. Very intense."

"It can be, yeah."

"So, I think it's not something I can do with Torey next door." *And Cynthia down the hall.* "I think it'll make me loud and crazy. I want not to have to hide that. And maybe, we should try when I haven't just come. That was almost like after a blowjob when the girl keeps sucking like she's going to town and it kind of feels good but kind of hurts more."

"Sorry. I thought it might relax you."

"No sorries." Ryan hugged him hard and kissed his temple against his hair. "It was a good idea. Just didn't work right. I really do want to try again. Sometime when we can wrangle an empty house for an hour?"

"I like that idea." John pressed in against his shoulder. "I'm sorry about the kids and Cynthia and all. I know none of this was what you were expecting."

Ryan grabbed the hair on the back of John's head and tugged hard enough to unearth his mouth for a kiss. "You could say that about the whole of the last six months. Some of it is much better than I ever could have expected, or imagined. The rest, um, comes with that."

"Mm." John didn't sound convinced.

Ryan kissed him again, harder. "I love the kids. Sure I want to turf them out for an hour here or there for screaming monkey sex. But they're great kids. I do wish your ex had someone else to go to, and I don't like the way she acts around us, like I somehow corrupted you."

"She doesn't."

Ryan sighed. "Yeah, babe, she kind of does. But she'll be gone in another week. You're only being the generous, compassionate guy that I love. So I'm good with another week of blowjobs and anything else we can keep quiet. And then we can plan for more." His confidence suddenly ran out. "If you want to. I mean, it probably sucks to have to go so slow and have me keep backing out on you. We don't have to try again."

This time the kiss was John's idea. "A week. I'll be looking forward to that."

They found a comfortable position, with enough skin contact for closeness but not too much to sleep. Ryan drifted, his mind flicking through parts of his day. It was almost surreal. Dancing, kissing John, fag-slurs and Donna and Tom, Brent, Andrea. There might be fallout later, but for the first time in a long time, his gut wasn't tied up with *what if they find out?* There was no one left to worry about, especially if Andrea spread the word around the firehouse.

He'd expected to be fretting about the bad parts of the evening, but instead he could feel some long-held tension unwinding deep inside him. No more lies and balancing and second-guessing. The future might not be easy, but it was that much simpler. Now he was determined to let everyone see how he felt about John without holding back.

The butt-sex part was disappointing. He hated failing at anything. But there would be another time, thanks to John's patience. He'd figure it out. He moved to press his leg closer to John's and fell asleep to the low rasp of John's breath beside him.

Chapter Eleven

A week later, John glanced around Torey's room in the new apartment. It was pretty bare, furnished with a bed and dresser. Nothing on the walls, no bookshelf. Much less personal than her room at the house. He felt a pang of regret. "Are you sure you don't want to bring some of your other stuff over here, honey?"

Torey glanced over from hanging her shirts in the closet. "No, Dad. I want that room to stay the same as always. I'd like to get my things from LA, but it's okay like this for now."

"Well." He stopped short of asking if she was really okay living here with Cynthia. She'd made the tough call on her own not to start an argument, or leave her mom alone right now. John was torn about it. Parents should take care of their kids, not the reverse. But Torey said it was cool. She liked being needed, and she was excited about helping set up a room for the baby. She and Cynthia used to be really close, back before Brandon. John told himself it would work out fine.

The apartment wasn't bad, downstairs in a four-plex only a couple of miles from the house. Six bus stops away— close enough to bike or even walk. But it wouldn't be the same as having her at home, seeing her at breakfast and dinner and hearing about her day. John had loved the last two weeks, with both kids underfoot and Ryan in his bed at night, and even just knowing Cynthia was safe too.

He'd fantasized about maybe putting an extension on the house for Cynthia so Torey could stay with both of them. He could keep his daughter, Cynthia could have her own separate space, and he could be around for the new baby if he was suddenly needed. In his saner moments, he knew that was a really bad idea.

He sometimes wondered if he went one step too far to keep the peace, to do what might work for Torey. He hated arguments, loud voices and anger, and always had, and Cynthia knew that. Ryan probably had a right to say she'd been taking advantage, even if John just felt like he was trying to keep everyone happy. He'd caught himself a time or two wishing they were different people, that Cynthia was more open-minded and Ryan less sharp, and then he'd been ashamed of himself for wanting to change Ry. This move out was probably a good thing. Definitely a good thing.

Ryan and Cynthia had managed to be polite if cool to each other for the whole two weeks, but there'd been moments of slippage— a disdainful look or comment from Cynthia or a provocative bit of snark from Ryan that had them glaring at each other. Ryan had gone out of his way to touch and kiss John around her, he was certain of it. And she'd made a clear point of looking away or walking out of the room. Underneath the wonderful family life, with everyone he cared about under one roof, he knew there was a powder keg that would explode if they kept it up too long. But it'd been so close…

Cynthia stuck her head in the door. "I ordered pizza. I got enough for you to stay and eat with us, John."

"Thanks," he said, before realizing he should stop and think. But hell, first evening in the new place should be a celebration for Torey, even if it didn't quite feel like one. "How about if I call Ryan and get him to bring Mark too?" They'd been over helping earlier, and then Mark had band, and Ryan needed to study. But they'd have to eat sometime. He could make this one more complete family meal, before he had to give those up.

Torey said, "Yay! Party."

Cynthia frowned. "I suppose that would be nice. I'll call back and put another pizza on the order."

"I'll pay, of course," he said quickly.

She shook her head. "I think we'll let this one be on Brandon."

They exchanged grim smiles of satisfaction. Maybe it had been extortion, but it'd felt like justice. He'd been so proud of her that day in the bank, meeting with Brandon. He'd come with her, the canvas bag with the cards over his own shoulder. He wouldn't have put it past Brandon to try to snatch them from her. But he'd hung back and let her deal with the man who would soon be her ex-husband.

Brandon was cold and controlled and barely on the edge of civilized, as they stepped up to the counter and made the bank transfer. His name obviously came up as some A-list customer, because the teller hurried away and a manager came over to help them himself. John made a mental note to suggest Cynthia find some local credit union, instead of a nation-wide bank that loved her husband.

Not that it was an obvious problem. The transfer was whisked through quickly. If the manager had any curiosity about why he was moving money between separate accounts for people with the same last name, he kept it to himself. Maybe rich folk did that kind of thing a lot. Cynthia had been cool and unhurried.

Once the money was in Cynthia's new account, after she'd taken out a hundred in cash and confirmed the balance, they stepped out of the building. Brandon said, "The cards?"

John handed him the bag, forcing him to reach for it. Brandon gave a grunt as it pulled him off balance, then moved off to one side to open the boxes and confirm a few contents. He slung it over his shoulder and sneered at Cynthia. "My lawyer filed the divorce papers. You'll get your summons any day now. Give some thought to settling for my terms because if it goes to court, my lawyer will bury you."

Cynthia's chin jerked up, and she gave him a thin smile. "We'll see what *my* lawyer says about that."

"You can't afford a good lawyer."

"You're not the only person with contacts."

"Hah." Brandon whirled on his heel and strode off, one hand clasping the top of his precious bag.

"Jerk," Cynthia muttered under her breath.

You married him and let him raise my kids. But John was impressed by her coolness through it all. "Do you actually have a lawyer?"

"Not yet. But I will soon."

"Might be smart," he'd agreed.

The money from Brandon, plus his own monthly child support, would pay for this small apartment for her, Torey, and the baby when it came, and living expenses for a while. She'd made sure she was still on Brandon's health insurance, until the divorce went through.

He did worry what Cynthia would do after that. He'd looked into California divorce law, and it sounded as though with such a short marriage, Brandon wouldn't have to pay alimony for long. Although if the baby had a disability, that might change the game too. He rubbed his face, thinking about all the possibilities. It was a good thing Cynthia was tough when she needed to be.

Leaving Torey to finish putting away her clothes, he went into the apartment kitchen. Cynthia was seated at the table they'd picked up secondhand for her, checking something on her new phone. She looked up and gave him a tired smile. "Thanks for your help, John. I don't know what we'd have done without you."

"Well, anything Torey needs, she gets. You know that. How're you holding up?" He'd noticed her bracing a fist against her lower back again.

"I'll be fine. But I just realized we only have four chairs, and we'll be five for dinner."

"We'll figure it out. One of the kids can sit on the couch or the floor or something."

She looked startled, then suddenly gave a small laugh. "Brandon would never have allowed that. Too lower-class. Oh John, why couldn't you and I have worked out together, huh? It would've saved so much heartache."

"Seems to me that most of the heartache was mine. You're the one who went out and found a better guy. You weren't fond of lower-class back then either." The memories tasted bitter when she suddenly looked like his lover of fifteen years ago. He'd stayed faithful. She hadn't.

"I know," she said. "I went looking for the fancy, the shiny, and to be honest, John? For someone who needed me more."

"I needed you." His throat ached.

She shook her head. "You were content to go along as we were, but that wasn't need. I was the mother of your children, and not much else. With Brandon, at first, I was everything, a lover, a help to his career, a real asset. He used all my skills."

I loved you. It was way too late for that. Too late to even *want* to go back. What he had with Ryan now was different and good and not tainted with all that old pain. "Well, he's the kind to trade in used assets for newer ones."

She nodded. "I did wonder if he has a new girlfriend already."

Like he had you, before we were even divorced? He didn't want to think about it. "Did you find a lawyer?"

"Not yet."

Torey came into the kitchen. "Hey, how long till pizza?"

He smiled at her. "Worked up an appetite?"

"Yeah." She pulled open the fridge and made a face. "We have no good food."

"We could make a quick grocery run," he offered.

"Fifteen minutes till dinner," Cynthia said. "No time now. I'll do it in the morning. Have you called Mark? Or Ryan?"

"Oops." He pulled out his phone. "Hey, Ryan?"

"Yeah? You about done over there?"

"Is Mark back from practice? We ordered pizza, and we thought you might bring him over here to eat. Break in the new kitchen."

There was a moment's pause, then Ryan said, "Sure. He just got back, but I bet he'd go out again if you ordered extra sausage."

John laughed. "I'm sure Cynthia knows what he likes. Fifteen minutes?"

"We'll be there."

John pocketed his phone. "They're on their way." He glanced around the sparse kitchen. "Anything else you want me to do?"

"Sit and take it easy? You've been hauling stuff all day and you're not twenty either."

"The furniture guys did most of the work." But he sat anyway. There was an ache in his shoulders that he'd been pretending not to notice.

Torey pulled out the third chair. "So, any bets whether the school bus will actually stop where it's supposed to tomorrow morning?"

"Let's not borrow trouble." John patted her arm. "If not, call me and I'll drive you, okay?"

"Thanks, Dad." She suddenly jumped up, sat on his knee and hugged him. "Coming back here is the best ever! Now if we could convince Char's mom to move to Wisconsin too, it'd be perfect."

"Have you talked to Char recently?"

"I sent her a picture of my room. She said it's dinky and boring."

That little stab of guilt hit again. John said, "Tell her you have two rooms, which are pretty big if you add them together."

"How's that going to work?" Torey looked at him, then Cynthia. "The custody stuff, I mean. Will I move back and forth when it's Dad's turn? Can I go over there when it's not? Maybe spend weekends there? It's different from when we had to fly back and forth. And will Mark stay here sometimes? Because there's no room for him except the baby's room."

"I guess we need to talk about it." John looked at Cynthia.

"Yes." She looked at Torey, not him. "But right now you've been at John's for two weeks, so you might stay here for a month? He has custody one weekend a month."

"A month? That's too long. Can I go over to Dad's as long as I don't sleep there?"

"I guess so. If you ask first, and you come home for dinner, or if I need you. And if it's all right with John."

"Of course, honey," John told Torey. "Anytime."

Cynthia added, "And if it's okay with Ryan?" Like she thought Ryan might throw Torey out on her ear or something?

John said, "You know Ryan loves you too. We'll figure it out."

Torey sucked the front of her hair into her mouth and mumbled, "Ryan's cool."

Cynthia said tartly, "Maybe, but that haircut he let you get isn't. If you keep chewing on that, we'll have to cut it all short."

John was surprised by how happy Torey looked at the idea. "I might want to. I could even up the sides a bit. Could I go back to the same place?"

"Why on earth would you do that?" Cynthia asked. "They cut it crooked in the first place."

"Yeah, but I asked Tina to. Tina was my stylist. She said it would be a wicked good look on me, and it is, but this one bit is kind of in the way. She said if I didn't like it, I could come back and she'd fix it more evenly and not charge me much. She was so cool!"

"She promised a discount?"

"Yeah. Tina said we could layer this piece up instead. Hey, Mom, can I get just a little color in it? Tina had lots of color in hers and it was so *sick*, but she said maybe a bit of copper and red in the underlayers, to brighten mine. Could I?"

"You see?" Cynthia shook her head. "That's the way those people work. She gets you back to fix the cut cheaply, and then you end up spending ten times as much to color it. It's a scam."

Torey pushed away from John and stood angrily. "Tina's not like that! She was being nice about the discount. She wouldn't scam anyone."

Cynthia shook her head. "You talked to her for what? Half an hour? Being nice is her business."

"It's not!"

A knock on the door interrupted them. Torey went and yanked open the door. As soon as Ryan and Mark came in, Torey said, "Ryan, tell her Tina isn't some kind of cheater!"

Ryan looked startled. "Tina?"

"The stylist. You remember."

"Oh." There was an odd expression on Ryan's face that John couldn't interpret, but he said, "It seemed like a decent place, and I didn't get any feeling that things weren't kosher. Why?"

"I want to get my hair evened up a bit, and Tina said she'd do it for cheap if I didn't like it, and Mom says it has to be a scam."

Torey was surprisingly intense, but then she often was these days. John said, "Relax, Tor. I'm sure she's fine, and as long as she doesn't talk you into colors, then it's a good deal."

Ryan frowned at Torey. "You wanted colors?"

She gave him an odd look in return. "Just a hint of red."

"Oh. Well, it would look good, but I guess that's your mom's call."

Cynthia said flatly, "We're not spending extra money right now. Mark, can you please set the table. Torey, do you need to wash up?"

The kids did as they were asked, and then the pizza arrived. Conversation was short-circuited by general face-stuffing. It wasn't until John was washing dishes, with Ryan drying to give Cynthia a chance to lie down, that he had a chance to ask, "What's so great about that stylist?"

"We'll talk later," Ryan said. "Where do the plates go?"

"Your guess is as good as mine."

They cleaned up and figured out Cynthia's kitchen layout in friendly silence. Out in the living room, the kids were watching a movie on Torey's laptop. The little apartment felt more welcoming now, full of people and smelling of garlic and sausage. It wasn't such a bad place, really, just small.

Ryan said, "I need to head home. I have a paper to finish for ethics class."

"Go ahead," John said. "Mark can ride back with me."

Ryan slid a hand into his hair and tugged him down for a kiss. "Later, then. You're a good man, John Barrett."

"What brought that on?"

He waved a hand. "This. Your extra dishes on the shelves and your food processor, because Torey uses it, and spending your whole Sunday helping your ex-wife move in? You know how few people would do that, especially after the way she screwed you over in the past two years?"

"She didn't..." John started, then sighed at Ryan's raised eyebrow. "Okay, yeah, she did. But this is for Torey too. This is where my kid will live, so I want it nice."

"I know. That's what makes you a good man."

John let Ryan out and then sat on the couch with the kids to watch the end of the movie. They all had to huddle together to see it on the laptop, which was okay, but as the movie ended he said, "We'll have to get a real TV for you, Torey."

Mark said, "You could give her the old one, and then we could get a big-screen, huh?"

"No fair!" Torey protested.

"Sure it is. If Dad's buying a new one, he should get to use it."

"You just say that because you want the big-screen for yourself."

"Well, duh."

John pushed out from between them and stood. "Enough. We'll see." He was suddenly tired. Tired from the long day and tired of everything being more complicated than it ought to be. "Tomorrow's a school day anyway. Mark, we should head out. Torey." He hesitated.

She jumped up and hugged him around the waist. "Good night, Daddy. I'm gonna see you lots now, right?"

"Sure, hon. It'll be great."

On the short drive home, Mark said reflectively, "It's kind of weirder to have me living with you, and Torey staying with Mom, now that we're so close. You'd think it'd be easier, but it feels more weird."

"We'll get used to it, I'm sure."

"Well, yeah. But, um, I won't have to live with Mom again now, will I? Like, ever?"

"Not if you don't want to. I think your mom has enough going on with Torey and the baby. She's not going to force you back if you don't want to go." *Hopefully.* The custody rules still meant she could try, but surely she would've picked a bigger apartment if she was going to fit two teenagers in it.

"I don't want to." Mark slouched in the seat. "It's okay to have Mom and Torey around. I don't mind. But I like living with you and Ryan."

"Good."

"And the band is going great again. Noah's really awesome on violin, and he likes my songs. It's not the same band as it was with Patrick, but I think it's going to be awesome. And maybe I grew an inch, I think. So things are okay."

"I'm glad." At least there was one kid he hadn't failed.

Mark looked sideways at him as they pulled into the drive. "You're still not, like, thinking about getting back together with Mom, right? You and Ryan are for real?"

John said steadily, "I'm with Ryan. That's real and not going to change."

"Okay." Mark clicked open his seat belt. "I thought so. Just sometimes, um, Mom seems like she might want you back."

"There's too much time and damage for that. I still care what happens to your mother, but I love Ryan very much, and he's who I want to be with. Can you understand that?"

"Yeah. Of course. At first, I really, really wanted you and Mom back together, but now it would be wrong if you weren't with Ryan. You'd be all different."

John breathed a silent sigh of relief. "You're right. Without Ryan, I'd be less than I am now." *And maybe I should tell him I know that.* If even Mark thought Cynthia had been over-friendly, then it hadn't been Ryan's imagination, and he owed his man a big apology.

He had to wait a couple of hours. Ryan was deep in writing on his computer, peering at the screen while intermittently attacking the keyboard a few words at a time. John left him to it, showered away the grime and fatigue of hefting boxes and got himself ready. The house felt emptier and quieter, but he was determined to see that as a good thing. He was falling asleep in bed when Ryan finally slid in beside him.

"Paper done?" he mumbled.

"Yeah. It's as good as it's going to be." Ryan spooned in behind him and kissed his neck.

"Tired?"

"Depends." Ryan's next kiss was wetter against his skin, with notable sucking action. "You have any plans?"

John pushed back against Ryan, feeling the beginnings of an erection against his back. He adjusted upward, did it again, so Ryan's cock pressed lower. "We have only one other person in the house, and he's got his music on."

"Mm." Ryan rocked against him in small slow movements that sent warmth flushing through him. "Probably still want to avoid making each other scream."

John raised his upper leg enough to fit them together more. "I know how not to scream."

"But a little moaning might be on the menu." Ryan set firm hands on John's back and leg, turning him slightly. "You up for that?"

John breathed faster as Ryan pressed closer, his cock sliding against John's ass. "Oh yeah."

"Although, I guess I'm the one who really needs to be up." Ryan's hard length rubbed over John's sensitive skin, leaving no doubt that he was already there. "You ready to take me, John?"

"Anytime. Any way you want."

They still just rocked together, no more than little shifts of position and short low breaths, bodies touching, teasing. Ryan kissed his neck some more, nibbling and licking under his ear, while his fingers explored John's chest and stomach. His cock slid against John in tiny nudging thrusts that went nowhere, except to build anticipation. Eventually Ryan leaned back, reached for the lube, slicked them both and eased into him, a slow, sensual possession one inch at a time. Then John did moan and gasp and lose himself in the sensation of being filled and taken.

Any other discussion he might have planned simply melted along with most of his brain cells. He knew nothing, thought of nothing but heat and skin, pressure and stretch and the slow, unstoppable build of fire along every nerve in his body. They came, eventually, Ryan first and John right after him, breath short and skin melding in the warm, dark, sex-drenched, perfect haven of their own bed. John was asleep almost before Ryan was done wiping him off. And though he woke once in the night, suddenly worried that someone was lost, Ryan's heavy arm over his shoulders and warm thigh along his own lured him back to sleep before the fear had time to go deep.

****

Ryan hitched his chair closer to the desk in his study, hit one more computer key and glanced at John. "So, we're really doing this?"

"Unless the baby comes at exactly the wrong moment, yeah, we are. You love your family. You need to be at Brent's wedding."

"Okay." He clicked the touchpad. Money winged off nonrefundably, committing them to two tickets to Houston and back. "Leaving Friday around seven p.m., an hour connection in Chicago, and we get in around midnight. Back on Sunday. Leave at noon, deal with O'Hare again, get in at six, back home by eight Sunday night. With luck."

"You sure you don't want to stay longer?"

Ryan gave John a look that he hoped came off as cool rather than pissed. "Since you've agreed to be the labor coach for a pregnant person, I'm keeping the odds as good as possible." Cynthia had only been out of the house a week, and she'd found a new way to entangle John in her life.

Maybe some of the annoyed part came through, because John looked apologetic. "She didn't have anyone else."

"I know." He *didn't* sigh, didn't say anything about how it was her choice to come all the way back here where she apparently hadn't made any good friends last time, to where John was her only support person. He didn't suggest women had babies in hospitals with professional staff all by themselves all the time. This was John and his once-wife's pregnant belly. Ryan thought his boyfriend had some kind of caring reflex so deeply imprinted nothing could change it.

He logged out of the laptop. "Well, I want to be here for Torey and Mark when the baby comes, anyhow." How weird was it going to be for them to have a half- sister whose mom they shared and whose dad they loathed? Particularly a special-needs kid much younger than them. They had to be wondering how much of their mom's attention they'd still get.

John bent and put a hand on Ryan's face to turn him for a kiss. "I love you."

"Say that again after we do this sweet family wedding." But he had to smile. "I do look forward to seeing you in a suit."

"Really?"

"Oh yeah. You know I love the jeans-and-T-shirts look on you, but it'll be nice to see you clean up all pretty."

"Pretty. Hah." John straightened. "So, are you sure you want to take Torey for her haircut? You did it last time."

"I'm sure." Torey had asked him to, and he had a feeling she wanted to talk about something. "I'll have a nice chat with my bisexual stylist again."

John's eyes narrowed. "The one who wanted the threesome?"

"Yep."

From the doorway, Mark said, "Wow, way TMI." He put one hand over his ear. "I'm not listening to anything threesomey."

John actually blushed. "It was a joke. We're not having a thing."

Ryan closed the computer and stood. "It was an offer, but we're still not having a thing. You ready to go, Mark?"

"Yeah." He hefted the guitar case in his other hand.

"Great. Let me grab my wallet and phone."

Ryan's car started right up, which was always nice when he hadn't driven it for a week. Mark put his guitar in the back and got in shotgun. "Hey, Ry, when I start learning to drive, you think you might do my practice hours with me?"

"I guess." He turned around in the drive carefully and then pulled out onto the road. "Because my car is smaller than the truck?"

"Well, yeah. Plus you don't worry like Dad does."

"Your dad wouldn't ever yell at you, though. I might."

"The way he gets all tensed up when he worries is worse than yelling."

Ryan said, "Okay."

"I'm gonna try to get all my hours this summer so I can take the test the day after my birthday, but Dad said that might not happen, what with the baby. People will be busy."

"How do you feel about that?"

Mark shrugged. "You sound like a shrink."

"You'd know that how?" He hadn't found a therapist before Mark's nightmares had faded to levels he said were *"no big."*

"*He* tried to make me see one, for motivational counseling. So the guy could fix me without anyone knowing I was defective."

"You're not defective, Mark."

"I guess. Anyway, the guy kept saying, 'How does that make you feel?' And I kept saying, 'I dunno.' I totally wasted Brandon's four hundred bucks."

"Good," Ryan said fiercely.

He surprised a laugh out of Mark. "Wow, I love that you say that."

"Anytime. What about the baby, though? Any thoughts?"

"Well, you and Dad aren't going to, like, babysit all the time, right?"

"I can't speak for your dad, but I don't think we'll take care of her a lot. Occasionally, yes. We like kids, and your dad will want to help your mom out now and then. But definitely not all the time. He has his work, I'll have my summer job" —and thank goodness the pediatricians' office position had come through, even if it was second best, or maybe a distant third. It was *here*— "and then school. We're not in a good place to add a baby to that mix."

"Okay, then it won't matter much."

From the way Mark was chewing his lip, it obviously mattered more than he was saying, but before Ryan could decide if he needed to push, they'd reached Cynthia's new place. Torey was waiting at the door, and she ran over and hopped into the back. "Drive, drive and don't look back!"

He laughed as he pulled away from the curb with a tiny bit of extra rev to amuse her. "Why?"

"Mom's talking about coming with us to supervise my haircut."

"Uh-oh. Driving right now."

"Luckily, the baby was kicking or something, and she decided to lie down."

"Nice that your sister is on your side."

Torey giggled, then said, "Sister. It still sounds so weird. I never had a sister."

Mark snarked, "I did. It's awful."

Torey kicked the back of his seat. Ryan said, "Cut it out. Or I'll tie you up and toss you both in the trunk."

"In this car? We wouldn't fit," Torey said. "Well, maybe shrimp-boy would."

"You'd still be able to hear Miss Loudmouth."

"Tie you both up with gags," Ryan clarified. "Give it a rest, guys."

Mark slouched in his seat, but Ryan caught a mutter of, "I grew a fucking inch last month."

He gave Mark's knee a light smack, half for the swearing, half for comfort.

They dropped Mark at practice and headed on to the hair salon. He was disappointed that Drake wasn't working, but it was probably just as well. He sat with his neuroanatomy flashcards, while Tina chatted with Torey and made a few judicious snips and cuts. After about ten minutes, Tina led Torey over to him. "What do you think?"

"Um." It didn't look much different, a bit less edgy maybe.

"We trimmed this." Torey demonstrated that the longer bit was now too short to reach her mouth. "But it still looks okay, I think."

"You look great," Tina said warmly. "I do good work."

Ryan stood, leaning on his cane because his leg had stiffened up. "Perfect. How much?"

"No charge." Tina smiled at them. "If someone changes their mind soon after, I don't charge for a minor fix."

"Wow, that's nice of you," Torey said.

"Good business. I want you to be happy you came here."

"Definitely," Torey said. "I'll probably be back lots, to keep it trimmed up like this."

Tina's smile became indulgent. "If that works for you. I'd say you'll need it freshened about every four to six weeks, if you want it to keep this shape."

"Better save your allowance," Ryan teased. When Torey suddenly noticed the price list and then looked stricken, he added quickly, "Just kidding. Haircuts are part of the parenting deal. Although we might make you chip in if you want the best every time."

"I can do that," she said quickly. "I'll be back here in six weeks, I guess."

"Right before Pride weekend. I'll look for you then," Tina agreed.

Torey was quiet in the car beside Ryan. Twice she started to swing her hair toward her mouth, and the end slipped through her fingers. The second time, she laughed. "I guess it was more of a habit than I realized."

"Looks like Tina fixed it," he commented neutrally.

"Yeah. I like her."

"That's good."

After another few minutes, Torey said with emphasis, "I *like* like her."

"What are you saying?"

"Um." Torey moved uncomfortably in her seat. "No. Yeah."

They were getting too close to home too quickly. Ryan found a quiet street, turned in and pulled to the curb, shifting into park so he could give Torey his attention. When he looked straight at her, she fidgeted and turned away, so he turned his gaze out the windshield and waited.

Eventually, she said, "I like Tina kind of how you like Dad."

Ryan took a moment, thought about it carefully, and started with, "She's a bit old for you, hon."

"Well, I *know* that." Torey hesitated. "Okay, not exactly like you and Dad, but, like, um."

She paused for a long, fidgety silence. Finally, he said quietly, "Like you're attracted to her?"

"Yeah." Torey's voice was almost too subdued to hear.

"Okay." He stopped there. He wanted to duck and run. She was twelve. Okay, almost thirteen, but still, so young. Shouldn't she be playing with dolls or something? Not talking about sex-type stuff with her father's boyfriend.

After a minute she said, "Is it?"

"Is it what?"

"Okay?"

"Of course, hon." He knew exactly what she meant and still took the cowardly route. "It's like having a crush on a celebrity or something. You're not going to actually ask her out, but it's okay to like her."

"She has a girlfriend anyway. But I like girls. Like that."

You're too freaking young! But then at thirteen, he'd been going for the gold-medal in the jerk-off Olympics and definitely thinking about girls. Maybe boys too. He had a hard time remembering when he'd decided girls were it. Back then, he'd spent a lot of time thinking about hands and mouths, without particular bodies attached, doing things Okay, thirteen might not be too young.

He realized Torey was practically holding her breath, waiting for him. He went with, "Well, you know I like guys like that. I love your dad like that. I'm not gonna think anything's wrong if you like girls. Or boys. Or both."

"Ohhh." It sounded like all her breath went out in one long sigh. "Good."

190

"Your dad won't mind either, at all," he promised. Seriously, this was John. He'd be there for her without any doubt. Even back when John thought he was straight, he'd never been narrow. "Your dad loves you. So do I."

"Mom might not be okay."

"Mm." He fumbled for something between optimism and truth. "Well, your mom isn't so cool with the gay; that we do know. Give her some time, though. She's a lot better with John and me than she used to be. We'll keep working on her."

"You can kiss Dad some more right in front of her." Torey's smile was watery but real.

"You noticed?" He laughed. "Yeah. If she wants John to help her, if she wants to be around Mark, she's going to have to get over us."

"Mark's not gay, is he?" Torey stared at him.

"Not that I know of," Ryan said. Judging by the porn he'd caught sight of once, Mark was definitely a fan of boobs, or at least trying them out. "I meant that he lives with your dad and me. You know, though, I wouldn't out him if he was gay, even to you, unless he was ready."

"Mom would have a fit if it was both of us."

"Maybe. Doesn't mean you should try to be something you're not to please her."

"I guess."

"But you also don't have to rush to come out." He put a hand on her shoulder. "Torey, I know you're almost thirteen, and it feels pretty grown up."

"Two more weeks and I'm in my teens." She flashed him a quick sideways look.

He winced silently. *Teenagers. Hormones. Oh yeah.* "Sure. But maybe give yourself time to figure things out before you take on your mom, okay?"

"It seems like now I know, I should tell her, or else I'm, like, lying. But I don't really want to yet."

"You do what feels right. It's your life. You can be lesbian or bi, or poly or whatever. And you can tell her, or definitely you can wait."

"I'm pretty sure I'm, um, lesbian. I like looking at girls."

He licked his dry lips. "Okay. Although you never know when someone can come along and tilt your assumptions. Look at me. I hardly thought about guys for fifteen years, and then there your dad was, and I fell like a rock."

"So I might end up straight?"

"If you like girls, you're not straight. But straight is boring anyway, right? You might be bi, though. You might find some boy you fall for later on. Who knows? You could wait to tell your mom until you have a girlfriend you want to talk about. Your call."

"I guess." Torey tugged at her hair and managed a smile. "I haven't even kissed a girl yet. Or anyone."

Oh, thank God. Ryan wasn't up to the sex talk. Although he did say, "You know about safe sex, right?"

She blushed bright red. "Yes, Ryan. Although, with two girls ?" Her voice trailed off questioningly.

He had no damned idea what you did without guy-type condoms. "I'll find you some information," he promised. "Can we not talk about sex anymore right now? My face is going to catch fire."

She giggled. "Oh wow. Mine too."

He started the car again because it made a good excuse not to look at her. "So, is Tina, um, the first girl you've liked-liked?"

"No. But I really like Hyoyeon, from Girl's Generation. She's such an awesome dancer. And Suzy from Miss A is really, really cute. Oh my God, cute. But I thought maybe it wasn't real, that I just wanted to be like them. Because they're famous and performers. Right? But Tina is, well, she's cute and great, but she's just a stylist. I don't want to be that. I just think she's, um, cool and, you know."

"You like her, as a girl."

"Yeah."

"That's fine."

"So really, I've known I wasn't straight for like a year. Except I wasn't totally sure and now I am. And I kind of want to tell everyone except I don't want anyone to know. Crazy, huh?"

Ryan chuckled softly. "Not crazy. When I started dating your dad, I wanted to show him off because he's such an amazing guy and he liked me, but at the same time I didn't want people to know I was gay or bi."

"And now?"

"It's taken me some time, but now I really want people to know we're together." Unbidden, a memory of a dark bar and the slurred sucker-punch of hate from a stranger came to mind. He swallowed and deliberately pushed past it. Fuck if he was going to let that guy affect him. Still, the thought of someone doing that to Torey was acid in his throat. "Remember, hon, I'm thirty years old and some days it's still not easy." He tried to imagine coming out at thirteen. "It's okay to go slow. It's okay to think for a while about what you'll tell to whom. It's hard to take it back, once you say the word 'gay' out loud."

"I guess."

"I'm really proud of you for wanting to tell your truth." Out of the corner of his eye, he saw her glance at him and smile. "I really am. But don't push yourself too hard, okay?"

"I guess," she repeated. "Ryan, will you have to tell Dad what I said?"

"Not 'have to,'" he said cautiously. "This is your private stuff. Do you want me to? Or not?"

He could tell she was biting her lip. "Not. Not yet. Is that okay?"

He held back a sigh. "Yes. I don't like keeping secrets from your dad, but I won't break a trust. You do know he'd be fine with it and proud of you too? Right?"

"Maybe after my birthday. I just want to wait a bit."

He could understand that. John loved her, but she was still his little girl. He imagined her asking John about female condoms and almost snickered. Poor John. Ryan had met Mark and Torey as teens and had no trouble seeing them that way, but John would want to lock Torey in a tower for a few years, gay or straight, the moment she started to mention sex. "That's fine. Let me know if you want to talk again, or want me to back you up when you tell someone else."

"Thanks." Torey played with her hair, fidgeted, then said, "Really. Thanks. It's kind of awesome just to say it to someone."

"Am I the first?"

"Yeah."

"What about Char?"

"She likes boys. She's all crazy about a bunch of the K-pop guys. Some of them are cute. I like G-Dragon, especially when he wears eyeliner and gender-bender clothes. But she likes big, bodybuilder guys too, and I don't."

"What do you think she would say if you told her?"

Torey shrugged.

"If she likes a guy in eyeliner, don't you think she might be okay with you?"

"Gay guys are kind of in right now. Lesbians, not so much. And she might think…"

"Think what?"

"That I was friends with her because of that. Because she's pretty."

"Mm." He almost asked, *Were you?* God, he of all people should know better.

They were silent until he'd pulled over in the parking lot of the apartment. He glanced over. "I meant what I said. Call me, anytime."

"Do you think you'll go to Pride? You and Dad?"

"I don't know." He hadn't planned on it, despite her earlier enthusiasm. "Do you want to go? You could come along as our family, I guess, and not have to be out yourself."

"Yeah. I thought, maybe. Tina will be there. She said it's fun. And there might be other girls."

"I'll talk to your dad about it."

She unbuckled her seat belt and leaned over to hug him. "You're the best other dad ever!" She jumped out and ran up the walk in her usual breakneck way. Pulled open the door. Turned, grinned, waved and disappeared inside.

"Thanks," he murmured to himself. Starting his quasi-parenting with teenagers was turning out to be one hell of an education.

Chapter Twelve

"Hey Dad!"

John turned just in time to catch a Frisbee awkwardly before it could hit his head. Torey ran over, grinning. "Sorry. Got away from me."

"You get a pass for being the birthday girl." He tossed it back. "Throw *away* from the house, though, okay?"

"Sure." She ran off, yelling at Mark, "Hey, you dork, watch what you're doing."

John leaned back on the porch steps, took a long swallow of his soda, and looked around the yard with satisfaction. Torey's real birthday was still two days off, but they'd decided to celebrate on the weekend. He'd spent all week, in any free moment he had, working on the garden to get it looking good. There were bright annuals in all the flowerbeds, the grass was green and weed-free. The bushes were trimmed back from their early spring sprawl, and he'd even fixed the broken rung on the tree-house ladder, just in case.

Across the smoothly mown lawn, a dozen teenagers tossed the Frisbee around with more enthusiasm than skill. After just a month, Torey had already made friends at school. He silently blessed the fact that one of his kids was easy-going.

Ryan came over, gripped the handrail, and lowered himself to the step beside John. "They seem happy."

"Working off the sugar high." The cake had been one of Cynthia's masterpieces and iced within an inch of its life. The kids had demolished it.

"I'm glad the theater class let Torey in. It's great that she's got people to hang out with."

"She still misses Char."

"Mm. But I don't think she regrets the move otherwise. She clearly loves having you and Cynthia both here to celebrate her birthday."

John gave Ryan a bump with his shoulder. "She owes you, big-time. You should be having peace and quiet to study, and I know you don't like having Cynthia around the house."

Ryan gave him a steady look. "I crammed all of yesterday. And I think I'm a big enough boy to handle having your ex here on the kids' birthdays."

"Still." John lowered his voice because he'd meant to say it for a while, and with Cynthia inside taking a nap on the couch and the kids busy, maybe this was the time. "I've been asking a lot of you, dealing with Cynthia's problems and the baby coming and all. I want you to know I'm aware."

Ryan's expression became closer to a frown. "You know what does bug me? That you don't seem to be aware that she's asking a lot of you too."

"I don't mind." Although there was a bit of a lie in there. He did, sometimes, but to keep both kids close by and happy? He'd willingly do ten times more than what Cynthia asked, and he'd still consider it a bargain.

"Yeah. Apparently you don't mind. Why is that, John? She fucked you over pretty bad, moving the kids across the country and all. I remember you crying in your beer."

He winced. "She didn't do it just to mess with me, right? She was following her husband, like wives do."

"And cheating on you? And not letting you have your visitation rights?"

John pushed to his feet. "So, yeah, maybe she was wrong, and we were both bitter about things. Maybe it wasn't good. But right now? My kids are home, and everything's fine. To see Torey and Mark play and laugh like that?" —he waved at the increasingly disorganized Frisbee game— "I'm willing to let it be water under the bridge to have that."

Ryan nodded slowly, but didn't say anything.

They watched as the game broke up. Several of the kids seemed interested in the tree house. John hoped to hell it was sturdy enough for everyone going up there, but he'd built it himself and checked it yesterday, and it should be fine.

Ryan chuckled.

"What?"

"Mark." Ryan's expression eased. "I think he's cruising that girl who's the lead in the middle-school play. What's her name? Vicki? He's poised to give her butt a helping hand up the ladder. Ah, young love."

John shifted uncomfortably. Mark was fifteen and Vicki was at least fourteen, but he still didn't want to think about it. He made a note to talk to Mark about respectful touch, although the girl didn't seem like she minded. "Young lust, you mean."

"No doubt. And speaking of which, here comes your fan club."

John saw three of the older girls headed toward them and sighed. "You mean your fan club."

"You're the one who carved that amazing tree-shaped jewelry box for Torey."

"You're the mysterious, handsome, older guy with the limp."

"That's not an asset."

"You wouldn't think." John grinned down at him. "Means you're slower to run away."

"Ew." Ryan made an evil eye gesture. "Let's not even talk about child molesting, eh?"

"You don't look anywhere near thirty."

"Well, I'm still fifteen years too old for them." Ryan started to get up, and John reached back a practiced hand for him. "Thanks."

The girls reached them and stood in a group, laughing self-consciously and chatting about John's wood carving while they darted glances at Ryan. When the topic ran dry, they discussed the school play as he and Ry deliberately let the conversation lag. John hid a grin when he saw Ryan finally realizing that, in fact, they were much more interested in getting to know him than in any kind of woodcarving. He didn't blame them. Ryan was very decorative.

One of the girls twirled her dark hair in her fingers and said, "I think it's so cool that you were a firefighter. Torey told us all about it."

"Oh?" Ryan's tone was shorter and colder.

"Yeah. And now you're in med school. I'm thinking about applying to med school too. Do you have any, like, advice?"

"Study like hell, volunteer, even if it's emptying bedpans, and know what you're getting into before you put over a decade of your adult life into getting there."

"Oh." She looked startled, then glanced up and behind them. "Thanks."

The girls walked off, and John looked toward the back door. Cynthia stood there, an arm across her stomach. She said quietly, "John? I'm having some cramping, and I think it might be smart for me to go to the hospital."

"Of course," he said, his own stomach tightening with anxiety. She wasn't due for a month yet. It was too early. "Should we let the kids know?"

She shook her head. "Not yet. I hope it's nothing much." Her voice was strained.

Ryan said, "Did your water break?"

She frowned at him. "No. Just contractions."

John said, "Okay, I'll get my keys. Ryan, you'll stay with Torey and the rest?"

Ryan lowered his voice. "You're leaving me with a dozen teenagers, including the giggling threesome? Maybe I can drive Cynthia and you can stay with Torey for her birthday and be here when there's more news."

John glanced across the yard. He wanted to do both. But Cynthia looked scared and she was wincing in pain, and he'd promised, because she had no one else. "You tell Torey what's going on, okay? But don't scare her."

Ryan sighed. "Well, keep me posted. They'll try to stop the labor first, and hopefully that'll work."

"Hopefully. I'll get back here when I can."

"I'll hold down the fort."

John really wanted to kiss him, but Mark was looking their way, and they'd promised Mark not to be obvious about the gay in front of kids who'd be at his high school next fall. "Thanks. You're amazing."

"Yeah, you keep remembering that." Ryan's eyes flicked up to Cynthia. "I hope it goes well for you. Try to relax in the car and do the breathing, right?"

She said, "Tell Torey I'm sorry about breaking up the party."

"Sure, they might not notice anyway. They should be okay for the next hour. I won't mention it until they miss John or you call with news. She's having a great party with her friends."

John followed Cynthia inside. "Anything you need before we go?"

"No." She grunted and clasped her middle for a moment. "Ouch. I just want to get there. I really am grateful, John. I didn't want Ryan to take me. He hates me."

"He doesn't hate you." He was pretty sure hate was too strong a word. "And you know— fireman, doctor— he'd have taken expert care of you."

He wasn't sure if her next grunt was pain or comment, but she stayed silent, leaning on his arm as he helped her down the steps and into the truck. They'd driven for a few minutes when she said, "He has a reason."

"Who what?" He focused on driving smoothly and not too fast, avoiding the winter-worn potholes that hadn't been fixed yet.

"Ryan. Has a reason to hate me. I made you miserable, and he loves you."

He spared a moment to stare at her. "Wow. I can't believe you said that."

"I don't get the gay, I really don't." She panted through her teeth for a minute. "But if you'd found another woman, and she looked at you like he does, I'd call it love. We were good together once, but even though he's a man, he makes you happier than you were the last year with me."

Maybe if you hadn't cheated, we'd have stayed happy. He pushed the thought back. Then he'd never have met Ryan, and he couldn't imagine not having Ry in his life. "I'm partly happy *because* he's a man."

"How can you *say* that?" She gripped the door handle and swore under her breath. "Ouch, ouch, dammit, fuck, ouch!"

He almost smiled, remembering that labor had always brought the profanity out of hiding in his prim-and-proper wife. Ex-wife. "Hang in there. Ten more minutes."

"Feels like hours."

"You know the drill."

"Yeah. Breathe." She took a couple of breaths and relaxed slightly. "Damn, I really don't want to have this baby early."

"I know. It'll be okay. They have good drugs. And even if they can't stop the labor, she's just a few weeks from term. She'll be fine."

"God, I don't think I can do the NICU again with another preemie." She rubbed a hand over her face.

John's gut tightened until his breath came short. *Daniel, sweet baby, miss you so much.* He managed to say calmly, "You'll do whatever it takes. You're a good mom."

"I hope. I try. Oh shit, not again. Ow." She sucked in a long breath, puffed it out, pulled in another.

"Not far now, hon."

"If something bad happens, you'll take care of the kids, won't you?"

He reached over blindly to pat her arm, steering carefully as they neared the emergency entrance. "Nothing bad will happen. But of course, I'll always take care of them."

"Even this one?" She touched her belly. "Brandon will just lock her up in an institution."

"Even that one. Hold on for the curb, there's a dip."

"I wish you'd married a nice girl who would help you with the kids."

"Now you're borrowing trouble." He thought of something Ryan had said, as he eased them toward the circle drive at the doors. "Anyway, wouldn't you rather I gave the kids another dad than a replacement mom?"

"Oh!" She sounded startled, but then they were at the door and it was time to get out, and he let the topic go.

He helped her out of the truck, then parked quickly while she went inside. He caught up to her at the admissions desk where she was given a quick assessment, a wheelchair, and an orderly. The receptionist said, "Sir, I'm going to give you a clipboard with the forms. You can go up with your wife, but please fill them out and pass them to the nursing station on her floor."

He grabbed the clipboard, didn't correct the assumption, and followed Cynthia's wheelchair into the elevator. When they got to Maternity, he was shunted to a corner of Cynthia's room as a couple of nurses got her into a gown and hooked up to monitors. A doctor hurried in, and one of the nurses stepped back to make space. John said quietly, "Are cell phones okay? I want to text the other kids at home."

She nodded. "Yes, they've lifted the restriction on this floor. And try not to worry. Your wife is doing fine and the baby has a strong heartbeat."

"Thanks." He juggled clipboard and phone, then retreated to a plastic chair and set the paperwork on his knees. He texted Ryan: *At the hospital. Okay so far. Baby is good.*

He got an immediate answer back: *I'm glad. Teens are eating us out of house and home. All well.*

Did you tell Mark and Torey yet?

Waiting on your word. The guests will be leaving in the next half hour.

I should know more shortly too. I'll keep in touch.

I can bring the kids there, any time.

Thanks.

He pocketed the phone and unclipped the pen, bending over the forms. He filled out what he could. He hadn't forgotten her birthday or her previous pregnancies or her allergy to penicillin. After it was done, he asked, past the scrub-clad bodies, "Hey, Cyn, okay if I dig in your purse for your insurance card?"

The doctor said, "Give us a minute, and you can talk to your wife while we get the ultrasound in here, all right?"

"She's okay, though?"

"Doing fine." His voice had that professional soothing sound to it. "We've given her an injection of terbutaline, which hopefully will stop the contractions. She hasn't progressed too far yet. She's doing very well."

Cynthia snapped from behind him, "Other than the damned, shit, fucking, won't stop, ouch."

The doctor said, "We'll give it a little while, all right? Meanwhile, we'll make sure everything looks good."

When the ultrasound cart arrived, John stepped out of the room to make space and headed down to the nursing desk to hand over the paperwork. He met the ultrasound tech coming back, and she gave him a smile and a thumbs-up. When he went back in the room, the doctor said, "We'll see how that terbutaline works for now. I'll check in now and then, and the nursing staff will be close by. I'm optimistic that we can help that little girl of yours stay warm and cozy in there for a few more weeks. If you put Cynthia's OB on the form, the nurse will contact him or her and I'm sure they'll be here shortly."

When the room was emptied out and quiet, except for the beeping of the monitors, John pushed his chair closer to the bed. Cynthia's hair was stuck to her sweaty forehead, and she gave him a harried look. "I am *not* having this baby early."

"That's the spirit," he said. "Hey, should I call the kids, or do you want to talk to them, maybe?" He held up his phone.

"Yeah, maybe this is a good time."

He dialed, and Ryan picked up right away. "Hey, Ry," he said. "We're waiting for meds to do their job. How's the home front?"

"Winding down. Three kids still waiting to go home, well, not counting Torey. How's the baby doing?"

"So far, so good, I guess. Heart beating along." The fast, steady beep of the fetal monitor was reassuring. "Cynthia wants to talk to the kids."

"Oh sure. Good thought. Give me a minute."

He handed Cynthia the phone and helped her adjust her pillows. She talked with both of the kids, telling them the truth but making it sound pretty minor. Once, she quickly passed him the phone while she panted and monitor-buzzed through another contraction. He held it to his ear. "Hey."

It was Mark on the other end. "Hey, Dad, Mom's okay, right?"

"Yeah, just needs some good drugs to relax her, I guess. I'll keep you posted. Don't give Ryan too much trouble."

"Da-ad."

He laughed. "Sorry, that was lame, right?" Cynthia held out her hand, and he said, "See you in a bit, son," and passed the phone back.

The afternoon wound into evening. He browsed online on his phone, not something he usually did much, but it passed the time. He texted back and forth to Ryan. Medical people came and went. The baby's heart monitor kept up a nice steady rhythm, only changing when it was squeezed by one

202

of Cynthia's finally decreasing contractions. The second shot seemed to be doing the trick.

He was standing at the window in the corridor, after a brief chat with Ryan, when a woman in a white coat came toward him. "Mr. Carlisle? I'm Dr. Leonard."

For a moment, he stared at her, wondering why she called him that. Then he realized the reason and decided this was where the ambiguity stopped. "No, I'm John Barrett. Cynthia's my ex-wife."

"Your But you came in with her?"

"Well, her current husband filed for a divorce a month ago, so I'm lending a hand."

"Ah. Well, I was going to tell you we'll be keeping her overnight, as a precaution, but she should be able to go home in the morning."

"How is she?"

The doctor looked uncomfortable. "If you're not her current next of kin, I really need her okay to discuss that with you."

"Never mind," he said. He'd ask Cynthia. "What I really need to know is will she need to have someone with her at home tomorrow? The kids will be at school, and I have work, but I can line up a care aide, I guess, if need be."

"No, she should be all right, as long as she takes it easy and doesn't overdo. And of course she should come back in if the contractions start up again."

"That's good news. She doesn't have to be on bed rest?"

"Not at this time. No lifting of any kind, though, and no vigorous exercise. Lots of liquids, small meals, plenty of rest. The medication sometimes only buys us a few days or a week, so she should have plans in place to come right back in if needed. Does she have young children at home?"

"No. They're teenagers."

"Oh, well, that's easier, then."

John nodded.

"I'll see her in my office on Friday, if all goes well."

"Thanks," he said, turning for Cynthia's room.

She was dozing, but she woke when he walked in and gave him a tired smile. "Hey, John."

"How are you?" He started to reach for her, then stopped and crossed his arms on his chest. "Doing better?"

"Yes. Thank goodness. I'd forgotten how much I hate labor."

"Worth it for the kids."

"Well, yes." She sighed. "Thank goodness you were around. I was scared."

"I know." *Me too.* But he didn't say it. He really needed some distance from this woman who was no longer his and the baby that never had been. He reminded himself of Ryan's warm, male voice on the phone. That was what counted most in his own life, along with his own kids. But it was hard to keep things separate.

Cynthia rubbed her face. "Will you keep Torey with you overnight?"

"Of course."

"She'll need to get to school in the morning."

"I'll see to it."

She smiled, looking blotchy and tired and far from her usual perfection. "I know you will. And they'll let me out around noon, the doctor said. Will you ?"

Before she could finish asking, he said, "I can run some fresh clothes over here in the morning before work. For the cab ride?" Or was that keeping too much distance? Maybe he was being too harsh. He'd give a good friend a lift, wouldn't he? "Or maybe I can come on my lunch break, if that would work."

Her smile faded. "The clothes I had should be all right. Maybe I can call you when they discharge me, and if you're not free, then I'll take a cab?"

"Sure," he said with relief. "That sounds good. That'll work. You get some rest now. I'll wait for your call tomorrow, or, you know, have them contact me if you need anything."

"Good night, John."

"Sleep well."

He left without looking back. The sky outside had darkened to indigo, with a faint wash of color to the west. He glanced at his phone, startled to see it was almost eight thirty. He texted Ryan: *All's well. Heading home.*

Eating Chinese takeout. Might save you some.

He laughed. *Twenty minutes. I want a fortune cookie.*

Maybe. If you're nice to me.

I can be very nice.

I'll hold you to that. Or hold that for you.

So TEN minutes, maybe.

Drive safely.

He put the phone away, located his truck, and turned for home.

The house was dark, other than the kitchen, when he pulled up. He went inside and found Ryan and the kids playing some card game at the kitchen table, but as he came in, Ryan scooped up the deck. "There you are." He stood, took a stiff step toward John and kissed him.

John was startled but went with it for a moment. Ryan sat back down, and John said to the kids, "They got your mom settled for the night. She should be able to go home tomorrow, maybe around lunchtime."

"Do I have to go to school?" Torey asked.

"Yes, hon. Your mother asked me to be sure you got to class."

"Oh."

"She's fine and so's the baby." He went and hugged her shoulder against his hip. "It was a false alarm. And you, young lady, have four more weeks of school before final grades come out and can't afford to miss any of it. All right?"

"Sure, Dad."

He pulled his chair around beside her, and Ryan brought him a plate. There was plenty of food left, and Ryan gave him a smirk as he dug in. "We tried to eat it all and failed."

"Good." He chatted with the kids about the party and teased Torey about her gifts. Slowly the tension in the room eased. Mark excused himself and went upstairs to his room. Torey got up and handed him a fortune cookie. "Open it, Dad."

He cracked it, pulled out the strip. *"You can only reach the stars by leaving the safety of the earth behind."*

He passed it to her, and she wrinkled her nose. "Is that a fancy way of saying you should try new things?"

"I guess."

"I don't like those kind of fortunes. I want the ones where they say, *'Tuesday will be a disaster'* or *'You will inherit a bunch of money.'* Ones where you can tell if it comes true or not."

He laughed. "I'd just as soon not expect Tuesday to be a disaster."

"I guess. Especially since it's my real birthday." She bent and kissed his head. "Thanks for the party and the awesome jewelry holder."

"My pleasure, sweetheart."

When she'd gone up to her old room, he turned to Ryan. "And what was your fortune?"

"This one?" Ryan held up a slip of paper and pretended to peer at it. "It says, *'Your partner will give you several blowjobs tonight while telling you how amazing you are.'*"

John laughed. "Right. It does not."

Ryan pulled an innocent face. "Right here in black-and-white. Well, dark red and off-white."

"Give me that." John made a snatch for it, and Ryan jerked his hand away. John jumped up and grabbed Ryan's arm in both hands, feeling the hard roundness of his biceps and the taut cords of his wrist. They wrestled for the paper until Ryan slipped and John pulled him into a tight hug, one hand on his wrist, an arm locked across Ryan's hips, and his interested dick pressed against Ryan's back. "I think you're lying," he murmured into Ryan's hair. "Show me."

"Never."

"I'm bigger than you."

"Bragging again?"

He pushed with his hips, enough of a nudge to show his interest. "Just saying."

"Take it upstairs and prove it."

"Not till I see your fortune."

Ryan said, "All right." When John let his wrist go, he quickly raised his hand to his mouth like he was going to eat the slip of paper. John snatched it from him and looked at it. "'*Love is patient, Love is kind.*' Huh."

Ryan took it back and pitched it into the trash. "Yeah. Pretty banal. I like my version better."

"I like this one too," John said. He slid a hand to the back of Ryan's neck and gave him a kiss.

"Well, it fits you," Ryan said. "You're patient and kind. I'm more like bitchy and jealous."

"No, you're not."

"Yeah. I am." Ryan kissed him, then nipped his lower lip, harder than he expected.

"Ouch! Of Cynthia?"

Ryan licked gently over the bitten spot, soothing him, stroking his neck. He slid his other arm around John and leaned back enough to meet his eyes. "Yeah. Of Cynthia. Of what she can give you that I never will. She's the mother of your children, forever. She's the one you grieved for Daniel with. Isn't that sick, that I'm even jealous of that?"

"Not sick." He dropped his gaze, trying to find words. "Sometimes I wish I'd been there when you were hurt, to help you through it."

Ryan stepped away and leaned against the refrigerator. "I'd have driven you off back then, like all the rest. This is better. But, even now, you look at her big round belly and you get this soft, longing look. I'll never give you a child."

"Or me you, Ry. You're the one losing the most. I already have children."

"You want more."

"I wouldn't mind more, but I'm not pining for them. Little kids are great, but they're a hell of a lot of work."

"See, I know perfectly well that the last thing I need in my life right now is a baby, but when you look at her like that, I practically turn green."

"I'm sorry."

"It's my problem."

He went to Ryan and pulled him in close despite the stiffness of his body that resisted touch. "No, it's not. I know I'm a bit messed up with the baby thing. Babies need to be cared for, and Brandon Carlisle deserves to be shot. But Ryan, I swear, I don't want Cynthia back. No way, not even if she was having my own child."

Ryan shoved at him. "Liar."

"No, listen. If the baby was mine, yeah, I'd want the child. But I had Cynthia, with two great kids and years of marriage, and we couldn't stay together. I'm not crazy enough to want that back."

"She divorced you."

"We grew apart. She was the one to leave, but only because we had such different needs we couldn't make it together anymore." He realized as he said it that it really was true. He'd almost been lulled by her current soft neediness, but really she was still the woman who wanted him to sell his art for money and give up work he loved for work with more status. That wouldn't change if she had a dozen more kids.

Ryan reached low and grabbed at the bulge of John's cock, which had faded to half-mast. "Well, we have pretty similar needs, right?"

John deliberately pushed into his hand instead of backing away and put his own palm over Ryan's groin. "That's not just a cute turn of phrase, Ry. We do. We fit, in lots of ways." He pulled Ryan close, slowly, until their hands were trapped between them. "You're the person I love and want to be with." He could feel Ryan relax and begin to respond to his touch.

"I love you too. I think those blowjobs you owe me might be sixty-nines. It'll keep the noise level down."

"Sure. After all, fortune cookies never lie."

"Never."

He slid his hand out from between them to turn out the under-cabinet light. "Upstairs? Or do you need to hit the books?" He remembered Ryan had one more exam to go.

"Upstairs first. Books later."

John followed Ryan out, eager and hopeful and plenty turned on. Nagging doubts lingered over whether he'd dealt with Cynthia and jealousy well enough, but upstairs in their bed, Ryan successfully drove any thoughts of other people out of his mind. By the time Ryan got up to go study for his exam, and John finally slept, he was lucky to remember his own name.

****

Being a dad meant learning to ignore a lot of noise, and yet being able to wake up suddenly and completely to the wrong kind of sound. John sat upright in bed a few hours later, his body tensing to the echo of something bad. The house was quiet again now. Beside him, Ryan slept in a limp sprawl, hands relaxed, his face calm and unlined. Probably not the one who'd cried out, then— his nightmares were pretty obvious, once you knew what to look for.

John had just decided he'd been mistaken when he heard it again, a muted whimper from down the hallway. He eased out of bed, tucking the blanket around Ryan, who muttered something but didn't wake. He had vague memories of Ryan joining him not long ago, dragging in from his books with a mumble of not being able to focus another moment. The guy needed what sleep he could get.

He'd assumed it was Mark having a rough night, but when he pulled on his robe and stepped out of the bedroom, he could see light under Torey's door. He paused outside her room, listening. There was no more crying, but he could hear her rustling around, clearly awake. For a minute, he hovered, not sure if she'd prefer privacy to comfort, but fatherly worry won out. He tapped lightly. "Torey, hon, do you want company?"

There was a moment of silence, then she said, "I guess."

He eased the door open, slipped inside and shut it behind him. Torey was sitting up in bed with a mug of something on her nightstand and several books strewn across the covers. She looked at him with an unfamiliar wariness. He leaned on the wall, thinking about his next line, but she pushed the books into a heap and patted the edge of the bed.

209

All right, then. He went and sat on the bed silently and let her lead. She lifted her mug, took a sip. "It's just peppermint tea."

"That's fine. Our only rule is no espresso after midnight. Unless you're Ryan pulling an all-nighter."

"I don't even like espresso."

"That's probably a good thing at your age. Black coffee is a filthy habit."

She snorted. "Right. I think it's more like a religion in this house. So…" Instead of continuing, she picked up her mug, staring into it, and took tiny sips alternating with inhaling the steam.

John held back a yawn and slid his eyes to her clock radio. Three a.m. He gave her a bit more time, but sleep was trying to drag him under, thick and muffling. He had to be up in a few hours. He said, "I heard a noise. Wanted to make sure you're all right."

"Mm." It wasn't a plea for help, but it also wasn't *"I'm fine, Dad, go back to bed."*

"Did you have a bad dream?"

"Kind of."

"About your mom and the baby?" he prompted. "They're doing fine, but I can imagine it felt scary."

"Yeah, no. Not exactly."

Well, that wasn't helpful. He kept quiet. It used not to take much to get Torey talking, but these days she was less open, more reserved. He missed her chatter, especially because he never used to worry that he didn't know what she needed. She sipped, set the mug down, fiddled with the pile of books that threatened to slide off the bed. Eventually a yawn did get past his clenched jaw muscles.

She said, "Sorry. I'm keeping you up."

"It's fine. Do you want to talk? Or I can sit here till you finish your tea."

"Stupid tea!" She shoved the cup hard enough to send it off the edge of the nightstand. It hit the floor with a thump. Torey burst into tears.

"No. Honey!" He wasn't sure which to reach for, child or mug, but she'd pulled herself into a tight ball around her knees, not inviting a hug. He knelt, picked up the mug and dabbed at the spill on the rug with a few tissues. "Look. All better. It's not broken, and there were only a few drops left. You can barely see it. We'll spray it in the morning."

For some reason, that made her cry harder. He sat back on the bed and tentatively slid his arm around her. At first, she shrugged as if trying to get loose, but before he could let go, she turned and grabbed him in a tight hug. Her arms clamped around him like she was drowning, and she hid her face in his shoulder.

He gathered her in, stroking her short hair. "Sh. It's all right. I've got you now, baby girl."

It took several long minutes before her sobs eased to something gentler and longer, before she softened in his arms and relaxed her hold around his chest. He eased her into a more comfortable hug and leaned his cheek on her hair. "Really bad dream, huh?"

"No. I…" She sniffed and rubbed her wet cheek against his shoulder. "No."

"You don't have to tell me."

"I *want* to. Fuck!"

They both flinched at the word. John laughed softly to let her know it was all right. "You'll be thirteen tomorrow. You get to use the four-letter words. In moderation. And probably not around your mother."

"Oh God, she's going to *hate* me!" Torey wailed and hid her face again.

"Baby, no, she would never hate you! Not for swearing, not for breaking the law. Not for anything."

Torey mumbled something indistinct into his robe.

"Hm?" He rocked her, pulling her more into his lap. *My little girl.* God, he wanted to make everything perfect for her. Not possible, he knew that. But this he could fix. "You kids are the most important thing in the world to your mom. No matter what. She will always love you, and so will I."

"I like girls."

At first her words didn't register, then he said, "Um? Sure. You are a girl."

She pulled back, then slid far enough down the bed that they weren't touching, braced her arms on the mattress and looked up at him, her face tearstained. "No, Dad, I *like* girls, like you like Ryan."

Maybe it was the lateness of the hour or just his own stupidity, because even then it took him a moment to parse all the *likes* and understand. To actually hear what she meant.

"Oh!" His stomach dropped, and his first thought was, *Oh, baby, no!* Along with visions of her being harassed in some school bathroom or dark alley by people calling her a lezzie and a dyke and threatening her. *No! Not my little girl.*

An instant later, he felt a hot wave of shame. He desperately hoped he hadn't let that reaction show on his face or in his voice. He said as steadily as he could, "I love you, always, no matter what. You know that, right?"

"I guess?" She sniffed and rubbed her eyes.

"No guessing." He reached out and touched her damp cheek with his finger. *My not-so-little girl. Oh hell, they grow up too fast.* He needed to say the right thing, right now. He'd actually thought about this, idly, wondering if Mark might bring home a boy someday, planning to be the perfect wise dad about it. He'd never thought of Torey that way. She was so *young*. He cleared his throat. "Whether you're, um, lesbian or bi or trans, or asexual or whatever you feel is right for you, you're still my one and only daughter, and I love you. Got it?"

"Yeah." She looked down, blinking. "So you're okay with that?"

"Torey, it's *your* life. It's not up to me or anyone else."

"Oh." She managed a weak smile.

"Just like no one else can tell me it's wrong to love Ryan."

"Oh." That was a happier sound. "Yeah."

"Now let me give you another hug, and we can talk some more. Or not, whatever you like."

She moved back into his arms, limp and spent with reaction, where she'd been so tightly strung a moment ago. He held her and murmured in her hair, "You're still not dating until you're fourteen. Maybe fifteen. Doesn't matter if it's girls, same rules apply. Maybe till you're twenty-four. Maybe I should buy a shotgun."

Torey gave a watery chuckle against his shoulder. "Dad, you're such a dork."

"I love you."

"Love you too, Dad."

They snuggled for a while. John forced himself not to think about all the possible issues, about how gay marriage wasn't legal yet and how the teasing could be bad and how Cynthia might react He made himself stay in the *now*, hugging this girl who had the guts to say at thirteen what he'd had a hard time saying at thirty-seven. "I am so proud of you."

"Really?" She pulled back enough to look at him. "Proud?"

"Heck, yeah. It's not easy to come out to someone, even when you trust them."

"I do trust you. I just I didn't want it to change the way you look at me."

"I understand." He paused, wondering. "Did it change how you see me, when I said I was bi?"

She hesitated. "Yeah. A bit. I wondered about you and Mom and if you were hiding stuff."

"And now? When you think about me as your dad who also loves Ryan, is it harder than a year ago? Or better? Or no different?"

She slid back in the bed to lean her elbows on the pillows and cocked her head, actually thinking about it. There was a long, silent pause. He realized he was holding his breath when his vision went sparkly. Damn, life wasn't ever simple. He took a slow, deliberate breath.

"Maybe better," she said slowly. "'Cause you're happier now, with Ryan, and I'm not still wishing you'd get back together with Mom when I really, truly know you won't. So it feels better."

He tried not to sigh too loudly. "Good."

"It was easier when I didn't even know I was into girls, though."

"Don't go for easy, go for what's right."

"No kidding. Way to talk like a fortune cookie, Dad."

"You want fortune cookie? Okay." He put on a deep, sonorous voice. "You will meet a fabulous woman when you're twenty-eight and have five children together." He returned to his own tones. "Which is why you don't need to start dating till you're twenty-four."

"Dad!"

He smiled, although he could feel unexpected tears hovering close behind it. "I'm kidding. Sweetheart, it's late, and we don't have to talk anymore unless you want to, but tell me, are you planning to let Ryan know? Or your mother? No pressure, if you're not ready. No rush." Especially with Cynthia. Was it hypocritical for him to hope Torey wanted to stay in the closet a whole lot longer, where her mother was concerned?

"Ryan knows."

"You told Ryan *first*?" He shut his mouth before he could make that sound worse, even though that hurt unexpectedly. It was probably a good thing that she liked Ryan and trusted him that much. It *was* a good thing.

"Is that okay?"

He'd hesitated too long. "Of course. You should come out to whoever, when you want. And later, if you decide you're more like bi, or even transgender…" He took a breath because he was such a bad parent, but he *really* didn't want to hear her say she was trans, that she wanted to change her body He was able to add, pretty calmly, "That's not what you're trying to say right now, is it, hon? It'd be perfectly okay if it is." He'd get some points for trying, right?

He managed not to sigh with relief when she said, "No, Dad. I'm happy being a girl. I just like other girls."

"So that's fine. I like another man. You must've known I was going to be okay with this."

That made her smile. "Yeah. I, um, telling Ryan first was like a kind of test run. I wanted to hear myself say it out loud. To someone else."

"I think I understand that." He remembered the first time he'd said the word "gay", looking in the mirror. It had been more difficult than it should have been.

"And Ryan is, like, not exactly a parent and he doesn't care as much, so it was easier."

"Ryan loves you too, hon."

"I know. But it's not the same."

He supposed that was true. Ryan didn't have this visceral connection, the way his kids were the best part of him, to be cherished and protected, so vital that anything that hurt them stabbed him too. "Well, I'm glad you told me now, and you know you still have to do your homework and you still don't get to date yet, and if I see naked sex pictures on your computer of *either* women or men, there might be trouble."

"What about half-naked?"

He tried to think about it, not wanting to be a totally straitlaced parent but considering that half-naked was a bit different if it was women then realized from the sparkle in her eyes that she was teasing him. "If you're not embarrassed to show them to me one by one, you can keep them."

She winced. "Burkas it is."

"Anything else I can do?"

She eased down on her pillow, pulling up the covers, and he lifted his butt to let her tug the sheet out from under him and up to her chin. Instead of closing her eyes, though, she said in a small voice, "Do *you* think I ought to tell Mom?"

He *knew* he should say it was her decision and help her think about the pros and cons herself. But it was late and he was off-balance, and what came out was, "No. Not now."

"No?" He thought she sounded more relieved than upset.

"I mean, it's your call, but she's pretty, um, hormonal and emotional right now. And even though she's better about me and Ryan, especially without Brandon around, she's still not, um, great."

"Yeah." Torey eyed him and in a more calculating voice said, "But if I do tell her, and she hates it, then I could live with you, right?"

For one moment, he had a flash of hope this was the actual reason she'd said, *"I like girls"* —as a way she might change custodial parents. And then he was *really* ashamed, because all that tearful, honest vulnerability hadn't been a lie. Watching Cynthia flip out over having a gay kid would be devastating for Torey, not an opportunity.

Which didn't make the custody question simple. "You're always welcome here. Yes, if you come out to Mom and she's anything less than okay with that, you come straight to me. If she fights it, we can go in front of a judge. But is that what you want? Once we start that fight, we can't stop it and make it go away. It could be a mess, especially with the wrong judge."

"I guess."

"You're still the same person who woke up in your mom's place this morning feeling pretty good. The same one who's been helping get ready for the baby and making plans for her. You have time to think it over." He wished like *hell* he could trust Cynthia with this.

"I'm so tired." Torey rubbed her eyes with one fist, like she had when she was three.

He felt a rush of tenderness so strong he could hardly breathe. He patted her ankle under the covers. "Go to sleep, honey. You told me, and I love you. Nothing else has to happen in the middle of the night."

"Okay."

"You think you can sleep now?"

"Can you stay, just for a bit?"

"Sure." He eased down the bed enough that he could get up without jostling her. "Try to sleep. I'll be right here."

She reached out to turn off the lamp. In the faint light from under the door, he couldn't see her clearly, but he thought her eyes were shut. Eventually, when he was beginning to believe she'd dropped off, she suddenly whispered, "I'm so glad you're bi."

He caught back a laugh that felt too shaky and instead murmured, "Me too." God, he was. For the chance to have Ryan in his life, and for this moment when he could be exactly what his little girl needed— someone who really understood.

He sat, watching over her, trying not to let his tired brain obsess over the thoughts that wanted to run through it. *Tomorrow.* It applied to him too. They could talk some more in the morning, when he might be wiser, more helpful at least more awake. He used the word like a mantra, a distraction— *tomorrow, tomorrow, tomorrow*— and eventually found himself slumping, his eyes wanting to close. Torey's breathing became slower and louder. He eased up off the bed. She didn't stir, and the rhythm didn't change. He carefully opened her door, slipped out into the hall and closed it behind him.

When he got back into bed, Ryan rolled over and put a foot against his. "Everythin' okay?"

"Yeah. Torey had a bad dream."

"Mmph."

He knew he should let Ryan sleep, but he had to ask, "She said she told you she, um—" He realized he didn't like the word *lesbian*. It was a noun, assigning a label, not just another adjective. It felt clunky and somehow more weighty than *gay*. It didn't come easily to the tongue. And Jesus God, he was overthinking all this! Even so, he finished with, "—likes girls."

"Oh." Ryan sounded more awake. "Yeah. She told you too?"

"Obviously. Just now."

He realized his tone had a little bite when Ryan laid a palm on his chest and said, "You know that she was more worried about telling you than me because you matter more, right?"

"I guess." That was what Torey had said. "I hate thinking she wasn't sure of me."

"Did she say that?"

"No. She did say she was glad I'm bi."

Ryan chuckled and moved in closer, pressing a kiss against his neck. "So am I."

"Hah. You should be."

Ryan stroked his chest and up over his shoulder. "So you're not upset, right?"

"Not really. I'm not sure what I think. She's my kid. Nothing changes that. But Cynthia It could get messy."

"Not right this minute, though." Ryan's fingers massaged his neck. Their feet brushed together.

"I guess not." Some of the tension in his belly melted at the feel of Ryan's skin against his own. He pulled Ry in tight against him, noticing the rub of fabric along his thigh from the pressure garment on Ryan's bad leg. Ry must have gotten up and put it on after he'd sucked John unconscious. He was wearing it more lately, and John wondered if he should ask about that too.

But fatigue was making him punchy, and he knew Ryan hated to be coddled. Frankly, John wanted to be coddled himself for a bit. He rolled over and pushed back into Ryan's arms. It was one of his joys, that Ryan immediately curved his body to fit, his thighs cupping John's ass, and wrapped his arms around him, holding him strongly.

"I love you," John murmured.

"Sleep now," Ryan whispered against his hair. "Love later."

"One-track mind."

"And you like that about me. Later."

Tomorrow. Tomorrow. You have time. He closed his eyes and tried to let it all go, relaxing his muscles one by one, his breaths slowing and easing. Nothing felt as hard or as complicated lying here in Ryan's safe embrace.

Chapter Thirteen

At five p.m. that afternoon, Ryan set his final exam paper in the growing pile on the professor's desk, gripped his cane firmly, and stepped out of the classroom. For the last time that semester! Done. A rough tackle from the side almost knocked him over, but he managed to wrap his arm around Donna and keep to his feet.

"Done, done, fucking done, all, all, all done!" she warbled. "That was evil but now it's done."

He laughed. "It did kind of suck, didn't it?"

"Like a deep, dark, sucking thing," she agreed, turning and looping her arm through his free one. "And now we're going to drown our sorrows at the Keg, right?"

"Not me," Ryan said. "If I try to drink right now, I'll end up facedown in my beer."

"Spoilsport. Oh well, you're probably right. Just the thought of bed makes my little heart beat faster."

"Or slower." They glanced at each other, chanted in unison, "Parasympathetic nervous system," and laughed.

Anita and Tom fell into step beside them. Tom said, "Keg?"

Donna said, "Sleep."

"The other good choice." Tom rubbed his eyes. "Was it just me, or was that last exam the worst?"

Anita said, "Oh yeah. Me too."

They reached the doors and headed out into the sunshine. Ryan pulled his arm away from Donna and turned to her. "Gotta go. My place Friday the tenth, right? Call me if there's a problem."

"Are you two dating?" Anita asked.

Ryan just shook his head, but Donna said, "He's gay, remember? He has the sexy bisexual boyfriend that I'm totally going to steal if they ever break up."

Ryan glanced at her. "When did I say he was bi?"

She shrugged. "Two kids? It kind of follows."

"Oh. Yeah. He's all mine, though. No breaking up happening." He hoped. Thinking about the wedding was giving him an ulcer.

"So," Tom gave Donna a warm look and put an arm around her. "What are you and Ryan planning, and if you're not dating, can I tag along? My summer's looking really boring."

"Only if you like babysitting." Donna shrugged him off. "I'm watching the kids so Ryan and his boyfriend can go to a family wedding."

"Oh?" Anita tilted her head. "How does that work? Do you each bring a date, or do you, like, go together? Won't people mind?"

Ryan didn't want to think about it too much. "We'll go together, but somehow we'll manage not to have gay sex in church during the ceremony."

Anita said, "Ew."

Donna laughed. "I've seen some weddings which would have been much more fun that way."

"Well, we'll still skip it."

"Might be smart."

As they approached the parking lot, Ryan turned aside with a nod to Tom and Anita. "See you guys in three months?"

Tom said, "Hell, don't be a stranger. Unless you have a summer job out of town?"

"Nope. Right here."

"Me too. We'll have to get together. I'm told a gay wingman is a great way to pick up chicks."

Donna and Anita each gave Tom a shove. "Don't say 'chicks,'" Donna said tartly.

"I didn't mean that to apply to you brilliant ladies," Tom said quickly.

"So you don't want to pick up women like us? Something wrong with us?"

Tom grinned. "My brain is too fried to answer that. I want beer and then bed. Later."

By mutual exhausted agreement they split up, and Ryan dredged up enough intact gray matter to find his car. Oh, yeah, there. He got in, located his key, turned it. Sat there. *Home. I'm driving home now. Right now.* He tried a quick slap on his cheek, which helped him focus enough to pull out his phone.

"Hey, John."

"Are you done? How was the exam?"

Somehow, John's voice helped clear some of the cobwebs. "Awful. But it's over."

"So you'll be home soon?"

"If I don't drive off the road in my sleep."

"Do you want me to come get you?" The sudden concern in John's tone warmed him. "Seriously, we can get your car tomorrow. Just say the word."

"It's not that bad." It wasn't now, just from hearing John's voice. "I'll go past the nearest drive-through for coffee. I'll see you in half an hour."

"All right. Be safe, though. Call if you need to. I'd rather come get you halfway than have them scraping you off an embankment."

"There aren't any embankments between here and there."

"You know what I mean."

"Yeah." He crossed his fingers. "How's Cynthia?"

"Back home. Still holding. No contractions."

"Great." He actually wasn't sure what he was hoping for. A baby was an acceptable excuse for dodging the wedding. "And Torey?" The morning had been a rush to get everyone where they were headed on time. John had played it very casual, after the nighttime heart-to-heart talk, and Torey had seemed relieved to just start her day like usual.

"Seemed fine. I didn't ask any questions, and she hasn't opened the subject again."

"Well, no rush."

"That's what I figured."

"Is she staying with us again tonight?"

"Nope. I dropped her off at Cynthia's."

221

"And she's okay with that?"

"She picked it."

"Ah. Okay." His brain wasn't up to sorting the ramifications right now. As long as it was Torey's choice. "See you soon."

He made it home intact and headed inside. John was in the kitchen, and Ryan staggered dramatically toward him. "Coffeeeeee. Mooooore coffeeeeee."

John smiled and wrapped an arm around him. "Are you sure? How about sleep instead?"

"Another good idea. Is Mark home?"

"Not yet."

"Want to come up and help me sleep?"

John hugged him. "I doubt you'll need help. You think you'll even stay awake long enough to get undressed?"

It was a good question. He thought about it for a minute, realizing he was leaning sideways only when John propped him up more.

"Come on, sleepyhead," John said. "One foot in front of the other."

"I have two feet?" He blinked hard. "I think one got lost."

"This way." John guided him up the steps and into their room before easing him down on the bed. He knelt at Ryan's feet to pull off his sneakers and socks. Then tipped him onto his back, unbuttoned and unzipped him. "Lift up."

Ryan raised his ass so John could drag his jeans down. "Thanks." He scratched at his hip where the denim had rasped down it.

John grabbed his hand "You keep doing that lately. Is it worse?"

"A bit tighter." He blinked, not watching his words. "Prob'ly should massage it more and wear the damned pressure garment more hours, but 's ugly. And hot. Hate it."

John bent, swung Ryan's legs up onto the bed and pulled the sheet over him. "We'll talk later. Get some sleep."

"Y'r a boyfriend in a thousand," Ryan mumbled. "Million."

John kissed him and moved away before Ryan's sodden brain could react to it. "Sleep."

****

Ryan woke to the dip of the bed as John got in. No, he realized. As John got out. Early morning sun lit the curtains and leaked in around the edges. "Wha' time izzit?"

John said, "It's six thirty. But you're off today. You can sleep in."

Ryan blinked and worked his tongue in his mouth, which tasted like something had crawled inside and died there. "Ugh. Morning breath. Sorry. I don't even remember you coming to bed."

"You were dead to the world. That's okay."

"I'll make it up to you tonight." He put a hand on John's thigh, and John gave him a wonderful smile.

"I'll hold you to that."

He lay back lazily and watched as John picked out clothes and got dressed. John really was a stunning man, and Ryan didn't even need to say *for thirty-seven* on the end of that. Those long workman's muscles combined with the intelligence and self-confidence were compelling, even mesmerizing. The glints of sunlight as he moved around the room picked up the red of his hair; the hint of stubble complemented his strong features. It was strange to realize that for fifteen years, Ryan had fantasized about rounded boobs and smooth skin, and now the coarse dusting of hair on John's hard chest could make Ryan's morning wood almost hurt.

"Better get that shirt on before I come over there and molest you," he said, although without the impetus to follow through.

John laughed. "I'll believe it when I see it." He tugged on a T-shirt and then came back to the bed. "Get some more sleep. Call me later. Maybe we can meet for lunch."

"Sounds good." Ryan turned his head to take John's kiss on his cheek instead of his mouth. "Believe me, you don't want to taste."

"Okay. I'll get Mark out to the bus. You take a day off."

"One in a million," he murmured again, cuddling into his pillow.

He tried to go back to sleep, but apparently thirteen hours were enough even for him. He lay in a pleasantly drowsy huddle, hearing Mark get up and head downstairs, the occasional thump from below, and a hint of voices. Then the front door opening and closing twice and the hum and rattle of John's truck pulling out down the drive.

His reader was on the bedside table and after a quick necessary bathroom run, he slid luxuriously back into bed and picked it up. He could read! Really read, not the rationed one-chapter-for-every-two-hours-studying that he'd been doing for what felt like forever. He dove into the mystery he'd been craving, and it was late morning before he came up for air with a satisfied grin.

Then the hot water tank for the shower was completely full, and he almost ran it out, just for the pleasure of standing under the sluicing water with no hurry and no deadline. When he got out, he took his salve to the bedroom with a big towel and stretched out on the bed. He worked the moisturizer into his leg and ass, pressing with his fingers and thumbs over the stiffer and more raised areas.

His skin itched, rough under his fingers. He hadn't exactly neglected this in recent months— he'd stuck with his routine. There was no way he wanted another round of surgical corrections and splinting and silicone, and pain and medications. But in the rush of day to day, he'd gone on automatic with the moisturizing and massaging and stretching, not really paying attention. He flexed and extended his knee, wondering if it felt tighter than usual.

Rolling further on his side, he worked the salve in over his hip and down his thigh. There were spots that were hard to reach, and he regretted not finding a new massage therapist in York. Stupid of him to have let it slide. His damned ego, to think he didn't need help. He realized his rubbing over the big patch on his thigh had turned into scratching again and uncurled his fingers. *Stupid!*

But he'd so wanted to be *done* with this. To go on with his life and move past it.

John had offered, several times, to help him. But he didn't want John touching him in medical ways. John had kissed him, here, there, had brushed his lips over that rough spot and even nibbled that little ridge with his teeth. Ryan was not going to change that into John worrying about which bit looked dry or tight. Fuck.

He blinked away a flash of those first weeks in the hospital. Not thinking about that. *Not.*

He did a good job, giving extra attention to the places that were tougher to reach. After he was thoroughly greased up, he did the stretches with slow care, pushing everything to the sharp edge of pain and holding it there. It was summer. He'd find a masseur, put in more hours, wear the pressure garment at night, and it would be good. No more fucking surgery. It would be fine.

When he was done, he lay in a limp puddle on the towel for a while. Eventually he pulled on boxers and wandered downstairs with his reader in search of brunch. He was leaning over, peering into the refrigerator when a voice behind him said, "Oh my God!"

He whirled, grabbing the counter for balance, to see Cynthia standing in the kitchen doorway, staring down at his bad leg.

Fuck, fuck, fuck. He never wore shorts out in public, or even around the house if anyone else was there. But he had no choice now, so he jerked his head up and stood straight and didn't quickly let go of the counter or try to hide. She might as well look her fucking fill. "What the hell are you doing here?"

"I'm, uh." It took another moment for her horrified gaze to rise to his face, and then she flushed. "I'm getting Torey her English book. She must have left it here on the weekend."

"So you just barge in?" He let anger rise, better than humiliation. "What if I'd been fucking John over the kitchen table?"

"You, he, God, he *lets* you?" Her face turned redder.

"He begs me." And then, because he didn't want to sound one-sided, "Of course, I beg him too. That's not the point. Privacy is the point. Since when do you have a key?"

"It's Torey's."

"Well. Fuck." He had no words.

"I thought you'd be out, in class."

"Yesterday was the last exam."

"Oh."

Sometimes the best defense was a good offense. "You know, key or not, it's good manners to ring the bell first, not just barge in. You don't live here."

"If I'd known you were home, I wouldn't have come."

"So you only have good manners if you know someone will find out?"

"That's not what I said." She sighed. "I didn't come here to fight with you."

"Just to wander around my house while I was out of it."

225

"I just need the damned book. And it's John's house, not yours."

Speaking of which "Yeah. And John is mine too. Baby or not, kids or not, he's not ever going to be yours again."

"Oooh, claws." She smiled thinly at him. "Worried?"

He held on to the ragged edge of his temper, his jaw clenched. There'd be no way for him to totally avoid Cynthia in the years to come. He didn't want to say anything unforgivable, no matter how tempting it was.

After a moment she said, "Look, I *know* he's with you now, right? You've both rubbed my nose in that."

Ryan relaxed a little at the word *both.* "No one's rubbed any noses."

"What do you call all that kissing when you knew I was watching?"

"Love?" He shrugged. "Okay, yeah, maybe that was partly for you to see. At least on my part. But mostly because you need to lighten up about the homophobia."

"I lived here for weeks and didn't say a single word. I still let Torey come here. I let John keep Mark. How much lighter do you need?"

"A whole fucking lot. Listen. Every time you turn away pointedly or leave the room when John and I touch, you're flashing *disgusting homo* in neon letters."

"I don't see why you care."

"I don't, personally." *You could fall off a cliff, as far as I'm concerned.* "But I care for John and the kids."

"It's not right to make the kids think that's, like, normal."

"It's essential to help the kids see that it's okay." He took a step toward her and stopped as she folded her arms defensively over her big belly. He needed her to listen, not retreat. "First, because John and I are together to stay. Forever. We're their family too, and they need to be good with that. Not worried because of how you react."

She lifted her chin. "Well, the kids don't seem to care anymore, do they? I guess you fixed that already."

"If they get teased about us at school, or maybe see us catching flak from strangers, they need to know, right deep down, that the homophobes are the ones who are clueless Neanderthals. That smart, good people know that love is love, in any form."

"But…"

He held up his hand. "Secondly, because they're going to have classmates and college friends who are LGBT. The time to teach our kids to be accepting about that is now. And thirdly for themselves." He pointed at her belly. "What if that little girl turns sixteen and she comes home and says, *Mom, I'm in love with this girl.* Do you want to have taught her brother and sister to hate her for it?"

Cynthia hugged herself tighter. "She won't. Anyway, she has DS. She'll probably never date."

"You don't know that. Some Down syndrome folk even get married." He'd done some reading, and that was very optimistic but not impossible. "But okay, what if Torey falls for a girl, or Mark decides he likes boys?"

She pursed her lips and glared at him. "They won't. They're normal."

"You never know. John's about as *normal* as any man gets, right?"

"No. Apparently he's not."

"Lady, you were married to the man for over a decade. If you don't know what a wonderful guy he is by now, then you deserve Carlisle."

She huffed out a breath.

"Look, I don't want to fight. But I'm asking you." He thought about Torey and changed that. "I'm *begging* you to, um" —get your head out of your ass— "think about this calmly and logically and see that the world is changing. Whatever you were taught about gay-equals-bad, that's not the world your kids will live in."

"So you say."

He shook his head. "If everyone around them was straight, you could probably keep your delusions a bit longer. But their father and I aren't, and there will be others in their lives who aren't either. You push your outdated views too hard, and you'll be the one to lose."

"Common decency is never outdated."

"True. Like not walking into someone else's house uninvited?"

"Don't equate that with what you do."

He had to laugh; this was getting ridiculous, and part of that was his own doing. "It was just an example. God, could you relax and let people be who they are and deal with your own life, huh?"

"The kids are my own life."

"Maybe. But you're only a part of theirs, not all of it, and they're growing fast. At least think about losing the bigotry, huh?" *Screw it.* He was done here. "What book did Torey need? You stay down here, and I'll get it."

"*To Kill a Mockingbird.* And her red notebook."

"Nice. Stay here." He headed for the doorway, and she stepped aside to let him past. He climbed the stairs at his normal speed, aware that she was watching and that his back view was worse than the front. But hell, he'd given her the full look when she first walked in. He wasn't hiding now.

He went into Torey's room and found the paperback and notebook beside her bed. In the hallway, he had a strong desire to go put pants on, but he refused to give in to it. Still in boxers, he headed back downstairs. "Here's the books."

She said, "Thanks," automatically as she took them, then dropped her gaze. "I'll go now."

"Drive carefully," he said, to prove he wasn't all asshole.

Her voice was low and matter-of-fact. "I don't know what John sees in you." It wasn't his imagination that her eyes drifted to his knee again. "But you and I have to get along somehow. I'll try."

He thought of John, thought of the kids, of the fact that he'd have to sit across from her in a few hours and play nice for Torey's real-birthday dinner, and managed to say, "Thank you. That would be good."

When he'd locked the door behind her, he leaned his forehead against it. Well, hell. Not his finest moment. He was an adult; he was over thirty, and that woman had him acting like a spoiled teenager. He scratched at his thigh, then stopped himself. Enough. No wallowing. Brunch.

He found a few leftovers in the fridge and ate them leaning on the counter. He was grinding beans for fresh coffee when he heard the front door shut. Teeth clenched, he flicked off the grinder and turned, slowly this time. But it was John who stood grinning in the doorway.

John's smile faded as his expression registered. "What's wrong?"

Ryan rubbed his lips and made himself relax. "Absolutely nothing, now," he said, aiming for a sexy drawl. "Get in here."

John raised his eyebrows but obeyed. *Three hours before the kids are out of school.* When John was within arm's reach, Ryan went for a fast kiss, then used the counter to lower himself to his knees. He wasn't sure how long he was good for. He'd just have to make sure John got off before his leg gave out. He framed John's already-hardening dick with his hands, looked up with a grin and then laid his open mouth over the bulge.

John said, "Mm. I *thought* a long lunch break was a good idea. Upstairs?"

"No. Here. I need this." He reached up for John's belt, unbuckling, unzipping. John looked like he might protest but Ryan closed one hand over the tented front of his briefs, and he moaned instead. Ryan shoved the briefs and jeans down to John's thighs in one motion and took that still-hardening erection into his mouth.

He could make the whole world go away, just like this. He could narrow his existence down to John. Nothing existed except John's satin-skinned cock, slippery with spit and salty with precome, gliding in and out of his throat, stretching his lips, flattening his tongue. He sucked, swirled his tongue, bobbed his head and felt John's hands land on his head and tangle into his hair. The musky male scent was in his nose. John's little grunts as he pumped were counterpoint to his own harsh, wet breaths, gasped around the fullness in his mouth. He closed his eyes, tightened his lips and hollowed out his cheeks.

"Holy God, Ryan, so hot." John froze for a moment, deep in him and let go of Ryan's head to stroke the hollow of his cheek with one finger. Ryan shuddered, needing, *needing something*, skin too tight and mouth too full and air fading to black spots behind his lids. He reached down to palm himself roughly, then pulled his head back most of the way and plunged down on John until his throat was filled past breathing.

John cried out and came, a trickle this time, salt-slick little pulses over the back of his tongue. Ryan swallowed convulsively and then eased his head back. John's softening cock brushed Ryan's neck, leaving a wet smear. Ryan looked up. John's face and chest were flushed, his mouth hung open through his shuddering breaths, his eyes were closed, auburn lashes almost invisible against the tanned, reddened cheeks. *I did that.* John looked like a man totally taken over the edge of pleasure, and Ryan shuddered at the sight. *Oh yeah.*

"Oh man." John's voice was barely more than breath. "How did I go thirty-seven years and never know sex could feel like this?"

"You hadn't met me," Ryan pointed out smugly, then coughed against the tightness of his throat.

"True." John opened his eyes. Their changeable hazel color was more gold than gray, his pupils still blown wide. He reached down and pulled Ryan to his feet and into a hug, kissing him thoroughly, the taste of come slick between them. They exchanged little gentle plucks of lips, touches of tongue, then separated enough not to have double vision. "That wasn't exactly what I planned."

"I'm a big fan of improv," Ryan said easily.

"I guess. So what's going on?"

"It's called a blowjob. Also a hummer, cock-sucking, fellatio, giving head…"

John shut him up with a wet, slow kiss with tongue and a little tug on his lower lip. "Show-off. I meant, is something wrong? You looked worried, or maybe angry, when I came in."

"Nothing's wrong except that you just came, and I haven't yet."

"I can fix that." John turned Ryan, easing him against the counter so he'd have some support, then slid down to his knees in turn.

There was one thing to say for wearing nothing but boxers— easy access. Ryan looked down at John's bent head, toying with his hair. The occasional strand of silver in the red made it feel more precious, more dear, to have this. John clasped Ryan's thighs in each hand, good and bad equally, and all his lovely, intent focus was on Ryan's needy cock. His head bobbed, trailing sweet heat and pressure over Ryan's sensitive skin. If he noticed the rough texture under his right palm or the fact that there was less muscle for his fingers to grasp, it didn't show.

Ryan leaned back and braced his elbows on the counter, breathing fast, working to take the sucking without trying to thrust too deep. John was so freaking good at this by now. "I love you," Ryan murmured, since his mouth was free to speak the truth. "Love you, love you, God, so much."

John didn't reply, but his answer was there in the touch of his hands and the pleasure of his mouth and the time and care he took.

****

Three weeks later, John shifted uncomfortably in the cramped, not-made-for-real-humans airplane seat, headed for Texas. Turning sideways, he slid his feet farther out into the aisle. Airline travel seemed to get less and less comfortable. Beside him, Ryan sat up straighter, their shoulders bumping.

They exchanged oh-my-God get-me-out-of-here glances. In the window seat beside Ryan, the little old lady said, "And then in nineteen eighty-three, my husband broke his hip. No, it was eighty-four. I remember because it was the same year Wendy had her youngest, and he couldn't carry the baby for a couple of months, and he was…"

John closed his eyes and let her voice wash over him. She'd barely paused for breath since they got on the flight an hour ago. He was glad he had Ry as a buffer.

Ryan said, "Hey, John, doing okay?"

"Sure. Just tired." He hadn't slept well the last couple of nights. He kept dreaming that Cynthia was having the baby, in a series of improbable disasters ranging from the front seat of his truck to the middle of a tornado. And that wasn't counting the times when he dreamed he was trapped in Texas, unable to get back home while storms crashed through and the kids drowned. He'd almost ducked out on this trip, just in case. But family and Brent's wedding were important to Ryan. He needed to be right here at Ry's side.

Ryan's hand landed warm on his, and he turned his palm over to lace their fingers together. He wasn't even thinking how it might look, until the old lady's chatter stuttered and stopped. He turned to see Ryan eyeing him, a tiny smile on his lips. Behind Ryan, the lady stared down at their joined hands. Ryan's smile just got wider. In a slow movement, inconspicuous to anyone but the three of them, he bent over, raised John's hand to his lips, and brushed a tiny kiss on his fingers.

The lady said under her breath, "Well, I never!"

Ryan leaned back again, closed his own eyes and relaxed, their clasped hands tucked down under his tray table. After a long minute of blessed silence, John did the same. Quiet reigned for a few more minutes, and then the woman said in a stage whisper, "Are you boys gay?"

John's eyes shot open, and he glanced toward Ryan, who looked equally startled.

The woman went on, in a chatty tone, "Back home where I live in Texas, we don't have any gay boys, or, you know, not any who are willing to show it. Which is a real shame. I've been reading these books by Suzanne Brockmann. Do you know her?"

Ryan said tentatively, "No."

The woman put a hand on his arm. "Oh, you should. She writes these wonderful romances, and I was cruising along reading about the girls and the men, and then all of a sudden, the gay agent, that's Jules, was falling for this actor…" She chatted on happily, rehashing the plot of what sounded like a dozen different books, all apparently with gay men in love. John left Ryan to find suitable monosyllabic responses to their neighbor. By the time the plane landed in Houston, she'd scribbled a reading list for them on the back of a receipt from her purse. "I'm sure there are others I'm going to be so mad at myself for forgetting," she said. "If I hadn't let the batteries in my Kindle run down, I'd be able to check. Oh well, those will be a good start." She handed Ryan the slip of paper.

"Thank you," he said, tucking it into his pocket.

They rolled up to the gate, and everyone began to pack their things and get ready to go. Once the exodus got near their row, John slid out into the aisle and reached down to give Ryan a boost to his feet, knowing he always stiffened up when he sat too long. He kept a hand under Ry's elbow until he was steady, then reached up to the compartment for their carry-on bags.

"You boys take care," the woman said loudly. "I hope you're very happy together, and don't you mind what anyone says."

The man ahead of them in the aisle glanced over his shoulder with a curl of his lip. John gave him a bland look in return. He noticed a couple of other people nearby whose expressions suggested they were not wishing a long happy life on two gay guys. Ryan gave John a nudge to get him moving, and they left the woman searching under the seat in front of her for some item that had fallen out of her overflowing purse. John heaved a small sigh as they got out of range.

"Yeah," Ryan murmured from behind him. "Her husband must be a very patient man."

"Or one with good earplugs."

"Well." Ryan stepped out of the plane and leaned on his cane with a low grunt he probably didn't realize he made. "At least she was an ally, right?"

"Yes." John turned to walk beside him and said quietly, "What possessed you to kiss my fingers in front of her like that? It's not like you."

"Impulse? Brain fatigue? A desire not to hear more about Wendy's third labor?"

"Well, that worked."

232

They glanced at each other, and both laughed. "In a way," Ryan said. "I guess I'm also, I don't know, trying not to hide when it's not necessary. We're older…"

"Speak for yourself."

Ryan nudged him. "You're old, old, old, and I'm not young."

John stuck out a foot, then caught Ry as he tripped before he actually fell.

"Asshole," Ryan said without heat, dropping his bag to cling to John's arm for a moment. "So. We're established, out to everyone we know. Random strangers frowning doesn't hurt us. So maybe they need to get the fuck used to it and we can help speed that up, huh?"

John picked up the handle of the bag for Ryan. "Sounds about right to me," he agreed, although he wasn't sure they needed to provoke total strangers. They'd never talked about that night at the off-campus bar, but maybe they should. Sometime. "You will remember this is Texas?"

"Not likely to forget."

"Getting people used to it is good. Getting the crap beaten out of us would be bad. Breaking up your brother's wedding also not good."

As they cleared the jetway and turned down the concourse, Ryan murmured, "I'll try to restrain my lust in public."

Despite the long day, John smiled. "We do have a nice, private hotel room. Maybe we can wear it out instead."

"I like a man with plans."

By the time they got through the airport, found their rental car, and drove to the nearby hotel, John's plans had faded to a warm shower and a bed with Ryan sleeping in his arms. The hotel room was run-of-the-mill, with one king-size bed. It was a big chain, and the clerk had barely glanced at them when handing over the two keys. Ryan stood his cane in a corner near the door, shoved his carry-on bag against the wall and collapsed on the bed. "Wake me in the morning."

John bent and swung Ry's feet onto the bed, pulling off his sneakers. "Want me to undress you?"

"I'm too tired to even take you up on that. Go have your shower if you want one."

Before heading to the bathroom, John pulled out his phone and checked for messages again, just in case. Still all clear. Nothing from home, nothing from Cynthia. She'd made it to her due date now, to everyone's relief, but in John's memory, babies had their own version of Murphy's law and tended to come when it was most inconvenient. Which would be tonight.

"Anything?" Ryan asked.

"Nope. All clear." It wasn't like he had to be there, of course. There were plenty of taxis in York, and in a pinch, Donna had promised to pick up Torey and give Cynthia a ride if she couldn't get hold of one. It wasn't Cynthia's first child and the hospital was nearby, with a very competent staff. It was just that he'd promised, and she had no other friends in town.

"Quit fretting," Ryan said. John glanced over, but Ry's eyes were closed, not even looking at him. "No flights back till morning anyway, so you might as well get a good night's sleep."

"Right. True." He set the phone with its charger on the desk and began pulling off his clothes.

"The kids like Donna. They'll be fine."

"I know."

"You don't have to take care of everyone, everywhere, tonight."

He knew that. It was a relief, in a way, to be stuck here with no one but Ryan to think about. He wanted a shower, but even more, he wanted to just stop for a minute, or an hour. To let go of all the roles he was juggling and simply be Ryan's guy. He paused, still in his boxers and eased onto the bed. He would have guided Ryan into a spoon against him like usual, or tried to be sexy if it looked like he wanted that, but Ryan reached out and laid a hand on his shoulder. Their eyes met, and Ryan said quietly, "Let's make tonight your turn, huh? Your turn to be taken care of?"

Tears prickled his eyes for no good reason at all, and he nodded. Ryan pushed him over on the bed, until he was facedown with his cheek on the pillows. Ryan leaned over him, hands rubbing his shoulders, smoothing his back. "Relax," Ryan said. "You're so tight. It's all right, take it easy."

The rubbing massage was good. Ryan's fingers were strong, and he knew some techniques that made John groan with relief. The moment when Ryan stopped, undressed and pulled him into a hug, wrapping him in strong arms, was even better. He let go of his worries— large ones, small ones, kids and weddings and bigots and all— and closed his eyes. For the first time in days, he slept the night through without waking.

Chapter Fourteen

Ryan stopped the rental car at the wide end of a long gravel driveway, pulling in behind a dusty pickup truck. He checked the time on his phone, looked for messages, put it away again.

John said, "Well, either they're having a big eleventh of June party, or this is the place."

"Yeah." Ryan still didn't turn off the engine, though. The AC blew cool across his face, but he felt sticky and unkempt. Outside, there was a shimmer of heat off the hood of the car, making the scene waver in the still air. The indicator in the dashboard said ninety-six degrees.

He was really irritable and not entirely sure why. Nervous about seeing Brent and Dad and having them talk to John again? Probably that was part of it. He didn't want a fight, but he could feel himself spoiling for one if they said anything even slightly off-key.

John said, "Do you want to try to park closer?"

"No." He switched off the car, pocketed the key. His leg ached from the long drive. He'd known it was stupid to insist on taking the wheel, but John had just shrugged and not pointed out the obvious. Sometimes he loved that man so damned much. "A walk'll be good. Anyway, parked up here, we can make a quick getaway."

John laughed like he was supposed to. Ryan wished he didn't think a sudden retreat was a real possibility. They got out and headed side by side up the drive.

The air was hot and dusty, but at least it wasn't humid. Up ahead, they could hear voices and music playing. Over the crest of a low ridge, the driveway led down toward a modest home with a cluster of outbuildings. There was a big tent set up on the front lawn, flanked by an orderly array of folding chairs and a flower-decked altar. The wide expanse of grass was a well-watered green.

As they approached the lawn, a young woman in a floral dress hurried up to meet them, smiling cheerfully. "Hi. Are you with the bride or groom?"

"Um, groom?"

"The right side of the seating is the groom's side." She pointed. "It'll be about ten minutes till we need people to start taking seats. Would you like some lemonade first? It's over there under the canopy."

"Sounds great."

She gave them a little wave toward the tent and whirled away. John said, "Nice to see someone having a great time."

"Yeah." They joined the cluster of guests in the shade, and John snagged them both cups of lemonade. The tart drink went a long way to restoring Ryan's mood. He sipped slowly, glancing around at the clusters of strangers in conversation. Or not all strangers. Drew's wife, Grace, caught sight of him and headed their way, with the boys in tow. Despite Drew's friendly attitude to John, Ryan stiffened and nudged John's arm. "Incoming. Sister-in-law at two o'clock."

Grace stopped in front of them and said happily, "Ryan! You came."

Logan said, "Hey, Uncle Ryan." Five-year-old Connor pulled his hand free of his mother's and leaped up at Ryan for a hug. Ryan fumbled the boy and dropped his cane, but John's hand at his back steadied them.

Grace picked up the cane. "Connor, you know we told you not to do that to Uncle Ryan."

Connor clung on, hiding his face against Ryan's shoulder, and muttered, "Sorry."

Ryan hugged him. "No problem, sport. I just need a bit of warning." He set the boy back on his feet.

Grace ran her fingers over the walking stick instead of passing it back. "I'd forgotten how cool this is." She looked up. "You must be John. We all admired the cane at Christmas. You have a real gift with your carving." She held out her hand to John as she passed the cane to Ryan.

John shook hands warmly. "Thank you. We'll hope Brent and Anne agree with you."

"Ooh, did you carve a wedding present? Can I see?"

Ryan felt a knot of something hard ease in his chest. "It's wrapped up. And since the fancy wrapping was my whole contribution to our present, I'm not unwrapping it for you. Speaking of which, where can John unload it?" He nodded to the canvas bag John had slung over his shoulder.

"You watch the boys, and I'll show him the gift table," Grace said. "Stay with your uncle, boys. Back in a minute."

Ryan had a moment's trepidation watching John walk off with Grace, their heads together as they talked. Hopefully they were discussing carving and art. Logan tugged at his hand to claim his attention. "I'm playing real Little League this summer, Uncle Ryan. I don't have to do stupid T-ball anymore. But Connor does."

"T-ball is fun," Connor protested.

"Where's your dad?" Ryan asked to distract them.

"In there." Logan waved at the house. "Mom says he's helping Uncle Brent look pretty, but guys aren't supposed to look pretty."

"Oh, I don't know." Ryan's mind went back to earlier in the morning, after the sweaty naked-in-bed fun, and the also-fun soapy, slippery shower. He'd turned from checking his tie in the mirror to see John standing across the room dressed in his own suit. It was a sharp, charcoal gray number that was probably not the latest fashion but it fit John perfectly. John had tugged at the sleeves, and said, "A relic from my corporate days. It's a bit tight in the shoulders now."

Ryan had said, "It's perfect. All the women and gay guys will be wiping the drool off their chins."

John had come over and stood behind him, looking at them both in the mirror. He'd put a hand on the shoulder of Ryan's own lighter-gray pinstripe and pulled him back enough to bring their bodies into contact. Ryan had leaned, secure in the certainty that John would support him. John said, "You're the perfect one. So pretty. How did I ever get so lucky?" And instead of objecting to the "pretty", Ryan had been forced to kiss him. Several times.

"Nothing at all wrong with a pretty guy," Ryan told the boys.

"Well, I want to be tough and play football," Logan said.

Ryan was spared having to decide whether to tackle that by Grace and John coming back. They seemed very pleased with themselves, which was good, or perhaps ominous depending on how you looked at it. Grace said, "Come on. Let's find our seats. Ryan, would you sit on the other side of the boys, please?"

"Sure." He'd planned to sit farther back, but after all, why should they? He and John followed Grace and took the two seats beside the kids in the second row. Out from under the canopy, the sun was hot. Ryan worked his shoulders and neck, trying to ease the stiffness of his new shirt collar. John had to be even more uncomfortable in his thicker, dark jacket. At least Ryan had Texas in mind when he bought his own suit last week. He allowed himself a touch of satisfaction at the memory of how his own old jacket hadn't come close to fitting across his shoulders or over his biceps. His leg might be fucked, but he'd improved his upper body even beyond his firehouse level.

He was broken out of his musing by his father's voice. "Ryan. John." His dad held out a hand to each of them, before sitting on Grace's other side. He leaned forward to talk to Ryan past her. "I'm glad you came."

"Wouldn't miss it," Ryan said cheerfully. "Brent, leg-shackled at last."

"Be nice," Grace said.

"What's leg-shackled?" Logan asked.

"It's a way to say married," Grace told him. "Not a nice way."

"Oh."

Connor looked over at John. "Uncle Ryan? Are you and Uncle John's legs shackled?"

"Neither of us is married," Ryan said ambiguously.

Grace added quietly, "Uncle John is Uncle Ryan's boyfriend, just like Aunt Anne was Uncle Brent's girlfriend, and now she'll be his wife."

Connor nodded, still looking at John. "Will you get married too?"

"Men can't marry men," Logan said scornfully.

"In some places they can," Grace told them. "But not in Texas."

"I don't like Texas," Connor said. "It's too hot."

"We're guests here," Grace reminded him, "So let's be polite. The flowers are lovely, aren't they?"

"The lemonade was good," John offered in his deep, easy voice.

"Yeah." Logan gave him a gap-toothed smile.

There was a stir in the assembling crowd as the music swelled and the groom and best man along with two more guys in tuxes came out of the side of the house. Ryan watched as Brent walked to his place in front of the alter, giving Drew beside him a nervous smile. There was something about a tux that made a guy seem more serious, more grown up. Ryan had never been one for weddings, but the sight of his brothers together like that caught his breath. He said softly to Connor, "See? Don't you think your dad looks pretty?"

"Yes," Connor whispered back, despite Logan's huff of disagreement.

Then the wedding march struck up from the speakers and the ceremony began.

Anne wasn't the kind of girl Brent had dated in the past. She was pretty, but her jaw was long, her figure was shapelessly rounded, and her dress was simple, worn with low, sensible heels. She walked down the aisle on her father's arm as casually as if she was taking an evening stroll. But the smile on her face when she looked at Brent was matched by the light in his eyes when he saw her. When she gave her father's cheek a light kiss and stepped to meet Brent, they came together simply and sweetly. Ryan decided he approved already.

The preacher had a thick Texas drawl straight out of a low-budget soap opera, but he stuck to the good parts of the Bible. He talked about love and faith, not brimstone and hellfire, and he smiled as if he was having a good time bringing this man and this woman together. Even Drew's boys paid attention and didn't fidget too badly. Ryan watched Brent kiss his lawfully wedded wife and didn't tear up or get sentimental or want to reach for John's hand. Much.

Then it was time for greetings and pictures and all the rigmarole. Ryan moved on down the receiving line. He shook hands with the bride's father, Eugene, and a manicured blond woman whose introduction he missed but who had to be the bride's mother. Anne smiled happily at him, and Ryan managed a quick peck to his new sister-in-law's cheek. She held his sleeve an extra moment and said, "I'm so glad you and John made it here. Don't run off, okay? We're going to try to fit in some family time."

"Sure. Whenever." He shook Brent's hand. "You're a lucky man, you bastard."

Brent's grin was wide and he pulled Ryan in for a hug like nothing had ever happened. Or like a man so high on the moment he couldn't remember, anyway. "I know it! Thanks!"

His own dad gave him a quick hug and shook John's hand again with apparent warmth. Ryan grinned at Drew and resisted the temptation to bow theatrically over the maid of honor's elegantly proffered hand. Eventually he ran out of receiving line and platitudes. John at his side buffered him out of the crush of people. They found a spot in the shade under the canopy, where small tables were set up.

Ryan fished out his handkerchief, mopped his forehead and stuffed it back into his pocket. "If we're ever tempted to do something fancy like that, let's not. We can have a potluck cookout instead. With lots and lots of cold beer on hand."

John's smile was surprisingly bright. "You've got it. Although if it was sixty degrees out instead of a hundred, it wouldn't be too bad. You stay here. I'll go find beer or something equivalent."

It was only after John had gone off to forage that Ryan heard his own words in his head. *"If we ever do that..."* Well, hell, maybe he did get sentimental at weddings after all.

A voice at his shoulder said, "Well, look who washed ashore. Ryan?"

He turned, gripping the cane unobtrusively in against his leg. Sure enough, it was Doyle, Brent's best friend and co-rabble-rouser from high school. And wait for it there was the glance down at his leg and cane, as if the damage would show through his tailored slacks, then the quick look back up and faux-casual smile. "It's been years," Doyle said, his handshake extra hearty. "How've you been? I mean, I heard you got..." He looked down at the cane again.

"I've been great," Ryan said, before Doyle could tie himself in knots. "I survived—" He allowed himself the evil of a moment's pause, watching Doyle get ready to be sympathetic, then went on, "—my first year in med school and painting Dad's house up to his standards in the same year. It's good."

"Oh. Excellent. Great." Doyle looked aside quickly. "Med school, huh? You always were the brainiac. Well, I'll see you around, right?" His clap on the shoulder nearly knocked Ryan off his feet.

"Have a beer," John murmured in his ear, steadying him and passing over a cold glass as Doyle strode off.

"Oh, thank God." Ryan took a long swallow.

"Someone you know?"

"Yeah, from high school. He hasn't changed a bit, unfortunately. How are you holding up?"

"Me? I have a beer, a friend, and no awkward acquaintances. I'm good."

"Have you checked your phone?"

John looked sheepish. "Yeah. While I was waiting for the beer. No messages."

Ryan sighed and tried to relax. Whatever came next, he'd managed to see Brent get hitched.

What came next was a few friends, a bunch of strangers and the occasional elderly relative. The call to eat rescued him from Great Aunt Marjorie's litany of all the family weddings she'd ever seen, with frequent hints that his should be next. John led the way to their table, which they shared with Grace and the boys and the sisters of one of the bridesmaids. The seating chart put one of the girls between him and John, and Logan on John's other side. Logan had clearly gotten bored with weddings and wanted to talk baseball. By the end of the meal, Ryan could feel every woman at the table melting over John's respectful attention to the little boy.

He's mine.

As if hearing the thought, John looked his way and smiled.

It was a pleasant meal. The toasts were good and the speeches short. The champagne was decent. By the time the cake had been eaten, he felt mellow with relief. The girls hurried off to fix make-up together. Grace said, "They'll start the dancing in half an hour or so. But we're wanted inside the house for a bit. Brent and Anne wanted a chance for the families to get together, since we're so spread out. Come on, Ry."

"I'll wait here," John said easily.

"Oh no, you don't," Ryan said.

"I thought we were going to be unobtrusive?"

"Not to the point of leaving you out of the family."

John raised an eyebrow at Grace. Logan said, "You haven't finished telling me about Willie Mays, Uncle John."

Grace nodded. "Ryan's right. There's unobtrusive, and then there's knuckling under. If Anne or Brent says differently, you two can stand on opposite sides of the room."

Despite his determination, Ryan felt the knot of tension retying itself in his belly as they went in the back door. Grace led the way into an open, vaulted living room. The bride and groom stood with all three parents near the fieldstone fireplace. As Ryan and John entered the room, Anne looked over with a smile. Brent's face was studiously blank. Ryan noticed John moving farther away from him.

The bride's mother came their way. "Grace, I brought down a box of Nate's old toys for the boys. It's over there by the couch." She turned to Ryan. "I was so glad to hear you were able to come. You and Brent and Drew do look alike, don't you?" She held out her hand.

He took it automatically. Did they look alike? Hair color, maybe. "Thanks for the invitation."

"Of course you were invited. Why, we're family now." She looked past him at John. "You are?"

"My friend John," Ryan said.

Her smooth forehead wrinkled perplexedly, but she said, "Welcome, John."

"Thank you, ma'am."

"Ryan, you should have a seat. Try the couch. It's pretty firm, so you won't sink into it." She gave a short laugh. "Eugene does love his deep easy chairs."

Ryan made his way to the couch and perched on the edge of it. John sat beside him but bent sideways over the arm to talk with the boys about their treasure trove of toys. Grace sat on the floor with her kids, and Drew dropped onto the couch on Ryan's other side.

Drew grinned up at Brent. "Whew. Next time you get married, bro, don't do it in the summer."

Anne said firmly but with a hint of a smile, "There will be no next time."

Brent kissed her cheek. "The boss has spoken."

A tall, heavyset guy about John's age came in and was introduced around as Anne's older brother, Nate. There was some stilted get-to-know-you chat about what everyone did or was doing this summer or thought of the wedding. Ryan participated with half his attention, the other half on the easy conversation John was having with the little boys.

Anne said, "We've gotten so many wonderful-looking wedding presents already. I'd love to rip into all of them tonight, but I just know I'll lose the tags and get the thank-yous all wrong. We decided to open the family ones now, though, so we can thank you in person, instead of with little cards in the mail."

"That's a lovely idea," Grace said.

Ryan looked over and met John's uncertain gaze. He couldn't do anything but shrug.

Grace turned to a sideboard with a few wrapped boxes and envelopes and lifted a familiar box with silver wrapping paper. "This is the biggest one." She gave Brent a happy grin.

"Go for it," Brent said. "Who's it from?"

She took out the card. "Ryan and John." Her voice didn't falter as she read both names. She tugged on the ribbon gently, then harder.

"You might have to cut it," Ryan said evenly. "I failed Wrapping 101, and I think there's a knot under there."

Anne reached for the scissors, and Brent steadied the package to give her a hand. They unearthed the cardboard box and opened it. Anne made a startled sound of pleasure. "Oh, look." She pulled out the bowl. "How gorgeous."

It was dark wood, a big piece that John said had started life as a heavy, crudely turned salad bowl. He'd rescued it from a garage sale, shaped and carved it, until the sides were waves, reaching upward in stylized curves. Along the rim, he'd put in fish and dolphins leaping, children swimming, a dog paddling with a stick in its jaws and a bird plunging for a fish, head and neck breaching the surface of a wave. He'd sanded and polished it and stained it a deep rich color, enhanced by the glossy finish.

Anne handed it to Brent, who gave John a startled look tinged with respect, then passed it on to his new mother-in-law. "Oh, that's a work of art," Anne's mother said warmly. "How beautiful, Ryan."

Grace said, "John's an artist."

Beside her, Connor looked up in confusion. "I thought he was Uncle Ryan's boyfriend."

In the sudden, stiff silence, Grace said calmly, "He's also an artist. He carved Uncle Ryan's cane and that beautiful bowl."

"Oh." Connor got up and went to look at the bowl, oblivious to the tension. "There's a dog on it. Would you make me a dog, Uncle John?"

Ryan had never loved John more than when he said, in exactly his usual voice, "Sure, I can carve you a wooden one, if you like."

"Yeah! Like Grandpa's dogs? I want one just like that."

"Like Sarge or like Solo?"

"Solo's prettier."

"Deal." John held out his hand, and Connor put his small one in it to be gently shaken.

Grace stood up. "Come on, boys, I think there's still plenty of wedding cake left in the tent. Shall we look?"

Logan jumped up. "Oh, good."

The adults all held still, waiting, as Grace ushered the boys ahead of her out of the room, with a backward admonishing glance that seemed to fall on all of them. When the back door banged shut, Anne's father looked at Ryan, at John, then at Anne. "Annie? Did you know about this?"

Her chin came up, and Brent moved closer to her. "Know that John is an artist?"

"Don't be like that, girl. You know what I mean."

"Then say it."

Ryan winced. John shifted against him on the couch so their thighs touched.

"All right." The patrician man gave the two of them another look, then turned back to his daughter. "Did you know Brent's brother was bringing his gay boyfriend to your wedding?"

"Of course." She still met his gaze defiantly. "He'd hardly be bringing his straight boyfriend."

"Annie!" There was a touch of appeal in that rough exclamation, and Ryan suddenly thought that this woman might have been a headstrong teenager. Her father, for all his bluster, didn't sound like he was sure he had the upper hand.

"Dad, this is the twenty-first century. People everywhere are gay and lesbian and have boyfriends and girlfriends. There are at least two lesbian couples out there among the guests too, you know."

"There are what?" His eyes strayed to the window, then back at her. "At least they're not rubbing my face in it."

"Neither are Ryan and John."

He waved a heavy hand at them. "What do you call that?"

"Two men sitting on a couch?" She sighed. "Look, Dad, don't make a big thing out of it, all right? As long as you don't have a fit, no one will care."

Her mother said, "Now, you know that's not true. There are a lot of us who just aren't comfortable with that kind of thing going on in our own homes."

"Arrgh. They are doing absolutely nothing that anyone should care about." Anne glanced around as if looking for support at last.

Drew said, "And even if they were holding hands or whatever, John is Ryan's serious boyfriend. They live together. They have a teenager, and they're a family. Whether you're comfortable or not doesn't change that."

Anne's father looked stubborn. "A wedding is not the time and place for this. I think they should leave now."

Her mother said, "All of our family is out there. Grandmother Seaboldt and everyone. We really can't have this."

Ryan said, "Look, we can just go. All right? We saw Brent get married. We brought the, um" —he swallowed the word *fucking*— "wedding present. So we're done."

"I think that's for the best," Anne's mother said, and her father nodded sternly.

John picked up Ryan's cane, stood and held a hand down for him. Ryan got to his feet as smoothly as he could. He hated seeming weak in front of these people.

Anne said, "Don't go. Brent and I want you here."

"Now, Anne," her father said. "Let's try to keep the wedding pleasant for everyone, including your mother."

Ryan held his gaze on Brent and waited. Brent flushed and looked down but said nothing. Ryan took a step over there and kissed Anne on the cheek. "Thanks for everything. You're a gem. Brent's a lucky man."

"I do know that," Brent said quietly as Anne hugged Ryan and gave John a smile.

Drew said, "I'll come with you, guys. Brent, you, you…" He broke off and strode toward the door. Ryan turned to follow, ignoring his father saying his name behind him. John stayed close at his side.

As they shut the back door behind them, Ryan took a sharp breath and bumped John's shoulder. "Wanna make out on the dance floor after all?"

"Not really," John said evenly.

Grace came over with the boys in tow. "Drew? Was it okay?"

Drew shook his head.

Ryan said, a bit manically, "Well, no one pulled out the shotgun or the tar and feathers. I don't even think there were threats of violence. We were almost glared to death, but it could've been worse."

Drew said, "I'm going to wring Brent's neck. He should've stood up for you."

"He should have stood up for Anne," John said quietly.

Ryan nodded. "He'll be lucky if she doesn't kick his ass for you."

Logan said, "Uncle Ryan said *ass*, Mom."

"Oops. Sorry."

"I think you're allowed just this once." Grace ruffled her son's hair. "But you're not, kiddo."

Ryan said, "We're going to head out now."

"Don't let those idiots chase you away," Drew told him.

"Those idiots are our hosts. Anyway, dancing isn't really my thing these days." He tapped his leg. It made a good excuse.

Grace said, "I wish we had more time together. The boys have really taken to John."

John smiled at the kids. "We'll have to do it again sometime. Maybe you could come out to Wisconsin. I have a good-sized house. We could put you up for a visit."

"I'd like that." Grace leaned over and hugged him. "It was really lovely to meet you. We've been worried about Ryan, but now we know he's in good hands."

Ryan waggled his eyebrows at her, and she laughed and hugged him too. "I don't want to know what that meant. Keep in touch, Ry."

"For sure." Ryan lowered himself to one knee carefully to hug his nephews. "Have fun, guys. Don't eat too much cake."

"How much is too much cake?" Connor asked.

"Whatever your mother says it is," Drew told him, reaching a casual hand down to Ryan. He pulled him up and into a hug. "Glad you came, bro, regardless. I know Brent is too. There would've been a hole in the wedding if you'd stayed away, no matter how gutless he was in there. And I'm sorry you-know-who spilled the beans."

Ryan said, "That's okay. In a way, I'm glad he said it just like that. Like it was nothing special. That was cool."

"He's a cool kid," John murmured beside them.

Drew gripped Ryan for another second, then stepped back. "You keep in better touch, all right? And we'll make that trip happen somehow."

"Right. Definitely."

The sun was slipping behind the buildings as Ryan turned toward the drive. It was still hot and dry. He thought briefly of another beer, or even lemonade, but in the end, all he really wanted was to be gone. John walked beside him silently. Ryan couldn't tell what he was feeling. Angry? Hurt? Bored? Just glad to be going home?

At the car, John held out his hand. "I'll drive back."

"Why?"

"Because you're moving stiff?" John suggested.

Ryan clenched his teeth, and from John's expression, it showed.

"Because that was your family vying for jerk of the year this time?"

He could still fucking drive. He pressed his lips together.

"Um. Because it's my turn?"

"Bzzzt." He could give that one the winning buzzer sound and hand over the keys. Truthfully, it would be so damned good to have the chance to stretch out and close his eyes. He walked around and got in the far side.

They'd successfully turned around and pulled out to the main road when he realized the thing he hadn't said yet. "Thanks."

"For?"

"Coming along. Taking it in stride. Being your usual self with everyone."

John shrugged. "I don't know how to be my unusual self. And no one got as far into frothing at the mouth as Carlisle did, so I figure we're even. You deal with my relatives, I deal with yours."

"The bowl was a big hit. I told you it would be." At least they'd admitted what an artist John was, before the shit hit the fan.

"It was a fun project. The original piece cost me a whole dollar."

"Well, it's an heirloom now."

"I like your sister-in-law. Both of them, actually."

"Me too."

"And the kids are great."

"Mm." Ryan couldn't help laughing. In a squeaky voice, he said, "Uncle John's not an artist, Mom. He's Uncle Ryan's boyfriend."

"Out of the mouths of babes." After a minute, John said, "I didn't mind, you know. Being outed. And there's something to be said for heading back to the hotel early."

"What's that?"

John gave him a quick glance. "You're not usually that slow. *Getting* back to the hotel early. While we're both awake and not too tired."

"Oh." John was right. He should have realized. "Yes. Definitely. A good compensation." For being persona non grata at his own brother's wedding. For *John* being treated like that. His anger threatened to rise, but he pushed it down. Useless emotion. He had better things to think about. "I'm going to close my eyes, lie back and think of all the things I'd like to do to you when we get there."

"So if you fall asleep, it's a sign that I'm boring in bed?"

"Hah." He patted John's thigh but let his eyes drift closed anyway. "If I fall asleep, it's because I'm power napping to build up my strength."

"Good idea, right," John said, his voice low and smooth. "You'll need that strength."

That sex-on-a-stick tone gave Ryan vague thoughts of having John pull the car over so they could get in a little foreplay. But he was too comfortable, with his eyes closed, his head tipped back and the AC running. The hotel wasn't that far away.

Chapter Fifteen

Ryan woke to John's voice in his ear. "Strength built up yet?"

He jolted, opened his eyes, then wiped self-consciously at the corner of his mouth. He suspected he'd been drooling, maybe snoring. They were parked in the hotel lot, near the side door up to their room. John leaned toward him, smiling slightly.

He unbuckled. "Yeah. Ready to leap tall buildings."

"Or maybe walk to an elevator?"

"Or that." He got out, tugging his jacket straight. The heat had abated somewhat, but he felt sticky and stifled in his suit. John still looked amazing in his, though, as he came around the car. "Mm. You look good enough to eat."

John smiled. "I wouldn't object to that."

They didn't touch each other in the elevator or going down the hall. Ryan was aware of John at his side, but not in the must-grab-you-now lust that they sometimes had. This was more mellow, a warm simmer of affection and desire. When they got inside the room, John reached to undo his jacket buttons, and Ryan caught his wrist. "Let me."

John raised an eyebrow but lowered his hand. Ryan made it a production, easing every button of that suit slowly through the fabric, sliding the weight of the jacket off John's wide shoulders. He tossed it aside and turned to the tie and then the shirt buttons. As those came open, he trailed his fingers over John's chest, brushing crisp, curly hair, and damp, warm skin. John said nothing, but he shivered once or twice under Ryan's hands. When the shirt was stripped away, baring him to the waist, he smiled, reached up to hold Ryan's head for a slow, deep kiss, and murmured, "This is really, really nice. A shower together would be even better."

"True." Ryan's own shirt stuck to his sides with sweat. "Great idea."

John reached for Ryan's buttons in turn, although he made it fast and matter-of-fact. There was something really sexy about that too, being stripped naked efficiently and quickly. John tugged Ryan's slacks and briefs down his legs together and then knelt for Ryan to step out of them. His roughened fingers stripped off one black sock and then the other as Ryan leaned on his shoulder for balance. When Ryan was naked, John looked up at him and smiled, his cheek inches from Ryan's growing erection. But he stood without touching Ryan again and turned away to unzip his own pants.

Ryan cleared his throat. "Give me a minute, and then I'll start the shower."

"All right." John tugged off his own slacks and socks, baring long knobby feet with a dusting of hair that shouldn't have been sexy but somehow caught Ryan's eye and shortened his breath. "Should I prep first?"

That added to the dryness in Ryan's mouth tenfold, but he managed to say, "No. I will."

John shot him a quick glance, his hazel eyes dark amber in the low light, but said nothing. Ryan turned and limped to the bathroom. He closed the door behind him and then, on second thought, locked it. His case was on the counter, and he got out the necessary equipment to get clean and ready. It wasn't like this was the first time he'd done it, and he knew John had a routine down and never complained, but for a moment, he really resented the necessity. Why was two guys getting together this little bit more difficult? Why couldn't it be simple? But then his innate optimism reminded him that it was also worth it. More than worth it. Sex with John, after a little preparation, versus spontaneous sex with one of his old female hookups? No comparison at all.

When he was done, he unlocked the door and turned on the shower to a moderate temperature. He stepped in, grateful for the hotel grab rail, and pulled the curtain shut. The blessed lukewarm water sluiced over him, washing the sticky, tight, lingering film of the day from his skin. He soaped himself and rinsed, eyes closed under the spray, hearing the door, then the toilet and then the ripple of the curtain along the rod. John's hand touched his back, as he murmured, "You're hogging the water."

Ryan laughed, and they did an adjustment, John's arm around his waist for security, until the water sluiced over both of them. Ryan watched John's red hair go dark in the spray. Watched the beads of water form on the tanned skin on the back of John's neck and then roll down to where the paler planes of his shoulders began. He leaned closer and put out his tongue to taste the water off clean skin. John sighed and slid his arm back around Ryan's hips. "This tub is too slippery for fun. Let me just get clean."

"I'll wait for you." Ryan climbed out and grabbed a couple of the big towels and the lube. In the main room, he set the bottle on the nightstand, spread the towels on the bed and stretched out on his back. They'd left the AC turned down for the day, and the room was still warm. The cooling evaporation off his skin felt good, and the occasional trickle of a drop down his neck or between his thighs made him twitch in anticipation.

John came out toweling his hair, then dropped the towel on the chair. "Now that's a sight to appreciate."

Ryan waved a hand. "How about appreciating from a bit closer?"

Oh God, he loved that smile from John. The one that was hot and happy and full of promise. Ryan took a quick breath as John came to the bed and slid onto the sheets beside him. John's hand, placed flat and heavy on his stomach, made Ryan shudder and his cock jerk in response. John slid his touch lower, slowly, his hand passing under the arch of Ryan's erection to brush over his pubes and around to his thighs. Ryan spread his legs, welcoming that touch lower. John said, "What would you like tonight?"

Ryan licked his lips. "I thought maybe, eventually, we might finally get around to you topping."

"And you bottoming. I like that idea. Eventually." John bent over, his damp hair plastered across his forehead, and opened his mouth to take the tip of Ryan's cock between his lips.

Ryan brushed those strands of hair aside, watching. He stroked John's cheeks as they hollowed even more to the rhythm of the sweet suction over Ryan's glans. Then John dipped his head, taking Ryan deeper. Ryan trailed his fingertips over John's head, brushing the back of his neck and the silken skin under his jaw, still smooth from shaving for the wedding. There was a tiny patch of stubble by John's ear, and Ryan rasped his finger over it, back and forth, as John's tongue teased back and forth in the same rhythm across the harp string of his frenulum. John pulled off and blew on the wet tip of Ryan's cock, making him shiver. Ryan murmured, "Oh yes, wonderful mouth."

He dug his fingers into John's hair as John took long sensuous licks over Ryan's shaft and across his skin to his hip and his belly. John said, between slow swipes of his tongue, "Remember the first time? When this felt so new so unlikely." He pressed the tip of his tongue into Ryan's slit. "So necessary."

"Oh yeah."

"Now it's like I can't imagine not knowing all the ins and outs of this, knowing the taste and smell of you." John nuzzled in against the softest part of his stomach. "And it's still completely necessary."

"God, John." John had always been braver when it came to words from the heart. The tender look in his eyes as he glanced up made Ryan's chest ache. He raised John's head, stroked his temples with his thumbs, then held him still and arched up in a crunch to kiss him. John leaned up enough to complete the motion. Their lips met, John's mouth slick and tasting faintly of precome. Ryan held the kiss, his whole attention on John, until his stomach muscles gave out and he had to drop back onto the bed. "It was never like this with anyone else."

"It doesn't get old."

"Not ever."

John gave Ryan's balls a nuzzle, then cupped them as he licked up and around Ryan's straining cock again. "I really don't need more variety, unless you want it."

Ryan tugged him upward, pulling insistently under John's arms until John's eyes looked down into his and John's weight was plastered over him. "I do. I absolutely want to. I'm sorry I'm making it a big freaking deal."

John kissed him. "Hush. Roll over, then."

He'd tried it on his side before and failed. Ryan rolled facedown instead, eyes closed, his face hidden in the crook of his arm. His erection was pressed to the roughness of the hotel terrycloth towel. It rasped pleasantly as he spread his thighs apart. John's hands gripped his ass cheeks, kneading them, pushing them together and then spreading him wide.

"Having fun back there?" Ryan asked, after several minutes.

"Yep." John's voice was calm. "Just playing."

"Well, don't mind me. Carry on." Ryan slid his good knee higher and found himself relaxing into John's touch.

He'd always loved the feel of John's hands. They were long-fingered and strong, rough with calluses because John did as much hands-on work as he could. And yet each touch spoke of care, of rapt attention. Even when John gripped him till he bruised in one of their rougher moments, Ryan never doubted that those hands meant to give him pleasure. Now the sensations were heightened with anticipation, until he swore the drag of fingertips over his skin left heated trails behind. John kneaded around over Ryan's ass, squeezing, moving deeper, first one and then the other hand dipping into his cleft to rub across his hole, or lower, to press on his taint until he felt the zing of that touch deep inside.

Ryan swore under his breath and squirmed, his legs spreading wider automatically to make more room. John shifted over him, reaching for the lube. Ryan felt the damp tip of John's cock slide a wet trail over the small of his back. Cool smooth lube trickled down between his ass cheeks. John's fingertip followed it, rubbing, smearing the slick, pressing over him and then slowly inside.

John shifted around, hairy legs brushing Ryan's spread thighs. One hand now slid under and gripped Ryan's balls, rolling them together with a pressure that was just short of uncomfortable and yet somehow perfect. The other hand delved inside him, two fingers now. The stretch wasn't bad, not even a burn, but the oddness kept hitting Ryan, his body insisting that things were supposed to go *out* there, not in. John crooked his fingers and rubbed over Ryan's prostate.

Ryan bit his lip and humped the bed, trying to get more friction on his cock. He felt unbalanced. Each touch over his prostate zapped him, but in a way that didn't match the arching, moaning hunger he got from John when he did it. This was electric, but it made him just as eager to pull away as push back. It unsettled him. "Enough prep," he muttered. "Do it now, John."

He was glad John didn't ask if he was sure, just eased his fingers out, reached for more lube and then lined up over him. Ryan stilled, his eyes squeezed shut.

The first press of John's cock was softer and easier than fingers. Ryan's body resisted, then began opening to it. They'd done this before, and he remembered the feel of it, the moment when easier became bigger and harder and hell-to-the-no. This time he breathed through the moment. John moved slowly and rhythmically, circling with his hips, pressing inward in small, steady increments. Ryan might've been fooled into thinking John was relaxed, but he could hear the huskiness of John's quickening breaths, and feel the fine tremor of John's forearm against his shoulder.

Ryan's body gave in at last, accepting the intrusion, no longer fighting the inward slide. John's motions got longer and smoother, thrusts rather than nudges. Ryan opened his eyes and rolled his head enough to see the veined strength of John's braced arm beside his head. He moaned then, the first sound he'd allowed himself.

John whispered, "Good, yeah."

Each slow stroke now brushed Ryan's prostate deep inside. The sensation took him beyond his instinctive resistance, shooting hot wanting needles through his body, pleasure and pain. He wasn't sure he liked it, and yet he found himself seeking it, shoving back at John, asking for more. The slide of friction across his rim was better, sexier, but that tingling jolt pulled him back to his core over and over.

John leaned down, his weight now pinning Ryan to the bed. John's chest was hot against his back. Ryan panted shallowly, glad of the grounding of that heaviness on him. Being fucked like this was making him fly, loosening his connection to anything but that center of himself where climax and distraction built together. John slid one hand over and pressed it on top of Ryan's, lacing their fingers together. Ryan fixed his eyes on that as John nudged his good knee higher and slid an arm under his chest.

Somehow, that still wasn't enough. John's weight pinned him to the bed. The terrycloth scratched against his nipples. John's hips rose and fell over him, invading deeper, impaling, opening him to heat and need and demand, but that was all physical. He wanted He needed Twisting his head, he tried to peer over his shoulder. They were too close; the angle was off. He saw a hint of rough cheek, of red hair. "John?"

"Mm?"

He squirmed and shrugged his shoulders, unable to find the words to ask, but John didn't seem to need them. He eased up and rolled them just enough to let Ryan turn a bit more, just enough for John to lean over so their mouths could meet. He kissed Ryan, once, and again, and then pulled back to look into his eyes.

It clicked. In that moment, they were one person. Giving and taking, possessing and being possessed. John's cheeks and forehead were flushed, his muscles tight, clearly balanced between the need to go harder and the perfection of holding on to this, right now. Ryan knew that moment; he'd felt it. The familiarity of it reached him, past the stretch and the discomfort and the new sensations. John had done this with him, now he did it with John. It was a gift they shared between them. The moment rang with crystal clarity, and he whispered, "Love you."

John kissed him again, slowly.

It was almost too much. The ache in his body and the ache in his heart became one living, clawing need. Discomfort was irrelevant. Topping was irrelevant. He turned his face into the pillow and tried to buck up under John's weight, to restart that driving rhythm. "More. Harder. Now!"

John kissed the edge of his ear, then nipped it. His breath came hot and fast against Ryan's cheek. He snapped his hips, repeated it, sped up. Each thrust now drove Ryan into the bed with a grunt, but he chased each withdrawal as far as John's weight let him, needing more. More something. Faster, harder, something to tip that ache over the edge. He whined again, moaned, begged, "Please, please." The heat kept building, stoppered up inside him, pressure and fire and want, unable to spill over. He'd never felt like this. Never lost himself so far inside that he couldn't tell what he was saying, or where half his body parts were, but only that he was stretched and full to bursting with John's cock, shaking, electric, hot enough to melt steel but unable, unwilling, impossible to let go...

"God, Ryan, come," John growled in his ear, slamming deep into his ass, driving him down hard against the bed. The tug of the towel against his shaft gave friction right where he needed it. John's voice filled his head. And it was enough.

His climax exploded out of him, the cork suddenly out of the volcano. It burned and ached and shook him, and yet it was the most exquisitely satisfying thing he'd ever felt. It left him shuddering, spots before his eyes, sweat dripping down his nose and trickling over his ribs. All he could do was lie there. He realized John had quieted too, but he'd been so out of it he couldn't tell "Did you come?"

"Hell, yeah." John kissed his neck. "And then some. Hold still now, babe."

255

"Wait. Don't go." He groaned deep and long as John eased out of him.

"You'll be sore anyway," John murmured. Then he collapsed over Ryan's back like a heavy, sticky blanket. Ryan pulled in slow breaths. The wash of tension drained out of him, in small shaking moments, until he was limp and boneless. He moved one leg, and the terrycloth slid over his sensitized cockhead. He shook again at the feel of the rough fabric. In a vague fog, he wondered if toweling off was going to become erotic from now on. His body managed a fractional twitch at the thought.

"So," John breathed against his cheek. "Good?"

He licked his dry lips, trying to chase down words in his fluttering thoughts. "Intense. Incredible. *Good* is the wrong word."

"But you liked it?"

Liked was the wrong word too. "How about you? Enjoyed topping?"

John nipped at his ear. "Yeah, I did. But I'm not sure I'd want to do that every time."

Ryan melted further in relief. "No?"

John slid over enough to take some of his weight off Ryan. "Sorry, I must have been squashing you."

"I liked that." Ryan threw an arm back to wrap across John's hips, holding them skin to skin. "That was almost the best part, having you on top, pinning me down. It was like I could fly, because you kept me from getting lost."

John moved farther, sliding one muscled thigh over to pin Ryan instead. He kissed across Ryan's shoulder. "I liked it too. Your ass is incredibly hot. But I missed having you inside me. I'd rather take turns."

"Works for me." Ryan rolled over, frankly snuggling in. John's arm across his shoulders was a comfort as he pulled him close. Ryan sighed and burrowed his face under John's chin, still off balance. "I'd actually rather not bottom too often."

"Did I hurt you?" John asked quickly.

"No! God, no. But it was almost too much, like all my nerve endings were exposed."

"Hm."

"I don't think my prostate works quite like yours. I couldn't decide whether to pull away or hump the shit out of the bed."

"I was the one humping the shit," John said, the humor sounding false.

"Don't get me wrong. I do want to do it again. But maybe only when…"

"When?"

Ryan hesitated. His thoughts felt as scrambled as his nerve endings, but he didn't want John to take this wrong. "When it's like this, just the two of us. When all I can see is you, and I need…" *Need what?* "Need to be pushed out of my head and filled with loving you."

"That doesn't quite track," John said, sounding more relaxed. "Although I like the sound of it. So you want to bottom when?"

Ryan shrugged and nuzzled in more. "Occasionally. When it's right. Fuck, I don't know." He suddenly had another revelation. "And now I have to get back up. Crap."

John laughed, damn his eyes. "Sticky ass?"

"Oh yeah."

"I could get you a cloth."

"I don't think that would cut it. Let me up."

John eased to the side, and Ryan wriggled over and struggled to his feet. By the time he was done in the bathroom, with a damp washcloth in his hand for John, he felt less shattered. He headed back to the bed. John had tossed the used towels in the corner and pulled back the covers. Ryan handed him the cloth and slid in behind him, taking his place as the big spoon. Once John was done wiping, Ryan dragged the covers over them both against the cooling room and hugged him in.

"I love you," he murmured against the back of John's neck. "So much. I'm crazy about being inside you or sucking you or getting sucked, or any of the things we do. And every now and then, I'll want to stretch out and have you pin me and fill me, just like that."

John twisted enough to brush a kiss back over Ryan's jaw. Then he sighed and pushed in close, his ass cupped against Ryan's thighs and one hand pressing Ryan's arm to his chest. "Sounds perfect to me," he said.

****

A knock on the hotel door next morning made John fumble his shirt button. But at least the maid hadn't come by twenty minutes earlier, when they'd been noisily occupied. He left his shirt unbuttoned and went to tell her to come back after they checked out, but when he opened the door, Brent, Anne and Ryan's father stood there looking at him. Brent looked nervous, Phil Ward was studiously blank, but Anne smiled. "Hi, John, any chance you might let us in for a minute?"

He froze, aware that the room smelled like sex, that Ryan was obliviously showering after fucking, that he was burningly angry with two of these people for treating Ryan the way they had.

"We have to get to the airport soon," Anne added. "Or I'd offer to come back later to take you guys to lunch."

"Shouldn't you be on your honeymoon?"

"Any minute now. Phil offered to drive us down to catch the plane, and I suggested we stop in and see you."

"How'd you know where we were?"

Phil said, "Ryan gave me your itinerary, just in case. Drew had your room number."

"Ah." He hesitated a moment longer, but could find no good reason to say no. He pulled the door open. "Excuse the mess." As they came into the room, he turned away, trying not to look hurried, and dragged the sheets up on the bed, at least.

"We won't stay long," Phil said. "I have to get these two on their way to Paris. Is Ryan around?"

Brent muttered, "This'll only take a minute."

John waved toward the bathroom. "He's in the shower. Let me just…" He needed to warn Ry. And no doubt take him some clothes. He doubted Ryan wanted to walk out of there naked in front of Anne or his father. John scooped up underwear, jeans and a T-shirt out of Ryan's suitcase and carried them with him into the bathroom.

The air was steamy, and Ryan was humming to himself under the water. John set the clothes on the counter and pulled the edge of the curtain open a crack. Ryan looked up at him, then smiled, swiping at the water streaming down his chest. "Gonna join me after all?"

"Not this time. We have some visitors."

He hated seeing the happy, easy smile fade off Ryan's face. "Who?"

"Anne. Your dad. Brent."

"Seriously?" Ryan shook his head. "Damn. All right. Will you be okay with them for a couple minutes?"

"No rush. I'm good. I brought you some clothes. I'll make sure Brent knows the real discussion waits for you."

He'd thought his tone was mild and casual, but Ryan reached out with damp fingers to touch his mouth. "Don't beat up my brother before I can get out there."

"So you can stop me from going too far?"

"So I can watch." Ryan managed a wry smile. "Five minutes."

Their three visitors were still standing awkwardly near the door when John stepped back out. He said, "Coffee anyone?" He waved at the little hotel pot. "If you can call it that."

Anne said, "No, thanks."

Phil shook his head. "Ryan raves about your coffee. Did you bring some beans with you?"

"I'm not that fussy." He actually was, but fiddling around starting two weak cups dripping in the stupid little pot was a way to kill some time. He buttoned his shirt and bent over the coffeemaker, tearing open the pouch, measuring water from the sink.

Behind him, Brent said, "Listen, John."

"Not now." He set the pot to work and turned around. "Wait for Ryan. Anne, tell me about your honeymoon. Where are you going?"

Anne obligingly filled the next few minutes with cheerful descriptions of the hotel in Paris and the little inn in Dijon that they'd picked out for their ten-day trip. Sight-seeing and dancing and wine tasting. It sounded pretty fun, actually. John had a moment's pang that he'd never done anything like that, had never been carefree and on vacation without kids and obligations. In the early years, after Daniel and before Mark was born, he'd been in college on a tight budget and since then Well, he didn't regret the kids, ever, but it sounded nice. Maybe he'd find a way to do that with Ryan someday.

Anne's description of a vineyard tour they'd signed up for petered out as the bathroom door opened. Ryan came out, rubbing at his hair with a towel. He wore the jeans but had the T-shirt tucked in one pocket. Muscles rippled in his arms and bare chest as he worked the towel over his head. He turned, tossed it back into the bathroom and smiled at John as if no one else was there. "Wrong shirt, babe. I wore that coming here."

"Sorry."

"No problem." Ryan dropped it into his case and pulled out a different one.

Brent said, "Wow, bro. You've really bulked up. That's, um, impressive."

Ryan threw him a sly look. "John likes it."

John sighed, realizing that keeping the peace was going to be a challenge. Ryan had done most of that muscle building in the year after his accident, getting every bit of upper-body strength he could without losing flexibility, to compensate for his leg. "You came to me like that," he said. "But I do like it. Brent, why are you here?"

Brent flashed a look at Anne, then said, "Because I was a douche yesterday?"

Ryan grinned fiercely. "Is that a question?"

"No." Brent dropped his gaze. "I guess I was."

John said, "You know, what struck me most was you leaving Anne out on a limb with her own folks." He looked at Anne. "We appreciated every word you said, just so you know."

Brent winced. "Yeah. Apparently it struck her too."

"Now, it wasn't all your doing," Phil pointed out.

"No," Ryan said in a sharper voice. "It wasn't. I can understand Brent not wanting to antagonize his new in-laws who'd spent how much for that lovely wedding?"

"It's not the money," Brent said.

Ryan shrugged. "But you, Dad. Where the hell were you when they were telling John and me we weren't welcome?"

"Thinking," Phil said.

"While we walked out the door?"

"Yes. Ryan, there's never one single answer. It was their home, their family and party…"

"And I'm not family?"

"Yes, of course. But Brent needs to get along with them for years to come. You never have to see them again."

"Oh, so that makes it all right?" Ryan turned away and yanked the new T-shirt over his head, his motions jerky. John realized he was hiding for a moment in the fabric.

"Why bother to come here, then?" John asked Phil, while Ry was still muffled. "If that's your planned position."

"I decided I was wrong," Phil said, without visible emotion. "I was caught between standing behind each of my boys, and I picked the one who seemed to need it more."

Brent flashed him a glance. "I what?"

Phil's expression became wry. "You had Anne, Ryan, and Drew against you, son. I wasn't going to add to that."

Brent looked down. "Maybe you should have. I just, you know, I didn't want a fight with my in-laws at my own damned wedding, especially over something like something that I still find…"

"Twisted?" Ryan asked. "Disgusting? Perverted?"

"Don't put words in his mouth," Anne said sharply.

Ryan actually dropped his gaze.

"It's more like, um, hard to accept," Brent said. "You and John. It's just, it's against nature, you know? And for you to change like that? I don't get it. I don't see how you can say you like girls one minute and then…"

Ryan took three steps to John's side. John stood still and let him call the shots. Ryan put an arm around his hips and leaned closer. "And then fall

261

in love? With someone who's strong and kind and smart and creative and honorable and damned sexy?"

"And a man!"

"Yeah. Caught me by surprise," Ryan said. "But I've never met anyone like John before. And it turns out the man part is a bonus." He turned and put a hand on John's neck, bending him for a kiss. John went with it, keeping it easy but putting some sweetness in it. Ryan's eyes met his for a second as they separated, and John smiled for him.

Ryan glanced at Anne, then at Brent, who stood with his jaw set and eyes stormy. "Tell me you never met anyone who was completely different from all the people you dated before and yet fit so perfectly you wondered what the hell you were thinking up till now." He looked pointedly at Anne again.

Brent looked at her too, then flushed, but said, "I didn't change teams."

Anne said lightly into the charged pause, "Now I have to ask who Brent was dating before me."

"Four-B's," Ryan said. When she raised an eyebrow he added, "Bottle blondes with big boobs. Believe me, you are such a step up, I'm amazed he had enough brain cells to recognize what he had and persuade you to marry him."

"Did you ever think that maybe I asked him?" she said. "Women are allowed to do that, you know."

"Touché." Ryan smiled, and John felt some of the tension drain out of him.

Anne glanced at her watch. "I hate to run, but we really don't want to miss this flight. Like, *really* don't." She came over and gave them a joint hug. "John, Ryan, it was great to meet you. I can't promise my parents will ever invite you over again, because their prejudices are set pretty deep. Still, you never know. I can promise you'll be welcome at Brent's and my house, and if we have kids, you'll be Uncle Ryan and Uncle John, just like you are for Andrew's boys."

Ryan hugged her back, but his eyes were clearly on Brent. "Does she speak for you too, bro?"

Brent muttered, "I'm beginning to think I should let her. She's better than me."

Anne went and kissed him thoroughly, then looped her arm through his. "No, I'm not. More open to Ryan's situation, sure, but you're a good man, Brent Ward. I wouldn't have married you otherwise."

Brent looked at her, and John could feel the way just looking at his new wife made the man melt. John leaned in against Ryan a bit more.

Brent looked back at both of them. "She's right. I don't get it. I don't like it. But I don't want to lose a brother over it, so I guess it's up to me to work on that. I almost lost you to that fire. I'm not gonna push you out of my life now for something that's really none of my business."

John would have been content with that, but Ryan said, "And John? We're both welcome?"

Brent said, "Oh hell, why not. Bring John, bring any gay friends you have, I'll trust Annie to step on my toes if I screw it up." He hugged her arm against him. "Am I good now? Can we go drink a bunch of French wine?"

"Sure," she said, smiling up at him. "Let's go honeymoon."

They headed for the door and out into the hallway. Phil lingered for a moment. "Ryan?"

"Yeah, Dad?"

"You're really serious about John, aren't you?"

Ryan's mutter of "You think?" was loud enough for Phil to hear.

"I'll try to give that the consideration it deserves."

John could feel Ryan's body tense. "John is not an *it* or a *that*."

Phil inclined his head just a fraction. "I'll try to give *him* the consideration you both deserve." He turned and followed the other two out of the room.

John closed the door behind him and looked at Ryan. Ry plastered a fake grin on his face. "Family. Can't live without them, can't beat the shit out of them."

John went back and gathered him close. "We could get Brent away from his fearsome wife and try."

Ryan did laugh then and hugged him back, then pushed him away. "I'd rather try to squeeze in one more round of making you scream instead. Except

I think I've had enough showers for this morning, and we have to sit on a plane for hours."

John went to one knee and put a hand on Ryan's hip. "I have an idea," he said. "I can be very, very tidy." He licked his lips and tugged Ryan's zipper down. Ry's refractory period was shorter than his. John would bet he could get Ry's mind completely off his family, at least for a while.

Chapter Sixteen

John had been looking forward to getting home, getting into sweatpants, and drinking a cup of real coffee while they watched something mindless on the tube. That plan went to hell in the gate area of O'Hare Airport, when his phone buzzed in his pocket. He pulled it out, checked the text. "Oh crap."

"What?" Ryan leaned closer to see the little screen. "Ah."

Torey's text read: *Mom just went into the hospital. I think she's really having the baby now.*

John started to text back, his fingers clumsy as usual on the little virtual keys. Then he said, "Forget it," and dialed Torey's phone.

She picked up right away. "Dad? Where are you?"

"We're in O'Hare, sweetheart. Right on schedule. We'll be there in about three hours."

"I wish you were here now."

"Me too, but you know, babies usually don't move that fast. Your mom was in the hospital ten hours with you and almost twenty with your brother." *And three interminable days with Daniel, before they lost the battle to keep him from being born prematurely.* He pushed those memories aside. This baby was safely past her due date now. "How long ago did she go in?"

"An hour? I called Donna. She gave her a ride and then brought me back here to our house."

"You're with Donna at home, then?"

"Yeah. And Mark's here."

"Let me talk to Donna?"

After a moment, Torey handed the phone over. John checked to be sure Donna was okay watching both kids until they could get back and then spent a moment reassuring Torey that everything would work out. When he pocketed his phone to line up for boarding, Ryan raised an eyebrow. "Is Torey doing all right?"

"Yeah. I think she can't decide whether to be excited or nervous."

"And you?"

"And me what?"

"Are you doing all right?"

"Of course." He made an effort to relax. "It's not my baby."

He thought Ryan muttered, "Keep saying that," but it might have been "You keep saying that," and he decided not to ask.

Boarding took forever. He never would understand why they made people wait to board in rows and then still let everyone pile up inside the jetway where it was hot and stuffy and you had to stand. The line moved forward a few feet at a time. Ryan leaned on his cane, frowning at nothing, a muscle in his jaw twitching. John wondered if he was thinking about his dad or Brent. They shuffled forward a few more feet.

Eventually, they were in their seats, squashed together in the body-warping space. John had noticed Ryan's leg bothering him when they got off the first plane and insisted he take the aisle this time so he could stretch it out. That left John in the middle with his knees digging into the seat in front of him. At least the window seat beside him held a small elderly man who seemed to be asleep. "Next time we spring for the first-class upgrade," he said, trying to find the most workable position.

"Yeah, I'm with you." Ryan pulled his leg back again as some late arrivals made their way down the aisle. "So, when we get back I can drop you off at the hospital, I guess, and then go hang out with the kids. But I have to work tomorrow morning."

"Donna said she could stay at the house until morning."

"And?"

"Well, then you could come to the hospital too."

Ryan turned to him. "Don't take this the wrong way, but I'd rather get rabies."

John stared at him. "You don't have to come. I just thought I'd ask. It'd be more fun, you know? There's hours and hours of nothing much happening except the mom pacing and panting and maybe swearing." He tried for a humorous look.

"Curiously enough, *I* have never been in a hospital bored stiff waiting for my baby to be born, so I *don't* know. And, oh yeah, this one isn't my baby either. Or yours."

"Look, I understand that it's sort of odd for me to be doing this for Cynthia, but she doesn't have anyone else around here. You *know* that."

"Yeah. Although she's been here a month and lived here a year before that, so if she has no friends, it's at least partly her fault."

"That's kind of harsh," John protested, even though he'd had the same thought once or twice. "Not everyone makes friends easily."

Ryan rubbed a hand on his lips. "Okay. Yeah, maybe. Anyway, I'm happy to bring the kids to meet their new sib when she's born. You can call me when the birth is getting close. I like babies, and I'll be pleased when this one is a separate person and not part of Pregnant Cynthia. But I don't want to spend hours watching you hover over her."

"You're jealous," John realized.

Ryan's eyes suddenly went flat and blank. "If you say so." He tugged his e-reader out of the seat pocket and focused on it, effectively shutting John out.

John sat there, feeling Ryan stiff and unresponsive at his side. He wasn't exactly sure what Ryan's problem was. Sure, he could imagine if some ex-girlfriend of Ryan's had come asking for help and demanding his attention, he'd have been annoyed, but he'd never have said *don't help her.* There was the baby to think of, and Cynthia was his own kids' mother, not just his ex. The baby was their sister. It was complicated. He was doing all this as much for Torey and Mark as for Cynthia. More, even.

He glanced sideways at Ryan, but the intent way he was staring at his book didn't invite more conversation. John leaned his head back and closed his eyes as an attendant went through the familiar safety lecture. He might as well rest now. He had a feeling it would be a long night.

They sat on the ground an extra twenty minutes waiting for clearance, which didn't make anyone happier. But eventually they made it out to the runway and lifted off toward home. When the seat belt sign went off, Ryan unbuckled and tucked his book away. "I'm getting up for a minute. That last flight tied me in knots."

"Good idea," John agreed. He watched Ryan struggle to his feet and into the aisle, then eased his own feet over into the opened space and sighed involuntarily.

Ryan suddenly smiled. "I think being squashed into this torture box is making us both grumpy. How about if we postpone discussing anything heavier than the baseball scores until we get off? I mean, get off the plane."

John felt an answering smile tug his lips, and he relaxed with relief. "Sounds good."

"So, how about those Brewers?"

"You know I'm a Cubs fan, right?"

Ryan said, "The underdogs. How could I forget." He leaned on the back of his seat, and they carried on a quiet, low-key conversation, more for the feeling of being easy with each other than for any real interest. When the attendants started coming through the aisle with the beverage cart, they had to squeeze back into their own seats, but this time Ryan's knee bumped John's, and their shoulders pressed together.

Their ease carried them through the flight, out of the airport, and all the way to the truck. John got in to drive the first bit, so Ryan could stretch out beside him. He'd checked his phone while they were still at the airport and there were no urgent messages. In fact, no messages at all. A quick call to Torey confirmed that they had no additional news. John figured he could probably safely stop home for a change of clothes and a shower but but. Things always seemed to happen at just the awkward moment. If the baby hadn't come while they were on the plane, it was a good bet it would happen the moment he stepped into a shower. So he drove directly to the hospital.

When he pulled up at the entrance, Ryan turned to him. "Keep in touch."

"Of course. Give the kids a hug for me and tell them I'll call when it's time to come over."

"Right." Ryan paused, then leaned toward him for a brief kiss. "Try to get some rest yourself, okay?"

John slid his hand behind Ryan's head and took a better kiss. "You too. Soak that leg in the tub, maybe."

They both got out. John waited beside the truck for Ryan to come around and took the moment when they were standing there, close together, to say,

"You're the one I'd rather be spending the night with." He eyed Ryan, hoping he'd be believed in that simple truth.

"Good to know." Ryan gave him a little push. "Go play midwife. As long as it's a one-time deal."

"Definitely," he said, relieved at Ryan's tone. He watched him drive off, then headed inside.

York General wasn't a very big place, two wings, four floors. It took him only a couple of minutes to get up to Maternity and then a few more to find a nurse who would direct him to Cynthia's room. He knocked on the door and eased it open. Cynthia was in bed, her eyes closed, a video playing on the small overhead TV. When he stepped into the room, she opened her eyes and looked over at him.

"Oh God, John, you *did* come." She rubbed away tears.

"Of course I did. Straight from the airport at that. Let me wash up, and then I'll come on over there, all right?"

She was silent as he scrubbed his hands and ran a wet paper towel over his face at the little sink. When he was done, he turned and went to her. She grabbed his outstretched hand in a fierce grip. "I was afraid…"

"What?" he asked after a moment.

She gave a short laugh. "Stupid stuff. Lying here just waiting, having contractions, nothing else happening, I guess my brain got paranoid. I thought maybe you'd be stuck in Texas, or your flight would be detoured to Kansas."

"Kansas?"

"Yeah. Well, I didn't say it made sense." She panted briefly, her hand tightening still more on his. When the contraction passed, she said, "Or that Ryan wouldn't let you come."

"Why on earth would you think that?"

"Well, he doesn't like me."

"And you don't like him. But he wouldn't keep me from helping you when you need it."

"He hates me." Her eyes filled with tears, and she let go of his hand to reach for a tissue and mop her face. She shoved her hair back and bit her lip, looking up at him plaintively. "I know I said some awful things that first time,

269

but he won't ever forget it. And he keeps pushing the gay stuff in front of the kids. And they still like him."

John managed not to say *I'm part of the 'gay stuff.'* More importantly, so was Torey, but he couldn't say that either. "You focus on having this kid right now. We'll sort things out with you and Ryan down the road, when you're not having a baby."

She sniffed hard. "Sorry. It's been a long afternoon. Are you really going to stay with me?"

"Really."

"All night? What about Ryan? And work?"

"Well, I'm sure as heck hoping you have that little girl before it's time for work."

"Aargh." She gritted her teeth, then puffed a breath. "Damn. Me too. Any time now. Shit. Ouch. Ngh."

"Has the doctor been in?"

She took a few more breaths, then said, "Yes. Fairly often, actually, and the nurses, of course. And the ultrasound. They checked the baby's heart a couple of times and said it still looks good."

"That's excellent news." He'd learned that Down syndrome kids could have heart defects.

She nodded. "But I'm still scared. What if they're wrong? What if she has problems when she's born? Maybe I should have gone to a bigger hospital with a better NICU. Maybe…"

He rubbed her shoulder, then slid his hand under her hair to massage her neck. "You're here now, and everything's going fine. Try to relax and breathe. Tell me something good. Have you decided on her name?"

"I want to see her first. Which can happen any time now." She patted her stomach. "Hello, baby, time to rise and shine."

"That's the spirit." He pulled over a chair and settled in beside her. "I'll hang out here, you get to work."

Cynthia snorted. "Typical man." But when the next contraction clamped down on her, she grabbed his hand. And when it ebbed, she gave him a wan smile and said, "I am so glad you're here, John. You have no idea. I felt so alone."

What he wanted to say was *well, you married a scumbag.* What he actually said was, "I'm glad I can help." He settled more comfortably in the chair and prepared for a long wait.

****

Ryan had been expecting to hear from John all through the night. There'd been one text close to midnight. *Progressing slowly. Sleep well.* He'd kept his phone at his bedside and he kept startling awake, grabbing for it, sure he'd heard the warble of an incoming message. Each time, it'd apparently been his imagination. So when the phone actually did chirp as he was making his morning coffee, he jumped a foot and spilled some of the water. He dodged the hot drips, set the kettle down and swore. Mopped up the spill. Poured the remaining water into the cone. Then reached for the phone.

Any time now. You could get the kids up and bring them in before work.

He texted back: *Everything okay?*

So far, so good. They'll check the baby over when she's born but strong heart, good ultrasound. Got to go.

Ryan set the phone aside. It was barely seven, and he didn't have to be at work till eight thirty. The kids were still upstairs, sleeping like, well, like teenagers.

He left the coffee dripping, went up and had a superfast shower and pulled on work clothes, then knocked on Torey's door. "Hey, hon, you awake?"

He got the expected sleepy grumble, then a quick yelp. "Is it the baby? Is she okay?"

"Any time now. Why don't you get up and dressed, and we'll go see."

The resulting thump and rattle suggested Torey was getting out clothes. He turned to Mark's door. It took three knocks to get a response and then it was a sleepy, "Don' wanna get up."

"Your baby sister wants you to."

"Aargh. Do I have to?"

"Mark." When there was only silence, Ryan tapped again, then tried the door. It was open, and he said, "I'm coming in," before actually doing so. This was a fifteen-year-old's bedroom, after all.

The room was dim, with the curtains drawn and the daylight barely filtering in. Mark was in bed, but when Ryan came in, he scooted up to sit against the headboard. His hair was disheveled, his chest bare and most of the covers hung off the side in a tangled mess.

"Tough night?" Ryan asked, pulling over the desk chair to sit down.

"Not 'specially."

"Your dad texted to say the baby will be born any minute. Torey and I are heading in to the hospital."

"Is Mom okay?"

"As far as I know, she's fine."

"Do I have to go?"

Ryan hesitated. "I guess not. Don't you want to?"

"I'm tired. I was up late."

"That's an excuse, not a reason." It was one of his own father's favorite sayings, and Ryan winced to hear it coming out of his mouth.

But Mark said, "It's just I'm tired of things changing. Can't life stay put for a minute and let me catch up?"

"Sounds like a song lyric," Ryan suggested.

After a moment, Mark looked less grim. "Maybe."

"You're right, babies are a big change. But more for Torey than for you."

"Uh-huh. Like Dad won't be all about the new baby now and taking care of her too. You know him."

Did he? Ryan couldn't be sure what John was going to do in this situation. They should've talked more, no doubt. He'd been kind of hoping it would all just go away. Cynthia would have the kid and fly back to her million-dollar home in California, divorce the creep, and live at a happy distance forever. It was a nice little dream, if he could pretend they'd keep these two kids. "We'll have to see. The first thing is to get her safely born, huh?"

Mark tilted his head. "What do *you* think Dad will do?"

"Like?"

"Is he going to move Mom and the baby back in here?"

"God, no." *Absolutely not; not if John wanted to live to thirty-eight.* "We didn't help pick out that nice apartment and get the nursery all set up just to bring them back here, and shoehorn all of us into this house."

"What if the baby's sick? What if it needs more care than just Mom?"

Yeah, what if? Down syndrome could come with a whole host of issues from heart defects to digestive problems to immune deficiencies and more. The list was scarily long for a parent. Which he and John were not. "We'll help her hire a nurse. Brandon's money has to be good for something."

Mark pulled up his knees and hid his face. "Is it awful that I wish there was no baby?"

Ryan softened his voice. "No, of course it's not awful. It's pretty natural. But since there is, I think you should go meet her. The thing about babies is that they're much harder to dislike when you actually see them."

As if on cue, his phone chirped. He pulled it out. *It's a girl. 6 pounds, 11 oz. Mom and baby doing well. The pediatrician will do a full exam after they clean her up, but you should get to see her in 20 min.*

He texted: *On our way.* "So, Mark, coming with us to meet your new sister?"

"She had it?"

"Not *it.* Yeah, baby production safely accomplished."

"Oh. That's good." Mark sighed. "Okay, yeah. Hey, does this mean I can miss school today?"

"Do you have any exams?"

"Nope. All review. Final exams are next week."

"Then I'd guess you might at least go in late. Your dad can write you a note."

Mark slid out of bed and stretched. "I'll get dressed."

Ryan looked him over. "Hey, you *did* grow some more, didn't you?" He'd been too tangled up in his own shit to even notice, but it was obviously true. He felt a twinge of guilt. He still didn't have the hang of family balance, clearly.

But Mark grinned at him. "Another inch. Finally. Not enough, though."

"We'll keep feeding you steak. You're on a roll." Ryan stood and ruffled his hair. "Ten minutes."

"Good luck getting Torey up in ten minutes."

But by the time Ryan got downstairs, Torey was already waiting. She bounced on her toes. "Can we go now?"

"Any minute. I'll bring your dad the good coffee." He went into the kitchen to fill the old tartan thermos. "By the way, your dad texted again." He passed her his phone.

Her squeal almost made him spill the damned coffee again, but he caught himself.

"She's here. She's born! Is six pounds little? It sounds little."

"Six and a half. That's pretty normal, really."

"He doesn't say her name."

"I guess we'll find out when we get there."

She glanced at him. "Aren't you excited? I'm super psyched to see her."

He said mildly, "Well, she's not my sister."

"I guess." Her effervescence dimmed.

He silenced a sigh, managed a grin instead. "But she is yours, so yeah, it's exciting. And for once, we're waiting on your brother."

Torey ran to the bottom of the stairs. "Mark! Move your ass! C'mon!"

Ryan screwed the top on the coffee and picked up his keys. "You'll have to watch your language around the baby."

Torey shrugged, swinging on the bottom banister. "I do around Mom anyway. You're a lot cooler."

He didn't feel cool. He felt bumbling and inept and out of his depth. He had a strong impulse to go hide under the covers of his bed and not come out. He could live off his disability pay, and play video games on his phone and never emerge. Not deal with babies and ex-wives and brothers and fathers and teenagers who were or were not gay and might be learning bad habits from him, and…

Mark came down the stairs, slower than his usual two-at-a-time rush, but dressed, with his hair combed. "Are we going?"

"Sure," he said. One foot ahead of the other; that was how he'd made it through things far tougher than this. "Torey's turn for shotgun."

As they pulled out of the drive, Mark stared moodily out the back window and Torey wiggled in the seat beside Ryan.

Torey asked, "Do you think she'll be blond, like us?"

"It's a good bet, since her parents are. Or more likely bald. A lot of blond babies are born bald."

Mark said, "Torey was bald, like an egg."

Torey twisted to stick her tongue out at him. "Was not. Anyway, you were two years old. No way you remember that."

"I've seen pictures."

Torey shrugged and sat back. "I can't wait to see her. And Dad. It sucked that he had to go straight to the hospital when you guys got back. Was the wedding fun, Ryan?"

"It had its moments," he said blandly.

"What was the bride's dress like?"

"Um, it was white? And long?"

Mark snorted. "Torey, he doesn't care about dresses."

"Well, some guys do. Like, especially gay guys. There's this show about wedding dresses on TV, and the person who does most of the fitting and choosing is a guy."

Ryan decided to be amused. "That's stereotyping, Torey. Imagine your dad picking out a wedding dress."

"For himself?" Torey held in a laugh for a second, then let it out. "Okay, maybe not. Do you have pictures?"

"A couple." He thought for a second about whether there were any she shouldn't see, but he hadn't taken fun pictures of John this trip. "Check my phone." Most of them would be Grace's shots of Drew's two boys, but she'd sent a couple of Anne and Brent. He figured there would be a few thousand official wedding pictures coming his way eventually, if he was still *persona grata* enough to be on the mailing list.

Torey fished his phone out of his shirt pocket and flipped through it. "Those are Connor and, um, whatisname?"

"Logan. Yes."

"They're kind of our cousins now, in a way. Right?"

"I guess so." Drew and Grace would love Torey, he was sure.

"Oh, there's the bride." Torey squinted at the screen. "At least she's not wearing strapless like every other bride for the last five years. She looks nice. I like her face."

"*She* was really great." Better than half his own family.

He'd been careless with his voice. Torey lowered the phone and looked at him. "Was someone not great?"

"Well, you know how it is. I rub my brother the wrong way sometimes. Siblings can be like that."

Mark muttered, "So here we are getting another sister. Yay."

Torey said, "At least it's not another brother." She looked back at Ryan as they stopped at a light, her expression older than her years. "Is it because you're gay?"

Mark looked up too. "Was it Brent?"

Ryan hesitated, but the kids were teens, and especially if Torey was bi or lesbian, she had a right not to have things too sugar-coated. "It was mostly the parents of the bride. They're older, they live in small-town Texas, they probably don't realize they even know any gay people. They have these prejudices. And Brent didn't want to fight with his in-laws at his wedding." In retrospect it sounded less painful than it had felt. "Which isn't unreasonable, really."

"Was anybody mean to Dad?" Torey asked in a low voice.

"Not mean, really. He and I just didn't hang around the people who weren't cool with us."

"I worry sometimes." Torey sounded sad. "Dad's just, well, he thinks good of everyone and he doesn't expect people to be less nice than he is. So with you guys being gay, I know *you'll* just tell them you don't care what they say, but it could hurt Dad."

"I think your dad's tougher than you realize," Ryan said, despite feeling that she'd found a truth, albeit sideways. John *did* think the best of everyone. While being kicked out for being queer hadn't seemed to faze him, it'd hurt Ryan to watch it. Plus that little scene at the wedding had burned even worse because John had seen Ryan's family disappoint the hell out of him. "We're probably more worried about him than we have to be."

"You too?"

"Yeah. A bit. Not because he really needs it, though."

Mark said, "I thought Brent was an asshole. Drew is cool, though."

Ryan said, "Drew is cool, and so's his wife, Grace." He let the first part of that go. He wasn't up to policing language or defending Brent right now. "The kids are fun too." He smiled. "In fact, we got outed because one of the little boys simply happened to say, 'Uncle John is Uncle Ryan's boyfriend.' For some people, it's just that ordinary."

Torey laughed. "That's great." And then repeated more quietly. "That is great."

"Yeah. Anyway, I think Dad and Brent are getting more comfortable with the idea. And things are changing. In another ten years, those older folks are going to look like dinosaurs." *Hopefully.*

"And what about Mom?" Mark said. "You think she'll get over herself too and forget that gay equals deviant child molester?"

Ryan wanted to curse as he felt Torey actually shrinking back in her seat. "That was Brandon's line," he said as mildly as he could. "And yes, I think your mother's attitude won't survive ten years around your father as a gay man. She's like a knife, but he's a rock. We know who wins that contest, right?"

Torey muttered, "Ten years."

"Or less. Maybe a lot less." Ten years was forever to a teenager, of course. He was screwing everything up lately. "I'll help. I'll be like abrasive sandpaper, rub that edge right off her."

At least that made Torey laugh. "I can imagine it."

"I'm good at being abrasive." He turned into the parking area. "And here we are. No more worries today, right? Let's go see a baby."

The gift shop in the hospital lobby was closed, but there was a novel kind of gift vending machine outside it. Since none of them had remembered to bring any of the dozen things they'd already bought for the baby, Ryan let Torey persuade him to pause and drain his credit card for a bunch of silk daffodils and a fuzzy teddy bear.

"Not a pink bear," Mark groaned as Torey hovered over the vending buttons. "Come on, Tor!"

"She *is* a girl." But Torey glanced at Ryan, then hit the controls for the rainbow one.

Ryan shrugged. "Works for me. Let's go."

They located the maternity wing, and a nurse smiled and directed them to the room on the end. The kids hung back, so Ryan rapped on the door that stood ajar. "Hello?"

John looked up from a chair. "Ryan! Hey, kids." He jumped up and came over, looking tired but happy. "Come on in."

Torey brought the flowers over to her mother. "Hey, Mom, we got these."

"How lovely. Thanks, honey." Cynthia nodded at the bedside stand, then looked down at the bundle in her arms. "Can you set them there? I have my hands full."

Ryan hung back, as first Torey and then Mark went to look at their new sister. From the little Ryan could make out, bald as an egg was about right. Otherwise, it was a baby. Cute and little, with a pug nose and eyes squinched shut. Cynthia was disheveled and tired looking, without her usual polish. She had little freckles of broken capillaries sprinkling her cheeks and forehead, but as she looked lovingly down at her new baby, she was softer and more attractive than Ryan had imagined she could be. For a moment, he finally saw what had appealed to John all those years ago.

John came over and slid an arm around his shoulders. "Thanks for taking care of the kids so I could be here for Cynthia."

"No problem. Here, brought you the good coffee." He passed over the thermos.

"My hero." John kissed the side of his temple and set the thermos on a shelf. "I'm going to stick around for a bit. I've called in to get the day off."

"I have to work. And I haven't called the kids' schools. Mark says no exams, so I said you might let them go in late today."

John laughed happily. "I think we can manage that."

Ryan lowered his voice. "It looks like the baby's doing well."

John matched his tone. "Yeah, pretty much. Likely there'll be some problems, eyesight and so on. But she just has a tiny heart murmur they're not too worried about and the rest of her physical was good, so it seems like the worst risks came out okay."

Cynthia was unwrapping the infant for the kids to see her better. Torey leaned in close, reaching to touch one tiny hand. John shifted as if he might go look too, but Ryan leaned on him harder and added, barely above his breath, "The kids will be glad she's okay, for her sake and for helping them keep some of Cynthia's attention and yours."

John looked away from the pretty tableau to stare at him. "You think they're worried about that?"

"Oh yeah."

John squeezed his shoulder, then stepped away. "Hey, Torey, Mark. It's good to see you guys. Did you have fun with Donna?"

Torey smiled at him, then came and hugged him. "Hey, Dad. I like Donna lots. She baked muffins."

"She did?" Ryan said. "How come I didn't see any?"

Mark grinned over at him. "Well she just made six, and…"

"Don't tell me. You ate them all."

Torey laughed, still hugged in against John. "Well, it was just two each."

Cynthia said, "Ryan, tell your friend how much I appreciate her help. She was very kind."

"I'll let her know." He cleared his throat. "Congratulations."

"Thanks." Cynthia looked at Torey. "Honey, if you want to sit in the chair, you can hold the baby."

"Really?" Torey hurried over and sat down. "How? What do I do?"

"Here, I'll help." John went to the bed to tuck the baby into her blanket and then lifted her skillfully from Cynthia's hands. "Hold your arms lower, sweetheart, and I'll put her in your lap."

Ryan backed up a couple of steps. "Well, I really should be heading to work."

John glanced over, the infant snuggled in his arms. "Do you want to hold her before you go?"

"Not right now. I've had the baby-burp-and-poo-explosion happen to me once with Logan, and I wouldn't have time to change."

John frowned but said, "Okay. Maybe tonight, then. Have a good day."

"You guys too." Ryan backed up more.

He stood outside the doorway of the room for a minute. John eased the baby into Torey's lap, showing her how to support the little head. Mark was paying attention too. They bent together over the infant, identical expressions of tender concentration on all three. Ryan could see an echo of John in both his children's faces.

A nurse stopped in the hallway behind him. "Such a lovely family. You can tell that man is a wonderful father."

"Yes," Ryan agreed. "He is."

"That's one of the best things about this job," the nurse said. "Watching babies being born into families that will really love and want them."

"I can imagine," Ryan murmured. He stood there awhile longer. After Torey had held the baby, Mark was convinced to take a turn. John juggled the newborn with such practiced hands as one teenager got up and the other sat down. Cynthia looked on, smiling, for once silent, letting John give directions. They moved together in harmony, orbiting around the wonder of the new child.

He eventually realized he was still hovering outside the room because he was waiting for John to look up, for one of them to glance over and see him. It was so fucking juvenile to wish that their little circle didn't seem so perfect and complete, to want John to feel the lack and come after him. Stupid! He'd said he was going off to work, and for all John knew, he was already out of the building.

He should be out of the building.

It was good the baby would be loved. Every child should have that.

Eventually it really was past time to get his ass to the car and head to his job. So he turned silently and left.

Chapter Seventeen

As he drove, Ryan tried to get his mind off the scene at the hospital and think ahead to his work. It was harder than he'd have liked. As a summer job, his was, well, okay. Not bad but not the externship he'd hoped for.

He was working in a medical practice, so it would help his résumé. It brought in a bit of cash, and now and then he got to listen in on clinical discussions. One of the six pediatricians really liked him, and would talk about her cases in general terms when she spotted him, which was nice. She'd spent ten minutes telling him her viewpoint in the debate over using antibiotics for simple ear infections, and he'd appreciated that. But mostly he was somewhere between nursing aid and janitor.

Today, everyone was running late from the word go, and the atmosphere was stressed. They seemed to have way more than their usual allotment of crying babies, and every toddler in the waiting room was hair-trigger primed for a tantrum. He circled around, cleaning exam rooms, sterilizing surfaces and toys, pulling fresh paper onto the exam tables, making sure there were new ear cones in the holders. And then doing it again.

His hands were powdery from the gloves he wore, his knee ached more than normal, and of course that made it the day he had to get down on his hands and knees again and again to pick stuff up. He struggled through it by using the furniture to haul himself back to his feet. He was not going to give in and get his cane. They'd asked at his interview if the job would be too much for his leg, and he'd be damned if it was.

The staff break room was in the back and blessedly quiet. When he took his hospital-lobby-bought lunch there, his favorite pediatrician was seated at the table. Dr. Bocovich glanced up at him from her phone, where she was texting one-handed while eating a sandwich with the other. She waved at a chair with her ham-on-rye. "You look tired, Ryan. Have a seat."

"Thanks." He sat down and unwrapped his vending machine version. The bread was sticky, the ham an unreal shade of pink, the lettuce limp. He sighed, tossed it over into the trash and tore open a pack of cookies.

Dr. Bocovich laughed. "A day when only simple carbs will do, eh?"

"Yep." He stuffed one in his mouth. "I'm not sure that was edible anyway. I don't need food poisoning on top of everything."

"Every what?" She finished texting and stuck her phone back into her pocket.

He shrugged. He wasn't about to whine to one of his bosses.

She said, "It's been a real Monday morning, eh? All the parents who didn't want to head to Urgent Care on the weekend are here with their poor, fussy, ear-achy kids."

"I guess."

"And no time for anything except scrambling round playing catch up and clean up." She eyed him and took a bigger bite of her sandwich. "You look a bit ragged."

"I don't mind," he said. "That's the job. It was just a long weekend. A wedding and a new baby in the family."

"Oh." She smiled. "Congratulations. That's lovely. If tiring."

"Yeah." He hesitated, then said, "The baby has Down syndrome."

"Ah, that's harder. Most DS kids do great, though."

"Mm." He bit another cookie. "I wondered. Do you know any gay pediatricians?"

"That's a bit non sequitur." She hesitated. "Doctors' personal lives are their own, but yes, of course there are some."

"Do you think it makes it harder? I mean, are parents really going to care who their kid's doctor sleeps with, as long as they're consenting adults?"

She leaned her elbows on the table and looked at him. "It shouldn't matter, but you know some of them would care. If they find out about it. Is this as personal as it sounds?"

"Maybe." Of course he hadn't been asked about his orientation when he applied for the job, and he hadn't told. But if he didn't ask his questions, he'd never know the answers. "Yeah. That baby? It's my partner's ex-wife's. My male partner's. And I'd planned to do pediatric neurology, and it shouldn't matter that I'm gay, but we've already come up against all kinds of stupid people and…" He stopped. For some reason, here, in the middle of work in front of his boss, of all people, he was close to tears. It made no sense whatsoever. "Forget it. I'm sorry. I should get back to work."

Doctor Bocovich put her hand on his arm as he stood. "Ryan. You're undoubtedly the brightest and most mature student we've had working in this office. That's obvious even after just a week. You'll be an excellent neurologist, if that's where your interests lie."

He managed a gruff, "Thanks."

"If you're asking, will it be harder to work in specialty pediatrics as an out gay man? Yes, I'm sure it will. I assume you do plan to be out?"

He took a breath, feeling steadier. "Yes. I don't need to flaunt it. I won't put rainbow flags all over my office. But I also don't want to hide it. Not just for the stress and the lying but, um, we have teenagers. I want them to know this is something worth telling the truth about, not something to hide like I'm ashamed of it."

"That's admirable."

He shrugged. "I'm a bad liar anyway. I tend to let the chips fly when I'm pushed to the wall. Better to start with the truth."

She met his gaze steadily. "You have a few years to decide. This country, at least, is getting more LGBT-friendly all the time. There are definitely other gay doctors who aren't totally closeted. I might be able to get you in touch with a couple who're in private practice."

"If you think they'd be okay with that." He really wanted to talk to someone further down this road than he was. "That would be great."

"I'll ask. But there'll always be fools and bigots, in and out of the clinic. Hell, we occasionally have a parent who doesn't want Lina touching their child, because she has dark skin."

"What do you do then?"

"We try to persuade them that she's an excellent nurse. Sometimes that works. But people have a right to be comfortable with their medical provider."

He bit his lip and nodded.

"The children come first. We accommodate the parents who think Dr. Kernos looks too young to know what she's doing or don't want a nurse like Mike, who's a man. We tell them they may have to wait, or reschedule to get the provider they want. If they're not too offensive about it, we offer them someone different."

"And if they *are* offensive about it?"

"If it's not an emergency, we can politely refuse their business. Part of our policy statement says we can refuse services to clients who are disrespectful or abusive to staff or other patients."

"Have you ever done that? For being racist?"

"Maybe once a year or so, yes."

"How does Lina feel about it?"

"How would you feel, if we showed a client the door for using homophobic slurs toward you?"

He shrugged. He'd think "grateful" should top the list, but the word that came to mind was "humiliated". "I guess it's a good policy."

"It is. Although Lina's a shy person outside of work and I think the whole thing embarrasses her, and she'd rather avoid the fuss. But we have a responsibility to both patients and staff to keep this clinic a safe, accepting space for everyone.. And we show any children who might witness the fuss that insults and threats don't make us give in."

He nodded slowly. "And now?"

"Now?"

He flushed, realizing that his own revelation had been forgotten already.

Dr. Bocovich hesitated. "Oh, about you being gay? Nothing has changed. Do you want me to keep this conversation confidential?"

Did he? He rubbed his face tiredly. "I don't care."

"Or shall I let Jennifer know you're taken, so she can stop running into the bathroom to fix her makeup when you're around?"

He stared at her, then laughed. "Sure. Yeah. Tell her my heart belongs to John."

"Does it?"

"Yes."

"That's lovely. Your John is a lucky man. Ryan, we're LGBT-friendly here. You're welcome to be out to whatever degree you're comfortable with. Hang on a moment." She pulled a note pad out, scribbled on it and passed the page over. "Here. She's the best clinician for Down syndrome patients in the area. Not the most recognized, but the one that parents and kids seem to thrive with for their specialty care."

"Thank you." He stuffed the paper into his pocket. "For everything."

"No problem." She added as he put his hand on the doorknob, "I'll leave it to you to tell people about John or not. Making big decisions on a frustrating day isn't always best."

"Right."

He headed outside to the patio, where the smokers went to get their quick fix. One of the nurses was there, but she just nodded to him, intent on finishing her cigarette. He wandered past her and around some planters to a quiet spot and leaned on the low brick wall.

He wasn't sure why he was suddenly hit with the urge to wave flags about his relationship. He could lie to himself and say he was doing it for Torey— her life would get easier with every person who came out as LGBT ahead of her. But while that wasn't entirely a lie, what he was doing didn't feel like supporting someone else. It felt angry. Selfish. And maybe scared.

He didn't *want* telling people about John to be a "big decision". He didn't want to pick and choose and weigh out his truths. And he didn't want some nice nurse looking at John with Cynthia and the kids and telling him what a lovely family they were.

He wanted to go back to that hallway and turn to that nurse and say, *Yes, my guy is a great dad, and he's also amazing in bed.*

Okay, maybe not that. Especially in a place where he might end up doing a clinical rotation And there it was, the coming-out dilemma coming around again. Jesus, he was petulant and whiny today. You'd think he was thirteen instead of going on thirty-one.

He could figure this out. One thing at a time, just like he'd managed to get his head out of his ass after the injury and learn to walk again. One step at a time. Finish work. Go home and eat with the kids. Talk to John.

Just the thought of talking to John made him hear an echo of John's deep voice, a hint of how his skin smelled. He thought of John hugging him in their kitchen. His tension eased in a way that was downright Pavlovian. Little steps. He'd spend the evening with John and they'd get a good night's sleep, and everything would make more sense in the morning. He straightened and limped determinedly back inside.

The afternoon went more smoothly, or perhaps he had his second wind. There were still crying babies, but the sounds didn't go through his head like a knife now. Dr. Bocovich had two clients willing to let him observe their child's exam, and he hung out in a corner of the room and listened to the discussions, the history taking, the way Dr. B dealt with her small patients. One was a complicated allergy case, and he felt a tug of interest in how mother, child, and clinician worked together. By the end of the day, he was tired, and his leg ached badly, but he was settled again in his med-student skin.

When he got home, John's truck was parked out front. He pulled in behind it and got out, feeling lighter and eager despite the damned leg. John was in the kitchen cooking, and he turned and leaned down for Ryan's quick hands-free kiss.

Ryan grinned. "What're you making?"

"Sloppy joes. Fifteen minutes?"

"Sounds good. I'll clean up." He went upstairs and showered away the sharp-odored cleaning chemicals and the strep germs and whatever else he might've brought home. He took five minutes to work extra salve into the scars over his hip and thigh and then dressed in sweatpants and a T-shirt. The kids were already at the table when he got downstairs.

They ate quietly at first. John had a brief conversation with Mark about his band's summer practice schedule, since high school would let out in a week.

It turned out his college-age bandmates all had jobs, which meant evening practices. "So you'll be free for some home improvement chores around the house," John said.

Mark groaned theatrically. "I was planning to sleep all day."

"I can help too," Torey said. "I love painting and garden stuff. When Mom and the baby don't need me, anyway."

"Thanks, sweetheart," John said.

"Are we going to go see them tonight?" Torey asked.

"Maybe for an hour. Unless you don't want to?"

"No, I do. It's good. We can bring the little blanket I made."

Mark muttered, "Is she going to name the kid sometime? We talked about it for, like, two hours this morning, and she still didn't make up her mind. We're gonna be calling my sister 'the baby' when she's a teenager."

"Not quite that long. I'm sure she'll choose soon," John said evenly. "I know she'll want to do it before they leave the hospital so all the paperwork can be filled out. A few hours isn't too long to think about something important."

"You think she'll let us vote?" Mark asked. "Because 'Ruth' is seriously not a good idea."

"We can go see." John stood and started clearing the plates. Ryan pushed to his feet too and went to the sink to wash up. He tossed the dishtowel at Mark, who caught it with a sigh and joined him. John looked at Ryan, a dip of his gaze showing he'd noticed the increased limp. "Are you coming with us, Ry, or do you want to stay home and stretch out and relax?"

Ryan was going to say a quiet evening at home sounded good, but stupid jealousy reared its head, and he said, "Nah. I'll come along. I want to find out what she names the baby too." *And I don't want you there bonding over it, smiling down together.* He seriously needed to rein in his imagination. He and John were solid. He knew that, and he had to start acting like he believed it again. Tomorrow.

The maternity ward was busier that evening, with visitors bearing flowers and balloons and stuffed animals. From many of the rooms, there was the quiet sound of laughter and joyful conversation. Ryan fell back to trail John and the kids and tried to wipe the frown off his face. Babies were good.

Cynthia was no longer pregnant and vulnerable and needy, and that was very good. Baby and ex-wife were now separate entities. He limped along faster, catching up to them at the door to Cynthia's room.

Cynthia and her baby could have posed for a painting of perfect motherhood. She sat up in bed with her child, looking much tidier than that morning, her hair sleek, her face clearer, and the shadows gone from under her eyes. The baby cuddled in against her, sleeping, one tiny hand fisted in the edge of her blue satin robe. The tilt of Cynthia's head and the curve of her lips looked loving, focused. Then she glanced up and smiled at them. "Come on in."

Ryan leaned on the doorframe as the others trooped into the room. John gestured at the lone chair. "Ryan? Want a seat?"

"Nah. Standing is good. The kids may want to hold her again."

Torey dropped into the chair eagerly. "Can I?"

The infant slept through the transfer obligingly. Mark said, "Does she ever wake up?"

Cynthia smiled. "Oh yes, no doubt about that."

"So have you, like, picked out names yet? You said once you got to know her?"

"Yes," Cynthia said. "Her first name will be Lily." Torey made a happy little sound, and Cynthia nodded. "Your suggestion. Short and sweet. And for a middle name, Johanna, after John."

"That doesn't suck," Mark said.

John cuffed the back of his head lightly. "Watch the language. But yes, it's nice."

Cynthia added happily, "And I was thinking. You know, Brandon doesn't want her. He's clearly not going to take care of her if something were to happen to me. So what if I just put your name, John, as her father on the birth certificate?"

"What?" John stared at her.

Torey said, "Oh, cool. We'd really be sisters."

John bent and picked up the baby from Torey's lap. Lily looked so tiny cradled in his arms. He gazed down at her, then glanced over at Ryan. Ryan tried to keep a smile on his face somehow, although it felt completely fake. John was so perfect with kids, and that baby needed a father desperately. A decent father who'd protect her. And yet Ryan wanted to yell at him not to do it. Not to say yes.

His stomach churned as John bent to blow softly on a scant wisp of hair on the baby's head, his expression foolishly fond. Without fully waking, the baby scrunched her eyes, whimpered and raised a delicate hand, fingers opening and closing. John held her closer and rocked her. It looked so natural, a practiced sway that had the baby relaxing in against him, small fingers closing on his shirt.

Ryan felt like a traitor. God, he sucked! John loved kids. If he wanted this one, wanted to love and care for her and have the right to keep her safe, how could Ryan say no? He'd sworn over and over that he'd bend to make John happy. Even if it meant letting Cynthia get a new hook in him If that hook was tiny, sleeping Lily, what right did he have to fight that?

He swallowed, tasted acid and held his breath so he wouldn't make the wrong sound. He was obviously a selfish, mean, unfeeling man, because what he really wanted was to shout *no!* and grab John and run. He blinked hard, his stupid eyes stinging and blurry. At least it kept him from having to look at the tender expression on John's face.

John bent and gently put the sleeping infant back into Cynthia's arms, easing his T-shirt fabric out of her precious fingers. He straightened, looked down at them for a moment and said, "No."

Ryan managed to be silent, but he clutched the door frame tightly for balance as relief flooded through him.

Cynthia and Torey both stared at John, who glanced at Torey and said in a gentle voice, "In the simplest terms, it's a lie. We don't want this little one starting her life based on a lie."

"But…" Torey sighed. "I guess. Okay."

John pulled out his wallet and took out a couple of bills. "Mark, I'd really like a soda. There's a machine down in the lobby. Would you and Torey go get me one and whatever you want for yourselves?"

Mark said sulkily, "If you want to talk to Mom alone, you can just say so."

"I want to talk to Ryan and your mom, alone. But this gives you two something to do and a time frame."

"Oh." Mark took the money. "Okay."

Ryan said, "Something with caffeine for me, please. I need it."

Once the kids were gone, with a backward look from Torey, Cynthia said, "I thought we could make this easy."

"It's all kinds of wrong." John met Ryan's eyes, then looked back at his ex-wife. "On the legal front, the divorce hasn't happened yet. You need Brandon to pay child support and her health insurance."

She dropped her eyes. "I guess."

"On the personal side, you said some pretty harsh things about me as a parent. You may have forgotten, but I haven't, even if I'm willing to work with you now."

She eased the baby against her shoulder and stretched a hand toward him. "John, I'm sorry. I overreacted. I didn't really mean all that. You surprised me, and made me think you'd lied to me."

He stepped back far enough for her reach to fall short. "I said I hadn't. You didn't believe me."

"Well, Brandon said..." Her voice trailed off.

"Yeah, you were all about what Brandon said. Which is fine, you were married to him. But you can't turn around and pretend that never happened."

"And if I'm truly sorry?"

"That's nice. Will you apologize to Ryan too?"

Cynthia turned toward him and gave him a stiff nod. "Sorry, Ryan. I really wasn't thinking back then. I didn't know you."

He nodded back silently. It was hardly a full apology, but this argument was between John and Cynthia. And John was doing just fucking *fine* by himself.

John said, "I'm still gay. I'm with Ryan. That won't change if you bribe me with a baby."

"I'm getting used to the gay stuff." Cynthia tried another smile. "Anyway, that's not what this is about."

"No?"

"No." She rubbed at her eyes. "I'm scared, John. I'm going to raise a special-needs baby by myself. Her real father hates her. Is it so wrong that I want to give her as much support as I can? I wasn't giving her to you. I was giving *you* to her."

"You can't. She's Brandon's child and yours. Maybe someday you'll meet another man, and he'll want to adopt her. Wouldn't it be a mess if my name was on there?"

Cynthia said, "I'm done with marriage."

"Maybe." John looked around again, right into Ryan's eyes. "But there's one more reason, an important reason why this is wrong."

"What?" she asked peevishly.

"It's wrong for Ryan."

"It has nothing to do with…"

"Of course it does. That's the whole point." John kept his gaze steady and warm on Ryan's until he felt his own smile becoming real. His chest loosened, and he could breathe again. He wasn't coming second to Cynthia and her baby for John, after all.

"Ryan and I are together. What affects me, affects him. Not only would that birth certificate be a lie about me, claiming I was with you, right at the beginning of my relationship with him. It would also put that baby and all her needs into the center of his life and mine, forever. Neither of us wants that."

"You do."

"No," John repeated. "I don't. It's wrong for me as well. That's not where my life is now. I want time to be with Ryan, as two adults, without that kind of responsibility. And I don't want to start over with another infant, and you as her caretaker."

"You still have children. With me."

"Yes, and Ryan and I both love my own kids and we'll always do our best for them. But they're not babies, thank God! Ryan has three years of med school left, but then he may need to move to another city or state. By then Mark will be off to college, and Torey will be driving."

Ryan saw John wince at his own words and forced a chuckle, looking into his eyes. "You want to take that lovely little thought back, don't you?"

"If she asks one of us to teach her to drive, it's definitely going to be you."

Cynthia said, "I'm not asking you to adopt Lily and take full care of her."

John didn't turn. "No, but you know I'd feel fully responsible. I don't want that."

"Being named her father doesn't mean—"

John rode over the top of her words. "If Ryan gets a great residency somewhere, I want to be free to move with him. If we get married and decide to honeymoon in Greece, I want to go even if Lily has a new class starting or is seeing a new doctor or you're busy and need childcare."

Cynthia took a sharp breath. "I really don't think I can do this alone."

John finally looked away from Ryan to say, "You're not alone. We'll help, and we'll find you other paid help. We'll be a safety net. Babysit now and then, do research for her needs, help you find specialists or daycare or whatever."

Ryan cleared his aching throat and said, "I have the name of the best pediatrician for Down syndrome kids in York scoped out."

"And if Brandon decides she should be put away somewhere?" Cynthia asked, her voice tight and high. "What if I can't protect her? What if I die?"

"Write a will," Ryan suggested. "Put us in as her guardians."

"Both of us," John said. "If you absolutely can't be there, then we'll be backup. Tell your divorce lawyer to sew it up tight."

Cynthia slumped. "I hate my lawyer. He's a wimp."

"Get a new one." Ryan had a sudden thought and pulled out his phone.

His father answered, his voice cautious. "Ryan? Everything all right?"

"I need a favor, Dad."

"Sure."

"I know Los Angeles isn't your backyard, but you know a lot of lawyers who know other lawyers, right? I need the name of a good divorce lawyer in LA."

"Most of the folks I know are in criminal law," his dad said. "I can ask around, though. Which county in LA?"

"I'll email you the details," he said. "It's for Cynthia, and for the kids, indirectly. Her soon-to-be-ex-husband knows all the sharks. She needs a killer whale."

Dad actually laughed. "I get the picture. Send me the details, and I'll see what I can do."

"Thanks. We'll have to talk again soon."

His father's voice softened. "I'd like that."

Ryan stuck his phone back in his pocket. "There. Resources deployed."

Cynthia stared at John, her fingers twisting the edge of the blanket around and around and around. "Well. What if I have to move away, maybe for Lily's needs sometime? What if Torey has to come with me again, far away from you?"

"Oh no, you don't," John said, low and hard. "Don't threaten me with Torey's custody situation. At worst, I will take a chance on going back to court. A lot of judges let a teenager have a say in where they live. And we might rethink child support based on my new salary. You don't hold all the cards, and you're not making me eager to help you."

"No judge will give child custody to two…"

"Don't," John snapped.

She subsided. "I was going to say, two men over the biological mother."

"You'd be surprised. But we can keep this friendly, for the sake of all the kids including the new baby. Or burn bridges you can't rebuild."

She took a long, shaky breath and burst into tears. "I'm just so t-tired, and so damned sc-scared."

Ryan thought that at least was genuine. John looked back and forth between him and Cynthia, and Ryan could almost feel his dilemma of loyalty and chivalry. So Ryan stepped over to the bed and passed Cynthia a couple of tissues. "You're exhausted," he said. The baby made a fretful noise, half-awake and rooting against Cynthia's stomach. Lily's tiny eyelids opened to reveal bleary blue eyes, and pudgy hands opened and shut. He reached down, and when Cynthia didn't block the gesture, he touched the infant's curved head, feeling the silk-soft warmth of baby skin. "She'll want to eat soon." A protective pang went through him. This little one deserved them all pulling together as much as the situation would allow. "John and I will go now, and you can focus on Lily for a while. Try to rest. It'll work out somehow."

She sobbed through clenched teeth, tears flowing down her face, looking away from him at John. But when the baby opened her little mouth for a surprisingly loud wail, Cynthia swiped hastily at her own eyes with the tissue and then gathered Lily close. "Hush, sweetheart. Mommy's here." The baby whimpered, and Cynthia pulled her robe over and looser.

"We'll head out and let you feed her," John said. "I'll check back in the morning."

Cynthia glanced up from trying to get Lily situated to nurse, sniffed hard and whispered, "Thanks, John. Really. I'd have been lost without you, like taking care of Torey yesterday, everything."

"You know I'll always take care of Torey and Mark." He held the door for Ryan and then closed it behind them.

They met the kids coming out of the elevator. Mark held out two cans of soda. "Is Mom okay?"

"Sure," John said. "Getting ready to feed the baby, for which she doesn't need an audience. You could go glance in to say good night, though. Knock first."

Mark shrugged, stopped and passed over the sodas, downing a big slug of his own without even glancing down the hall. Torey hurried off, though, and disappeared inside the room for a minute. When she came back she was smiling fondly. "Lily is sooooo cute."

"Yeah, she is." John gave her a one-armed hug, and they turned back to the elevator. "So Torey, you'll stay with us for at least another night or two. We'll see when they let your mother and Lily go home."

"You're really sure you don't want to be Lily's daddy too?"

John smiled with apparent casualness. "Yep. We figured out that if I did, Brandon wouldn't have to pay his child support."

"Ooh," Mark said. "Yeah. Bad move."

"Uh-huh." Ryan let his grin have a touch of fierceness. "No way he's getting out of that. He owes Lily clothes and bicycles and orthodontists and ponies and castles." *And speech therapists and eyeglasses.*

"I didn't get a pony," Torey said.

"Maybe we can tell him they only come in pairs and make him spring for two."

"I wish." But she grinned. "Anyway, I'm kind of growing out of ponies. I'd rather have a motorcycle."

"No," Ryan and John said together.

"When I'm sixteen, of course."

"Dream on," Mark scoffed.

They drove home, chatting easily. The kids both opted for heading up to their rooms, and Ryan wasn't sorry to make it an early night. When he got into bed with John, though, he couldn't get to sleep. His leg itched, and his head spun with too many thoughts. It was warm and he pushed the covers off his side down to the sheet and slid away from John because shared body heat was not helping tonight. He rolled on his side, then on his back.

After half an hour of trying and failing not to wriggle around, John asked him, "Are you all right?"

"Sorry. I'm keeping you up. I should probably just go sleep in the spare room, because it's not happening here."

"No way." John rolled to face him, sliding one leg so their knees touched under the sheet. "What's up?"

"I don't know." But that was only partly true. "I was actually scared for a minute."

"Scared?"

"That your goddamned chivalry would make you feel like you had to take care of Cynthia and the baby, at any cost, forever."

"Oh."

He heard the hurt in that little sound and pressed his own lips together.

John said, "I thought you would know I'd *never* do something like that without you being okay with it."

Ryan tried to keep his tone level. "Yeah, but if you'd wanted to be a father to a little baby who otherwise gets Brandon Carlisle, well, how could I possibly say no?"

"Who's chivalrous now?" John pressed a hand to Ryan's chest, over his heart. The touch was warm and damp, but Ryan leaned into it. "I know I can't be everything for everyone, no matter how much I might want to. You, Torey, and Mark are the ones who get everything I have. The baby? Well, she's family of a sort, like if your obnoxious brother had kids and they needed help. We'd do what was right, be there for them, but not the same as their real parents."

"You really feel that way? You didn't say no just for my sake? You seem to like Cynthia a lot more than you like Brent."

"Sometimes, but..." There was a long silence. Then John said, barely in a whisper, "She's also the woman I used to love who sat there and asked if I'd given her AIDS *while we were married.*"

"Oh." In all his dismay at the homophobia flying around the day he met Cynthia, he'd missed the way that must've cut John, who was nothing if not faithful. He grabbed John's wrist, pressed that calloused palm in harder, feeling it trembling against his chest.

John said in an unsteady voice, "And who said I wasn't fit to be around my own kids, even if she has changed her mind since then. So no, most of the time I don't particularly feel like doing her favors on my own behalf either."

Ryan lunged closer and kissed him, mashing their lips off-target in the dark, before adjusting and finding that perfect fit. They kissed, hard at first and then softer, tongues meeting, stroking, lips plucking, slowly easing, eventually separating enough to talk.

"I love you, John." That was the thing he needed most to say. "And I wouldn't trade this complicated life of ours for anything."

"Nor would I."

He let his tone get contemplative. "Although I wouldn't say no to a summer in Greece."

"A summer ? Oh." There was a pause as John no doubt remembered the word *honeymoon,* then John said, "It sounded good to me too."

Ryan slid his hand up to brush over John's lips. He wanted to both kiss and talk, and this was as close as he could come. "I was thinking the other day that there's no good word for what you are to me. Partner, lover, boyfriend, none of them sound right."

John said "Mmp," against his fingers.

"Then I realized that there is a word, and it's 'husband.' But we can't legally do that here."

John captured Ryan's stroking fingers, lifted his hand away, but continued to hold it. "Some guys do the wedding anyway, for the meaning if not the tax breaks."

"Ye-es." He couldn't find the right words, but he had to try. "I want to, and yet, I don't. It's not about the tax breaks. It's like, if we fake it, we're saying it's okay that we don't have the legal right. It feels like giving in to second-class status."

"So you want us to wait until it's legal? That could be a long time."

"I know. Although we're finally considered real people in five states; there's momentum building. But yes, I guess when I marry you, I want to do it right, legally, in front of everyone. I don't give a crap for floral arrangements and tablecloths, but I want the right to the same wedding as Brent and Anne had."

"I can understand that. I don't mind waiting either. There's just one thing missing in this process right now."

Ryan frowned. "What's that?"

John said nothing, just brought Ryan's hand to his mouth and began to kiss and lick over his knuckles, wet and suggestive, sliding his tongue around Ryan's ring finger…

Ryan laughed. "God, I'm sorry. That was the most inept, egotistical, assumption-filled proposal ever, wasn't it?"

John's laugh was deep and sweet. "I kind of liked it. Ryan Ward, someday, when the state of Wisconsin joins the twenty-first century, will you marry me?"

Ryan's chest was suddenly tight, his whole body suffused with warmth. "Yes. John Barrett, someday, when that stupid bigotry falls, will I get to call you my husband?"

"Yes."

They kissed again, a seal on a promise. John said, "In the meantime, I can think of other things I want to call you. Sexy, smart, wicked." He slid a hand into the waistband of Ryan's boxers. "Naked?"

Ryan lifted his hip for John to strip them off him. "Yeah."

"Hot, hard." John's hand made sure of that. "Wonderful, bossy, accepting, sharp, caring, generous." He paused, stilling the motions of his hand. "Mine?"

And there was a word that would do, until the law changed. Ryan kissed him, hard and fast. "Yours," he said.

Epilogue

A brief morning rainstorm had cooled the late-June air, even if it also left annoying puddles and mud behind. John tried to make sure Ryan had the least slippery part of the path to walk on, without being obvious about it. York's Pride in the Park was crowded with cheerful people undaunted by the earlier showers. Unfortunately, the decorating committee had obviously been working on a low budget and the multitude of paper rainbow banners hung in sodden clumps.

Mark muttered, "Looks like a unicorn puked all over."

"Marcus," John said. "Be nice."

"I'm here." Mark grimaced. "I think that *is* being nice."

John noticed Mark was lurking beside him, hunched as if to seem smaller. He nudged him. "And we appreciate it. Do you want to wander around on your own instead of hanging out with the old fogeys?" It *was* a step forward that Mark had actually chosen to appear with Ryan and him, at a public gay event.

"You wouldn't mind, Dad?"

"Not a bit."

"Okay, then. Maybe I might, um, go look at the bumper stickers." Mark headed off quickly across the grass toward one of the tents.

"Well, I *like* hanging out with you," Torey said to him. "Come on, Dad. You haven't met Tina yet. She said she was doing face painting."

They walked along the path through the park, past stands selling food and others with books or pamphlets, with artwork and health-club memberships. A few handmade signs said, "York loves New York", a nod to the sixth sane state to pass marriage equality, just two days earlier. *Momentum.* The whole event was bigger and busier than John would have expected, with a wide mix of ages. There were a surprising number of families, even people pushing strollers with toddlers and infants. A mother lifted a tiny blond baby to see a shiny wind chime, brass tubes suspended from a rainbow arch. The baby reached up an open hand, falling far short but laughing anyway. John was reminded of Lily. Not that she was laughing yet, but she was a happy, easy baby.

Apparently he wasn't the only one who saw that byplay, because Torey said, "Lily might like one of those. It's shiny and musical."

He said, "Mm hm. But I don't think it's baby safe."

"I want to get her something rainbowy. I wish we could've brought her."

"We'll see what we can find that's appropriate." Torey was really in love with Lily; she'd have carried the baby around 24/7 if she could have. Sometimes John's heart overflowed, watching them. But he always reminded himself he was still glad it was Cynthia getting up at two a.m. for feedings and worrying if Lily was eating enough and whether that spit-up was normal or not. He was glad it wasn't his job to reassure and debate and worry with her. Lily was his almost-niece, not his child. Torey, though— God, she was growing up good.

Torey pointed at a tie-dye stall. "I bet they have some kind of baby clothes. A T-shirt, maybe. We don't have a ton of stuff for her, yet. Mom would totally have to let Lily have a Pride romper if we bought her one."

John caught Ryan's eyes ruefully.

John hadn't been sure whether to applaud or restrain Torey's enthusiasm in the last few weeks leading up to Pride. Around Cynthia and Mark, so far, she'd claimed she was just being open-minded, but he could feel her impatience with being cautious and going slow. He sometimes wished she'd turn it down a notch. When she had friends over, she made a point of introducing her two dads. Mark did a lot of wincing, and when Cynthia came out of her baby stupor to notice, she looked irritated. Torey's rainbow sparkling was becoming more deliberate at home, and he worried about the approaching moment of truth with Cynthia.

He forced himself to relax. Here, at least, she fit right in. She should get to enjoy that.

Suddenly, she alerted like a pointer spotting a pheasant, and grabbed his hand to tug him forward. "There. She's over there." He let her propel him down the path, with Ryan leaning on his cane and following more slowly.

The stylist was set up with a small makeup table and chair. Her hair was as bright as Ryan had described it, with what looked like sparkles on the ends, and she was putting the finishing touches on a pink heart on a child's cheek.

She smiled at Torey and said, "One sec," as she added a trailing red ribbon bow to the heart. The child craned her neck to see herself in the mirror and grinned widely. Once her mother had put a donation in the PFLAG jar on the table, they headed off down the row. The stylist got up and gave Torey a high five. "You made it."

"Of course I did." Torey pulled John closer. "Tina, this is my dad. Ryan's his boyfriend."

Tina said, "Hi, Ryan's Boyfriend."

"Hi," he said. "Torey's been thrilled with the way you cut her hair."

Torey said, "Da-ad," with some agony of teen embarrassment, but Tina said, "Thanks. She has great hair to work with."

Torey asked, "Is your girlfriend here?"

"Sure." Tina pointed down the row. "She's working the popcorn stand right now."

"Did you bring the bike?"

"Are you kidding?" Tina nodded to a clump of trees behind them. Parked in against them was an electric-blue motorcycle.

"Are you going to ride it sometime?"

"We rode here, took it round the park a couple of times, and we'll ride it home. But there's no formal parade."

"That sucks."

"Maybe next year. What actually sucked was getting caught in that downpour on the bike. I had to totally redo my hair when we got here."

John said truthfully, "It looks very cheerful."

Tina laughed. "Hey, Torey, I brought you something, in case you made it to Pride. Have a seat in the chair." She patted it.

Torey sat eagerly, and Tina picked up a comb. John said tentatively, "Nothing permanent, right?"

"Don't worry." Tina reached under the table and pulled out a set of little strands of hair in rainbow colors. "I'm going to clip these in underneath, so they flash through. What do you think, Torey. Spaced around, or all on the one side?"

"One side," Torey said. "Where it's longer."

Tina's agile fingers got the colored bits into Torey's hair quickly, then snipped with scissors to even them up. Torey looked in the mirror, tossed her head to make the strands swing beside her cheek, then bounced up out of the chair and hugged Tina. "I love it. It's perfect."

John pulled out his wallet and dropped a bill into the jar, even though Tina tried to wave him off. A mother with two small girls stopped, looking at the sample flier for the face painting, and Tina said, "Oops, customers. It's been nice and busy despite the wet. You should enjoy the park. Stop on back if you get bored. Happy Pride, Tor." She turned toward the mother and girls.

John saw Torey droop for a second before she recovered her smile. "So, Dad, what do *you* want to do?"

"Soft pretzels?" he suggested.

"Get me a plain one?" Ryan asked him.

He and Torey stood in line, then the three of them took their booty off to a shady area to stand and eat. The spot was far enough back from the path to be quiet, but the colorful swirl of people and booths made a pleasant view. Torey nibbled on her pretzel, licking the salt crystals off the surface. Eventually she said, "Tina's great. She's been with her girlfriend for three years now."

"That's pretty solid," Ryan said. "She seems happy."

"Yeah, she is, I guess. Like you and Dad."

John said, "It was really kind of her to bring those hair things just in case you were here."

"They're called extensions. It was so freaking cool that she remembered. I told her it would be my first Pride."

"Ours too," Ryan said. John looked at him, and Ryan lifted his chin and smiled. Despite the public space, John really wanted to kiss him.

"Yeah, ours too," he agreed.

"You're not sorry, right?" Torey said. "You don't want to be, like, not gay?"

"Well, it's not always the easiest thing," he said. "But I'm happier than I've ever known, being with Ryan, and that means the gay is here to stay."

"Hm." Torey ate more of her pretzel. John could tell she was mulling something over, and clearly Ryan had picked up on her signals too, because he ate his own pretzel silently and waited.

Eventually, Torey licked the last salt off her fingers, looked down and said, "I still like girls best." She flicked a glance at him, then toward the entrance to the park. "No matter what people say."

He and Ryan followed her gaze. Three dark-clad men who hadn't been there when they arrived stood side by side just inside the decorative fence, silently glaring at the happy throng, holding signs that said "God hates FAGS," "Sodomy is the devil's work" and "The wages of sin are death".

John thought he'd never wanted to hit anyone quite as much as he wanted to punch the smug look off those men's faces. His little girl's first Pride, and they were sliming it with their hate. He wanted to march over there and, and—

Ryan closed a hand on his arm and muttered loud enough for Torey to hear, "I want to take away their signs and shove them up their sanctimonious asses. Then we'll see if they care what goes up my ass."

John choked, and Torey stared at Ryan.

Ry shrugged. "Well, they're the ones thinking about sodomy. You have to wonder, how do they know the devil does that kind of work? Firsthand experience? You think he does it well?"

Torey giggled.

John said, "Ryan."

"What?" Ryan raised his eyebrows in an exaggerated way.

Down by the fence, a group of men and women approached the protesters. A woman began tossing rainbow leis at them and their signs like some gay floral version of horseshoes. A man gestured, his hands held low. Another pointed at the signs, his palm over his infant's eyes. The men in dark suits shifted back a step.

Torey said, "Looks like the forces of Pride are on it, huh? So who cares what three morons think?" Her voice was almost steady.

He felt an overwhelming rush of love for her. His little girl. She should be too young to be worrying about this, except obviously she wasn't. He remembered again, with stomach-twisting clarity, the first time a stranger spewed hate at him and Ryan, just for who they were, who they loved. He couldn't make the world accept Torey, but he vowed then and there to do what he could. "Let's leave the morons to people who look like they have a plan." He turned away from the scene, drawing her with him. "So. I clearly need a bumper sticker for the truck. And maybe a T-shirt. You want to help me choose? You have better taste than me."

Ryan said, "When it comes to clothes, everyone has better taste than you. But yeah, come on, Torey, I need something tasteful but clearly gay to wear to work. And then there's all the Pride stuff we're going to get Lily."

"Oh." There was an odd tone of wonder in her voice. Abruptly, she hugged Ryan for a second, then turned and caught John hard around the middle, driving the breath out of him. He wrapped an arm across her shoulders, pulling her close and looked at Ryan over her head. Ry smiled wryly and gave a slight shrug.

After a moment, Torey pushed away. He pretended not to notice when she brushed the heel of her hand across her eyes. "So, Dad? Rainbow shirts?"

"Definitely."

"And a romper for Lily?"

"Yes." Cynthia was going to have to get used to it, right the hell now.

"Maybe you'll see a cute girl here," Ryan suggested.

John elbowed him. "She's too young to date."

"Lots of kids my age are dating," she said, "including, like, half my class. I *am* a teenager."

"Don't be in too big a rush to grow up," he said, knowing it was futile. God, he remembered thirteen— painful, constantly changing, confused, mostly consumed by a burning desire to be sixteen. Oh God, he was in trouble. He reached out and took Ryan's hand, comforted by the strength of those fingers between his own.

Torey shrugged, then her face brightened. "Hey, there's Donna and her boyfriend!"

"Donna has a boyfriend?" Ryan asked.

"Yeah. She told us about him. He sounds really smart. I'm gonna go say hi." John thought he heard a hint of relief in her tone as she hurried off across the grass.

He blew out a slow breath. He wasn't really sorry to have a moment's break from the intensity of that conversation either. A quick glance over his shoulder showed him that the protesters were moving back, out of the park now and onto the sidewalk. The signs were half-hidden by bright balloons bobbing at the same height, held by the people surrounding them.

Ryan followed his gaze. "I have to hand it to the local committee. They seem well organized. Good planning."

"We might help out next year," John suggested.

Ryan squeezed his fingers tighter. "We just might."

They turned and watched as Torey went up to Donna and a tall dark-haired man. Donna's smile was genuinely welcoming. Torey pointed down the row of booths toward Tina's, then at the clothing booth next to them. Donna said something they couldn't hear. Torey laughed, went over and held up a T-shirt against herself, the bright image curved across her chest.

Down by the park entrance, there was a loud ripple of applause. John looked back to see the three protesters climbing into an SUV, stuffing their signs in the back. The much larger crowd around them on the sidewalk waved, cheered, blew kisses, and clapped as they pulled away. Through the side window of the SUV, the word FAGS momentarily showed clearly. Then they were gone.

John groaned, hit by another realization, and leaned his forehead on Ryan's hair. "I sent her back to live with Brandon. Right after he said all that homophobic nastiness to us, that she heard. I didn't want to have a big custody fight, and I didn't think I could win, so I made her go back there." Remembering Torey's reluctance hurt to the point of nausea. "I didn't think it would be that bad for her."

"We can't change that," Ryan murmured, letting go of his hand to wrap his arm around John. "You barely managed to keep Mark without a big battle. You didn't know. It seemed best at the time."

John jolted with a sudden thought. "You don't think Marcus…"

"What?"

John looked around and spotted Mark, in a group of teens. He looked comfortable, relaxed. "Is gay too?"

Ryan actually chuckled. "I doubt it. He could be bi, but he's had two pretty convincing crushes on girls that I know of, and his porn features boobs."

"I don't want to think about my son's porn." John closed his eyes and let himself lean on Ryan for a moment.

"I don't want you thinking about boobs either." Ryan still sounded amused. "Maybe you can think about the positive side to Torey being a lesbian. No teen pregnancy. A lot fewer STDs."

"Ouch. No, no." He pulled away. "You don't talk about Torey and sex." It was mostly meant as a joke, to cover a real internal wince.

"For what it's worth, I think you have some time. She's still thinking romance and crushes, mostly. Now Mark…"

"You're just mean." He gave Ryan a shove. After a moment, he asked, "You don't think I need to have another sex talk with him, do you?" He'd had one years ago, and it had been pretty uncomfortable for both of them. He was pretty sure he'd covered condoms and respect. He couldn't be sure about the details, though. He'd kind of blanked out the memory.

"I'm yanking your chain a bit. Although, he's fifteen, so you never know. Maybe put a box of condoms in the main bathroom? An open box."

"Aargh," John growled. "Yes. Good idea." And another talk about the value of waiting and being careful. He and Cynthia could be an object lesson.

Ryan took his hand again. "You're a good dad."

"I seem to spend all my time lately flying by the seat of my pants."

"You're doing okay."

"I miss the days when the kids were small, and all they needed were playgrounds and Band-Aids. I went to work, I came home to my family. Life ran along so smoothly."

Ryan didn't comment, just tugged him to walk back toward the path.

John let the thought spool on. "It was simple. And for a while, it was good and sweet and easy, but then it wasn't. It got, I don't know, tense. And boring and unsatisfying."

Ryan's chuckle sounded forced. "Well, at least we're managing to avoid boring."

John stopped him with a tug on his hand and stepped in closer. "Also unsatisfying. Ry, I do miss the lack of stress, but I wouldn't trade now for then. And I surely wouldn't trade you for Cynthia. Ever."

Ryan's eyes met his, but he thought he still saw a shadow in them. He cursed himself silently. He'd been thinking aloud, but something had clearly hurt Ryan. "I look forward to someday coming home to my husband and an empty house. And all the things we can do in it."

That got a better smile. "Hold that thought. Mark has band practice tonight."

"Mm." He walked on, still holding Ryan's hand in his. Here, if anywhere, they could do this. Hell, they *should* do this, for themselves and for all the kids like Torey. He looked around. There were other same-sex couples in the crowd. Two women old enough to be his grandmothers sat on a park bench, arms around each other, leaning together. A pair of shirtless teen boys stood at the hot-dog stand. Both had body paint on their hairless chests— "I'm his" and a bright red arrow.

"I don't think I'd have come here on my own." He raised their joined hands to kiss the back of Ryan's. "But I like this a lot."

Ryan gave him a grin. "Me too. Torey's waving at us." He pointed with his cane at a wildly beckoning Torey. "Let's meet Donna's boyfriend."

John strolled beside him. Ryan slipped on the mud, but John's grip was enough to steady him. His leg had been bad at the end of term, but he said the new massage therapist was helping. John was considering a summer course in massage. Even if it ended up being just for fun. Another reason to have his hands on Ryan couldn't hurt.

The summer sun was warm on their shoulders. Ahead, Torey tossed her hair, and the rainbow stands caught the light. She was taller every time he looked at her, and her thin shirt hinted at new curves. *Changes.* Everything changed. He was still her father, though, always would be, and he was going to do his best to give her what she needed.

"We'll work on Cynthia," Ryan murmured at his side, as if by telepathy. "Get her to see how great this is, for Torey's sake. Or maybe try bribery. Blackmail. Home cooking. More babysitting."

John tugged on his hand to stop him, then let go of his fingers and touched his cheek. "I love you. You're perfect for me." He bent and brushed their lips together, with that rainbow crowd around them.

Ryan tilted his head. "Back at you, John Barrett. This time a year ago, I was looking ahead at years of intense study, of never letting anyone see me weak, or look at my leg or feel sorry for me. Maybe a bit of anonymous hetero sex. A long, slow grind toward a distant future that might be better. One day."

John's chest ached at that vision of Ryan's life. "And now?"

"Now the future's already here, it's rainbow-colored and scary and different and full of everything. Full of family, the kids and school and you."

"And that's good, right?"

Ryan glanced to their left. John followed his gaze. Donna and her nice straight boyfriend were still looking their way, with Torey bouncing on her toes beside them. They were all smiling.

It was Ryan's turn to touch his face and focus his attention back to just them. Ry's green eyes shone in the summer sunlight. "It's exactly, imperfectly perfect." He rose stiffly on his toes, bringing their mouths together. John caught his elbow and held him there, for a long kiss.

Then Torey's voice broke in, clearly deliberately loud. "Dad, quit kissing your *boyfriend* and come meet Donna's boyfriend."

Ryan grinned against his lips and dropped back down on his heels. A young guy walking past said, "Nah. Keep kissing. Your boyfriend's hotter."

One of the two elderly women, coming down the path in her quiet, ordinary clothes, murmured, "It's so nice to see our families out like this, together. So fucking *nice*."

Donna gave Torey's hair a ruffle and said, "Don't interrupt your father when he's busy."

Her boyfriend said, "Hey, I'm totally hotter!"

And Ryan leaned in against John, warm and solid in his arms, and laughed, while Pride in the Park sparkled on around them.

#######

About the Author

I get asked about my name a lot. It's not something exotic, though. "Kaje" is pronounced just like "cage" – it's an old nickname.

I was born in Montreal but I've lived for 30 years in Minnesota, where the two seasons are Snow-removal and Road-repair, where the mosquito is the state bird, and where winter can be breathtakingly beautiful. Minnesota's a kind, quiet (if sometimes chilly) place and it's home.

I've been writing far longer than I care to admit (*whispers – forty years*), mostly for my own entertainment, usually M/M romance (with added mystery, fantasy, historical, SciFi...) I also have a few Young Adult stories (some released under the pen name Kira Harp.)

In 2010, my husband finally convinced me that after all the years of writing for fun, I really should submit something, somewhere. To my surprise, they liked it. My first professionally published book, Life Lessons, came out from MLR Press in May 2011. I have a weakness for closeted cops with honest hearts, and teachers who speak their minds, and I had fun writing four novels and three freebie short stories in that series. I was delighted and encouraged by the immediate reception Mac and Tony received, and went on to release other stories.

I now have a good-sized backlist in ebooks and print, some free, some indie and professionally published, including Amazon bestseller *The Rebuilding Year* and Rainbow Award Best Mystery-Thriller *Tracefinder: Contact*.

I'm always pleased to have readers find me online at:

Website: https://kajeharper.wordpress.com/

Facebook: https://www.facebook.com/KajeHarper

Goodreads Author page: https://www.goodreads.com/author/show/4769304. Kaje_Harper

Other Books by Kaje Harper

Self-Published/Indie:

Tracefinder: Contact *(Tracefinder #1)*
Tracefinder: Changes *(Tracefinder #2)*

Second Act

Rejoice, Dammit

The Family We're Born With *(Finding Family #1) - free novella*
The Family We Make *(Finding Family #2)*

Unfair in Love and War (in the charity anthology *Another Place in Time*)

Not Your Grandfather's Magic (in the charity anthology *Wish Come True*)

Re-releasing in 2017:

The Rebuilding Year *(Rebuilding Year #1)*
Life, Some Assembly Required *(Rebuilding Year #2)*

Sole Support

Gift of the Goddess

Audiobook:

Into Deep Waters (Narrated by Kaleo Griffith)

From MLR Press:

Life Lessons *(Life Lessons #1)*
Breaking Cover *(Life Lessons #2)*
Home Work *(Life Lessons #3)*
Learning Curve *(Life Lessons #4)*

Unacceptable Risk *(Hidden Wolves #1)*
Unexpected Demands *(Hidden Wolves #2)*
Unjustified Claims *(Hidden Wolves #3)*
Unsafe Exposure *(Hidden Wolves #4)*

Storming Love: Nelson & Caleb

Full Circle

Where the Heart Is

Ghosts and Flames

Possibilities

Tumbling Dreams (in the anthology *Going For Gold*)

Free series stories:

And To All a Good Night (*Life Lessons #1.5*)
Getting It Right (*Life Lessons #1.8*)
Compensations (*Life Lessons #3.5*)

Unsettled Interlude (*Hidden Wolves #1.15*)
Unwanted Appeal (*Hidden Wolves #2.5*)

Can't Hurt to Believe (*Into Deep Waters #1.005*)

Stand-alone free novels:

Into Deep Waters

Nor Iron Bars a Cage

Chasing Death Metal Dreams

Lies and Consequences

Laser Visions

Changes Coming Down (in the free anthology *Hunting Under Covers*)

Stand-alone free short stories:

Like the Taste of Summer

Show Me Yours

Within Reach

A full list and links can be found at:
http://www.kajeharper.wordpress.com/books/

Made in the USA
Coppell, TX
30 June 2021

58368128R00177